SEDUCER FEY

CULLYN ROYSON

Booktrope Editions
Seattle WA 2013

Cover Design by Greg Simanson
Edited by Dawn Pearson

This is a work of fiction. Names, characters, places, brands, media, and incidents are either the product of the author's imagination or are used fictitiously. Any resemblance to similarly named places or to persons living or deceased is unintentional.

PRINT ISBN 978-1-62015-141-9
EPUB ISBN 978-1-62015-237-9

Library of Congress Control Number: 2013946827

To Kris Locke

Contents

PART ONE

PRESENT: IN WHICH THERE IS A GENETIC FEY

If you encounter a beast with a mane of kelp stepping out of the sea foam never confuse it with the goddess of love. Its allure will be your demise. Refrain from partaking in the food of the feys. If you dine, you will serve them forever.

–CASSIDY ADISA

CHAPTER 1
SPYING, FLIRTING, PURCHASING

WHEN TABAN STUMBLED to the kitchen breakfast table at nine in the morning on May Day he did not expect to hear: "Would you go to the other side of the continent, make friends with a particular person for me, and be back by dinner tomorrow?" from his housemate and best friend, Eadowen.

"Why?" Taban replied as he poured milk on the rim of his cereal bowl splashing it over the table.

"Well, we're having vegan black pudding." Eadowen set a tall mug of coffee in front of Taban. "And I want you to try it."

"No, the other thing, Ea," Taban replied addressing Eadowen by his nickname. "Who is this person I need to befriend?" He stared at his reflection in the mug. Even in the black coffee his azure eyes shone back at him. He suspected that when he was a young child, his father had paid a small fortune to have the color of his eyes genetically enhanced to appear more striking in contrast to his dark skin. It was one of the few procedures his father had done to him that he found acceptable.

"Edana Reyes is my third cousin once-removed. I've done some research on her, it appears she prefers to be called Danny and uses female pronouns," Eadowen explained. "It seems Danny will be coming here to Nova Scotia to visit our university during her Spring

Break. This is a problem because you know what might happen if they get a hold of her genome."

"So, you think she's like you? Gonna live forever and all?"

"Forever is an exaggeration." Eadowen laughed and poured a cup of tea from a silver teapot. "She might not be like me, but I'm not going to take any chances."

"You want me to make sure she trusts us enough to believe us when we tell her about her heritage?"

"Affirmative."

"You seem to know more about her. Why don't you go?"

"Her parents would not be happy if they knew I was associating with her," Eadowen explained with a small smile.

"Oh, gotcha." Taban raised his mug and tapped it to his friend's tea cup with a wink as the ceramic clinked together. "Let's see, I have to book a round trip flight, get to the airport, and figure out how to get close to her in under thirty-six hours?" He shrugged. "Sure. I wanted to skip class today anyway."

* * *

Taban arrived to unusually hot spring weather in Victoria, British Columbia. This was unfortunate because he had worn an excessive number of layers and a hood to avoid being recognized by Danny while he spied on her. He'd completed the disguise with brown contacts and by tucking his blond bangs under a baseball cap. Prepared for a long wait, he reclined on a city bench across from the apartment Danny Reyes shared with her father. He slid a pink visor over his eyes, both to protect them from the sun and to review the images of Danny and her father. As he swept his finger along the edge of the visor to change images, he noticed a man who resembled Danny's father's pictures, walking down the sidewalk. Taban checked the time, which also matched when Mr. Reyes would arrive home from work at a local design studio.

Shoving the visor into his pocket, Taban jumped to his feet. "Hi, you must be Mr. Reyes." Taban waved with an intentionally goofy smile on his face. "I go to school with your daughter, Danny."

The petite, dark-haired man altered his course to join Taban by the bench. "Nice to meet you," he said extending his hand in greeting. With his hands in his pockets, Taban pretended to hesitate by looking around bashfully before returning a bright-eyed gaze to Mr. Reyes. After all, he'd decided to play the part of a love struck boy who had just met the father of his crush.

"I ... I ..." Taban made himself stammer as he rubbed the back of his neck. "I was wondering if she might want to hang out this Spring Break?"

"I'm sorry she's headed to Nova Scotia to visit her mother and some universities with her friend."

As Taban let his face fall at this piece of information, he fiddled with his hoodie zipper. Mr. Reyes' brow furrowed as he regarded Taban with sympathetic brown eyes.

"What's her friend's name? I might know her too," Taban said quietly.

"Cassidy, and she's from Washington State, not my daughter's school."

"I was *really* hoping to see her. When does she leave?" He let a strain into his voice. "Maybe I can catch her before then."

"She leaves in the early morning."

"So when could I get a hold of her?"

"Don't you have her contact?"

"No and that's the problem," Taban replied, wringing his hands to emphasize his feigned pain. "Look if I don't ask her out now. Someone else will. I've liked her for a really long time, but I've always been so shy. I'm kind of a ... well I read a lot of books and don't play sports. Why would she go out with me?"

When Mr. Reyes placed a comforting hand on his shoulder, Taban had to slouch to conceal his toned neck and arms from Mr. Reyes' touch. Luckily the thick fabric of his hoodie helped to hide his true frame. "My daughter could really use some friends. Especially some who could help her get better grades. Don't tell her I said that part about the grades."

Barely able to hide his smirk, from the satisfaction that Mr. Reyes had bought his corny love story Taban continued his facade. "I'd absolutely tutor her!" he said, his voice dripping with earnest.

"Her flight leaves at 8 a.m. so she'll be leaving here a few hours before then. So, you'd have to be here in the pretty early morning."

"I'll do my best, but don't let her miss her flight because of me."

"If you like my daughter, then you should get up the courage to tell her," Mr. Reyes said patting Taban on the back.

Once Danny's father was out of sight, Taban flopped down on the bench. He decided to remain close by until she got home because identifying her on the plane would be easier if he knew what she looked like in person. A message alert beeped in his borrowed headphones. He preferred the thin audio strip attached to his mandible to the heavy old-style noise reduction headphones, but anything he could do to conceal his identity the better. He slipped his visor on and read the message from Eadowen on the lens: **How's everything going?** Through the pink-tinted visor, Taban saw several teenagers walk by cuing him in to the fact that school had just let out. Danny could walk by any minute. He switched messages from Eadowen to auto-audio read, so he could keep a look out for her.

Hey Ea, it's fine, Taban tapped a response on his Ogham, a rectangular electronic device strapped to the inside of his right forearm. The actual device was only as big as the palm of his hand and paper thin despite opening up to two screens to provide a larger surface or three-dimensional viewing. A slim, rectangular box on the top side of his forearm was attached to the same strap as his Ogham. The compartment had replaced the wallets he'd seen in old movies; however, it was made obsolete because most financial exchanges and identifications were done digitally. Taban crammed his compartment full of salt packets, which he added to almost everything he ate. His contemporaries wore utility belts to hold bigger personal items, while older adults clipped their Oghams to their belts and continued to carry purses.

Do you have the same flight as her? Though Eadowen had not explicitly asked how Taban had managed to get the same flight as Danny, he knew his friend would quiz him if he didn't provide some explanation.

Yes, Taban confirmed. **I *accidentally* bumped into her father on his way from work and started a conversation.** Taban took care to be vague when communicating electronically. Message protection was not secure, because privacy had been sacrified years ago in favor of accessing text messages under the ruse of identifying criminal misconduct. Unlike most people he could afford some privacy and high account security, but that didn't make his online profile unhackable.

A petite teenager dashed by him, her long dark hair flying behind her in a loose ponytail. Her large T-shirt and baggy pants, both black, looked like a single piece of billowing fabric. She was too far away for him to make out her facial features, but her broad shouldered silhouette matched the photographs he'd found. Slumping so that his hood fell farther over his head, he took a video by nonchalantly tilting his visor on his head. He paused the video, lowered his visor over his eyes, and zoomed in on her face. Narrow brown eyes, sharp features, and freckles dusting a dark complexion—yes, she was definitely Danny Reyes. He didn't need to use his facial recognition software to confirm. She bounced up and down in front of the door of the apartment until a taller girl, wearing red bucket-topped boots and a matching blouse, joined her.

I suppose I could bump into Danny now, he considered. *But that would seem contrived. Running into her on the plane gives me a great excuse for having the same general destination.*

There weren't many empty seats. Taban typed to Eadowen. **I bought an extra seat in business class, so that I can convince whoever is sitting next to them to switch places with me during the flight.**

Them?

Oh, apparently, a friend of hers is going with her.

Taban zoomed in on a frame he'd caught of Cassidy. The crimped waves of her cropped hair just covered the tops of her ears. Though he didn't find either of the young women particularly appealing, he admired the mahogany shade of Cassidy's face. Despite acne blemishes, her skin tone complemented her honey-colored eyes agreeably.

I'll be home tomorrow. Late, he tapped out.

I'll leave dinner in the fridge for you. What would you like? Eadowen replied.

You know what I like.

Salt?

Ha. Ha. Thanks, Taban replied, not appreciating Eadowen's commentary on his culinary habits.

Are you sure you'll be able to make a good impression without the usual repercussions?

I'll just channel you and everything will be fine, Taban replied.

Thank you.

Anytime, Taban tapped, but erased before he clicked send.

Running his hand through his bleached hair, Taban purchased his tickets and packed his tablet. He hated that the bleach made his hair feel like straw and that the swimming pool often altered the color. He desperately wished he could stop dying it, unfortunately that was not his choice. At least bleaching took less maintenance than nano-dye and more efficiently reversed than gene therapy.

The sunlight caught the red in his stone ring. He moved his hand allowing the shine to jump along the red flecks scattered on the dark green surface. Absentmindedly he slid the ring to his knuckle, revealing a band of lighter skin around his ring finger. Fondling the rough edge of the stone, he pushed the ring against his knuckle knowing it would not come off. It was a place holder, one that he never wanted to replace. Sweating in his grey hooded jacket, he rolled up his sleeves to cool himself. He glanced at his bare arms, saw the teal ink on the inside of his right forearm, and quickly pulled that sleeve down to cover the hideous mark on his dark flesh. When he wasn't wearing long sleeves, he wore his Ogham on his dominant arm to cover the tattoo. To his dismay, it was never completely hidden by the strap.

A solar-powered public shuttle slowed, he flagged it, and got inside. As he swept his Ogham across the scanner for payment, he caught the eye of the scowling shuttle attendant.

"Where are you headed?" the middle-aged attendant grumbled, her face aged by her sour expression.

Taban leaned over the scanner toward her. "Next stop." The lines around her face softened and her cheeks colored as she coquettishly patted her hair. He didn't know where the shuttle was headed and he didn't care—he had the rest of the day to kill.

CHAPTER 2
OF STRANGERS IN NOVA SCOTIA

CASSIDY WATCHED THE MORNING LIGHT glint orange off the city's windows as the soft patchwork of the land fell away beneath the plane. She shifted uncomfortably in one of the tiny plane seats. To distract herself from Danny's snoring from the seat beside her, Cassidy decided to play some music. She commanded her Ogham by the label she had given it: "Sunset: playlist six." The energetic beat of her favorite *Knots of Avernus* song, "The Lady's Jester," reverberated from the skin-toned audio strip on her jaw.

The plane ascended into a dense cloud and breached over a sea of ivory. Ripples with crests of magenta extended toward the horizon broken only by a towering cumulus. To Cassidy, the clouds seemed like castles on the sea with pearl-white architecture. She stroked the audio strip to repeat the song and took a small journal out of her trench coat pocket. The violet cover, highlighted by shiny gold spirals, had caught her eye in one of the airport shops. She unlocked the journal with the key hung around her neck.

Name: Cassidy Isaac Adisa, she wrote. *Date: May 2nd*

I've never written in a journal before, but Anna-Mom recommended it, since I've been so anxious about school lately. My other parent, Rona-Mom, also encouraged me to do this. I haven't written by hand since elementary school so my handwriting is atrocious, but I do like the feeling of the physical page beneath my pen. It's very different from the voice recording I usually use.

I came to Victoria from my home in Port Townsend, Washington State, to visit my friend Danny. We met at a martial arts summer camp when we were both fourteen. A few months ago, I mentioned to Danny that I really wanted to check out universities in Eastern Canada and the East Coast of the United States. Conveniently, her mother lives in Nova Scotia and offered to take us on a trip over Spring Break.

I'm seventeen, so in many places I would be in my third year of high school, but I am taking classes at the local junior college. I will apply to specific programs of study at universities this fall.

Shaking out her hand, Cassidy looked at her friend, Danny. The woman, who had sat in the aisle seat next to them during takeoff, had gone to the restroom, returning only to get her luggage. Cassidy assumed the woman had found a better seating arrangement. Taking advantage of the extra space, Danny had sprawled across both seats.

I'm an only child. Danny's what I imagine a younger sibling would be like: annoying sometimes and a little weird, but I'm glad she and I stayed in touch through our Me-Sites.

Thinking of her Me-Site, Cassidy glanced at the rectangular dual-screen device strapped to her arm. Her Ogham, which had a projector, camera, voice recognition, and financial capabilities, was also her connection to friends and family. For voice commands, Cassidy had chosen to dedicate her Ogham's name to the spectacular evening skyscapes she enjoyed while kayaking on the Puget Sound. "Sunset accept: Birthday recommendations for Rona-Mom."

"Your mother recently read several articles about the up-and-coming magician, Harlan Eldin. Popular with young audiences, he is known for his eccentric costumes ..." Cassidy touched her Ogham to silence it. Most children received their Me-Site around the age of six. Schools required them; however, some people updated more often and put more information on their Me-Site than others. She had observed a current trend at her school to include as little information as possible to seem mysterious.

Cassidy picked up her pen and scratched it along the page but no ink came out. She gently tapped the pen to the page wondering why a pen she had just bought wasn't working. It took her a moment to realize that pens with ink function differently than the stylus she used to draw on her tablet or Ogham screen. A little ashamed of herself, Cassidy sat up tilting the pen down and the ink flowed onto the page.

To be fair, we're both too stubborn to ignore, too honest to adore, too kind to abhor. I'm more of an introvert than Danny, but those traits are probably how we became friends at the camp in the first place. I just wish Danny was as nervous about applying to university in the fall as I am.

Cassidy looked out the window wishing she could go play in the clouds instead of worrying about the future. "I wish I could fly," she murmured to herself.

Danny responded with a snore. That sound did not disturb Cassidy's whimsy, but a cheery male voice from the aisle did. "You *are* flying."

"I meant like a bird." Cassidy whirled around from the window to face the intrusive speaker.

A young man rested his arm on the headrest of the aisle seat as though he owned the plane. The blue audio strip on his jaw contrasted with his dark—gold skin and matched his V-neck and eyes.

"I got up to get some coffee and I couldn't help but overhear your comment." He gave her a radiant smile. "I feel the same way when I look at the sky."

Another snore from Danny made both Cassidy and the young man jump.

"Looks like your friend could use some caffeine. Would you like coffee, soda, or anything?"

As he leaned toward Cassidy, a wavy forelock fell between his eyebrows. One glance into his uncannily bright eyes made the temperature rise in Cassidy's cheeks.

"Nope. Thanks. Bye." She plastered on a smile.

"Are you sure?"

"I prefer black tea with a little bit of honey and lots of sugar in the morning." Cassidy covered her mouth. *I can't believe I told him that,* she thought.

"I'll see what I can do."

She waited until he was out of sight to poke Danny. In her sleep, Danny knocked her hand away. Cassidy shook her friend gently. Danny rolled up into a ball and turned away from Cassidy. As a last resort, Cassidy clapped next to Danny's ear.

Sitting bolt upright Danny grabbed both of Cassidy's hands. "Don't do that, my head will be ringing for hours."

"There's a guy, who is ... getting us tea."

"How nice." Danny folded into her seat in a perfect imitation of a pill bug.

"Don't go back to sleep," Cassidy commanded, shaking her friend's shoulder vigorously. "I don't want to talk to him alone."

"We didn't pre-purchase a meal, did we? They won't let us have drinks unless we pay for the whole meal."

"That's true. I hope they don't get mad at him."

Fishing around her bag for her glasses, Danny gave up on any hope of a nap. She had managed to tune out most of the noises on the plane, but the vibrations coming from Cassidy's audio strip made it hard for her to sleep.

"What're you listening to?" Danny asked.

"Nothing in particular."

Danny located her glasses and slid them up her tiny nose. She usually didn't wear them outside, but it was nice to see detail up close. Danny sighed. Every time she put on her glasses, she was reminded that she had been born without any testing or corrections. Genetic enhancements were extremely pricy and not all legal, but vision correction was often performed through gene therapy. Her mother had been against Danny getting her genome sequenced at birth, though it would've been useful for health purposes. Plenty of anti-discrimination laws existed to ensure a genome couldn't limit someone's career choices, in case someone managed to get that private information. A breach of confidence of that type was almost unheard of because the medical community kept genomes in strict confidence. *I don't understand Mom's prejudice,* Danny thought. She started picking at the seat cushion. A few years ago, when she'd contracted a bad flu, her father allowed the physicians to process her genome. Her mother was furious when she found out, but evaded questions as to why. Not long after Danny's illness, her mother moved back to Nova Scotia. *I wonder if my parents separated because of me,* Danny thought. *They never told me why my genome was so important.* The scratching sound of wheels brought Danny back to the present. A trolley rolled down the aisle and stopped at their row. The attendant, a tall ginger-haired gentleman, poured black tea into two compostable mugs. Danny moved to the middle seat and put the tray table down. The attendant set the two drinks on the tray.

"Have a good morning," the attendant said as he rolled the trolley away.

"Thank you," Cassidy replied.

"You too." Edana encircled the cup with her tiny hands, feeling its warmth. The bitter scent of black tea made her nose wrinkle. She preferred green tea with honey, or as Cassidy had put it, honey with a spot of tea.

"I'm sorry you don't like it," Taban said, returning to see Danny's expression.

"It's fine, thanks. I'm Edana, but you can call me 'Ed' or 'Danny.'" She thrust her hand out in greeting.

"Edana?" Transferring his mug of coffee to his left hand, he took her hand in a firm shake. "That's pretty?"

"Thanks."

"I'm Taban Mir. I was visiting relatives and now I'm headed home." Taban leaned over Danny. "Pardon me." He offered his hand to Cassidy. "What's your name?"

"Cassidy." She cautiously accepted his hand.

"Nice to meet you. Do you mind if I take a seat?"

"Not at all," Danny said.

He placed his mug on the tray and sat down. As he did this Cassidy noticed a scratched stone ring with specks of red on his left ring finger. The dark color and abrasions clashed with the rest of his apparel and demeanor, so she pondered it, but wasn't comfortable inquiring about the object.

"What were you talking about?" he asked.

"Music," Cassidy replied.

"There are some bands playing in Nova Scotia. Who's your favorite?"

"Knots of Avernus," Cassidy said. Then coughed and felt the heat in her cheeks spread to her ears. "I mean, I like a few of their songs. I wouldn't want to see them in concert though," she lied.

"Knots of Avernus? Aren't they the teen band that people make fun of?" Danny asked, without a note of judgment in her voice. She didn't care if Cassidy liked the band or not. In fact, if Cassidy liked them, that was a point in their favor, in her opinion. She searched the name of the band and had some information about them transferred to her glasses. "What do you like to listen to?" Danny asked Taban and closed the viewer on her glasses.

Soon Danny and Taban were looking up bands on their Oghams and joking like they were old friends. Cassidy pretended to message someone on her Ogham, so she wouldn't have to interact. What were initially cheerful butterflies in her stomach when she met Taban, abruptly transformed into spiteful, wasps, as she watched him listen to her friend. *Danny's enthusiasm often puts people off,* Cassidy reasoned. *It's nice that someone appreciates her.* Angry at herself for being jealous of her friend, Cassidy tried to look out the window, but her attention kept returning to Taban. She couldn't quite put her finger on it, but Taban seemed like he came out of a mid-twenieth century film that used a blurred halo effect to suggest glamor.

"What about you, Cassidy?" Taban asked.

"What?" Cassidy replied, having managed to distract herself with pictures of attractive people on her Ogham. She hid the screen with her hand when she realized Danny had disappeared from the middle seat. He slid into it.

"Danny told me you go to junior college." Resting his elbow on the tray table Taban tilted his head and regarded her intently.

Cassidy nodded.

"I go to Dalhousie. Danny said you were touring. Maybe I'll see you there." He tapped a code to unlock his Ogham. "Here, take my contact information." She set her Ogham to receive mode and slid it across his.

"That'd be awesome!" Danny said when she rejoined them. "We should hang out."

The seat belt sign beeped to on and the pilot announced the descent. Taban let Danny sit in the middle seat to Cassidy's dismayed relief. She wanted to learn more about Taban, but using the face scan feature to look someone up on the Ogham was considered rude. Plus, most people bought a certain level of privacy from face identification technology.

* * *

As they exited the plane, an Ogham buzzed. Cassidy and Danny instinctively checked theirs, before noticing Taban looking at his.

"I need to take a message. It was nice to meet you both." He walked far enough away that Cassidy couldn't make out anything, but Danny heard: "Yeah, she's here."

"Who's he talking about?" Danny asked aloud.

"What?"

"Oops, I shouldn't have been eavesdropping. It's nothing."

"Tell me."

"He said, 'she's here,'" Danny explained.

"That's weird. Maybe he was talking about someone else."

"Must be."

Cassidy tapped his name into her Ogham. Since his last name rhymed with 'purr' she tried both 'Mar' and 'Mir'. The latter yielded professional photographs that resembled the young man they'd encountered. At a glance, Cassidy could tell he'd put his privacy settings to high and paid a six-figure sum for an inclusive privacy service.

"A13 accept: Message Mom: At Baggage Claim," Danny said.

"Why is your Ogham called: A13?"

"The number I've broken."

Danny's mother met them at baggage claim. Her hair was grey with the last hints of black tied in a bun.

"I'm so glad you could come, I missed you!" She wrapped her arms around Danny. "Cassidy, it's nice to see you again too."

Danny's mother, Sarah Reyes, lived close to the airport in a compact, yellow, mass-production house. She drove them to her home in a small electric-solar car. When they entered, Danny noticed the walls painted ivory and grey. The dull interior contrasted with the colorful apartment her father had painted in Victoria to such an extent that Danny connected the dissonance to her parents' separation.

While enjoying a sandwich Ms. Reyes made, Cassidy noticed her friend's frown across the table. "You okay, Danny?"

"Yeah." Danny didn't feel like mentioning the estrangement in front of her mother.

"You sure?"

"Yeah."

"So, what have you two been up to?" Ms. Reyes said.

"I've been trying to stay on top of my school work, but it's really hard," Danny replied.

"I volunteer at a mediation center," Cassidy said.

"Do you still do Aikido?"

"Not so much lately. I've been surf kayaking, though." Cassidy decided she should attempt small talk. "What brought you to Nova Scotia, Ms. Reyes?"

Ms. Reyes continued eating her sandwich, as though she hadn't heard Cassidy's comment.

"Mom, didn't you take me here when I was little?"

"No. You must be mistaken," Ms. Reyes said. "I grew up here." She finished her sandwich and left the room. Remaining at the table, Danny and Cassidy exchanged uncomfortable looks.

"Want to play a video game?" Cassidy asked.

Danny offered to watch, but Cassidy preferred to choose something they both wanted to do. At last they settled on their tried and true pastimes: watching martial art comedies, sparring, and eating pizza. School work and other productive pursuits could wait until after break was over.

* * *

When they had completely exhausted their eyes, Cassidy and Danny got ready for bed and made their way upstairs to the extra bedroom. Ms. Reyes had covered the king size bed with a bright-green quilt, which cheered her daughter.

"Sunset: sleep mode," Cassidy commanded placing her Ogham on the bedside table. Sleep mode turned her Ogham to vibrate and informed senders on her contact list that she was unavailable.

Danny switched her Ogham to sleep mode, by sliding her finger across the screen. She owned an Ogham-Flex, which, as the name indicated, had a flexible screen that made a cuff on the user's arm. Cassidy looked at it carefully because it was much less popular than the Ogham with a strap. It had no compartment and tended to come off accidentally more often than the regular model. Giggles usually accompanied an Ogham falling off in public, because Oghams, being both waterproof and comfortable, were only taken off under specific circumstances by their owners.

They awakened to a loud knock at the downstairs door. Cassidy and Danny glanced at each other. *Who on Earth would come by this late at night?* Cassidy wondered. She crawled to the bedroom door, kneeling next to Danny to listen.

Ms. Reyes opened the door. "You aren't welcome here."

"We know she is here," a quiet but authoritative voice answered. "It is essential that we talk to her."

"No! I'll make sure she doesn't have to be part of this. She will be safe as long as she doesn't know. Who's to say that she's one of you anyway?"

"How can you think ignorance is going to protect her?" The stranger growled. "She is very likely a Tuatha de Danann."

"A Tooua de whatta?" Danny mouthed to Cassidy.

"If I knew how that was spelled I could look it up."

"Shh! You will wake up the girls. Leave now!"

Danny heard clattering that sounded like her mother pushing the stranger out of the door.

"We're in trouble if they find out about one of us," he said. "You chose the worst time to bring her here. And make sure she doesn't get sick!" he added desperately.

The latch on the door clanked as it locked into place. Danny and Cassidy listened to the clicks of latched windows and rustled curtains. Ms. Reyes' footsteps resonated, as she ascended the stairs making her way to her bedroom. Neither of them dared to move for about five minutes. Eventually, they crept away from the door to communicate in whispers.

"I just spelled it out phonetically and came up with Tuatha de Danann," Cassidy said. "Supposedly that's a race in Celtic mythology."

"That doesn't make any sense," Danny replied.

They huddled, silently searching on their Oghams for anything that sounded like what they heard, but yielded nothing promising. A break in the cloudy sky allowed a sliver of moonlight to illuminate the bed. The surreal light emphasized muscle definition on Danny's dark arms and added an elegant shine to her hair. To Cassidy, Danny appeared uncharacteristically serene and powerful.

"Why did mom say I shouldn't know? I want to find out more, but I trust my mom."

"Knowledge is power," Cassidy whispered. "How can not understanding what's going on actually be good?"

"I guess."

A cloud blocked the moon causing the room to darken considerably. A thought occurred to Cassidy, "Was that Taban just now?"

"No. I'm positive it wasn't him. The voice was too high."

"I didn't think so." Cassidy rolled over on the mattress. "Now that your mom's not here, let me ask you again: 'Are you okay, Danny?'"

"Yeah ... I'm mad at Mom for keeping something from me, though. I'm glad you're here."

"Me too. We'll figure this out."

"I'm not sure I can sleep." Danny stretched her arms over her head. "Ugh. The plane made me so stiff."

"Would a shoulder rub help?" Cassidy offered.

"Definitely. I'll give you one too."

As Cassidy worked on a couple of knots on her neck, Danny tried to remember if she'd been to Nova Scotia before. As she reached back into the depths of her mind, she heard that word—Tuatha de Danann—echoing through a large house. The call of a bird in the distance, a twig breaking in the breeze, and a scratching below the floor boards distracted her from the vague recollection. She made a mental note to tell her mother about the rats under the house and drifted off to sleep.

CHAPTER 3
WELCOME, TUATHA DE DANANN

FOLLOWING THE SCENT OF BACON, Danny charged down the stairs. Cassidy trailed after her with much less enthusiasm. Sunlight flooded the pastel-yellow kitchen through floor-to-ceiling windows. Ms. Reyes stood in front of the stove, her hand moving mechanically as she scrambled the eggs. The plates clanked as she set the table with unsteady hands. Cassidy saw the dark shadows under Ms. Reyes' eyes. Ms. Reyes wouldn't relinquish control of the frying pan to Cassidy, who tried to relieve her of the duty. A sizzling pop caused Ms. Reyes to jerk away from the stove. "Ouch!" Danny rushed over to help, her sudden motion causing more grease to jump out of the pan. Danny dodged the grease, but her mother moved sluggishly in her insomnia-induced stupor, so she suffered another burn. Apologizing profusely, Danny retreated back to the kitchen table. Ms. Reyes finished breakfast and served the girls.

"So Danny, where's our first stop?" Cassidy asked. She ducked her head to give thanks for the meal.

"Dollhorse University," Danny replied with a piece of bacon hanging out of her mouth.

"Pardon?"

Danny swallowed the bacon. "Dalhousie University."

Ms. Reyes glanced at her Ogham. "We're going to be late!" She snatched Danny by the collar and headed to the door.

In the car, the company sat in silence. The mystery at hand was the only subject on Cassidy's mind. *I shouldn't message with Danny about it on our Oghams because Ms. Reyes will get suspicious,* Cassidy thought. *I don't even know what I'd say.* Instead of focusing on the legal news read by her Ogham, she found herself doodling on her hand using her relearned knowledge of how pens functioned. She noticed Danny checking her Me-Site every few seconds and offered to watch a movie, to distract them both.

"Are we there yet?" Danny asked.

"Look out the window."

Sitting up, Danny saw a brick tower and realized her mother was looking for parking.

"You have a tour scheduled in a few minutes," Ms. Reyes said. "Message me an hour before you'd like to be picked up."

After carefully tucking her slacks into her boots, Cassidy tried to walk like a sophisticated upper-classman across the green. She thought about how great it would be if someone mistook her for a local student. Her concentration on poise was broken, as Danny sprinted past her. She sighed and tried to keep up with her friend.

In her excitement, Danny overshot the building designated for tours. As she veered around a corner to rejoin Cassidy, she barreled over a university student, losing her glasses in the process. Danny pushed her head off his chest, mumbling apologies.

"That's quite the greeting for your tour guide," he said in a cool voice she immediately recognized.

"Taban?" She squinted from her position on top of him and brought the blur of gold and teal into focus. He sported a style of shirt she'd seen advertised recently. Comprised of two thick straps and many thin ones, Danny liked the wide variety of ways the Strap-Shirt could be worn. A special spray lotion or an undershirt could be used to protect against tan lines. Based on the sheen of his skin, Taban had elected to apply the former option. He had pulled the smaller straps over his shoulders and coiled the two large straps so tightly around his waist that his stomach didn't move when he breathed.

"Hi, Danny." Taban brushed tangled hair out of her face to slide her thick glasses up her nose. She grinned at him. He returned with an equally broad smile.

"What are you doing here?"

"I go here. Remember?"

"Oh, right."

"Let's go find our tour group," Taban beckoned. "Shall we?"

"I found our guide!" Danny shouted when she saw Cassidy.

"She knocked your tour guide flat," Taban corrected.

"Is it just us, or am I in the wrong spot?" Cassidy's eyes widened when she saw Taban. "Uh, hello, again?"

"Morning," Taban said. "Spring Break is usually busy, so there are a lot of students on staff, but I think most people are still sleeping in. The school will get really crowded later. I saw your names on the list for tours today and asked for you because I thought you'd like to see a familiar face."

"Uh ...," Cassidy said.

"You didn't want to see me again?" He blinked his wide, blue eyes seeming completely taken aback.

"I don't mind," Cassidy assured him. "I was just surprised to see you again."

"Good." Tracing her arm with his fingertips, he gave her hand a quick squeeze. The ink from her doodle smudged on his fingers, turning the ends black. "I wanted to give you the best college experience. There's a guest speaker at the university this afternoon. The presentation was so popular I had to reserve spots. My best friend, Ea, pulled a few strings so we could bring guest students. Are you interested?" He tapped his Ogham and they leaned in to read.

May Savali, Professor of Anthropology, presents: The Power of the Tuatha de Danann

Cassidy tried to conceal her gasp with her hand. She jerked her head up in time to catch a knowing smirk on Taban's face, before he hid it under a warm expression. *While you're pulling helpful things out of nowhere, I'd like a sandwich,* Cassidy thought.

"What's the matter?" he asked.

"Nothing, um, how is this pronounced?" Cassidy asked.

"Tooua-De-Dhan-Un."

The young women exchanged a confirming glance. Afraid Danny would mention the event from the night before, Cassidy said, "Sure, we'd love to go."

"Wonderful."

They remained a couple strides behind Taban.

"Should we ask him?" Danny mouthed.

Cassidy gave her friend a blank look. She felt like her brain wasn't functioning at full capacity around Taban, and worst of all, it wasn't entirely unpleasant.

"A13: Message Mom: Cassidy and I are attending a featured lecture, could you pick us up at three?"

After visiting the library, main office, and other points of interest they headed back toward the tower at which they'd started. As they walked across the campus green, a long-legged woman in bright running shorts hailed Taban.

"This probably sounds weird, but were you in a commercial recently?" she asked.

"I was," Taban laughed. "If there were any parts of me they didn't CGI. Honestly, I think they only used my voice."

"I work for the school media. Do you think you could do some commercials for the school?"

"Sure. I'm giving two prospective students a tour right now, so I have to go."

"Wait, I don't have your contact info," she said, resting her hand on his arm. "I'm Michelle, by the way."

He touched his Ogham and quickly tapped it to hers.

Cassidy grimaced. It took all of her self-control not to dislike the pretty athlete talking to Taban. She reminded herself that Michelle had given her no reason to despise her.

He's in commercials too! Cassidy wrote on her Ogham and showed to Danny. *That explains all the pretty pictures I found when I searched him,* she reasoned.

"Well, he *is* charismatic."

"Thank you, Danny," Taban said.

"It's true," Danny shrugged.

"Wait." Michelle jogged up to Cassidy holding out Cassidy's key necklace. "You dropped this. The chain is broken, but let me fix it." Michelle took small pliers out of her utility belt, which she used to press the links together. "Here you go."

"Wow, thanks, so much," Cassidy replied. Michelle waved and dashed off.

An uncomfortable silence around them was shattered by a growl from Danny's stomach. "I'm hungry! What's for lunch?"

"Good timing. We could meet Ea in the dining hall and then go to the lecture together."

"I think I smell food. Is the dining hall this way?"

"You're right. Lead the way," Taban laughed.

* * *

Cassidy opened the oak door that led to the dining hall, holding it for Danny and Taban. About two-dozen students sat in clusters around picnic-style tables, for eating, conversing, and or browsing tablets. Cassidy cautiously crept into the spacious hall, feeling that all eyes would be on her if she made a sound. Taban stumbled in his platform sandals, surprising Danny, who knocked over a basket of bagels, which tumbled to the floor, spilling its contents. All the students looked up to see the source of the commotion. A tall teenager, carrying a grey chinchilla, rushed over to help them. He too, sported platform sandals and a Strap-Shirt, but he'd used the wider straps to form a red v over his shoulders to downplay his lanky figure. Taban took the basket and headed toward the compost bin by the door.

"Sorry," Danny said.

"Don't you mind it." The teen brushed a few purple strands of his face-framing hairstyle off his aquiline nose. "My name's Stag."

For a moment, Danny contemplated his soothing American Southern accent. She guessed he hailed from Georgia.

"I'm Danny and this is Cassidy. Can I pet your chinchilla?"

"Of course. Her name's Grenadine."

While Danny and Stag bonded over the rodent. Cassidy noticed a latte machine in the corner next to the table on which the bagels had been sitting, before they met their untimely demise.

"Thanks for helping," Cassidy said and offered Stag a latte she'd purchased.

"You're so kind. Thank you."

"Where's Ea?" Taban asked stiffly. For the first time in their brief acquaintance, Cassidy didn't see a pleasant expression on Taban's face. It wasn't directed at her, but at Stag, who didn't look pleased to see Taban either.

"Over there." Stag pointed to the far end of the hall. "I need to let this little one rest," he said, indicating the chinchilla. "Maybe I'll see you at the lecture." He carefully placed his rodent in a pet carrier that he'd left on a far table.

Danny waved to Stag, while Cassidy purchased four more lattes. She kept one for herself, handed one to Danny, and gave two to Taban. "For your friend," she explained.

"You don't need to … alright let me introduce you to Ea. This way."

Eadowen, wearing a pressed dress shirt and a green sweater vest, gave a delicate wave from his table. Freckles lined his even cheekbones and a Windsor adorned his throat. His chestnut bangs were cut with precise care just above high arched eyebrows. The same diligence seemed to apply to his unassuming smile. One feature distracted from his conscientious presentation: thin scars running from his left cheek, down his neck, and into his starched collar.

As they approached, Danny detected a crisp floral fragrance, which evoked the memory she'd been trying to recall the night before. She couldn't elicit any details, except for an image of her mother crying.

Setting the lattes down, Taban strolled to the other side of the table. He draped his arms around Eadowen and rested his chin on his shoulder. Eadowen patted Taban's arm in greeting. As he did this, Cassidy noticed a stone ring on his left hand resembling Taban's. Complementing his crimson tie and hazel eyes, the ring seemed better suited to Eadowen than to Taban.

"Sorry, I couldn't make it over in time to help," Eadowen said. "It's a pleasure to meet you Edana and Cassidy. My name is Eadowen Tolymie." He shook their hands. "Please sit down we still have a few minutes before we leave for the lecture."

"How do you say your first name?" Cassidy asked as she held out a latte.

"Thank you. And it's 'EE-doe-in,' though Taban calls me 'Ay-ah.'"

The soft intonations of his voice immediately set even the socially anxious Cassidy at ease. He spoke with an accent Danny recognized as "mixed-national". Usually students developed the accent from prestigious pre-university schools with impressive student diversity. She hadn't noticed it in Taban's voice before, but when he started speaking with Eadowen, she could identify similar inflections. Yet, their mixed accents were still different. Taban pronounced most words like Cassidy did. In contrast, Eadowen's accent was infused with the long o's of some Canadian speakers and a subtle Scottish burr.

"Do you prefer Danny or Edana?"

Danny thought for a moment. Eadowen pronounced her name, "eh-DON-a" instead of ED-anna. "I like the way you say Edana," she decided.

"Cassidy, do you have a nickname?"

She shook her head.

"And your preferred gender pronouns?" Eadowen continued.

"She and her," they answered in unison. Cassidy appreciated his attentiveness.

"Mine are xie and hir," Eadowen said.

"By the way, thanks for getting us into the lecture," Cassidy said.

"You're welcome. Edana, it's very important that you attend it. Afterward we can probably explain everything, but if I try without any background you won't believe me."

"Um," Cassidy began, but she didn't even know what kind of question to ask or whether it was a good idea to reveal the details of last night. Everyone waited patiently for her to respond, but she couldn't come up with anything that wouldn't draw suspicion.

Discomforted by the lull in conversation, Danny blurted, "Eadowen, do you do commercials too?"

"Hm. I never considered it." He pushed on the table. Danny and Cassidy's eyes widened as Eadowen rolled backward. Their reactions to his wheelchair caused Taban to start giggling next to Eadowen's ear. Cringing, Eadowen pulled him, still laughing, into the seat next to him. He told Taban to compose himself and they finished the lattes Cassidy had provided.

* * *

Eadowen settled into a spot at the back of the rapidly filling lecture hall. Leaning on the railing, he gestured for everyone to sit in the three empty seats next to him. Cassidy wanted to sit next to Taban so badly that it made her uneasy. Resolving to take the farthest seat from Eadowen, she pulled Danny into the seat next to her. Taban took the last seat available between Danny and Eadowen.

One of the lower doors opened and a woman dressed in grey entered. Cassidy touched the acne on her cheeks when she noticed the woman's flawless skin. Adjusting an amethyst pin in her hair, the woman in grey scanned the audience. Even though Cassidy sat in the back, she caught a twinkle in the woman's chocolate eyes.

"Good afternoon, students and faculty of Dalhousie University. My friend and colleague, Dr. May Savali, just contacted me and she is running a few minutes late. My name is Abigail Crane." The audience cheered. "For those who do not know me, my research team and I are asking students with Celtic ancestors to volunteer their genomic records. Many of you had those records taken at birth to determine allergies and health risks, among other things. We have excellent privacy regulations, so rest assured ..."

"Dr. Abigail Crane is also known for writing the fastest genome sequencing software program to date," interrupted another person from the doorway. Though the other person appeared composed in her sport coat, her black hair clung to her forehead from perspiration. The colleagues greeted each other with a friendly side hug, and then Crane ducked into a seat in the front row.

"My apologies for my tardiness, my name is May Savali. I thank you all for your patience," she began, in a voice accustomed to presentation. "Today, we will be discussing the history of the Tuatha de Danann."

The lights dimmed, Savali pressed a button on the podium and with a whirring noise the screen slowly lowered from the ceiling. The light of the projector from her tablet illuminated an image of Ireland and Scotland on the screen. At least the coastlines looked like Ireland and Scotland, but the names were unfamiliar. Cassidy could see the name "Caledonia", in the Northern part of Scotland. She leaned over and whispered to Danny. "Caledonia? That looks like Scotland?"

"It was the name the Romans used for Northern Scotland, when they started their conquest of the Gauls in the First Century BCE," Eadowen answered quietly.

"Thanks," Cassidy whispered as Savali began:

"The peoples of Ancient Ireland and Scotland relied on oral tradition, so much knowledge and culture has been lost. The Romans were the first to formally record the traditions of the Celtic people." Savali tapped her tablet and the image changed to a caricature of a grinning leprechaun. A ripple of laughter echoed in the spacious hall.

"When I say fairies you probably think of gold-hoarding, pop culture leprechauns, little girls in pretty dresses, and shoe-making elves. But today, we will discuss some of the ancient gods of the Celtic world. The two groups I will discuss today are the Tuatha De Danann and the Fomori.

One particularly interesting aspect of Irish mythology is that the deities were not necessarily immortal. They had extended lifespans, much like some of the early myths about mermaids. The Tuatha De Danann are mentioned in all Celtic mythologies: however, only a few texts from the Celtic world survive. Existing before humans in Ireland, the Tuatha De Danann were said to be the last race of deities to inhabit Caledonia. According to legend, the Danann battled and defeated the other races including the Fomori. The Tuatha De Danann had a formidable adversary in the Fomori, who were described as deities from the sea. Most accounts suggest the Fomori's physical appearance was revolting to behold, though some retellings list attractive exceptions. When humans came to Ireland, it is said that Tuatha De Danann became the intermediaries between the other world and the human world.

The afterlife of the Celtic mythos is different from the afterlives of other mythologies that you might be familiar with. They believed in reincarnation. The other world was merely a lovely place where one could reside before one's next life began. It was said that a living human could stray into a residence of the Tuatha De Danann—the other world between life and death. Some legends feature a Tuatha De Danann producing offspring with a human during the human's stay in their realm."

Wracking her brain for some connection between Danny and the Tuatha De Danann, Cassidy glanced at her friend, who looked just as baffled.

"Wow, what a cute couple," a student in front of Cassidy whispered to his friend.

His friend looked and nodded.

Cassidy followed the student's gaze and saw Eadowen absent-mindedly stroking Taban's cheek, while Taban napped on his friend's shoulder. She knew many people who were affectionate with their friends, but there was something intimate about the way Eadowen touched him. She wondered why Taban had referred to Eadowen as a friend and not as a partner. Frustrated with herself for letting her thoughts stray to an irrelevant issue, Cassidy swallowed her disappointment. She forced her attention back to the lecture.

"Interestingly enough, some people have theorized that the Tuatha De Danann and other ancient gods were not gods at all, but exaggerated heroes or even another race of humans. This is absolutely ridiculous, of course. The Tuatha De Danann are primarily an Irish myth; however, there are many entities with similar attributes across all Celtic mythology. For example, who knows what a Kelpie is? Yes, you in the front with the purple hair."

"A Kelpie is a mythological river horse that lured children onto its back. It would take the child under the water," Stag explained.

"Excellent, Kelpies are similar to the Each Uisge, which exist in Scottish folklore. They are said to be beasts of the ocean, shape shifters that can appear as alluring men or horses.

Many aspects the mythologies of the Celtic World are still unknown. The meanings of the Pictish symbols can only be guessed. The traditions of the tribesmen and many ruins remain enigmas."

An image of a few Pictish symbols appeared on the projector. One looked like a hand held mirror, another appeared to be a comb or a tool of some sort, and one was definitely a spiraled snake. Cassidy's mind took another trip to la-la land as she pondered the image that reminded her of a mirror. *Did they have those back then?* she thought.

"On a recent research trip to the University of Aberdeen, I came across evidence that one Roman officer may have learned the Pictish language from a native and recorded aspects of their lives that we do not yet know. Unfortunately, the documents he recorded have been lost to time, along with answers to many Celtic mysteries. One source indicated that the documents were last seen in 1840, in Ireland, just before the potato famine. It is possible that the documents immigrated to the United States with one of the many people who came from Ireland.

"So, if you have Celtic heritage feel free to check your parents' attic," Savali jested. The audience responded with chuckles.

"All kidding aside, I highly recommend submitting genomes to my longtime friend, Dr. Abigail Crane. You will receive both monetary compensation, as well as a full genealogy chart of your ancestors. If for some reason you did not have a genome taken as a child, Dr. Crane can take a cheek swab. She will be available next door to take swabs for the next hour."

As she spoke, Abigail beamed at the audience from her seat at the front of the room.

"I hope you enjoyed my presentation, please have a lovely evening," Savali finished as the screen slowly ascended toward the ceiling behind her.

The audience clapped as Crane and Savali glided out of the room. Several people in the audience started to go through the consent procedure to submit their genomes. Eadowen leaned over his sleeping friend. For a moment Cassidy thought he was going to kiss him, but instead he retrieved Taban's water bottle. Eadowen poured some of the water onto his hand and let it drip through his fingers onto Taban's face. Taban sat up so quickly Eadowen barely had time to move the water bottle.

"Why do you always do that?" Taban groaned.

"Only way to wake you. Would you prefer Donovan's method?" Eadowen asked. "My youngest brother pours a bucket of ice water on Taban to get him up," he elaborated for Cassidy and Danny's benefit.

"Don't ever let Donovan wake me up again," Taban shivered. "He doesn't even wait for the ice cubes to melt. It hurts!"

Cassidy and Danny snickered.

"Did you enjoy the lecture?" Eadowen asked.

"I'm going to submit my genome analysis to Abigail's project," Danny added excitedly. "I can't wait to take more biology classes."

"Edana, please don't," Eadowen begged. "Your information is particularly vulnerable."

"Eadowen's right," Cassidy nodded. "That's a lot of personal information to volunteer."

"But it sounds so interesting."

"It's fascinating, but there are some things you need to know first," Eadowen said. "Will you—"

Before he could finish his sentence, Stag came charging up the lecture hall stairs. After acknowledging Cassidy and Danny with raised eyebrows, he scanned the chairs in which they had been sitting. "Follow me outside now!" Stag commanded, yanking a couple of Danny's hairs out of the backrest.

"They're going to come find you because you answered that question," Taban growled as they hurried out into the hallway.

Stag didn't speak again until they had crossed almost to the other side of the now crowded campus. When he did speak, it came out as a rapid stream of consciousness directed at Eadowen.

"I'll keep 'em sidetracked by submitting my genome and telling them all the Celtic history and mythology you've taught me. They'll probably pick me as the most likely sample group at this school and then Savali will move on to the next school. It's too bad this is Crane's home base. I've been checking around campus this week. This afternoon they're paying students to approach people who fit the phenotype of someone with strong Celtic heritage. The students get money for each sample they collect, so some of them try to cheat and take hair samples they find. Even though only cheek swabs would hold up for analysis, if they found anything."

"Thank you, my dear," Eadowen sighed. "Oh, and just to be safe, could you find out if Savali was doing anything important that caused her delay?"

"Anytime." He and Eadowen exchanged a quick peck on the cheek. "Take care of yourselves." Stag nodded to the girls and departed.

"What the heck is going on?" Cassidy said, feeling thoroughly uncomfortable and confused.

"Where are you going next?" Taban asked.

"We're—" Cassidy started to explain, but with considerable effort she stopped herself.

"We're going to meet—" Danny began, but Cassidy dug her fingers into Danny's arm.

"We're not telling you anything until you explain what's going on," Cassidy said firmly.

"I assure you that we will," Eadowen said. "Please, come to our house this evening for dinner and we'll explain everything you need to know. Though, if you mention my name to your mother she'll never let you go." He spoke so softly that Cassidy had to lean in to hear him. "Listen closely, Danny. You and I are from the same family tree, so we're both at risk. I just want to help you." He drew back as a young woman approached Danny.

"Hey do you want to submit your genome?" she asked cheerily. "All you have to do is sign here, little lady."

"We're in a hurry," Cassidy replied more than ready to escape from all the bizarreness that had occurred in the last hour. "Come on." Cassidy and Danny bolted giving no one a chance to stop them.

"What if I want to find out about my genome?" Danny jogged next to Cassidy. "Maybe Eadowen and Taban are trying to trick me?"

"We don't know anything. No one is going to touch your genes until we do," Cassidy assured her.

* * *

When Cassidy and Danny reached the parking lot, they saw Ms. Reyes furrow her brow as she read something on her tablet. She turned the tablet around and showed it to Danny. "Is this the lecture you went to?" she asked fiercely.

Danny swallowed and looked at her mother. Ms. Reyes towered over her with worry and anger shifting in her eyes.

"Yes," Danny answered hanging her head.

"That was the lecture that was offered to us on the tour," Cassidy explained. "It was just a talk about Celtic mythology."

"Were you both awake last night?"

"Not the whole night," Danny replied.

"Don't be smart with me, Edana Arthur Reyes. Did you overhear anything?"

Both Cassidy and Danny stood petrified. Inspecting the ground Danny kicked a rock. Cassidy tried to make her expression as vapid as possible, which was challenging, since she liked to display intelligence.

"You did hear him. I should have known, with your hearing, you would. I thought when I married your father—he was nothing like them—I thought I'd never have children like you." Ms. Reyes braced herself on the car door and covered her face. "I'm so sorry honey. I have to cancel your trip. You are going back to Victoria and staying there. Victoria is far away from them." She looked at Danny's hurt expression and softened her voice. "Get in the car, both of you. This isn't your fault."

"Who are 'them'?" Danny pleaded.

"Please, just get in the car."

Danny heard the clopping of platforms hitting the pavement behind her.

"There you are!" Taban ran up to Ms. Reyes with a winning smile. Huffing, he extended a hand, which she accepted warily. "You must be Danny's mother. It's a pleasure to meet you. I hope that Danny and Cassidy will have time to join us. Do you think you could drop them off at Dal later this evening?"

"What?"

"Oh there's this dinner thing for prospective students. It's held at my friend's house. He's part of student government."

"I'm afraid not."

"But mother ..."

"No buts, Edana!"

"I would be happy to pick them up if you are unable to drop them off." Taban edged closer to Danny's mother. "Cassidy is *so* clever and Danny is *so* enthusiastic. I think the University would like *really* benefit by having these two *brilliant* ladies as part of the incoming class."

A tremble on Ms. Reyes' lips almost turned into a smile. "That might be okay," she said.

"Thanks so much," Taban purred.

"You're, um, welcome." Ms. Reyes held her forehead as though she had no idea what had happened.

Danny almost knocked her mother over when she threw her arms over her mother's shoulders to show her gratitude. Feeling a warm hand on her arm, Cassidy looked up and caught a wink from Taban as he brushed past her.

CHAPTER 4
WHEN WINNERS WRITE HISTORY

AS TABAN CROSSED the freshly mowed lawn, he heard the sound of quick footsteps behind him.

"Taban! Hey!"

Taban recognized the athlete from earlier that day. "Hello, again." He tried to look pleased to see Michelle, while maintaining a distracted air. "I need to get going, but was there something you wanted?"

He already knew what she wanted. Her minimalist workout clothes showed off her legs and chest. She was very attractive; it was a pity that if he complied, she'd probably regret it.

"I just ...," Michelle began, then looked down and ran her fingers through her hair. "I wanted to know if you wanted to go out sometime—maybe to coffee?"

Taban folded his arms so that his left hand caught the sunlight. Her eyes darted to the ring.

"As friends is fine." She smiled sadly. "I guess you *are* with Eadowen. Hir's such a lovely person."

"There's a guy with purple hair running around." Taban walked away from her. "He'd be happy to help you with the commercial and anything else you might need," he added over his shoulder.

Taban spotted his friend sitting under a maple tree with a black teapot, two tea cups, and a couple of scones on a cloth napkin next to him. A five-fingered leaf floated down, landing on the stack of worn papers in his friend's hands. Eadowen brushed the leaf away, letting it fall onto his folded wheelchair, and continued reading. Taban jogged to his friend and knelt beside him. On the off chance the young woman was still watching him, he slid his hand under Eadowen's. Intertwining his fingers with Eadowen's, Taban touched his lips to the back of his friend's hand.

"You have no audience right now," Eadowen said flatly. "I prefer it when your affection is sincere or whatever the equivalent of that is for you."

Taban laughed, letting Eadowen open his hand. He pressed his palm to Eadowen's. They had almost the same hand size. Eadowen's index finger was much longer than his own, but his ring finger extended past Eadowen's. While Taban compared their anatomical differences, Eadowen pushed a cup of tea toward him and continued reading.

"Not gonna play up that sexy Scottish accent for me?" Taban feigned whining. "You sure put it on for them."

"Thought they'd find it intriguing." Eadowen flipped to another page. "Canadian is just as fetching."

"I can't believe you're reading that on paper."

"You know why I can't make an electronic copy. It's too risky. This is the only copy I made of the stone tablets in our vault."

"I still can't believe that's the Roman officer's journal that Savali was talking about." Taban tasted the tea. He didn't have to check the temperature because Eadowen never offered him anything that would burn him.

"Right."

Looking over Eadowen's shoulder, Taban saw the familiar Latin script. He didn't want to learn how to read it, because he would know the exact words, and for Eadowen's sake it was better that he didn't. Taban had gathered from Eadowen's allusions to the content of the writing that it was a Roman officer's journal from around 100 to 150 AD.

"I needed to reread it after Savali's lecture."

"You have it memorized—you read it like a favorite novel," Taban teased. "These look delicious." He picked up a scone, but Eadowen blocked his arm.

"I put those in an insulated container, so they're still hot," Eadowen said and continued on the other topic. "It *would* be my favorite novel if it was fiction."

"Still have a crush on the Tuatha de Danann in it?" Taban lay down in the grass next to his friend with the tea and scones between them.

"I don't have a crush on Endymion or the Tuatha de Danann descendant he encountered." Though Eadowen spoke in his usual pleasant tone, Taban detected harshly tapped r's in his friend's accent. He smiled up at the tessellated leaves. It had taken him years to hear that subtle change. It was hard to provoke Eadowen, but the challenge made it deliciously satisfying to do so. Attempting to snatch a scone while his friend was preoccupied, he was again thwarted by Eadowen.

"Endymion?"

"The Roman officer's name."

"If it's such a risk to keep those old tablets around, why do you?"

"They're the only clue to my family's origins. They meant so much to my parents and so many other people. I can't imagine destroying them."

"Whatever you say." A leaf rested on Taban's chest. He plucked it off and tickled Eadowen's cheek with the fan, catching a rare glimpse of Eadowen's teeth in his smile.

"You can eat it now." Eadowen brushed the leaf away from his face. "You know what's most fascinating about this piece? Endymion asserts that the Each Uisge and the Fomori were one and the same."

"Whoa, wait. I don't know much about Celtic mythology, but that's wrong. One was ugly, the other could morph into a hot guy." Taban ripped open one of the salt packets he kept in his Ogham compartment and sprinkled it over his scone.

"That's just it. Endymion says the descendant of the Tuatha de Danann he met told him this. In a weird way it makes sense; the Tuatha de Danann won against the Fomori and ..."

"...and winners end up writing history," Taban finished his sentence. "Interesting thought."

Before Eadowen could reply, his Ogham flashed. He answered it using a metallic bio-feedback device that looped over his ear to align with his temple. Taban always thought the device looked like an intricate gold earring, which didn't bother him. However, not knowing when Eadowen was going to answer his Ogham could get annoying at times.

"Message from Stag: Dr. Savali's delay was for a family member, it had nothing to do with the research."

"What was the family matter?" Taban demanded.

"Message from Stag: I don't think it's relevant. That's another person's personal inform—"

"If she told you it can't be that secret," Taban said.

"Stag," Eadowen said. "I admire your ethics. Just to be sure, is there anything you'd be comfortable sharing?"

"Message from Stag: Her son was looking at surf kayaking gear and they missed a shuttle. Like I said, not important."

"Thank you," Eadowen replied.

"Message from Stag: By the way, a beautiful person named Michelle started talking to me about a commercial. What did you do?"

"Consider the pretty girl a thank you present," Taban said. "Have fun."

"Message from Stag: Don't treat her like a commodity, that's horrible."

"You know, Stag, most guys would kill for my cast offs. Just go talk to her," Taban replied.

"Cast off is such a disrespectful term—"

Taban cut Stag off by ending the conversation with a tap on Eadowen's Ogham.

Taban tried to soak up the sun, but he felt cold. He envisioned himself falling asleep beside Eadowen and never waking up. There was a vial under his bed back home that would make that possible, but for now, he had two people to protect: Eadowen and Telyn, his younger sister. Rubbing his tattoo, Taban thought of Telyn, still in the clutches of the most charming monster he'd ever met.

"If you dislike your tattoo so much, why don't you get it removed?"

"Can't. I mean ... I just hate that it looks like the Loch Ness Monster. I think the symbol is even called the Pictish Beast."

"I see a dolphin."

"Dolphins aren't always nice to people," Taban explained. "They've been known to ..."

Eadowen kissed the mark and Taban felt warmth suffuse his entire body. Taban's Ogham buzzed. He checked the name at an angle Eadowen couldn't see. The chill crept up his spine again. "I have to go," he said.

"Bye."

* * *

Taban jogged to the Life Sciences Centre, where a woman, waited for him, while fiddling with her hair pin.

"Hello, Taban."

"Hi, Abigail. What's going on?" He placed his hand on her hip and guided her into the cool shade of the building. He glanced around, as though Eadowen could see across campus. Wrapping his arms around her waist, he pulled her into a long kiss. "Any news?"

"Yes." Dr. Abigail Crane's eyes sparkled with excitement. "May Savali found some evidence that the journal came to North America during the Irish immigration caused by the Potato Famine."

"Hm?" Taban ran his hands down her sides, so that she wouldn't notice that her comment made him shake.

"She may have pinpointed the geographical location of the journal."

"Did she tell you where that was?" Taban asked.

"No, because it's not official. She won't share anything that she isn't sure about."

"Thanks for telling me," he purred. "You know how *fascinated* I am by your work."

She looked around to see if anyone noticed their affectionate touching. A couple of students walked by and she stepped back to a more platonic distance.

"You're my intern, so you're an important part of this project."

"Well, my interest isn't just in the project." He embraced her and rested his chin on her soft hair. When they separated, he saw her face had fallen. "What's wrong, honey?"

"You know how I found the unique genes in the group of people I studied who were all between the ages of 110 and 120?"

"The deca-centenarians. I know." Taban nodded.

"Well, if someone had a combination of several different genes my team identified, they could live a lot longer. I found a couple people with a higher percentage of the genes out of that group."

"Fantastic. What's the problem?"

"My theory about the descendants of a mythical race is going to sound like a crack-pot theory, unless I have a piece of historical evidence. I need that journal and I need it soon," she sighed.

"I'm sure your genius will be appreciated someday," Taban assured her. "Is Dr. Savali around?"

"She's not on campus," Abigail replied. "She told me she was headed for Ottawa," she added when she saw his quizzical expression. "I don't know if she's leaving tonight or tomorrow night."

"Is she close to her family?" Taban asked.

"Very much so, why?"

"Oh, no reason." Taban remembered Stag's comments about Daisuke, May Savali's son. "Is her son still around?"

"I think so." She tapped her chin looking thoughtful. "He should still be on campus? I think he's staying in Halifax for a while."

"Great," Taban turned to go.

"Goodbye, then?" she said disappointedly.

"Oh uh, do you want me to come over tonight? It'll have to be pretty late, but ... what's wrong?"

"It's childish, never mind." She waved her arms in front of her face. Taban took both of her hands between his and massaged her palms with his thumbs. "Who was the boy you were sleeping on in the lecture hall?" She asked. "Are you involved with him?"

"Who?"

"The brunette in the sweater vest," she clarified.

"Oh!" Due to Eadowen's gender identity, Taban was accustomed to people referring to his friend as person rather than boy. "No, no," he assured her. "Xie—that is 'he,' the boy you saw, is just a friend. I was like really tired today. I don't have any lovers other than you, of course."

"Sorry, that was ridiculous of me."

"It was," Taban accused. "Do you want me to come over?"

"I only want you to come over when you want to," Abigail tucked a strand of hair behind her ear. "I probably shouldn't even be having this kind of relationship with you."

"That's as ludicrous as your idea that I'd be getting it on with some stuffy guy." Taban turned his blue eyes skywards. "We've been through this. I love you, Abby."

"I didn't mean to …"

"It's because I'm a young guy." He pretended to swallow back tears and let his voice crack. "You don't think I can be in love! That's it isn't it?"

"No! I'm sorry if I gave you that impression. I respect your feelings …"

To his amusement, she continued to apologize. He waited until she was almost out of breath before silencing her with a kiss. "Thanks. I'm so glad we had this talk. See you around midnight tonight."

Once he was out of her sight, he wiped off his mouth and looked at his Ogham. It would only take a few social media searches and some asking around to find Daisuke on campus. Taban started to brainstorm ways to get Daisuke to share, and continue sharing his mother's findings. He could probably talk him into giving something away by accident, but it would be better if Daisuke owed him his life. *I think I can put him in a situation where he needs to be rescued before lunch tomorrow,* Taban thought. *I wonder if he knows about Martinique Beach.*

CHAPTER 5
PREPARING TO DINE WITH FAIRIES

"I THINK WE'RE GOING THE WRONG WAY," Cassidy said from the passenger seat of the Reyes' car.

Ms. Reyes' Ogham had been indicating Cassidy's statement for the last fifteen minutes, but Ms. Reyes slammed on the brakes, as though Cassidy was the first to mention it.

"We're sorry," Danny said. "Please, tell us what's going on?"

"I'm sorry, dear, it's better for you to not know, that way you don't have to worry about it."

"But I am worried!" Danny exclaimed, but only silence answered her plea. She fidgeted in her seat as though struggling to find a new topic of conversation beneath the seat cushion. "How are you doing?" She asked Cassidy.

In reply, Cassidy mumbled something that sounded like a combination of okay and fine. She opened her journal. Danny stopped squirming to admire Cassidy's repose as she wrote. The key necklace highlighted Cassidy's bronze neck, which smelled of fresh lavender.

I don't really feel like writing right now, but I'm afraid Danny's mom will read into anything I say or send to Danny.

Asking for another person's genome is so invasive that I can't believe Crane and Savali are getting away with it. Genomes are kept under high security and only accessed if legal or medical needs require it. I'm glad Eadowen stopped Danny, but I still don't know whether to trust hir anymore than Crane and Savali.

I looked up Taban and Eadowen again. Because of their high privacy protection, I couldn't find much about them, except that before Dalhousie they went to a prep school in Malibu. I hope I get into a good university. junior college is really hard. There were lots of tests to make sure students have the skills to go to junior college. I was too busy with school to think about asking someone out. Actually, it doesn't feel like anyone gets in relationships anymore. I envy Taban and Eadowen. They seem to really be in love and I've never even kissed anyone.

She looked up from her journal and took a deep breath.

Geez ... why am I thinking about Taban at a time like this? What's wrong with me? My friend might get in trouble. Yes, that sounds more like me. Danny's safety takes priority.

As Ms. Reyes eased the car into park, Danny leaped out. Her mother yelled after her to wait until the car had come to a complete stop, but Danny had already made it halfway up the steps to the front door.

Checking herself in the hallway mirror, Cassidy sighed. Since she shaved her head every four months to six months, her hair usually puffed up at an awkward length right before she decided to cut it. She patted her hair futilely trying to compress it, while attempting to ignore her pimples in the reflection.

Danny stood next to Cassidy. "I think you look great."

"You're just saying that!"

"Why do you care how you look right now?" Danny asked. "You don't usually stress about your looks."

"I don't. Well I do. But ..." Cassidy swept a mascara brush over her eyelashes and dabbed tinted sunscreen on her cheeks with a sponge.

"Are you getting dressed up for Taban?" Danny's tone dropped at the end of her question.

"No! Well, I just want to look nice since we're meeting new people. I like your colored lip balm by the way."

"Thanks." Danny applied the ruby shade generously to her full lips. "It's pomegranate."

"Are you sure you want to go?" Cassidy whispered.

"Yes, I ..."

Cassidy realized Ms. Reyes was dusting a bookshelf next to them and finished Danny's sentence. "Really want to learn more about Dalhousie. What was your favorite part about the school?"

The shift in topic perplexed Danny until she noticed the swish of her mother's duster behind her. "Oh, I liked the science building. Biology is really fun," Danny replied hastily.

"Yeah, I'm into law, but it would be cool to overlap it with patents."

"Wow. You actually have a plan," Danny commented. "I don't know what I want to do with my life or even school."

"I wouldn't call it a plan. I have to get into a pre-law program at a university. Those are really competitive." Cassidy's palms felt cold as she thought about applications.

As Ms. Reyes continued to hover around them doing various chores, Cassidy and Danny continued to talk about anything but Celtic mythology. As their conversation segued from the recent implications of string theory to a popular old cartoon about ponies, they heard the crunch of gravel.

Danny jumped onto a window seat and peered through a slit in the blinds she created. "Taban's here, I think." The clang of the doorbell resounded through the house. From her perch on the window seat Danny looked at Cassidy expectantly, but Cassidy, only an arm length from the door didn't open it. Danny trotted over to let Taban in.

"Good evening." Taban stood close enough to hug Ms. Reyes. "Thank you *so* much for letting them come."

"No problem, bring them back …"

"Is eleven okay?"

"I suppose," Ms. Reyes answered.

"Wonderful. I'll wait outside."

"Well, he seems … nice," Ms. Reyes said after Taban shut the door.

Cassidy breathed a sigh of relief when she saw a small white electric-solar car. She had imagined Taban showing up in something with a prancing horse logo. Taban was holding the front passenger door open. "Danny said you could have shotgun 'cause you get car sick on windy roads."

Worried it would seem rude to sit in the back with Danny, Cassidy accepted.

As he gripped the steering wheel with his right arm, Cassidy saw that his Ogham strap was empty.

"Did your Ogham fall off?"

"We don't use Oghams at our house, but it'll be okay if you keep yours just for tonight. Do you both want to listen to music?"

"Sure. Just don't turn it up too loud," Danny said.

"Play song from *Knots of Avernus*," Taban commanded to his car. "Your favorite, right?"

Cassidy looked down not knowing whether she was more embarrassed about liking the band or that Taban remembered.

The road began to wind more often. It narrowed from two lanes divided by a double yellow line to an unmarked paved road. The size of the deciduous trees in Nova Scotia couldn't compare to the giant evergreens to which Cassidy was accustomed. Yet, as they drove farther from Halifax the trees seemed to come in larger sizes. She attributed the sensation of a dense forest of giants to a trick of the waning light.

Danny tuned out the electrical beats of *Avernus* and concentrated. The same memories the floral aroma evoked earlier that day returned, but this time she couldn't identify the trigger.

"Almost there." Taban turned the car directly off the paved road into what appeared to be forest. Cassidy yelled at him to stop. As the car pitched forward, she saw vehicle tracks on a narrow path into the woods.

"Oh, I'm sorry. I should have mentioned that the Tolymie's driveway is hard to see." Taban laid his hand on her arm; his touch soothed her and made her skin bristle at the same time. It reminded her of sandy waves splashing in her face when she surf kayaked.

The trees created a canopy, shading out the sunlight. They pulled up to a two story cedar house with an attic tower. The maple and oak grew so densely it was apparent where their limbs had been removed so as not to penetrate the house. To Cassidy the Tolymie's residence seemed like it had been preserved from another time. Perhaps it was the warm firelight in the windows, or the bare wood instead of paint, whatever the reason, she wondered if she should've checked for white rabbits. Taban attempted to open the doors for Danny and Cassidy, but Danny had already exited the car and played valet to the passenger side.

"Welcome," Eadowen said, from the doorway.

They removed their shoes in the hallway. A red tapestry with golden knots woven through it hung across from an armoire with a full length mirror. Three long teardrop crystals dangled from a chandelier. A long rug similar in appearance to the tapestry, but worn in places that the design was obscured, covered the polished wood floor. The mirror on the armoire reflected a fire blazing in a round green marble hearth in the center of the living room. A couch made of red leather, semi-circled the fireplace.

"Make yourselves at home." Eadowen gestured toward the archway leading to the living room. "I haven't quite finished making dinner. Perhaps Taban can show you around."

Cassidy and Danny followed Taban past the hearth. A loveseat, matching the couch, faced a large screen surrounded by speakers and various electronic gaming devices. The screen flashed brightly as the image of a race car zoomed around a track. Unable to contain her interest in old-style video games, Cassidy inspected the equipment before noticing a teenager playing the game. Mud caked his sports jersey and a long lacrosse stick leaned against the sofa. He had pink sunburn on his broad muscular shoulders. The skin on his hands looked raw and dry, as though he'd scrubbed them too vigorously while washing.

"Donovan, greet our guests," Taban shouted.

The teenager did not respond. Taban took off his large noise-canceling headphones. Donovan glared up at him with steel blue eyes. "What?" he asked in a bass voice.

"Say 'hi.' "

"Hi," Donovan replied, running his hand over his crew cut.

"Cassidy, this is Ea's youngest brother. Cassidy likes to play video games, so we're going to join." Taban patted the seat next to him for Cassidy to sit down.

* * *

Meanwhile, Danny stood next to the fire. She detested that style of gaming because she could never coordinate the buttons with what she saw on the screen. The modern versions with simulation gloves and visors suited her better. Fortunately, the golden knots in the hall tapestry interested her, so she returned to it. As she ran her hands over the fabric, she heard a scratching sound underneath her. At first she thought it was a rat, but the sound was too decisive to be a rodent. She started to kneel to put her ear closer to the floor when she felt Eadowen's wheelchair rolling along the carpet.

"What's wrong?"

Turning to address him, Danny wondered if Eadowen ever changed expressions. His face reminded her of how a spokesperson for a new medicine looked after listing the possible side effects: sweet, trustworthy, and blank.

"I don't like video games. I suck at them."

"Would you like to join me, while I put the last touches on dinner?"

Danny could hear Cassidy's laughter from the living room as she followed Eadowen. Her throat burned as she pictured Cassidy's beautiful smile directed at Taban.

"I have more concern for your comfort than for possessions," he replied. "You must be curious about all that has happened. Come with me. I'll explain."

She followed him into the kitchen. Danny had not yet seen a door, aside from the front door in the Tolymie's house; neither kitchen nor living room had doors separating them from the hallway. The kitchen was the same dark cedar as the rest of the house with brass and silver pots and pans hanging from the walls. The brass and silver shimmered as though they had never been touched, but their hangers had been worn by many years of use.

Eadowen rolled over to the sink. "Get comfortable wherever you like."

A lamp with a red shade lit the kitchen from an oak table. A basket of round bread rolls, a glass bowl containing a spinach salad with vegetable toppings, and plates of rice noodles, covered in almond slices and peanut sauce surrounded the lamp.

To prevent herself from rudely eating the food, Danny settled on the low countertop next to the sink. The same black-green as the hearth, the polished countertops reflected the little white candles burning on the window sill. Danny enjoyed the lilac scent permeating from the candle smoke.

"Why is Mom so scared and who are you?" Danny asked.

"You and your mother came to visit nine years ago. Do you remember?"

Eadowen filled a kettle with water from the sink. With his closer proximity she detected the other floral scent she recognized from earlier that day.

"I smell something that gives me *déjà vu*."

"Hm. You were pretty young when you came over." He bit his lip. "Please describe the scent."

"Fresh and earthy. I think it's on you."

"Oh! Why didn't I think of that?" Eadowen set the kettle on the stove with a soft, but punctuated clang. "When I was a kid, my parents took me to Scotland. I liked the smell of the hawthorn and thistle flowers, so my dad taught me how to extract the smell and wear it. I had it back then too."

As he glowed with enthusiasm, his dull expression melted, but to Danny's chagrin, he snapped back to his original demeanor almost immediately.

"Let's see if we can jog your memory." He tilted his head to the side and stroked his neck directly under his ear. "This is where I put it on."

She leaned forward and inhaled above the place he'd indicated. The memories started to patch together. *Mom was in a heated argument with two people in front of that nice fireplace in the Tolymie's living room,* Danny thought. *When the argument escalated, eight-year-old me heard someone crying and followed the sound. I found a kid whose whole body was covered in bandages.*

"There was a kid crying," Danny summarized to Eadowen.

"I was upset because my parents were arguing with your mother. You comforted me. My father found us asleep together. I wasn't going to show you this, but since you remember ..."

He took a printed photograph out of a drawer and held it up for her to see. Danny recognized her younger self in the photograph curled up with a severely hurt, but identifiable Eadowen. The picture approximated her mental image of the event. She scanned it with her Ogham.

"Your mother was angry because she didn't want to be part of our secret cohort, but she wanted to have children. She moved to the other side of the country and married someone she thought didn't have the genes. Your father is mostly Hispanic, correct?"

"Yeah he is, but my mom is Hispanic too. I guess they have some other genetics in there. I mean I have some Irish way back in my genes from both sides of my family, but everyone has a mix." Danny gestured to the stereotypically Irish freckles on her dark skin.

"That's part of what makes this so complicated. The human race is so mixed; anyone could have the genes not just people who identify as Irish or Scottish. I think your mother felt your father would be less likely to carry the genes or she may have just wanted to remove you from the Celtic part of your heritage."

"It doesn't matter. The Tuatha De Danann aren't real. Mom's just being weird."

"The Tuatha De Danann are a myth. However, there is a grain of reality, in every myth. Sometimes evidence of a human condition is the only fact, but sometimes there was a person or event from which the fairytale stems. The Tuatha De Danann did exist as a humanoid race. My family prefers the term Genetic Fey or just GF, because we are humans who carry some genes from the Danann. The actual Danann race is long extinct."

"I'm confused."

"Do you follow scientific discoveries in the media?"

"Yeah."

"Well, perhaps you've heard of the various groups of humanoid skeletons they've found all over the world?" Eadowen returned his attention to the kettle. "There is evidence that there were once multiple species of humanoids on the planet, but the other species died off. My family knows relatively little about the GFs, but fortunately, no one without GF ancestors knows about them—at the moment. I fear that may soon change, with people like Dr. Crane so adamantly looking at genomes. She must have noticed some consistency in the DNA of those who lived for a long period of time, because it appears she suddenly started targeting people of Celtic heritage."

"Dr. Crane wants to find my DNA?"

"Based on the journal of a Roman officer, it was possible to interbreed with a group of humans who had unusual traits—traits that came perhaps from ancient interbreeding between two species of humanoids, namely human ancestors and the Tuatha De Danann. Your traits and some people in my family are similar to those described by the solider."

"So even at the time of the Roman officer the Danann race was already extinct, but certain people were their hybrid ancestors?" Danny clarified.

"Exactly. Would you like some tea?"

"No, thanks."

He poured a mug of hot water and put a sheet of rolls in the oven. "Would you pass me the tin of tea and the honey jar behind you?"

"What were the unusual traits?"

"A long lifespan, based on genealogy records my family kept. There may be other inherited traits, but it is difficult to tell with the few of us that exist. There's a distinct possibility that more of the genes that code for olfactory receptors are turned on in us."

"Humans sure missed out on the smell sense," Danny said eyeing the honey as Eadowen stirred some into his tea. He took a bowl and spoon from a rack by the sink and gave both to her. She unscrewed the top on the jar, poured the honey into the bowl, and started to eat it. "Thanks."

"If I have a longer lifespan, does that mean my development is slower? I thought I was mostly done with puberty," Danny groaned.

"From what I've seen of my family you probably developed a little bit slower, but not very much. Our organs just don't seem to degrade as quickly as other people. Unfortunately, that doesn't protect us from diseases induced by both viral and genetic mechanisms. Do you see why Dr. Crane getting a hold of your genes is a problem?"

"They would want to study me to find out how my body does things differently?" Danny asked. "Wouldn't that be good?"

"Well yes, but ..."

"Oh wait, a longer life span might not be good for the human race," Danny interrupted. "We could have even more over-population problems."

"Not to mention it might ruin your life." Eadowen stroked his chin with the back of his fingertips as though it surprised him to be talked over.

"How?"

"Conflict of interest, my dear. The corporations that fund these types of research are in it for money. Unfortunately, there aren't many of us. If we are discovered and try to have some control over what happens to the discoveries, it would be easy to make us disappear. Once our DNA is stored, our lives aren't very important and if a family member tries to claim rights to the DNA, they have revealed themselves as also being a GF."

In nervous contemplation, Danny tugged at her ponytail, which came undone releasing long wavy hair down her shoulders. "Someone would actually murder for the rights to DNA?" she wondered aloud.

His face somber, Eadowen stared at the floor. "It happened to my mother ... she managed to get away ... but ..." He rubbed his eyes, then continued with a rasp in his voice. "She died of her injuries. A friend had her body cremated." With fingertips wetted from tears, he stroked the ends of her hair. "I don't want the same to happen to you or anyone else."

From her perch on the counter, Danny reached down and laid her hand on the soft wool of his sweater vest that covered his shoulder. "I'm so sorry to hear that," she heard herself say.

"I'll be alright," he assured her. They sat together in silence for a few minutes until the oven chimed. Eadowen took the rolls out of the oven and set them on a vacant counter space. Resting his arms on the counter next to her, he looked up at her affectionately with eyes still rimmed in red from crying. Danny enjoyed the aroma of the bread mixing with his scent. "How did you find me?"

"Edana, I need to apologize. I horribly invaded your privacy. I promise you that I never looked up your Me-Site. Your home address, in Victoria, is in my family's contact list. When I started to hear about this research project, I got in touch with your mother, which is how I learned about your visit. You can probably guess she told me to stay away from you. I blatantly disregarded that request." Eadowen regarded her, his whole body stiff, as if he expected her to punch him.

"Well, I do feel uncomfortable knowing that, but for now I'm going to ..." Danny searched for the right words.

"All I ask is that you give me the benefit of the doubt. If I betray your trust, do as you see fit."

"I can do that," Danny replied as the oven beeped. "The person who came to my house last night said something about how I should try not to get sick or something."

"Just take good care of yourself. You seem strong, I'm sure you'll be fine," Eadowen said hastily. "Dinner's ready. We can talk about it later."

* * *

"You're not half bad," Taban said as Cassidy raced them around the virtual track. "Donovan, she's givin' you a run for your money!"

"Uh huh," Donovan agreed in monotone.

"You know Cassidy, Donovan has a crush on the guitarist from that one band you like."

"But the guitarist is a guy—"

"I'm gay," Donovan said coldly.

"Sorry," she mumbled to Donovan. Scolding herself for making assumptions Cassidy wondered, *Am I really that desperate for someone to have the possibity to be attracted to me? Must be Spring Break that's got me feeling like this ...* Still playing the video game, Taban tilted his whole body to make his car round a particularly sharp turn. *Though it started when he showed up.*

"'I'm gay'—two words, really stretching yourself there, Donovan," Taban laughed.

"Three. A contraction." Donovan cut off the car Taban controlled sending it into a spin.

With her attention diverted from the game, Cassidy realized Danny was no longer standing behind her.

"Where's Danny?"

"Probably went off with Ea," Taban explained. "She might be in the dining room."

"Dining room? Oh no!" She imagined her friend destroying delicate table decorations. Ashamed that she had forgotten Danny, she made her way down the hall, until she heard voices from the kitchen. Peeking around the doorway, she saw Danny sitting calmly on the counter, kicking her feet. Danny listened intently to something Eadowen said, but Cassidy could not hear him over the running water as he filled a kettle. She returned to the living room and sat on the sofa next to Taban. They continued to play the game until Eadowen called them to dinner. When Donovan stood, he dwarfed Taban who Cassidy estimated to stand six feet tall without his platforms. *He looks like he has trouble fitting through doors,* she thought, noticing his no longer hunched shoulders. *In both directions.*

"He's six feet ten inches." Taban responded to her unstated question. "Can you believe he's sixteen ... or seventeen?" Taban checked his Ogham. "He turns seventeen in a couple weeks, but still."

CHAPTER 6
OF RITUALS & PERFORMANCES

CASSIDY PASSED A TABLE only large enough to accommodate a vase containing a single stalk of orange foxglove. Beneath one of the tapering table legs, she observed a piece of particularly frayed rug. The table seemed to be placed specifically to conceal the tattered fibers worn away by repetitive use.

"*Entre ici*," Taban bowed in front of an archway in mock formality.

A chandelier with seven crystals hung from the vaulted ceiling. The soft light illuminated the ivory tablecloth covering the oval table in the center of the dining room, but the apex of the ceiling remained shadowed. Between two silver candelabras, ripe pomegranates lay on a bed of apple blossoms. A silver plate with two forks on the right and a spoon and a knife on the left comprised each place setting. From a tray in his lap, Eadowen handed Danny glasses cut to refract light into an aria of color. Danny filled each glass with sparkling water. Donovan transferred the salad bowl, noodle container, and bread basket from a wheeled trolley onto the table. Behind Donovan, Cassidy noticed a harp next to a double casement window framed by violet curtains.

"Would you like to take a seat?" The tips of Taban's fingers touched the small of her back to encourage her to move out of the doorway.

"Sit next to me." Danny pointed to a spot between her and Donovan. The water she poured spilled over the edge of the goblet. "Oops, sorry!"

"Just water," Donovan replied.

While Donovan mopped up the spill with his cloth napkin, Taban sat on the other side of him. There was another place setting between Taban and Donovan, but the chair for that place was in the corner of the dining room, as though its master rarely joined the table.

Eadowen gave Donovan a separate plate of noodles. "Please, help yourselves."

"He's allergic to nuts," Taban clarified. "Which is kinda funny when you think about it."

Donovan turned toward Taban. Even though Cassidy could only see the back of Donovan's head, a chill went up her spine. *I never want to be on the receiving end of his death glare,* she decided.

Eadowen lifted himself into the seat between Taban and Danny and pushed his wheelchair behind him to the wall. "I wish Aydan would join us."

Taban opened the window. "He'll smell the food."

"I don't usually like to interrupt him, but we have such wonderful company. How are you doing, Cassidy? I trust Taban and Donovan behaved."

A spicy aroma wafted from the large helping of noodles Cassidy had just served herself. "I had fun." She bowed her head to give thanks. Everyone stared at her except for Eadowen, who placed his hands together to show he understood.

Cassidy reached for a bread roll.

"Don't take one yet," Taban said. "Unless you want to do dishes later." Cassidy stopped, fearing she had done something impolite. Donovan took a bread roll and passed the basket to Taban, who also took a bread roll and set another at the empty place. He handed the basket to Eadowen, who unfolded the white cloth in the basket revealing several more bread rolls.

"Now you can have anything you like." Eadowen gave the basket to Danny, who took three. Taban turned the crisp roll in his hands and smiled at Donovan, who flipped his over on his plate with a fork and sighed. Cassidy craned her neck and noticed a round burned spot on the otherwise flawlessly baked crust. "Whoever gets the black mark does the dishes," Eadowen explained. "If we kept a schedule, everyone would avoid their day, but this way it's random."

"How appropriate that it's based on a ritual to determine a sacrifice," Taban commented.

"Is this your house?" Danny asked.

"My brothers and I inherited this house. This house and almost everything in it is generations old."

Cassidy reached for her goblet, but stopped when she realized it might be a family heirloom. "Don't worry about breaking anything—Aydan dropped everything on this table when he was learning a tablecloth trick," Taban assured her.

"This is lovely, thank you,"Cassidy said.

"You're welcome." A light thump came from the open window behind Taban. A small person perched on the sill, his face shadowed by long black locks.

"Won't you join us, Aydan?" Eadowen beckoned to the figure. "These are our guests Cassidy and Edana, who prefers Danny."

Aydan alighted on the floor. A black velvet coat concealed his body, just as his hair hid his eyes. A thin hand whipped out of his coat and pulled out the last chair available between Eadowen and Taban. The candlelight shone on an intricate silver broach fastened under his pointed chin. Still standing, Aydan snatched up the serving plate of noodles and dumped the entire entree onto his plate.

"Manners, Aydan!" Eadowen ordered just as Taban slurped a noodle.

"Oh, and you want me to take lessons from him?" Aydan asked, pointing at Taban.

"Please take a seat," Eadowen said.

Aydan disregarded his sibling's request and consumed several bites of pasta. Sweeping his hip-length hair behind his head, he secured it loosely with the salad fork. Heavy stage makeup highlighted his cheek bones and emphasized his wide mouth. The silver and black eyeliner, applied to the edges of his lids, gave his narrow eyes a cat-like appearance. Nodding to recognize the guests, he shrugged off his coat revealing a black garment Cassidy decided was a cross between a short dress and a tunic. He took a deck of cards out of his thigh-high boots, set it on the table, and flopped into his chair.

Well, no more empty places, Cassidy thought. *That means the gang's all here.* The new arrival made her uneasy. Before, if anything weird happened, she and Danny were close to evenly matched. She felt guilty for not including Eadowen, but his movements were limited enough that she didn't consider him a physical threat and Danny had been present while the drinks were prepared. The way Donovan wolfed his food suggested to her that he was more focused on returning to his video game than anything else. She glanced at Taban—he gave her a sincere smile—he was so easy to trust.

"Good evening," Aydan said in a husky counter-tenor. "I just got back from doing a magic show." The firelight reflected in his ebony eyes, as he scrutinized Danny. "You're the one who didn't know you were a GF?"

Recognizing his voice from the night before, Danny stared back at him, her cheeks stuffed like a chipmunk. "Maybe." She swallowed the lump of pasta. "I'm not sure I believe it."

"I understand this is confusing. I hope you will return tomorrow night. We'll do what we can to prove it to you." Eadowen said.

Cassidy shifted in her seat; she wasn't sure she how she felt about returning tomorrow night. She wanted to see Taban once more before she and Danny had to leave, but she still found the concept of the mythical Tuatha De Danann hard to grasp, and what was all this about being a GF?

Aydan picked up a pomegranate. He made a small slice with his knife and ripped it open, spraying red juice over a startled Taban. Danny, feeling threatened by Aydan, decided to show off. She shoved her fingers into the top of another pomegranate and tore it in half without the aid of cutlery. Cassidy guarded herself with a napkin.

"Edana, you're so powerful." Eadowen clapped delightedly and turned to his left. "Aydan, that's barbaric, clean it up." Eadowen sipped his drink, ignoring the almost identical irritated and incredulous expressions with which Taban and Aydan regarded him.

This interaction eased Cassidy enough to ask, "Where do you put your Oghams?"

"Everything is recorded by Oghams and tablets, both communication and location. No one is supposed to be able to access Ogham company records, but a good hacker would have no problem getting to them. That's why we don't talk about GFs in our Oghams and we have an apartment near the university where we store them and receive all of our mail," Taban explained. "It's a good place to do homework."

Danny heard Aydan mutter in a low voice, "By homework, he means women." His lips pursed in satisfaction when he realized she alone could hear him. A fan of playing cards in front of Aydan's plate replaced sustenance. His attention focused on a single playing card that he flicked back and forth from one hand to the other.

Eadowen let his hand rest on Taban's. "Ready for dessert?"

"Definitely!" Danny shouted.

"Me too. By the way, who plays that harp?"

"I attempt to play the clàrsach," Eadowen answered as he repositioned himself in his wheel chair. "I'll play for you, if you like."

"Should I sing?" Taban asked, following Eadowen into the hallway.

The shadows cast by the candlelight seemed to close in around the table once Taban and Eadowen left the room. A breeze caused the shadows to dance around the room. The fluttering card Aydan tossed, added a heartbeat of sound to the otherwise silent table. Cassidy tried to keep her eyes fixed on the moving card, but she shivered each time she felt a shadow slide past her.

Donovan shut the window. "Better?"

The fire shadows slowed to a gentle promenade.

"Much. Thanks."

"Nice card-thingie," Danny said.

The queen in Aydan's hand halted, he scooped up the deck that lay fanned on his plate. Then he shuffled, cut the deck, and fanned half in each hand so that Danny and Cassidy could see every card.

"Can you shuffle?" He asked, rolling up the velvet sleeves of his jacket. He pulled the silken collar from around his neck and covered his eyes with it.

She cut the deck several times and pushed the cards together.

"Now discreetly pick a card."

Feeling Danny's breathing in her ear, she held the cards up to show her. Danny pointed to the ten of diamonds.

"You have it?"

"Yes."

"Hold onto that for now," he said, still blindfolded, as he cupped the flame of one of the candles in his hand. The flame flared bright yellow for a moment then receded to a small orange flame, revealing a silvery card in Aydan's hand. The shimmering card, much more elegant than the simple cards Cassidy held, had ten golden diamonds etched in it. Aydan flicked the card and it landed face up in her lap. He removed the blindfold with another swift movement.

When Cassidy stood to give Aydan the card, she realized he was more petite than she had originally assumed. His eyes were level with her collarbone, while wearing boots that had a slight heel. "That was spectacular," she said, instead of remarking on his stature.

"Keep it."

Cassidy nodded in thanks as Danny's chin dug into her shoulder. She handed Danny the card to inspect.

Taban returned with Eadowen. He placed a chocolate mousse covered in cherry sauce, with a sliced strawberry adorning it, in front of her. She plunged her fork into the chocolate and took a large mouthful then her eyes widened, "This is amazing!"

"It's tofu," Donovan grumbled.

Aydan snickered from behind a fan of cards.

Eadowen ran his fingers across the strings of his clàrsach producing a sweet chime.

"What should I sing?"

"Fionn samhradh," Eadowen replied.

The melody began softly, like a distant ocean lapping an ivory shore, then it crescendoed to a flowing river. The high ceiling caught the sound and reverberated it off the walls. Even Danny stopped eating to listen. Aydan closed his eyes and pulled his hair behind his ears to better enjoy the sound. Donovan rested his head in his hands and stared at the crystals which glimmered as the music caused them to spin slowly. Cassidy watched Eadowen lean into the harp and caress each string as though they were cobwebs and he was brushing away the morning dew. As the bubbling brook faded, Taban's tenor voice harmonized with the soft chimes of the harp. As his voice flowed over Cassidy, she felt as though she was transported to an exotic island where she was submerged in a pristine sea. She could see the iridescent light playing on her legs as yellow fish darted around her hands.

Danny also felt that she was in an ocean, but the clear water was cold as ice, and a shadow pulled at her feet. The light did not reveal the form of the creature that swam below her. It remained amorphous and terrifying. Tearing herself away from the sound, by covering her ears, Danny noticed that Aydan had opened his eyes and was glaring in Taban's direction. Danny tried not to make eye contact with anyone. She stared at a candle flame—its irregularities comforted her as she was surrounded by patterned sound.

Eadowen slowed the melody to ripples of rain on a deep lake. Taban allowed his voice to fade to a mist that was swept away by the wind of the final note. Framed by the drapes Taban and Eadowen ducked their heads to each other and their audience.

"Please, enjoy your desserts," Eadowen said, waving at the nearly untouched mousses. Cassidy savored the tart cherry on bitter chocolate, cleansing her palate with sweet strawberry. Taban laid his head on the table and closed his eyes.

* * *

"May I help you clear the plates?" Cassidy asked.

"I have everything taken care of," Eadowen replied. "It's almost eleven."

Donovan poured the remainder of the sparkling water in the pitcher over Taban's sleeping face. Taban jerked out of his stupor and jumped when he realized how close his face had been to one of the candles. He grabbed a long bronze candlesnuffer and gingerly suffocated a flame. Aydan rolled his eyes, licked his fingers and put out the candelabras.

Next to the tapestry, Danny tied up her tennis shoes and Cassidy slipped on her boots.

"What are you doing tomorrow?" Taban asked.

"Mom offered to let us go surfing, since she already called a plane to get us home the day after tomorrow."

"I think you'd *love* Martinique Beach, especially if you go in the morning, right before *lunch*," Taban purred. "The water's *lovely*."

"Will you both come over tomorrow night too?" Eadowen asked.

"Yeah," Danny replied, glanced at Cassidy and added, "Probably."

As the trees lining the road thinned and became smaller, a figurative weight lifted from Danny's shoulders. The trails in Strathcona Park back in Victoria had much bigger trees, but Danny had never felt the same connection she did to the boreal forest near the Tolymie's house.

* * *

As the car pulled up to Ms. Reyes' house, Taban touched the dashboard to unlock the doors, so that Danny could jump out early. She raced into the house waving a quick goodbye to Taban. He returned the gesture and slowly brought the car to a stop. Cassidy grabbed the door handle and tried to say she had a good time, but he was suddenly closer to her. With an intent expression, he held her gaze. Then he grinned and hugged her around the shoulders. "See you."

Cassidy felt light-headed as she carefully stepped out of the car. Trying to conceal her vertigo, she gripped the railing as she walked up the three steps to the house. She kicked off her boots, ran to the spare bedroom, and flopped onto the bed. The butterflies she felt when she encountered an appealing person were nothing compared to this discombobulating reaction.

"What's up?" Danny said, crouching on the bed over Cassidy like a vulture.

"Nothing, I'm fine. So, what did you find out? What's a GF? "

With energetic hand gestures, Danny explained everything she'd learned about the genetics and the risks.

"Sounds like bad science fiction, but I guess it's plausible," Cassidy said. "Do you trust these people?"

"I do. Mom was lying. I've been to their house before, when I was little. After I remembered xie gave me this picture."

Danny showed Cassidy the photograph on her Ogham.

"Are you sure? It could be doctored."

"Eadowen's neck smelled good. I remembered him from before. It makes sense 'cause smell connects strongly to episodic memory."

"When did you smell Eadowen's ..." Cassidy had to remind herself that Danny tended to say things out of context. "I'll visit them tomorrow if you will. It's better if we stick together ... err sorry about getting caught up with the video game."

"I understand," Danny shrugged. "It's okay."

"I'm jealous of you."

"Why?"

"Because you get to be something special that people are after," Cassidy scratched the back of her neck. "I know that's really bad, isn't it."

"I don't think I'm special. Maybe I get to live a little longer life, but all my friends will be gone and I'll have to hide that I'm still alive ... that kind of sucks. Do I seem immature to you?" Danny blurted.

"You're just petite." Cassidy tried not to look amused. Danny did appear youthful, but to Cassidy she didn't seem young. The sharpness of her features and her proportional figure made her age ambiguous. When she thought about it, Cassidy realized, her friend could pass as twelve or twenty-seven. Most peculiar of all, Danny's eyes seemed ancient, as though she had witnessed the world far longer than her chronological age.

"No, I meant me not my appearance," Danny explained. "The kids at school call me that when they think I can't hear them."

"Sometimes a little?" Cassidy attempted both honesty and diplomacy, but Danny's face fell. "I like you the way you are," she added.

"You *like* me as a friend?" Danny ventured, picking her words with great care.

"Of course you're my friend." Cassidy shook Danny's shoulder gently. "You're awesome!"

"Okay." Danny rolled up into a ball. She attempted to convince herself that she didn't know why Cassidy's kind sentiment frustrated her. "I'm scared. What's going to happen?"

"It's going to be okay. It's not like we're getting attacked by 'Egg Friskies.' "

"What?"

"You know those things from the lecture that were like Kelpies, but lived in the ocean," Cassidy said. "Promise me you won't let yourself get lured to the ocean by any horse-men, okay Hon?"

Danny laughed. "We'll have to look up the pronunciation sometime. Let's get some sleep."

"Good night, Danny."

Cassidy played with the card Aydan had given her. She watched the shine jump from diamond to diamond as she bent it. Still not sure she could allow herself to entertain the possibility that Genetic Feys were real, she lay awake, thoughts of Taban creeping into her mind. The harder she pushed them out to make room for planning, the more persistent the images became. At last, she fell into a dream in which she swam around cotton candy clouds in a blue sky.

PART TWO

FOUR YEARS AGO: IN WHICH TABAN'S ORIGINS ARE REVEALED

"There was a Fomoriian Prince who was as seductive as an Each Uisge—strange in what forms attractiveness can come. He was also the father of a Tuatha de Danann. It would seem we are all connected."

–EADOWEN TOLYMIE

CHAPTER 7
IN WHITE MARBLE HELL

IT WAS TABAN'S FINAL YEAR at Talbot Mir Academy in Malibu, California. He'd received his acceptance letters to universities and celebrated his eighteenth birthday three months earlier, in January. He should've been walking down the dorm halls with head held high. Instead, he was running at full tilt with a framed certificate clutched in his hand. Halting at a hallway intersection, he peered around the corner. A young woman carefully read the numbers on each room. She was between him and the door to his room. He ran back to a glass door at the other end of the hall, slid his Ogham across the identification pad, and exited into the garden. The dorm surrounded a small enclosure for students to plant and tend. Taban leaped over patches of lettuce and cabbage and grabbed the trunk of a sapling cherry tree to assist him in a sharp turn. Pink petals showered him, as he slid on newly plowed soil. As he transitioned the certificate to his mouth, he located the second-story window of the room he shared with Eadowen Tolymie. Placing both hands on the first-story window ledge, he vaulted. Balanced on the first-story window, Taban gripped the top of the frame. Then he put one foot on the side of the window, pushed his weight to the top of the frame, and snatched the bottom of the second-story window. With the assistance of a tree branch he hauled himself onto the second-story window ledge. Seeing no one in the room, his anxiety heightened. He tucked the certificate under his arm and crammed his fingers beneath the window pane. His arm burned, as he yanked up on the glass forcing the window open. In a rush of adrenaline, he dove through the open window. His platform sandal caught on the ledge causing him to fall face first onto Eadowen's bed.

The room was only large enough to contain two beds, dressers, and desks. Taban dropped the certificate on Eadowen's desk with a resounding clack. He quickly traversed the meter-wide space between their beds and threw open the restroom door. Listening to his tablet, Eadowen reclined sleepily in a bubble bath surrounded by beeswax candles. Open flames in the dorm room seemed to be the only rule Eadowen broke.

"Knocking is usually considered polite, especially since listening to Wodehouse isn't the only way I relax," Eadowen reiterated the warning Taban frequently disregarded.

"Consider the sound of my face-plant a knock," Taban huffed. He reached into Eadowen's bath and pulled the drain. To his surprise the water was ice cold, but he had more important issues to bother asking why. "There's a girl who's probably going to come by any minute. I have to hide!"

"Again?"

"I can't help it—it just sort of happens," Taban begged. He sat on the tile floor facing his friend. Hanging his head to avoid Eadowen's gaze, Taban felt Eadowen brush the petals out of his loose brunette curls.

"That's no excuse," Eadowen replied, taking off his reading glasses. "I'll help her."

"I'd appreciate that."

"For her, not you. I'd make you face her, but you'd lie. She'd believe you because everyone seems to and it would get worse."

Taban averted his eyes, as Eadowen hoisted himself out of the bath. He maneuvered into his wheelchair and entered the room. Taban shrunk behind the door, but watched from the sliver created by the door hinge. Just as Eadowen finished buttoning up his shirt, there was a knock.

"Coming," Eadowen called cordially as he dried his hair with his towel.

Eadowen opened the door to reveal the same girl with tear stains glistening on her face, slouched shoulders, and clenched fists. "Good afternoon, what can I do for you?"

"Hi. I need to talk to Taban."

"I'm Taban's roommate, Eadowen. What's your name?"

"Marja."

"Would you like to sit down, Marja? Anywhere you like."

"Thanks." She sat at the foot of his bed.

Facing her, he crossed then uncrossed his arms. Marja imitated his motion and relaxed her shoulders. They sat in silence across from one another for a while. She fussed with her blond pixie cut.

"What can I help you with?" Eadowen asked.

"I need to talk to Taban. This isn't your problem."

"I'm sorry, he can't speak with you right now."

"Okay—I guess I'll have to come back. Sorry to intrude." Marja pushed herself off the bed.

"You seem distressed. Just rest for a minute." Eadowen held out a hand to indicate that she should sit down, which she obeyed. "What's your focus in school?"

"I just started at UCLA, public health and international relations."

"Wow. You must have great time-management skills." Eadowen tilted his head in order to look up at her with his warm eyes. "Taban acts like a disrespectful, narcissistic, amoral imbecile. *I* will do whatever *I* can to help you."

"So, it's a more efficient use of my time to talk to you?"

"Definitely."

Marja sighed. "I slept with Taban last night. It was my first time and ...," her voice cracked. "I don't feel good about it." She looked down and scratched her arm. "I didn't feel like I had control of myself, but I didn't have any alcohol and I know he didn't drug me."

Lightly touching her forearm, Eadowen made a comforting sound. "If you believe Taban coerced you, it may be a good idea to report him."

I didn't pressure her. Thanks a lot, Eadowen, Taban thought.

"Actually, I'm surprised he managed to have sex. I wasn't aware he was that coordinated."

Marja gave a small snort in response to Eadowen's snide remark. "I think I was the one who came onto him, so I don't feel like I should be upset, but he just lingers in my mind. It's weird," she explained.

"That's not true at all. An intimate experience has a lot of emotions involved. I'm so sorry he's too pathetic to talk to you about this. It's very irresponsible of him. Fortunately, there are plenty of better places to go if you need support."

She tucked a strand of hair behind her ear and inspected the certificate on Eadowen's desk. "You won a cooking competition?"

"I did. Do you want to try a dessert?" Eadowen retrieved a tiny square cheesecake from a mini-refrigerator under his bed. It was decorated with an elaborate Celtic knot drizzled in caramel and sprinkled with coconut. He took a fork out of a circular container on his desk and handed it to her with the cake. She carved a morsel of the delicacy and took a bite.

"This is really good."

"That means a lot to me. How are you feeling?"

"I guess I liked him more than I thought I did." She tugged on her hair. "You do this a lot, don't you? That was rhetorical," she added hastily, when Eadowen gave her a pained look.

It always amazed Taban how quickly people opened up to Eadowen. Marja conversed with him for an hour and a half. Taban's back started to ache from crouching against the tub. Quietly, he unclipped his strap shirt releasing his stomach from the tight wrap around his torso. In the mirror, hanging on the restroom door, Taban inspected his reflection. Years of swimming and he still had little muscle definition and his diet had caused a pudge around his waist. He thought it was odd that his skin was darker than his hair, though modeling agencies seemed to like his diverse look. Besides contrast, he couldn't see anything particularly special about his face; he didn't have a defined jaw or nice cheekbones. It was a mystery to him why people seemed so attracted to his average looks.

"I really appreciate everything. Thanks for letting me unload."

"I'm glad I could be there for you. Take care of yourself."

"I will." She said and shut the door decisively.

"You need to take responsibility for your actions," Eadowen said as Marja's footsteps faded down the hallway.

"I would but— most people get weird around me," Taban said flopping onto his bed. "I just took her on a nice date. You know I'm not disgusting enough to ply someone with alcohol or drugs. Right?"

"Maybe you should act like you are a drug."

"I don't have magic pheromones. All I did was sweet talk her a bit."

Taban glanced at the time. He pulled creased slacks out of the bottom of the dresser bringing a variety of other articles of clothing out of the drawer with his motion. He let the designer garments fall in a pile on the floor.

"Stop doing that."

"Doing what?" Taban asked pausing halfway through putting on his belt, as though Eadowen had been referring to his action of dressing.

"Letting it go. Your behavior is inexcusable."

"She's fine now." Taban latched his belt buckle closed with a clang. "I brought you your certificate from the contest, since you were at physical therapy all morning." Taking a formal shirt from a hanger on the door, he threw his Strap-Shirt on the pile of clothes. Taban looped a red tie around his neck. The knot untied itself when he tried to tighten it. He made another attempt with the same result and let out a frustrated groan.

Eadowen motioned for Taban to come toward him. Pulling Taban closer to him by the loose ends of the tie, Eadowen carefully folded it into a large knot. "Eleanor was in here sobbing for five hours last week because she thought you loved her." Eadowen flattened Taban's tie to his chest. "You seem nervous. Where are you headed?"

"Dad summoned me."

"Oh … can't you decline?"

"I'll be fine," Taban replied. "What're you up to today?"

"Book Club is having high tea in an hour."

"Do you need anything that's not on our regular grocery order?"

"Wattleseed, maca powder, and we're out of salt again."

The first year they'd roomed together, Eadowen had managed to coax out every secret Taban kept, usually with food. Fortunately for Taban, Eadowen kept his lips sealed.Taban tried constantly to stay on good terms with him, so that behavior would continue. Taban didn't mind doing little favors for him, if said benevolence didn't involve going out of his way. He owed Eadowen for the complication with Marja.

"The only place I can get wattleseed is a half-hour away from here," Taban whined. "Can it wait?"

"Have a nice drive." Eadowen opened and closed his hand in a cutesy wave.

* * *

Taban parked his black Ferrari under Talbot Mir Tower. The tall, white-marble building stretched toward the sky above all the other buildings. The mixed-use tower contained only the offices of the most respected faculty and administrators. He flashed his digital identification to the security guard standing in front of the French doors. The elevator beeped, as it ascended toward the heavens. At the 56th floor Taban exited the elevator and entered a small elevator with golden gated doors. He flipped to his identification screen on his Ogham and swiped the Ogham across a pad. Taban felt his stomach stay on the 56th floor while the rest of his body ascended to the 57th. Given a choice, he would rather have stayed with his gut than see his father. The elevator doors clanked open; Taban paused before entering the penthouse. The hot sun blazing through the windows was intensified by the polished white marble walls and floors. Taban noticed a photograph, the size of his desk, hanging on the wall. It was a picture of him—sort of. The highlights in his hair glowed, his skin didn't have pores, and his eyes were enhanced to cartoonish proportions. This was the "photograph" all of his father's associates saw.

His father, Tynan Mir, was waiting for him in an executive chair behind a gigantic desk. The gold stenciling around the desk shimmered. Taban used this as an excuse to shield his eyes so he would not have to look at his father. Instead, he inspected a pearl-toned half-couch under a circular window with small rectangular prisms radiating out from it. The prisms cast scattered rays of multicolored light in a panorama across the fabric of the couch in a way that reminded Taban of the bottom of an outdoor pool.

"Make yourself comfortable," his father purred.

"I'll stand."

"Suit yourself. You haven't come by for a visit in a long time, Taban, so this is a pleasant surprise."

"You asked me to come."

"I did, but it was nice of you to show up."

"If I didn't, all the teachers and everyone would be harassing me because they all want to make you happy."

"Of course, I own the school."

"Everyone does what you say, even if they regret it."

Tynan Mir rested his head on his folded hands and regarded his son with azure eyes. "Is that so different from you?"

Taban cringed. "I don't use people intentionally—mostly!"

"You don't?"

"I don't do what you did to me."

"Ah. What things did I ever do to you?"

"When you wanted me to go into commercials ... and what you told me to do with that photographer ..." Taban touched the tattoo on his arm as his stomach churned.

"You certainly didn't get the most recent national commercial, because of your appearance or talent. Clearly you've warmed up to the idea. This is good because I need you to do a little something."

"What I did was *my* choice. I won't be your dog." *Anything to earn enough money to get away from you.* "And as for talents, mine are in chemistry."

"You're good at manipulating people and you enjoy it."

"No ... I ... don't." Taban knew his father could see through the lie, but he told it anyway.

"Your science background will be good for what I want you to do."

Taban marched to Mr. Mir's desk and slammed his hands on the cold marble surface. "If you want to screw someone, in all the ways that implies, then do it yourself!" he shouted. Taban saw the reflection of his own blue eyes in the white marble between his fingers. He did not want to remember the number of people who had told him that he had his father's 'beautiful' eyes.

"Unfortunately, our gift fades quickly with age."

"If this is what you wanted to talk to me about, I'm leaving!"

"Then don't you want to know why people do what you want? It's a gift."

Taban's curiosity pulled at him like a rip current, but he resisted. His father waved a tablet tauntingly. Biting the bait, Taban snatched the tablet away from his father and retreated to the door while he read the screen.

The screen was open to an article in an e-zine entitled, "The Universe Explained by Psychology." He read the article tagline.

Recent speculation that there are a set of genes for charisma may be confirmed in the next few years. This could revolutionize the science of attraction.

"They might find a gene for charisma. So what? This is just a pop psychology article, anyway. They find this kind of stuff every other week. Makes great press."

"Have you noticed that certain members in our family history always got what they wanted?"

"So?" Taban scoffed. *I've noticed that everyone seems to go into entertainment, finance, or politics,* he thought.

"You and I have genes that are very rare in the human race. We don't know much yet, but we believe these genes help us to produce some kind of subconscious signals making us more appealing."

Taban punched the fancy door. "Who is 'we'? And what the hell are you talking about?" Feeling the numbness creep into his fist, Taban stared at his father. He searched his father's face for any indication of sarcasm, but his laugh lines were smooth. To his surprise, his father's expression was more serious than he'd ever seen.

"If I were to believe what you say ...," Taban said cautiously.

"We still don't know much yet. I have more important things to do than pay attention to the science stuff. I leave that to your Aunt Rhiannon in Australia."

Taban vaguely recalled his relatives from a visit to Australia when he was still a preteen.

"What's the big deal about scientists researching charisma?" Taban feigned a yawn to sound uninterested.

"If they discover the origins of our genes, then we will be investigated. They may learn to copy or make synthetic versions of them."

"Do you enjoy the royal we?"

"The other people we could find with our abilities, specifically, your aunt and cousins."

"So?"

"So!?" His father raised his voice, but immediately dropped back to his calm purr. "If we are investigated, I may lose all that I've gained. Not to mention that a synthetic version of our abilities could be used as a weapon or sold as an aphrodisiac."

The colored light from the prisms shifted across the marble desk. Taban's eyes followed the rippling light until he unintentionally looked at his father's face and saw his sparkling eyes had faded. Taban tried to dig at the vulnerability his father had exposed.

"You're afraid of losing your hypothetical edge?" Taban leaned against the door as casually as he could manage.

"Do you want everyone to know what you can do?"

"I think you're crazy. I want no part in this!"

"You will become the intern to the head researcher for the charisma research project."

"What? No!" Taban answered as he pushed open the door.

"I've arranged for funding to be cut on the charisma research program, but I can only delay the work. You must convince the head researcher to do work for your Aunt Rhiannon's new project. Your aunt has discovered that certain people live a long time. She could make quite a pretty penny if she could figure out why, so she's funding a research project on the subject."

Again, Taban's curiosity pulled him back into the room, but this time his rage anchored him to the open doorway.

"Abigail is waiting downstairs. I'd like you to introduce yourself. She's a bit fat, but not horrible looking, so you'll be fine."

"I won't do it."

"If you won't help me, Telyn will have to do." His father chased a beam of light from one of the prisms with his finger.

Taban looked at the golden elevator door only a few feet away. Then he thought of his sweet little sister living in Seattle with his estranged mother. When he considered her abilities, he realized everyone adored Telyn—strangers doted on her like she was a princess, even when she threw tantrums. "She's only twelve."

"Exactly, she'll do everything I need. Also, if you don't help me, things could start going wrong in your life."

"Telyn has nothing to do with this," Taban yelled, clenching his fists at his sides.

"Well, if our genes are discovered, her life will definitely not be a pleasant one."

"Where is this researcher?" Taban growled.

"Waiting for you downstairs," Mr. Mir repeated. "When I told her my wonderful son was interested in genetics, she was more than happy to meet with you. You're not that good looking. It's a pity your mother made it difficult for me to get you more suitably engineered. You know, you have a voice that'd be good for a pop star ..."

"I know I'm not that good looking! My roommate has better abs than I do."

"Yes, what was that crippled kid's name again?"

"You suggested we should be roommates!" Taban retorted through gritted teeth. "And Eadowen isn't crippled. Eadowen has a physical disability, but it doesn't impede hir."

"Why's he in a wheelchair anyway?"

"Xie doesn't tell anyone. And it doesn't matter!" he snarled.

"He's attracted to you, isn't he?" His father's eyes sparkled with mirth as though he were presenting a child with a new toy. "Does whatever you ask?"

"No!"

"Well, don't get involved with him. It might mess up his devotion to you."

"Why not?"

"I have reason to believe that boy might have the longevity genes. Thanks for bringing that hair sample a few months ago. I sent it to your aunt."

"That's ridiculous." Taban tried to hide his glee when he realized he'd given his father fake samples out of spite. His aunt had some random guy's hair from his gym class instead of his roommate's.

"Now listen, son," his father said in a soft voice. "If you don't do as you're told, you know what I'll make sure happens to your sweet little sister. If that's not enough, your friend will have an incident. And if you, Taban Mir, are heartless enough to let that happen. I will take everything else you hold dear: starting with your face."

"I'm going to the store."

"Abigail is on the fourth floor in conference room A. I hear she likes blonds. We'll have to do something about that."

Without saying another word, Taban lunged through the door, slammed his Ogham across the scanner, and jumped into the elevator. Meeting with this Abigail person could not be any worse than spending another moment with that hateful man. He switched to the main elevator and watched the numbers decrease as each floor took him farther away from the penthouse office. The more he recalled the way people acted around him, the more real Mr. Mir's words became. Taban gripped the knot on his tie for comfort.

CHAPTER 8
OF TATTOOS & TABOOS

A FEW MINUTES LATER, Taban reluctantly opened the door to the conference room. At the far end of the glass oval table a seated woman read a thick paperback book. The cold blue of the backrest contrasted with her warm skin tone. The ruffles of her peach silk dress accentuated her impressive hourglass figure.

"Good evening," Taban said tentatively. He wondered two things: if she was Abigail Crane's assistant, and if she was available.

"How can I help you?" She closed the book and held it to her chest.

"I'm looking for Abigail Crane. I was told she was waiting in this room."

"I *am* Abigail Crane," she giggled.

"Wait you're not … I mean I wasn't expecting someone so … well … dressed?" Remaining near the door, Taban waited for her to glance away so he could observe her better. He couldn't find a location on her beautiful curves that could make him consider her fat, but he was happy to continue searching. Her blazer obscured some of his view, so he felt behind his back for the thermostat panel, located it, and subtly dragged his finger over the panel changing the room from air conditioned to heated.

"Thanks. I thought you were going to say 'young.' I did accelerated programs in school because I knew what I wanted to do, so I'm only twenty-eight."

"Again, sorry for the mistake, you look very sophisticated. I was being stupid," he sputtered as he grabbed the chair next to her. "I'm surprised to see someone reading a physical book."

"I just like the feel of it."

"Would you recommend it?"

Abigail looked at the floor and Taban thought he saw her cheeks flush. "I don't think you'd like this genre."

"I like paper books too," he bluffed since he'd only touched one or two his entire life. "It feels like I've accomplished something as I turn the final page." He made a large flourish with his hand as he finished the sentence. His motion knocked the book out of Abigail's hand and it fell to the floor with a thud. Instinctively, he dove for the book, hitting his head against Abigail's, since she had followed similar impulses. Applying pressure to the dull pain where their foreheads had collided, he remained seated on the floor, next to her.

"Are you okay?" he asked, steadying her with his arm around her shoulders as she knelt down holding her head. He reached for her book with his other hand. As she accepted the book, she gave him a radiant smile. He realized how close his face was to hers and jerked away, dropping the book into her lap. "I'm sorry."

"How's your head?" She rubbed her forehead as she tried to stand. Jumping to his feet, Taban caught her arm unnecessarily. He let go again and she sank into her chair.

"Do you need some ice?" Taban asked. "I think there's a medical office on the fourth floor. I'll go get you some!"

"No," she protested. "Really, I'm fine."

Taban noticed a container of filtered water next to the door and pressed the lever to pour some of the water into one of the glass cups he took from the top of the filter. The container made a satisfying gurgle as he released the lever. Taban offered Abigail the glass over the table.

"Thank you." She took off her blazer to Taban's delight. "So, your father said you might be interested in becoming my intern?"

"Well, I don't know that much, but it seems like an interesting subject."

"Here's my information."

"Thanks." He held out his arm and she brushed her Ogham over his.

"Since the funding for my charisma research has been cut, I'm going to move back to New York City to finish my PhD. Your father said Dartmouth might be a good place for me to propose a similar research topic, if I find a new source of funding."

"That's the school Mr. Mir wants me to attend."

"Don't you mean your dad?" she asked.

"Yeah." Taban bobbed his head grudgingly. "It was a pleasure to meet you. I'd stay longer, but I really have to get to the store."

"No worries." Fanning herself, she walked toward the door checking the thermostat on the way out. "This must be broken."

"Oh, you're right. It is." He stood behind her as though to inspect the temperature settings. He rested a hand between her shoulder blades where her dress didn't cover her bare skin. "I'll personally go down and ask them to fix it. It's terrible that they'd let a lady wait in a heated room on a day like this."

"I really appreciate it." Her Ogham chimed a reminder alarm. "I need to catch my flight. Stay in touch." She lingered by the thermostat, even after Taban removed his hand from her back. With the aid of several alarm reminders, she broke away and headed to the elevator.

"Wait! You forgot your book!" He caught the elevator door and returned it to her. She held the door for him invitingly; he pretended he had a good reason to take the stairs.

* * *

On his way back to the dorm from the grocery store, Taban's Ogham informed him that the road he usually took was congested and listed several alternative routes. Ignoring all the suggestions, he drove to the Academy's recreation center.

The indigo sky tinted to violet, the silver-lined clouds turned golden, and jets created pink trails in the atmosphere. The sunset reflected on the still surface of the vacant outdoor swimming pool. It had closed earlier that day, but thanks to his family connection, Taban used his Ogham to open the gate.

Throwing his tie, shirt, belt, and shoes into a pile, Taban stared at his frame against the dark sky reflected in the pool. With a shudder of disgust, he let his pants fall off his hips and flung himself into the water. Feeling the icy water stream over his warm flesh, he kept his body rigid to slide to the bottom of the pool. Turning on his back, he ran his hand over the tile, contrasting the smooth ceramic surface with the rough cement. Five meters of water pressed against his chest. He screamed. Beneath this liquid barrier, he was sheltered from the human world. No one could hear him. No one could hurt him.

When he went surfing, he would allow himself to get caught in a riptide that would sweep him out to the open ocean away from everyone. No matter how far out or what the conditions were, he knew he could always swim back to shore. Sometimes he'd watch for attractive women caught in the current to rescue before the lifeguards could get them. The women would always do nice things for him after he brought them to shore. Mr. Mir wanted him to compete nationally in distance because he knew that his son could outswim anyone. Taban carefully kept his times above state qualification, so he couldn't compete.

The air in Taban's chest started to push on his lungs. He exhaled and watched as air pockets ascended like silvery jellyfish to the surface. He pushed off, propelling himself to the surface. Throwing his head back, he launched beads of water off of his hair. Taban swept his hands across his face to remove the chlorinated water from his eyes and flopped onto his back. Hopefully, no one would walk by and notice that he was in his underwear and not a swimsuit, although the thought of being caught thrilled him slightly.

The last rays of sunlight glinted off the chicken-wire fence. He squinted and tried to picture his sister, Telyn. She resembled him with the same dark skin tone and hair, but with sweet, brown eyes. He lay his arm across his eyes and let his body sink into the pool. The water felt like ice as it rushed over the skin he had exposed to the warm air. As he retreated from the world again, he wished she weren't so distant. His parents lived together during his early childhood and always fought with each other. He and his sister would hide away together. From the few messages he received from his mother, Taban gathered that Mr. Mir showered Telyn with gifts and treats. It was so easy for Mr. Mir to buy a child's affection. That was how his father convinced him to move to Malibu. It wasn't until recently that he realized why his mother no longer wanted anything to do with him—he reminded her of his father.

His arm throbbed from his birth control injection. He glanced at the green marker on his forearm, which indicated his injection was up-to-date. Under the mark he saw his tattoo, and a memory he had locked away rose to the surface. It was an ancient symbol known as the Pictish Beast that would have been a beautiful nod to his mixed Scottish-Moorish heritage if his father hadn't marred it. Taban felt throbbing pain in his arm, as he remembered being strapped to a chair by two men his father hired. He thrashed in the water when he relived the moment the needle pierced his flesh. "This way you will always remember what you have," his father had said. Scratching at the mark, as though he could remove it with his nails, Taban tried to remember what had triggered that action from his father. He'd probably refused to smile for headshots or some other minor rebellious act. If he didn't do exactly what his father instructed, he feared what would happen to Telyn, Eadowen, or worse, himself.

As the last glow of crimson faded from the outlines of the clouds, a chilly breeze made wakes on the pool. With a single stroke of his arm, Taban slid through the water to the edge of the pool. He placed his hands on the edge of the pool and pushed to a standing position on the deck in a fluid motion. Running his hands down his chest and arms, he attempted to skim some of the liquid off. He buttoned up his shirt, hung the tie around his neck, and headed back to his car.

CHAPTER 9
WHEN WATER IS BURNED

SLIGHTLY OFF-PITCH HARP MUSIC greeted him when he opened the door to his dorm. A large red candle on the windowsill above Eadowen's bed, made the room inviting. The flame appeared to sway along with the soft harp melody. Taban remained silent, so as not to interrupt his friend's strumming.

"Is the pitch wrong?"

"You play in many pitches." Taban hummed to help his friend, but Eadowen over corrected.

"What's wrong, Taban?"

"Nothing. I got you truffle oil too." Taban held up the cloth grocery bag. "I know how much you like to use the stuff."

"Thanks. I didn't know truffle oil was sold by the liter."

"What's that song called?" Taban continued.

"Ea." Eadowen watched his friend through the strings of the harp. "Taban, what happened this afternoon?"

Taban unceremoniously moved the harp and got on his knees in front of Eadowen to put the groceries in the mini-fridge. Maca didn't look like it needed to be refrigerated, but he put it in anyway. "What's Ea mean?"

"It means 'little fire.' What's your father trying to force you to do this time?"

"He wants to use my body to get something he wants." Taban stood hitting his head on the wooden frame of Eadowen's bed. "So, like I said, nothing new."

He sat down on the bed next to Eadowen, who bent over to get a well-used ice pack out of the mini-fridge. Holding the cold pack on top of Taban's head, Eadowen waited silently.

"Look. I know I sleep around." Taban took the ice pack from Eadowen and squeezed it in his hands. "I receive really nice gifts and sometimes cash from the rich women I date, but that's my choice—no one is making me do it. And it's certainly not my fault if those gifts are Ferraris and trips to the Bahamas."

"You say that like I've accused you of something." Eadowen smirked. "More importantly, is there a reason you haven't reported your father's abuse?"

"With my dad's connections, I'd end up in an even worse situation if I tried to tell anyone. The only reason I tell this stuff to you is because I know you won't gossip about it." Taban rubbed the bump on his scalp. "It's not that big a deal."

"Taban ..."

"My head is fine," Taban answered with a grin knowing the result of his momentary lack of coordination was not what most concerned Eadowen. He slammed the restroom door shut before Eadowen had a chance to ask any more questions.

Instead of soothing him, the hot water made his blood boil. He wanted to do something—anything that his father would hate. Taban turned the shower's temperature to an icy cold to enjoy the evanescent pain that accompanied the shock of transitioning from hot to cold. With a single lunge he shut off the water to the shower, watching as the remnant swirled down the drain. After loading his chlorine-dry hair with leave-in conditioner and throwing on pajama pants, he returned to the main room.

A dish towel with traces of hair clippings lay on Eadowen's lap. The small scissors Eadowen used expertly to trim millimeters off of his bangs flashed in the candlelight. "Mirror," Eadowen muttered to his tablet, mounted on his bed post. The tablet switched from his homework chemistry lecture to a reflection. Checking his face from all visible angles, Eadowen picked up the scissors and made a few quick upward cuts. He clenched the strands with his fist for a moment, then released, making his bangs flare across his forehead. Removing his glasses, he paused the chemistry lecture. Then he rolled up the towel and placed it at the foot of his bed. Eadowen dabbed his perfume on his wrists and neck and returned the cologne bottle to its place next to the candle on the windowsill.

"Can I dim the lights some more?" *Maybe if I darken the room, Eadowen will sleep instead of asking questions,* he thought.

"You look like you're going to cry."

Taban wiped drops of water from his wet hair off his forehead. The situation reminded him of the conversation they'd had two years ago, after he'd received the tattoo torture. It had culminated in him sobbing with his head on Eadowen's lap. He'd cried about petty things around his roommate, but that was the only time he'd completely broken down. Taban decided he would rather not repeat that episode. Eadowen moved to allow his friend room to sit next to him on his bed. It was such a hot night that Eadowen's shirt was undone, revealing the scars on his neck and chest. Taban inspected his friend's muscular abdomen and round, freckled face. Taban determined that Eadowen, though not beautiful, was a pleasant plain. *There are lots of people better looking than me,* Taban thought. *What makes me so appealing? Does it work on everyone? Does Eadowen find me attractive like other people do?* Running his finger over his lower lip, Taban contemplated what his father had said about Eadowen. Now that he thought about it, he knew very little about his roommate. Eadowen came from somewhere in Canada, had to try in school, and wasn't rich. If he hadn't been awarded a scholarship, because he'd scored extremely high on the International Emotional Intelligence Test, Eadowen would never be able to afford the school. It seemed strange that his father had forbid him from "getting involved," with Eadowen who seemed relatively harmless. Though the thought had never occurred to Taban before, a devious idea began to form in his mind. He could test his supposed appeal and completely go against his father's wishes and the only test subject he needed was sitting next to him. Taban slid closer to Eadowen. First he had to ask for something Eadowen would refuse to give. Then he'd see if he could get Eadowen to reveal it.

"What happened to make you wheelchair-bound?"

"I don't want to talk about it." Eadowen noticed how much closer Taban had moved toward him. "Do you want something to eat?"

"How about you?" Taban let his eyes fall to Eadowen's chin before looking into his hazel eyes.

"I'm not hungry," Eadowen replied without a trace of sarcasm. It was impossible to tell if Eadowen ignored or missed the innuendo. "Would you help me with a chemistry question?"

"Sure."

"I can't keep these straight." Eadowen indicated two structural diagrams on the screen.

That's acetylcholine and that's norepinephrine. They're both neurotransmitters and both are involved in decision making." Taban pointed to a nonapeptide molecule on Eadowen's tablet. "Know what that one is?"

"No, but it looks familiar." Eadowen scratched his cheek in frustration. "I really should know this one."

"That's oxytocin." Taban rested his hand on the wall next to Eadowen's shoulder. "I can show you how that one works in a way you'll never forget."

"Eh? You know what," Eadowen replied. "I think it's coming back to me." Grabbing Eadowen's wrist, Taban pressed him against the head of his bed. The swift motion caused Eadowen's hand to knock against his tablet screen turning it back to mirror mode. "What're you doin—?" Taban touched his mouth to Eadowen's lips. "Well." Eadowen turned his head so that Taban's lips slid to his cheek. "I'll certainly remember now."

Taban ran his hand across his friend's collarbone slipping Eadowen's shirt off of his shoulder, then he pecked Eadowen's neck. As he did this, he noticed his reflection in the tablet-mirror. His large blue eyes looked almost violet because his pupils were dilated more than seemed natural. Leaning back to look at his friend, Taban noticed Eadowen's pupils were also dilated. Unfortunately, the room was dark enough that the sympathetic reaction would not necessarily indicate attraction. Starting with cartoonish pupils, a list was beginning to form in his mind about factors that might play into his attractiveness. Taban nuzzled Eadowen's shoulder, inhaling his friend's unique floral scent, which reminded him of a class lecture on pheromones. Many high-end colognes included androstadienone, a chemical naturally occurring in humans. Though only that morning he'd denied special pheromones, he decided it wasn't impossible his body produced a surplus amount of that chemical. Though he knew very little about the subject, he'd heard that hormonal fluctuations in people affected others close to them. Taban thought it seemed more likely that his hormonal shifts affected others more strongly than most people, rather than the idea that he produced super-pheromones. He needed more data.

"Kiss me," Taban commanded.

"We just did."

"That wasn't a kiss. That was a handshake with our mouths."

"Taban, what's provoking this?" Eadowen raised his high-arched eyebrows.

"You are."

Pushing up against his friend's body, Taban let his tongue touch Eadowen's lower lip, but Eadowen used his teeth as a barrier for further intimacy. Taban could feel drops of water sliding from his hair onto Eadowen's face. "You find me, like, attractive and stuff, right?" Taban brushed some of the water off of his friend's forehead.

"You have an appeal."

"What exactly do you like about my features?"

"Well," Eadowen said. "We just learned about facial symmetry in psychology ... your face is incredibly even."

"And body symmetry too. My body is even too, isn't it?" Stroking Eadowen's chest, Taban attempted to give him a deeper kiss, but Eadowen declined to open his mouth. *I can't make you cooperate, if you don't cooperate.* "Come on, gimme a real kiss," Taban tried.

Eadowen pushed Taban away and held him at arm's length by his shoulders. Taban froze. His friend's default expression had changed to a penetrating stare. The candlelight played around his hazel iris which was almost completely eclipsed by his pupils. As Eadowen straightened his broad shoulders, his flushed lips parted. Taban couldn't pinpoint what had changed about his friend, but suddenly he was both intimidated and captivated.

"Are you using me to experiment?" Eadowen asked.

"Yes," Taban replied. *But not in the way you think,* he added to himself.

"And you really want to osculate?" Eadowen let his voice deepen to his natural baritone.

"Duh." Taban nodded as he puzzled over his friend's metamorphosis. The eerily alluring Eadowen, seemed to deliberate. Then he tilted Taban's head back and fulfilled the request. For a moment, Taban lost himself in a rush of pleasure. Eadowen was such a fluid kisser that he struggled to remind himself that he had a goal. They caressed one another for a few minutes. Undoing the strap on his Ogham, Taban let it fall on the bed, and reached for the latch on Eadowen's arm. The devices contained the owner's medical history and could quickly indicate if a potential partner had not been checked. Taban started to feel queasy. The canoodling was great, but Eadowen's excellent body didn't appeal to him. It was inconvenient that the peer who didn't concede to his wishes and served as a 'take that' to his father was not his type.

Eadowen pulled away abruptly and refastened his Ogham. To Taban's relief Eadowen had almost returned to his mild presentation. "Okay, we're done," Eadowen said.

Too focused to interpret what his friend said, Taban ran his fingers through his own conditioned hair, and slipped his hand under Eadowen's waistband.

"Ah! Let go." Eadowen grabbed his wrist. "Stop."

"But you're enjoying it. I can feel your—Ow!" Taban felt searing pain on the back of his neck. Reaching behind his head, he touched a stream of hot wax cooling on his flesh. Eadowen returned the large candle, still burning, to his windowsill. The musty scent of singed hair irritated Taban's nose.

"You groped me—my body reacted. That doesn't mean I like it. If you touch me one more time, I'll report it as sexual harassment."

"Uh ..." Taban retreated to the middle of the bed.

"You'd better not have ever treated anyone else like that. No one should ever have to refuse more than once. I thought you were better than that." Eadowen emphasized every 'r' and dropped his 'g's as he continued to admonish Taban. "To top it all off, I can tell you're uncomfortable. You were trying to get me to do something you wouldn't feel good about. Why on Earth do you think I'd find that acceptable?"

"Geez, I'm sorry. I thought you'd like it!" Taban said desperately trying to appease him. "You said I'm attractive and you're pansexual, right?"

"That's not how it works. I have the potential to fall for anyone. How can you not understand that?" He stared at Taban in disbelief. "Why are *you* pouting?"

You messed up my experiment. This is why people use rats, Taban thought. "I'm sorry. No one's ever rejected me, so I've never pushed before. I won't do it again. But ... why did you kiss me like that?" He asked cautiously.

"I was still trying to figure out what was going on. You're a very convincing actor."

"What makes me a good actor?"

"Not sure." Eadowen motioned for Taban to move to his own bed.

He obeyed. Sitting across from his roommate, Taban pondered acting. "Try to tell a lie."

"How do you know I haven't?" Eadowen flashed his usual pursed lip smile. The skin around Eadowen's eyes wrinkled, which was usually a sign of sincere happiness. However, on reflection, Eadowen used that smile for almost every situation, including situations where he wasn't happy. If he could consciously control his face that would partially explain why he could tell when Taban lied. *It would also support my ability to deceive anyone I want,* Taban concluded.

"Control of micro-facial expressions ..." Taban noted under his breath.

"Pardon?"

"Just thinking aloud." Since Eadowen had calmed down, Taban decided to test his hypothesis. "I'd really appreciate it if you'd tell me how you came to be in a wheelchair?"

"I'd rather not discuss it."

"If you aren't into me, why were you willing to room with me the last three years?"

"And risk unleashing you on someone else?" Eadowen let the candle flame lick his fingers. "I applied here after I met you at the recruitment fair because you remind me of the person who probably donated his Y chromosome to me."

"Wouldn't that be like your dad?"

"No, my dad is the one who raised me—he was with me when we first met." Eadowen chuckled giving Taban a sidelong glance.

Taban pretended to glare back. He could see Eadowen mentally replaying the awkward way they'd met at the Canadian recruitment fair for the Talbot Mir Academy held in Ontario. A little kid with long, dark hair had tripped him and he'd fallen onto Eadowen's lap. Though that encounter seemed to be chance, Taban remembered how adamantly his father pushed their friendship.

"You and I aren't as different as you think we are," Eadowen said, blowing gently on the candle flame so that only the blue at the core of the flame was visible.

"Are you kidding? We're like night and day." Taban picked the wax off the back of his neck.

"Not many twelve-year-olds can provoke a group of people enough to make them chase a preteen off a three-story building. After that, my dad contacted a friend of the family in Scotland to come talk to me. He helped me a lot. My dad said something to my mom and the other man about forgiving them. After that, I noticed some physical similarities I had with him and figured it out."

Did Eadowen just tell me? Does that mean what I did actually worked? Taban wondered. *I despise inconclusive data, but I'm not going to try that approach again.* "Didn't you have your genome sequenced at birth?" Taban asked aloud. "Unless he signed a waiver, your dad should know who your father is."

"I don't have my genome sequenced. My parents waived the entire procedure."

"Is that why you never got a treatment to help you walk? I read about those things the other day. They seem to work pretty well for most trauma injuries, but they require lots of time, money, and your genome. I have a lot of money from the commercials I do. I'll pay for the procedure if you can't afford it. Just get your genome sequenced because they require that for any big medical procedure."

"You see me as needing to be fixed?"

"No! You're very capable, but I'm sure it's an inconvenience."

"That's kind of you, but I can't. We have our reasons. My mother took me abroad for treatment. They used specialized enzymes to inhibit scar tissue and neural growth factor to allow my body to partially regrow the spinothalamic tract over a period of years."

"So you can feel in your legs?"

"Somewhat, yes."

"Can I ask how your dad feels about not knowing whether or not you're his biological child?"

"He loves me as much as my brothers who are, without a doubt, his biological children." Eadowen bit his lip in thought. "Assure me you won't come on to anyone who doesn't want you ever again."

"I never have and I won't," Taban held up his hand. "And since, apparently, you're the only person who can see through me, you know I mean it."

"Good, because I want you to come home with me over Spring Break. You need a chance to get away from all this."

"Wha—" Taban started, then recovered himself. "I'm supposed to be partying in Miami, but I guess I can do that all summer. I'll just book a flight from Florida, so my father won't notice that I changed my plans. Where do you live Vancouver, Toronto, Ontario?"

"Toronto is in Ontario. I live in Nova Scotia."

"What province is Nova Scotia in? Do you like speak French? 'Cause that'd be hot!"

Eadowen rubbed his forehead and sighed.

"Hey, how do you think I'd look as a blond?" Taban asked.

In response, Eadowen raised an eyebrow and wrinkled his nose in disgust.

"That bad, huh? I thought I pulled it off when I dressed up as that country-pop singer from the 2010s to sing for your eighteenth birthday." Taban admired the short white dress hanging in his closet over a pair of silver stiletto heels.

"I guess you did pull off those ringlets pretty well. I liked the way one of your heels was dangling off your ankle while you faked playing the guitar. That was a nice touch."

"Oh, that was because I broke the strap when I fell trying to get to the stage. Connor had to escort me so I wouldn't rip the dress. He's had a giant crush on you for forever, speaking of which why aren't you and he dating?" Taban peeled more wax off of his back. "I walked in on you two making out Sophmore year and he's followed you like a puppy dog ever since. He's an A-list actor now; get with him and you're set for life."

Eadowen shook his head.

"I do commercials so I stay anonymous because fame looks really annoying, but you could handle it. It's not like the tabloids are going to have anything juicy to go on with you if you were his significant other. I mean come on, Connor Haswell is gorgeous, if I was into sleeping with guys he'd be at the top of my A-list."

"I have an obligation to someone else. Acquiescing to his advances was a lapse in my judgment." Eadowen covered his eyes with his hand. "You need to understand, Taban, you and I are like drugs—people can basically get addicted. The people you've been intimate with will struggle to find satisfaction in other partners."

"Even if that's true I'm not going cold turkey."

"Then wait seventy-two hours."

"What?"

"If someone asks to sleep with you make them think it over for seventy-two hours away from you. That will give them a chance to think it over with their rational mind." Eadowen explained. "Also, you won't have much trouble with this, but only have sex with the same person once or twice."

"Won't stop most people, but sure I'll do it unless she offers me a Lamborghini with gull wing doors like my Ferrari. I've been wanting one for a while."

"You can do the seventy-two hours thing too, right? I'll help you get someone. What do you find attractive?" Taban said cheerily. "Like really, what *do* you like?" If he couldn't attract Eadowen, he had to know who could.

"Good. Bring me a fairy."

"Huh?" Taban chuckled. "A folklore fetish? That's hilarious."

"More of a kink," Eadowen clarified. "Leave me to my fantasies and I'll leave you to that tentacle stuff you watch." He put on his glasses and searched something on his tablet. "By the way, it says here that oxytocin can be released through massage. I would've preferred that."

"Shut up, Ea," Taban mumbled into his pillow.

"Ea?"

"You poured candle wax on me. It suits you, 'little fire.'"

Eadowen tapped the lights off and blew out the candle. Soft light from the city shone through the window making a small rectangle on the floor between their beds. The shape was disrupted only by the dark shadow of a branch tapping against the glass in the breeze. Taban reviewed his mental list of attractive traits he might have inherited genetically. Eadowen did seem to fit most of the same categories. There were more factors involved, of that he was certain.

Chapter 10
How Guardians Disappear

DURING TABAN'S FIRST EVENING visiting Eadowen at his home in Halifax, he joined his friend for an evening walk to loosen his muscles from the long plane flight from Florida. Taban shivered and wondered how he could be cold when the sun was shining in a clear sky.

"Here, take my jacket." Eadowen handed him a windbreaker he was carrying in his lap.

"You're not cold?"

"I'm wearing more than you."

Taban wrapped the jacket over his Strap-Shirt. It certainly wasn't an ideal piece of clothing, but it was in vogue. *Eadowen looks like he's dressed from a hundred years ago,* Taban thought as he looked at Eadowen disapprovingly. *If he really is like me, maybe he wears it to seem not as attractive. Although, he also seems pretty intent on covering those scars on his neck and chest.*

"You don't seem to mind cold swimming pools," Eadowen remarked.

"I move really fast in the water," Taban replied. "We've roomed together since we were fourteen. It's going to be weird not living with you this fall." The reality that he and Eadowen would be separated hit Taban like a kickboard accidentally launched by someone who had tried to hold it underwater. Aware of how much more difficult his life would be without Eadowen defusing whatever toxic reactions he had stirred up in others, Taban touched Eadowen's arm affectionately. "You're going to Smith and I'm headed to Dartmouth—not that I should be."

"What do you mean?"

"Mr. Mir's an alumnus. He made a few calls because he couldn't stand the idea of me going to a place without a title."

"Are you saying you're going to miss me?" Eadowen said, a hint of disparagement in his voice.

"Of course." Taban punched his friend's shoulder in a failed attempt to seem chummy. *Just the other night, you tell me, I'm not alone because you're like me and now you're leaving me,* he thought.

They made their way back to the house in silence. With the sun still high overhead Taban had trouble believing it was evening.

Eadowen went to the side of the house that had a ramp, while Taban took the front steps. Eadowen's father, Daray Tolymie, opened the door. His broad-shouldered but otherwise slim frame was silhouetted against the orange glow of the chandelier. The accent of a violet tie highlighted his narrow, grey eyes. A silver pin held his black hair, which fell over the shoulders of his double-breasted suit. The swanlike way he poised in the doorway completed the elegance of his appearance. Barely taller than Taban's sternum, Daray commanded a presence that filled the room. The tremors in Daray's hands and the slow pace at which he moved contrasted to the rest of his youthful appearance. *Ea did say Daray raised him from birth. Was he younger than me when Ea was born?* Taban thought.

"Good evening, Mr. Mir." Daray intercepted Taban's train of thought. "Did you enjoy your perambulation?"

"We did."

"I'll have dinner ready in a half hour. I hope you will excuse us for a moment. I need to speak to Eadowen privately."

"Not a problem at all."

"This way." The flickering light from the circular hearth illuminated Daray's delicate features.

"Donovan took your luggage upstairs for you." In the far corner of the room Eadowen's father leaned over another couch facing a television. "Donovan, have you finished your homework?"

"Yes."

"This is Taban, Eadowen's roommate. He'll be staying with us all week. Please help him to feel welcome," Daray said. "I'll let you know when dinner is ready." Daray picked up a walking stick by the door and used it as he exited the living room.

"Hi, I've seen you on Eadowen's video calls, remember me?"

Donovan looked at him for the first time. His grey eyes widened and he snapped back to his game.

"What're you playing?" Taban touched Donovan's arm. Recoiling, Donovan fumbled with his game controller and turned away. Taban was surprised by such a vehement negative response, until the color of Donovan's cheeks clarified the situation. When he looked around for something else to occupy his time, he noticed another person had entered the room. She had her back to him, seemingly entranced by the flames of the hearth. Her little black dress had long sleeves and showed off the curve of her waist. She turned as though she sensed his gaze. It was then that Taban remembered Eadowen also had a fifteen-year-old brother. Though Daray was the senior, Aydan looked like a rough sketch of his father that had been taken out and hung in the rain, which was by no means an insult. Donovan and Aydan had both inherited their father's long face and eyes set a little too high. These features made them striking, but looked a bit odd on further inspection.

Seeing the way Taban carefully inspected him, Aydan held up his palm with his thumb, pointer, and middle finger extended to form a bar sign used by heterosexuals primarily to make their sexuality known to potential partners of the opposite sex. Taban showed Aydan the same sign, but with the back of his hand to resemble the British sign for "up yours."

"You there, come help me with my boots," Aydan commanded. He flopped onto the sofa and stuck a stiletto boot out. Taken aback by the address, Taban went over to the circular sofa. Fearing removing a boot while standing would send him into the fire, Taban sat on the floor to assist.

"Hi, I'm—"

"Taban Mir. Eadowen told me to watch you like a hawk and to tell you I can throw a card at forty-five meters per second with accuracy." Aydan unfastened a large clip letting his hair fall out of an updo. "That might not seem intimidating to you, but it will if I also inform you that I prefer knives." He flipped his wrist; the clip opened revealing a blade. He took the small razor out of the clip and hurled it across the room into the center of a knothole. Smiling at Taban like a slasher film villain, he cocked his head to the side.

"You must be Aydan." Taban pulled off one boot. "Nice to meet you too."

A pointed boot toe tilted Taban's chin up. "A pleasure."

Up close Taban noted the makeup contouring Aydan had used to sharpen his features, as well as eyeliner, mascara, and eyebrow penciling to enhance his appearance. Knowing that Aydan was not naturally as striking as he at first appeared, Taban liked him a little better, but distanced himself from the magician anyway. *He has pointy things,* Taban thought, rubbing his tattoo. *I don't like sharp things.* Browsing the shelves, Taban occupied himself with a book on Greek mythology. An hour later, Daray came to invite them to dinner.

"Sorry for the delay. I burned some of the food," Daray explained.

Taban hadn't smelled anything burning, but he acknowledged that the house must be well ventilated considering he wasn't bothered by the fire burning in the marble chimney.

Though the dining table was set elaborately, the details faded out of Taban's attention the instant he saw Eadowen's bleak expression. Taban grabbed the chair next to his friend making as much of a commotion as possible to get his attention. At last, Eadowen blinked and glanced around the room as though to orient himself. When Eadowen noticed Taban staring at him, he plastered on a face that was stiffer than his usual polite smile. "Uh, hi Taban, h-have something to eat."

"You okay?"

"Of course," Eadowen replied, squeezing Taban's leg under the table to suggest that Taban not broach the subject at dinner.

Donovan sat hunched over a plate of sweet potatoes, carefully avoiding eye contact with Taban. As Taban accepted a silver platter from Daray, he noticed that Daray also seemed troubled. He rested his delicate pointed chin on his long-fingered hand, as though he were showing off a bracelet.

"Mr. Tolymie, where did you get your suit? It's very nice."

"Thank you. Some students ..." Daray paused. His eyebrows pressed together with concern.

"Some students studying fashion at Dal made it for him," Aydan finished the sentence. "He likes to just be called Daray."

Daray looked at the table as though ashamed that he hadn't been able to formulate his thought. The somber mood during such a delightful feast reminded Taban of the funerals he'd attended throughout his life. He decided to make conversation in the hope that someone would reveal the elephant in the room.

"You know, Eadowen's accent is kind of more Scottish-y than you guys." Taban indicated Daray and Aydan. "Did you guys used to live in Scotland?"

"We only visited. Mom was around more before I was born. She's from Glasgow so it must've rubbed off," Aydan explained.

The mention of the Tolymie's mother triggered a breathless silence. Daray put his head in his hands while his three children exchanged comforting looks to each other. Racking his memories of the few video chats Eadowen had let him join, Taban recalled a robust fifty-something woman who he had considered an unusual match to Daray's youthful beauty. Annoyed that no one had bothered to tell him what had happened to Eadowen's mother, Taban decided to continue the conversation on the topic.

"So, um, what does Mrs. Tolymie do?"

"She ... worked ... at," Daray slowly attempted to answer the question.

"*Dr.* Artio Tolymie *was* a psychologist, who primarily worked in the United Kingdom," Aydan said in such a way as to make clear that Artio Tolymie was not to be addressed in any other way.

"So, how'd you meet Dr. Tolymie?" Taban attempted to redirect the conversation to Daray who seemed more compliant than Eadowen's pesky younger brother.

"I was shoved in a locker at a high school. Artio was a foreign exchange student from Scotland. She chewed out the people who put me in there and made sure I got home safely ..." Daray trailed off.

"—then she asked him out," Aydan helped his father finish the story. "She didn't know he was a psychologist hired to work on the bullying problem at the school. They didn't form a relationship until we met many years later, at a conference in Scotland."

"Why would someone shove you in a locker?" Taban asked.

This remark temporarily brought Eadowen out of his daze. He went into an involved narration about the horrors of bullying. Tuning out his friend, Taban wondered if it was considered bad form to ask a trophy husband his age.

"Um, Daray, how old are you?"

"How old do you think he is?" Aydan said coyly.

Aydan's just happy I'm not asking about his mom anymore, Taban thought as he did some quick addition in his head based on Aydan's age. "Thirty-three," he tried.

"Hm. Must be slipping. I usually get twenty-six, but I'm somewhere in my early nineties … I've lost count." Daray ran his fingers up his cheek. "Would you believe incredible plastic surgery?"

"Not for a second," Taban replied. *Dad forced me to get some plastic surgery. The only way to get a face like that is to sell your soul,* he thought.

The pieces started to fit together. Taban recalled that Daray had met his father briefly during the prep school fair in Toronto where he'd first met Eadowen. It didn't matter if Daray was thirty-three or ninety-four. *Whatever age Daray put down when he registered Eadowen at the school must have infuriated my father, because his appearance and appeal, or "gift" as he calls it, is fading so quickly with age. That must've been why Mr. Mir told my aunt about the Tolymies,* Taban concluded. *Now my aunt wants to get a hold of their DNA … and I'm working for Abigail and since my aunt is funding her work, I'm working for my aunt.* Taban glanced uneasily in Eadowen's direction.

"I missed you all. It's good to be home," Eadowen added in a voice that sounded more like a farewell than a loving remark.

Daray touched his cheek to cheer him, a gesture to which Eadowen responded by lovingly resting his hand on his father's hand. As Taban watched the sappy display, something seemed to block his throat making it impossible for him swallow his mouthful of rice. Daray's steel-grey eyes focused on Taban, he tilted his head as if to say, *Did you want to join?* Hastily, Taban found his plate of sweet potatoes fascinating, but not before noticing that despite his father's comfort, Eadowen looked more upset than Taban had ever seen him.

* * *

"Should I help with the dishes?" Eadowen asked.

"Spend time with your friend," Daray said. "Aydan and Donovan can take care of it."

Taban followed Eadowen into the living room. Once he thought they were out of earshot of the rest of the family he ventured to repeat his earlier question. "Are you okay?"

"Well, for now I guess I'm fine." Eadowen gazed into the fire.

"Look Ea, I really care about you. I know you're not fine."

"I want you to enjoy your first evening in Nova Scotia. I think I need to turn in early, though." Eadowen went to the lift next to the staircase. Taban took the stairs and met him on the second floor.

"Ea, what's going on? Something happened to your mom didn't it?"

Eadowen hid his face.

"Tears? Ah! You're crying!"

"Thanks for clarifying."

"You can't cry!" Taban said. *You're the one who comforts me—and everyone else. I have no idea what to do,* he thought.

"I'm going to bed. The guest room is behind you."

Ignoring the hint, Taban watched from the doorway as Eadowen got into bed without changing his clothes. Taban looked around the unfamiliar room and noticed a closet. Fumbling in the dark, he rummaged for something that resembled pajamas. He draped soft clothes over Eadowen, who was lying motionless on his bed.

"Here change into these."

"Wait," Eadowen said his voice muffled by his arm. "Shut the door." Taban pulled on the knob. "I won't be going to Smith, anymore."

"What? Why?"

As he walked back toward the bed, Taban stumbled on a woven rug, and fell on top of Eadowen. The clothes he had laid out sloughed onto the floor.

"Ow. What're you doing?" Eadowen said angrily.

"Don't hurt me. I fell." Fearing Eadowen might misinterpret his clumsiness as an assault Taban quickly explained, "I'm one of those people who makes walking look challenging. I don't belong on land." He rolled over and lay next to his friend so that he could see Eadowen's profile in the dark. "You okay?"

"Yeah," Eadowen assured him, but his voice cracked.

"So." Taban propped himself up on his arm. "Why aren't you going to the school you tried so hard to get into?"

Eadowen tapped a message into his Ogham and showed it to Taban: **Do you know sign language?**

"Only a few signs," Taban replied verbally.

Eadowen wrote another message: **This house isn't very soundproof. Dad's going to take Aydan to his performance soon. Then we can talk.**

The flash of headlights in the driveway answered Eadowen's message.

Taban felt in the dark for his friend's shoulders and waist. He sat up pulling Eadowen with him as he leaned against the headboard. Eadowen's hot tears ran down Taban's neck into his shirt.

"I told my dad I'd stay and take care of my brothers," Eadowen said in a strained voice.

"Is he going somewhere?"

"Yes."

"Where? For how long?" Taban asked, his curiosity growing.

"Probably Scotland, and no idea," Eadowen gulped.

"He wouldn't leave. I saw how much he loved you."

"Someone knows how old my dad actually is. My dad really is ninety-three. You know how my dad said he didn't meet my mom again for many years. It was forty years. That's how they knew they were the same."

"The same what?"

"We're fairies."

"That's funny. I'd almost believe you if your whole family looked like your dad. He's like a high elf infused with anime character."

"Physical beauty isn't part of it. That's just Dad."

It was hard not to believe someone as honest as Eadowen. Taban decided to at least pretend he accepted the idea, which wasn't hard to do after what he'd learned about himself only recently.

"So, why does he have to leave?"

"As you could probably tell, my dad isn't functioning so well. He probably has a neurodegenerative disorder from his human genes. Aydan has to help him dress and I had to do most of the meal we ate tonight. If someone comes looking for him and we aren't around, he won't be able to defend himself." Eadowen mumbled into Taban's shirt.

"Who do you think is after him?"

"The same people who murdered my mother." Eadowen mumbled into Taban's shirt.

"What?"

"My mother was shot a few weeks ago in the UK, but Dad didn't tell me until now because he wanted to tell me in person." Eadowen explained in a strained voice. "The police think it was a mugging gone wrong, but my mother managed to escape. Before she died of her injuries, she told a trusted friend in Scotland that her assailants were discussing her longevity. That friend contacted my father."

Taban cringed, it wouldn't surprise him if his aunt had tried to kill Dr. Tolymie so that Dr. Tolymie couldn't interfere with the use of her DNA. In fact, it seemed the likely turn of events. "So why do you think these people also know about your dad?" he asked.

"There was a break-in at the apartment in the town that my family uses to get our mail. Based on the information they stole they were interested in my father, not commodities. The person trying to locate my father probably doesn't have this address, which makes sense because we try not to report this address anywhere. I doubt they'll try another break-in, because the police now have their prints and DNA on file."

"I think you're right," Taban agreed. His aunt seemed to have refocused her energy on a nationwide scale instead of just targeting the elusive Tolymies. *That fake hair sample I gave my dad probably convinced my aunt that Eadowen doesn't have the genes,* Taban congratulated himself on accidently foiling her. "Should you all leave?" Taban whispered.

"That would raise suspicion. Donovan, Aydan, and I are much better documented than our parents. We do still minimize our online footprint though, and our parents were able to veto our genome sequencing." Eadowen's body shook in his arms. "I know I can take care of my brothers. I'll take a year off from school and then transfer to Dalhousie—it's a great school. If Dad sees me like this he'll never leave!"

"Just let it out."

"I miss my Mom. I feel so alone" Eadowen cried, gripping Taban's shirt in his fist. Taban felt the elastic fibers of his shirt stretch. *Maybe Eadowen would be safe for longer if I stay close to him. It might be possible to convince my father that Dalhousie is the best place for Abigail to do her research instead of Dartmouth,* Taban decided.

"You won't be alone," Taban said into his friend's hair. "I'll live with you. I'll go to Dalhousie. They have, like, a chemistry program, right?"

"Will your dad let you go to Dal?" Eadowen asked.

"Yes. After I talk to him," Taban assured him. Taban had already concluded that he could persuade Abigail to submit her research proposal to Dalhousie.

"You don't have to."

"You're gonna need money."

"I can work and my parents have money to leave us too."

"You're going to need more than that and with me you can still afford to go to school. I have a bank account that my father doesn't know about. It's where I put the money from selling the cars and other gifts my lovers give me."

"Where did your family get all your money anyway?"

"Originally, tricking people out of their money; from what I understand, it was white collar crimes," Taban explained.

Eadowen groaned and shifted his weight.

"What's wrong?" Taban asked letting his embrace slack so Eadowen could move more freely.

"Something's digging into my hip."

Confused, Taban felt his pocket and identified the culprit of Eadowen's discomfort. He took out two stone rings that he'd found surfing. Since he had no need for them at the time, he'd turned them in to lost-and-found. The morning he boarded the plane for Florida, he'd received a package from the lost-and-found with a note saying no one had claimed the items. To see if one fit, he wriggled it onto his finger. Since Eadowen was still crying, Taban wondered if he could distract him with the trinkets. Taking Eadowen's hand, he slid one of the rings onto his finger. It was loose, but it fit.

"Pretty sure this is made out of bloodstone. It'll look nice on you. Uh, you're going to have to take my word for that until morning."

"Rings?"

"Sure, why not? There's two. Guess we were meant to be together."

"This isn't a separate ring, see the rough edge," Eadowen answered running his hand over the smooth raised stone. "There must have been a flaw in the manufacturing."

"Aren't you going to ask me how I got these?"

"I'm accustomed to you doing this kind of thing." Eadowen sounded exasperated, but Taban could tell he wasn't shaking as much as before.

* * *

Taban opened his eyes, his mouth tasted sour and he realized he hadn't brushed his teeth the night before. Running his tongue over his unclean teeth, he sat up. His clothes felt crusty, he noticed stretch marks on his shirt from the night before and realized he was wearing the same clothes as yesterday. Stretching his hands over his head he looked to his left and saw Eadowen fast asleep next to him. Shivering, Taban slid back under the covers, resting his head on Eadowen's bicep to enjoy his body heat.

"Eadowen, it's time to wake up," Daray called from the hallway. Taban wasn't sure how to answer, since he wasn't Eadowen and it didn't look like Eadowen was going to wake anytime soon. Eadowen's father opened the door and stared at Taban, who became cognizant of the condition of the bedding. The sheets were spread in all directions and only a corner of the quilt remained on the bed. To make matters worse the clothes he'd gotten out for Eadowen lay sprawled across the floor.

"We'd prefer you used the guest room."

"Sorry, I guess I'm so used to living with Ea—Eadowen."

Daray surveyed the scene trying to piece together what had happened the night before. Taban was relieved that both he and Eadowen were fully clothed, even if their attire wasn't in the most presentable condition. He wasn't sure he liked the Tolymie household. Aydan, Daray, and Eadowen didn't react to him the way everyone else did.

"I'll show you to the guest room." Daray beckoned Taban.

"Dad, wait," Eadowen said groggily. "I was stressed and Taban stayed to help me. We just fell asleep."

"Well, Eadowen Ursula Tolymie, make sure it doesn't happen again," His father scolded. "Breakfast is ready."

The ring Taban had given Eadowen had fallen off on the bed sometime in the night. He retrieved it, hopped back on the bed, and shoved his legs under the sheets.

"Ah! Your feet are freezing!" Eadowen yelped. "I guess it's decided then. You're going to live with me."

Taban wrapped himself in the blanket. "Yeah," he replied returning the ring to Eadowen's finger.

"What'd I ever do to deserve this …" Taban brightened until Eadowen concluded with, "—nightmare." In a split second Taban watched Eadowen shift back to the dark alluring Eadowen he'd discovered during his misguided exploration of his abilities. Eadowen laced his fingers into Taban's newly bleached hair, pulling just hard enough that Taban could feel the tension in his roots. "And just to make one thing clear, you can kiss me, but if you ever ignore when I or anyone else says 'no,' I will make sure you have to answer to authorities. Understand?"

Eadowen's hand still dictating the majority of the motions he could make with his head, Taban gave a stiff nod. "I'm surprised you're even willing to do that much with me," he commented.

"Contrary to what you seem to think, I have physical desires and with you I don't have to worry about heartbreak."

"Ha. Well, this seventy-two hour wait thing is harder than I thought. I'd be fine having some fun. Just promise you won't fall in love with me."

"It's a deal." Eadowen released Taban who massaged his own tingling hair follicles.

The sound of someone clearing his throat made them both look toward the hall. "I really hope Donovan has better taste in guys than you do," Aydan remarked to his older sibling from the open doorway. "Dad told me to check on you two. He won't let me have breakfast until you are downstairs so hurry up."

PART THREE

PRESENT: IN WHICH THERE IS SABOTAGE

"The sea is also a place of life. Do not let the monsters that dwell within it deter you from experiencing the wonder of the ocean."

–CASSIDY ADISA

CHAPTER 11
RISK TAKER

THE GREEN SEA SHIMMERED below Cassidy as she soared through her dreamscape. Thin streamers of cirrus clouds wove around her bronze arms. She surrendered herself to the velocity of a downward spiral; the wind blew marks on her face away—she was perfect plunging through the atmosphere. The ocean reflected this image, as it swirled upward to consume her. She drew in her breath, titillating with anticipation for the caress of water, but Danny yanked her out of the dream by slamming the door as she raced downstairs.

"Mom says we need to get up if we want to go to the beach!"

Cassidy removed her face from her pillow. Heavy rain washed against the window at a slight angle. *Well, it's probably not going to be crowded,* Cassidy thought as she headed downstairs. *I don't really mind the rain. Not looking forward to the wind though.*

"Mornin' Cassidy," Danny's bushy ponytail stuck out behind a precarious stack of pancakes covered in bacon.

Cassidy took a seat next to Danny but not too close, so as to avoid flying chunks of pancakes. The savory flavor of butter melted together with the sweet syrup. She tried to ignore the carnivorous noises from Danny's direction.

"Thanks for letting me borrow your surf kayaking gear," Cassidy said to Ms. Reyes. "Danny, are you going to bring a wave ski?"

"A what?"

"I showed you one at summer camp. It's a flat kayak that looks like a surfboard, except it has indentations to sit in," Cassidy explained.

"I'm not bringing one," Danny mumbled. "I just don't like being in water when I can't see the bottom." Leaving her chair wobbling, Danny raced upstairs.

"Okay, your loss," Cassidy responded, steadying the chair.

"Which one did you pick?" Mrs. Reyes asked.

"Martinique Beach. I searched it on Taban's recommendation," Cassidy replied. "It looks like a nice spot."

Cassidy neatly scraped the last morsel of pancake off her plate and spooned up the last drops of maple syrup. The sweet woody flavor remained in her mouth as she took her plate to the sink and sponged the sticky surface. Real maple syrup tasted completely different from the light-brown sugary substance she used on her pancakes back home.

Unzipping her suitcase in the guest room, Cassidy pulled out several layers of clothes, in preparation for the torrential rain. She sighed and tried on a bright red halter top over a one-piece swimsuit. She turned in front of the mirror. Usually she would ignore the colorful concentric circle design across her waist, but today she felt self-conscious about her voluptuous figure. She sighed and picked up her journal.

Hello Self! she wrote. *It doesn't matter what clothes Taban would want to see. I pick what I like. He's not going to be at the beach anyway. Why does he fill my head like this? It's annoying. We barely know each other … why am I so into him? Now I know what my friends were talking about when they described their first love …*

Cassidy stared at the page and hastily blacked out *first love.*

"Are you ready yet?" Danny said as she entered the room, a towel draped over her hair. Cassidy noticed Danny's defined abdomen and hid her stomach with her arm.

"Does your tummy hurt?" Danny hopped around trying to put on a black peasant skirt while standing.

"No.You're slim and buff," Cassidy said. "I'm not."

"You're curvy."

"Curvy is just a nice way of saying fat."

"No, It's not! You take great care of your health and it shows." Danny gazed at Cassidy intensely. "I think you're really beautiful

Cassidy." she said, her dark eyes shining. The fervor with which Danny spoke made Cassidy feel flattered and a little anxious at the same time.

"I can see why you always used to get mistaken for a male-bodied person at camp," Cassidy said. "Wait ... I didn't mean that. Sorry, I'm just upset about my figure."

"I know. I do it on purpose sometimes. When people mistake me for male they seem to like me better. Honestly, I just wish I could get clothes that fit me. My boy hips, huge shoulders, and being short make it impossible for me to find anything that fits and I can't afford a tailor."

"I'm really sorry. I think you look amazing," Cassidy said trying to make amends for her tactless comment. "Let me go take a shower and screw my head on properly."

When Danny heard Cassidy close the door sharply behind her, she looked at her bare torso in the mirror. Danny flexed her abdomen so that she could see six indentations, tilted her body back, and placed her hands on her chest. If she pushed her breasts flat with her hands her torso resembled a male upper body which she couldn't decide if she preferred to her female one.

In the shower, Cassidy turned on the news on her Ogham. She clipped it to a holder on the tiled wall. The most popular news snippet involving different countries MeSite privacy policies played while she scrubbed her hair.

* * *

"You're right—the Canadian Prime Minister's decision could be problematic." Cassidy continued her conversation with Danny about the news segment she'd listened to in the shower. She pulled the car into the sandy parking lot of Martinique Beach. "You certainly don't need any of your information leaked, since you're probably going to have to live as privately as the Tolymies."

"I know. I feel like I already have too much of a presence online," Danny said. "I don't know how the Tolymies do it."

"Me neither." Cassidy mused. "We practically live in the virtual world. Honestly, it was kind of pleasant to have dinner and talk to people face-to-face."

"Yeah, I've barely spent any time on my tablet or Ogham the last couple of days. It's weird."

"We'd better put a message or post a photo, so no one thinks we died." Cassidy stepped out of the car and started unclasping bungees from the rack on the van. As Cassidy donned her wetsuit, she noticed Danny still hadn't gotten out of the car. "What do you think, Danny?"

Danny stared at the small grey crests breaking white on the shore, the Ocean seemed like it could swell up and devour her at any moment. "There are no lifeguards."

"Yeah, according to the site they keep changing the amount of supervision at this beach." Cassidy clipped on her helmet.

"Please be safe," Danny muttered, making no motion to leave the car.

"It's okay. I'm used to unsupervised beaches."

"I'm going to stay on shore."

"You want to hang onto this for me?" Cassidy undid the little gold key around her neck and refastened it around Danny's. "Does that car look familiar?" Cassidy commented looking at a vehicle parked in the shade of an oak tree in the far corner of the parking lot.

"Yeah, it looks like Taban's car, but that model's pretty popular."

I wish I could remember numbers better, so that I could check the license plate for reassurance, Cassidy thought, as she carried the flat kayak over the spiny grass leading down to the beach. *I wonder why he recommended this beach?*

"Be careful!" Danny called. She lay out a rainbow beach towel and took out her tablet, searching for any movies on the subject of linguistics.

Cassidy pushed her kayak into the water, fastened the ankle and waist straps, and paddled vigorously toward the open ocean. As she sliced through the surf, the boat lurched as waves broke over the bow, spreading foam over her neoprene-covered legs. Her shoulders ached, reminding her that she hadn't kayaked since autumn, but she didn't care. The surf was tall and rough, but she assessed that she could handle it. She struggled through the breaking waves to get to the calm, open ocean. A crest broke on the side of her kayak. She caught a breath of air before she capsized. Upside-down in the surf, strapped to her kayak, she heard pounding surf overhead. Her helmet scraped against a rock, but she barely noticed in the icy water. Using a technique that had taken her years to master, she pulled her paddle beside her, then around her body creating momentum to flip the boat right-side-up. She gasped as she broke the surface. Her core muscles ached as she hurried out of the breakers. *I really don't want to have to do that a lot.*

One other kayaker paddled in the distance, farther out than Cassidy would have considered ideal for catching waves, but perhaps the person didn't want to surf. However, his boat seemed flat small like hers, not long and slim like a kayak designed for regular paddling. She saw a swell that humped promisingly behind two smaller swells. She allowed the first swell to elevate her, when her kayak dipped after the first swell, she slipped her paddle deep into the ocean and pulled back sharply, rotating her kayak to face the shore. When the second swell passed underneath her, she took two strokes with her paddle to reach the point right before the second swell started to break. She waited. When the third wave touched the back of her boat she paddled as hard as she could. Her momentum carried her with the crest of the wave until she felt the water pull underneath her. She let out a cheer as the wave carried her toward the shore. Before the crest broke, Cassidy drove her paddle into the top of the wave as though she were slaying a wild animal; this motion rotated her boat. With one stroke, she freed herself from the wave and began to paddle back toward the open ocean.

When she reached the place where the swells started to break, she looked for the other kayaker. Paddling a little farther out, she continued to scan the horizon for the person she'd seen. Finally, she spotted the kayaker farther down the shoreline where the swells broke more unevenly. He didn't have a lifejacket, nor did he use his torso to paddle, instead he strained his arms against the water. The rain beat against Cassidy's face. She used her Ogham to get a close-up picture of him. She cringed. He wasn't wearing a helmet and had fastened himself into the wave ski. Cassidy watched the raven-haired man fumble to catch a wave. He missed the first, but timed his speed with the second swell. The wave carried him gently until it broke sharply forcing his boat into a nosedive. Cassidy saw the boat resurface after the wave had passed, but it was upside-down. *Was he able to unclip himself?* she thought. *Sometimes ankle straps are hard to undo. What if he hit his head like I did?* She started to paddle hurriedly in the direction of the boat, but the current inhibited her speed. "Sunset, emergency report: kayaker may be injured at Martinique Beach," she yelled to her Ogham.

"Sunset accept: Emergency response: Please briefly explain the emergency."

"There is an indication that a kayaker is stuck under his boat."

"Emergency Response: May we locate you via your Ogham?"

"Affirmative," Cassidy said.

"Emergency Response: A helicopter is on its way."

"Message to Edana: I saw someone who might be injured. I'm going to check on them."

"Message from Edana: Alright. I'll direct any help your way. Be safe."

Cassidy's arms and core burned. Icy water flew off her paddle and stung her face like needles. Brine scorched her throat and wind-swept rain blurred her vision. She looked toward the shore to protect her eyes from another wave and saw someone running along the beach. Rubbing her eyes with the sleeve of her wetsuit, she continued to paddle, but watched the figure remove a teal shirt and kick off his shoes. Another wave arched over her, so she shut her eyes and used her paddle to navigate through it before it broke. She kept her eyes on the person who was now running into the surf. Once the water reached his torso he dove under a wave and did not resurface after the wave. *Oh great, someone else to worry about.* As she approached the boat, the body of the kayaker resurfaced, face down, farther out in the open ocean. *Good, he managed to unstrap himself, but why is he so far out?* she thought, until she noticed a table-sized clump of seaweed moving steadily out to sea. *A rip current! If I get caught I might not have the strength to ride it out then paddle back to shore, but at least I can hold him above water until a helicopter arrives.* With strength she didn't know she had, she paddled into the rip current and reached the unconscious man. Concerned that he might have spinal injury, Cassidy carefully turned him over. A bleeding gash ran from his temple to his eyebrow. *I think he's alive, but I don't know how to get him to breathe better. I can't use CPR in the water.*

A tap on the front of her kayak broke her concentration. She looked down into azure eyes. "Taban?" She identified the swimmer she'd seen in the distance.

"What're you doing out here—I mean—nice to see you, Cassidy," Taban said, cheerfully treading water. His bleached hair, wet and tangled with seaweed, emphasized his brunette roots. "Give him to me and I'll get him to shore."

"You're caught in a rip current. Hang on to my boat and stay calm." Her hand started to numb in the cold as she held the young man's head. "There's a helicopter on the way."

"I'm fine. I'll just get out of it a little farther out where it calms down." He casually swam over to the boy and relieved Cassidy from holding him. "Looks like Daisuke isn't breathing. You'd better let me get him to shore."

"You know him?" Cassidy asked. She couldn't wrap her head around how he'd managed to reach her so quickly from shore even with the aid of the rip current. "Wait, I have an idea." Cassidy unfastened the clips on the wave ski and jumped into the water.

"What the heck are you doing?" Taban shouted.

"Watch out." She overturned the wave ski so that she had a flat surface, save for the three fins at the stern. "Help me get him onto my wave ski. If you take his hips and I take his shoulders we can keep his neck and back straight," Cassidy instructed.

Only a little smaller than Donovan, Daisuke could have been a college football linebacker. They struggled, but Taban's inexplicable ease in the water accelerated the task of moving Daisuke onto her wave ski. *It's almost as if Taban can time his pushing precisely with the shifts in the ocean,* she wondered as she leveled Daisuke's head onto her boat.

"Hold my kayak as steadily as you can." Cassidy straddled Daisuke. The boat pitched and she fell forward.

"You okay, Cassidy?" Taban asked. "I have it now."

"Keep holding it." It had been years since her mothers had signed her up for a basic water safety and first aid course. She opened Daisuke's mouth and scooped out some seaweed blocking his throat. Starting the chest compressions, she briefly considered asking Taban if he knew how to preform CPR, but realized she wouldn't be able to hold the boat as steadily as he could. "Help me count compressions."

"Aren't you going to give him mouth-to-mouth?" Taban asked.

"That. Doesn't. Help. Unless. Well. Trained. I'm. Not. Better. To do. This." Cassidy said, each word punctuating a pump to his chest. Daisuke started to cough, and then he made a gagging sound. Cassidy tilted his head so his vomit wouldn't clog his airway. The contents of Daisuke's stomach spilled out onto her kayak. When Daisuke opened his dazed eyes, Cassidy experienced the most gratifying sensation she'd ever felt. He continued to choke, and she guessed he'd received a concussion, but it looked like he'd live.

"Message from Edana: Are you ok? I hear a helicopter."

"Message to Edana: We're fine. I see it," Cassidy shouted over the sound of the surf, salt water splashing into her mouth. Soon she also heard the whirring of a helicopter. She waved at it and smiled at Taban. He returned with an expression that made her heart melt.

The helicopter hovered overhead, causing the ocean to froth and the rain to swirl. A securing line dropped down followed by a stretcher with three EMTs aboard. While two EMTs transferred Daisuke onto the stretcher, the other attended to Taban and Cassidy.

"May I take your contact information?" she asked. Cassidy and Taban slid their Oghams across the EMT's Ogham.

"What hospital are you taking him to?" Taban asked.

"We're taking him to the Queen Elizabeth Health Sciences Centre," she replied. "What you both did was very heroic. Do you need assistance getting back to shore?"

Cassidy noticed that she could easily paddle out of the rip current now that they were far enough out to sea. "Nope," she said.

"Should be fine, thanks," Taban added.

As the helicopter ascended, the ocean churned, forcing Cassidy flat on her wave ski. Taban ducked under the water and reappeared only when the whirring had faded far in the distance.

"Are you sure you're going to be okay?" Cassidy asked Taban, who was noticeably shivering.

"Yup. See you on shore." He dove under the water.

Cassidy used a function on her Ogham to monitor the rip current, so she could maintain a safe distance. As she started to paddle to shore, she saw Taban bob up for a breath over twenty meters ahead of her. *Geez, he's fast,* she thought. *He looks like a happy, little blond seal from here.*

Despite her fear of the water, Danny ran into the shallow foam to assist Cassidy. When she stepped out of her kayak, Cassidy felt overwhelming exhaustion in every muscle of her body. She embraced Danny, resting against her.

"I'm so glad you're safe." Danny stood on her tip toes, so that she could whisper in Cassidy's ear. "I heard everything. That was so heroic."

"I am. Everything is okay. Would you be willing to carry my kayak and paddle? I don't think my arms will work anymore."

"No problem."

Danny carried the wave ski onto the higher beach, while Cassidy flopped onto Danny's towel. To her delight, the wind had died down and the rain poured down in large drops. Cassidy retrieved a dry towel, from a plastic bin, in which she had stored the wet suit. Danny returned to help peel Cassidy out of her wet suit. As she threw her halter top over her swim suit, Cassidy checked the ocean for Taban. *He was ahead of me before.* She spotted him doing backstroke. *Did he just decide to swim a few laps? Guess he's fine.*

"Here." Danny handed her a chocolate bar. "I helped Mom pack snacks."

"Seventy percent cacao with lavender," Cassidy read. "My favorite!"

"How're you doing?"

The chocolate bar having sufficiently rejuvenated her, Cassidy decided to prove to Danny that she felt completely fine. After she made sure there weren't any rocks under the towel, Cassidy stood. "So, you were practicing your Tae Kwon Do?"

"Yeah," Danny said standing beside her.

"Good." Gently twisting Danny's hand Cassidy flipped her onto the towel. Danny landed skillfully guarding her head. "See, I'm doing better already," Cassidy laughed.

"Yeah?" Danny jumped to her feet, placed her hand on Cassidy's chin, and put one foot behind her knee. "Take that!" She pushed Cassidy over.

Shifting to her knees, Cassidy held out her hands. Danny knelt facing her and placed her palms against Cassidy's. They started to practice a basic Aikido technique, in which both participants attempt to make the other lose her balance. Eventually, Cassidy pinned Danny on her back. "Ha! I have you now," Cassidy snarled playfully.

"Not yet!" Danny wrapped her legs around Cassidy's waist and rolled over. They looked at each other and burst into giggles. Through their laughter, Danny heard irregular splashing. "What was that?" She and Cassidy turned toward the ocean to see Taban wading through the sea foam. He carried Daisuke's wave ski under one arm.

"Oh, don't stop on my account," Taban chuckled. "Please."

"We're sparring!" Danny and Cassidy clarified in unison.

"Spawning?" Taban scrunched his hair in noticeable confusion. He walked up the beach to set the kayak down on the shore near Cassidy's.

"How long was he standing there?" Cassidy whispered through her teeth to Danny.

"Not long. I just heard him."

"We need to think of a good comeback for that sort of comment," Cassidy said.

"Agreed."

"I just thought I'd go back out and get his kayak thing," Taban commented, rejoining them.

"You *swam* out there again?" Danny asked in disbelief, waving in the direction of the rip current.

Taban nodded genially.

"I saw you do it the first time," Danny said. "How did you get there so fast?"

"I'm a good swimmer."

"But you looked like an Olympian!"

"I'm a very good swimmer," Taban said sweetly, but Cassidy thought she caught a smirk flash across his lips, as though he knew something they didn't. She equated it to the time he'd invited them to the lecture. "Aren't you cold?" He shivered. "This weather is miserable, but you two inspired me to come to the beach today."

Danny wrapped him in another towel from the bin and he nodded appreciatively. "Cassidy's from the Pacific Northwest, she can handle it."

Cassidy had started to get chilled, but the skeptical look on Taban's face afforded an opportunity she couldn't pass up. "Yeah. It feels fantastic doesn't it?"

"And I'm from even farther North." Danny leered as the rain washed over her face.

Shaking his head, Taban collected the shirt he'd discarded on the beach. He pulled a duffle bag out from behind a log and changed out of his wet clothes under the towel. When he rejoined them, Cassidy saw a piece of green kelp hanging from behind his ear.

"Uh, Taban, you got a little something." Cassidy combed the seaweed out of his hair. She showed it to him to prove she hadn't made up an excuse to touch him.

"Thanks." He stroked her cheek. "Will you and Danny be coming over this evening? I'd *love* it if you did."

"Uh … I … yeah I'm pretty sure …"

Burning with jealousy, Danny looked away to pretend she didn't see the way Taban touched Cassidy. Then she noticed something different about the two wave skis. "Hey people!" She pointed to Daisuke's boat. "Two of the fins on this kayak are broken and one's missing."

"Hm. Must've hit a rock or he didn't put them on correctly," Taban mused. He returned his borrowed towel to the bin.

Cassidy joined Danny. "That's odd; these two fins have a very clean break." She ran her finger over the fin. "Maybe it was a flaw in the manufacturing, but it has striated marks like someone used a—"

"I'm going to take this to the hospital so he can get it back, but I have to hurry to my internship." Taban yanked the boat out from under their scrutinizing and headed up the beach. When he reached the parking lot he shouted, "See you tonight!"

Taken aback by his hasty departure, Cassidy and Danny waved.

CHAPTER 12
FISHING FOR INFORMATION

TABAN FINISHED STRAPPING the small surfing kayak to his car. He clambered into the driver's seat and threw the two broken fins under his seat with the other fin from Daisuke's wave ski. Convincing him to surf Martinique Beach had been a snap:

After leaving Abigail the day before, Taban tracked down May Savali's son. He figured Daisuke was his best way to access information about what his mother knew about the Roman officer's journal. Though he had found Daisuke's sexuality listed on his MeSite, Taban decided not to use seduction in case Abigail discovered his affair. Using Daisuke's interest in trying surf kayaking to his advantage, Taban applied a few smiles and enthusiastic anecdotes to persuade him. He attempted to cover as many interests Daisuke might have as possible. "In fact, I'm headed to the beach tomorrow. Perhaps we'll meet up?"

Sure enough, he encountered Daisuke in the parking lot the next morning. He concocted a story about losing a sentimental item. When Daisuke started to comb the beach for it, Taban inspected his kayak. He removed the center fin and carefully sliced into the other two. Though Taban had never tried surf kayaking, he knew the fins enhanced the stability of the boat. He also reversed the release mechanism on the straps, so Daisuke would have more difficulty getting out of the boat.

"I've surfed before." Taban remembered Daisuke explaining. "Why do all the instructional videos for wave skiing suggest all this safety gear?"

"Yeah, I never wear a helmet surfing," Taban had agreed. He stalled Daisuke until he saw Mrs. Reyes' car enter the parking lot, then encouraged him to surf.

For a while, Taban had worried that Danny and Cassidy wouldn't show, due to the miserable weather. Honking, a car zoomed past him. Brought back to the present, he glanced in his rearview mirror and saw a line of cars tailgating him. He increased to the speed limit and the cars fell back to a safer distance. As he made a right hand turn onto Pleasant Street, a glint of red caught his attention. Looking at the passenger seat he noticed a crimson thread. He picked it off the seat and rolled it into a ball between his thumb and index finger, feeling the familiar cotton fabric of Cassidy's trench coat. She seemed responsive to his flirtations, but very reserved, so she probably did not trust him enough yet to follow his advice. *The more people involved in this the messier it's going to get when Abby and May get ahold of that journal. There's no hope for Danny, but at least I can get rid of this girl,* Taban thought angrily. *Cassidy was supposed to see me be all heroic and save him. I was trying to get a two-for-one deal. Who even does a water sport in the freezing cold that requires so much gear? Those girls are frickin' crazy.*

"Ea, why did you have to drag her into this?" he asked the open road. "Are you really that desperate for allies? She has no business being here. She's just an extra person I have to work around."

As he drove toward Dalhousie, Taban tried to clear his mind by humming a beat that resembled the drumming of the ocean. When that failed, he shouted to his car. "Instruction: play recent song." The bouncing music of *Knots of Avernus* boomed from the speakers. "Instruction: turn up volume to five." The music increased to a deafening cacophony, into which he plunged his mind, to purge his thoughts.

* * *

Taban made his way through the crowded Life Science Centre on the Dalhousie campus. At the end of the hall, he swiped his Ogham across the scanner and entered the reserved room. He froze in the doorway. The light from Abigail's tablet highlighted the outline of her figure in black under her white lab coat. Tugging on the plastic cap covering her hair, she hunched over hundreds of miniature test tubes containing cheek samples.

"Oh, hello." She turned around. "I didn't know you were coming in today."

I didn't know you were going to be here. I need to run a sample of Danny's hair, but I can't do it with you in the room, Taban thought. "Nice to see you," he said, taking a lab coat out of the closet and pulling it on over his clothes, "How is the survey working?"

"Savali's lecture brought in tons of samples from people whose genomes weren't sequenced at birth. Even more people submitted their documented genomes," Abigail said excitedly. "Best of all, Savali finally cleared me to put the lecture online."

"People really want to know about themselves." Taban picked up a new tray of samples and placed them on the lab table next to Abigail.

"Yes, they do. All the better for us." Abigail smiled. "Unfortunately, nothing seems to be matching the usual genes I found in people who live to over 120. I hope Savali's right about the journal. If I knew for sure, I could get a grant to test people in Scotland and Ireland. Even though lots of people have emigrated and immigrated, that area would be the best place to locate those genes. Honestly, it's like finding a needle in a haystack right now."

"At least the technology is good enough that you can work in bulk."

"Yeah thank goodness I can run nuclear and mitochondrial DNA simultaneously in minutes for each sample. But I just wish ..."

"Wish what?" Taban asked preparing the enzyme to copy the DNA.

"I don't have any funding. I need support from gene therapy organizations. I can taste the discovery. I'm just not quite there yet." Removing her gloves, she walked to the other side of the room. "Can you double check this?" She indicated a mounted tablet. "The software we use to check for specific gene sequences in the submitted genomes had an upgrade, but it seems to be running slower."

"Sure," Taban agreed, though he didn't know more than she did about the software. *She's such a lab rat. How am I going to get her out of here?* he wondered.

While he inspected the software, she removed his cap and tried to untangle his curls. "Your beautiful hair's a mess. Did you take a dip in the ocean earlier?" She tugged on one of his salt laid curls. "You're like Elatha."

"Who?"

"Oh, nothing. May Savali has been teaching me more about Celtic mythology. Probably wouldn't interest you."

"Actually, it would. Please, tell me more."

"Elatha was a Formorian prince who was handsome, unlike the other Formorians. He was more like an Each Uisge, really."

"And?"

"Well, he was a sea god. So he probably swam like you do and most accounts of him describe him as blond." She cheerfully ran her fingers through his forelock.

Frustrated with the software and still fuming over Cassidy's impressive rescue, Taban snapped at her. "What is it with you and blond hair?"

She looked at the ground in a way that reminded him of a small child. "When the other kids teased me for studying all the time, there was this one boy who was nice to me. He just happened to have platinum-blond hair, so it makes me happy when I see it." Abigail glared up at him. "You don't understand what it's like to feel like you only have one thing you're good at. I may be a science prodigy, but I didn't have any friends growing up. I spent my life in a lab because it's easier."

"I'm sorry," he said with true sincerity. "I didn't know. Look, I'll run the next set of samples to make it up to you. You can go to a bar or something and have fun."

"It's okay. I'm fine now." She put on new gloves and handed him another plastic cap. "Besides, I'm supposed to supervise and I'm no good with people."

"You're great with me and I'm a person." Taban touched his chest to remind himself of that fact. "I love you," he tried, but her expression didn't improve. *What would Eadowen say?* Taban wondered. "You look tired." He faked a yawn to inspire one from her. "You know taking care of your mental health is incredibly important. You should do something nice for yourself that makes you feel good; social or otherwise." He escorted her to the door. *Yay! I'm becoming fluent in Eadowen,* Taban thought. *It's gotten more and more difficult to control her. Maybe my abilities diminish with a long-term relationship.*

"No! I need to do more work," she said.

"Well, I suppose we could do it right here to save time. That'll help you feel better." With a suggestive smirk, Taban glanced at an empty lab table.

"That's not sanitary and there are security cameras." Abigail waved her arms in embarrassment. "Alright, alright. I'll go. You're very sweet to do extra work for me."

"That's right. You aren't going to make any discoveries without being in your best health." Taban kissed her and took her lab coat. "I'll take care of everything." As soon as the door clicked shut, Taban rushed over to the samples. Hurriedly, he set a new gel and took a vial out of a small pocket on his duffel bag. With his gloved hand, he carefully laid out the hairs he'd collected from Danny. He noticed enough follicles on the ends of the hair to run a tissue test similar to the cheek sample. Under a microscope, he removed the follicles and placed them into test tubes for replication. Capping the tubes, he balanced each in the centrifuge. After obtaining the extracted DNA he applied it to the polyacrylamide gel to separate the DNA. When the electrophoresis process finished, he ran a photograph of the results through the software. While he waited for the results, he set the rest of Abigail's samples on another tablet and tidied the laboratory.

"Data complete," the tablet informed him.

"Run an ancestry on both mitochondrial DNA (mtDNA) and nuclear DNA for sample 'Danny,' " Taban commanded. He read the screen. *So, Edana Reyes has roots of Aztec origin that follows with her father being Mexican. There's the Pict and the Scythian that goes with the GF theory. Huh, she's got some Indonesian in there too. It looks like she has some genetic material from the ancient people of Flores.* He laughed to himself. *It'd be funny if she got some special abilities from that.*

Taban touched his Ogham to bring up a hidden file containing DNA samples from the Tolymie family. He compared the chromosomes that contained genes for longevity Abigail had marked. *Ugh. I wish genetics was like it is in comic books: one magic gene. There are tons of these little things on different chromosomes.* "Mark longevity genes on sample 'Danny.'" After studious inspection, he concluded that Danny's marked genes most closely matched Aydan's. None of the four samples had inherited the exact same set of genes. *This is good. It means only someone with a high percentage of these genes will show up on Abigail's radar.*

Connecting his Ogham to the tablet, Taban commanded: "Transfer data to connected Ogham." He removed his Ogham. "Delete all data related to sample 'Danny.'" Taban verified several times that the software erased the data, and then he checked through the system to make sure there wasn't any evidence of his work. Then he loaded the program with samples from Abigail's set. As he finished cleaning the room, another idea struck him.

Online, he found the old research Abigail had published on charisma. *There's a gene on the fourth chromosome that she only found in two people out of the thousands of samples she has gathered,* Taban thought as he read through her notes. *One of the people was a highly successful actor and the other a Fortune 500 business woman. I wish Abigail didn't have to keep their identities anonymous. The gene they possessed seemed to be linked to facial movement control.* Taban swabbed his cheek and prepared his own DNA sample. This time he marked the gene listed in her work. Recalling Eadowen's assertion that he too had inherited capacities similar to Taban's own, Taban reconnected his Ogham to the tablet and marked Eadowen's genome. Taban read the screen and sighed. *Well Ea, it appears we have at least one thing in common.* He checked Donovan and Aydan, neither yielded the gene. *It's just us, Ea.* Taban wiped his eyes on a strap under his lab coat. He had to find out how close May Savali was to locating the journal. With any luck, she hadn't yet connected to the characteristic to the Tolymies, but if she did, she could claim it as a historical artifact. Then she and Abigail would have the evidence they needed to get backing from the major gene therapy financial contributors. Seeing his disheveled reflection in the laboratory window, Taban decided he needed to clean up before plying Daisuke for information. He locked up the room and headed to the gym to shower. *The problem with being a swimmer is you spend half your life in the pool and the other half in the shower.*

* * *

A freshened Taban entered the Queen Elizabeth Health Sciences Centre. Based on the head injury Daisuke received, Taban trusted the staff would keep him for at least most of the day.

"May I help you, sir?" the receptionist asked.

"Good afternoon, Jake," Taban read off of the name tag. "I rescued a guy earlier today and I'd like to make sure he's okay. I'm so worried about him." In the shower Taban had avoided scrubbing his face, so that his tear stains remained visible.

The receptionist's brow furrowed with concern. "We heard about that, but we don't usually—"

"Would you be so kind as to go in and ask him if he'll take a visitor?" Taban begged. "It'd mean the world to me."

"Yes, I think I can get someone to do that," he said. "May I see your identification?"

"Yeah." Taban touched his Ogham and held it out. "I appreciate it so much," Taban gushed as the receptionist scanned it.

A few minutes later a nurse went to speak with Daisuke at the request of the receptionist. Taban settled into one of the hospital chairs, prepared to wait awhile for a response, but the nurse returned almost immediately. "Mr. Savali says he can see you now," he reported.

Taban followed the nurse down the hallway to Daisuke's room. An IV in his arm, Daisuke reclined on the sterile hospital bed, watching a documentary about heavy artillery. "Hi there," Taban said. "I'm really sorry," he added when he saw the bloody bandages around Daisuke's head.

"Don't be sorry." Daisuke muted the sound on the film. "It's not your fault. Thanks for helping to rescue me."

"I brought your kayak-thing. I'll put it on your car when I leave," Taban offered. "How're you doing?"

"I have a concussion and needed a few stitches. You want to sit down?"

"I'm so sorry." Taban grabbed a chair to sit next to the bed. "Good thing you're tough."

"It's no big. They won't let me leave though, because they don't want me to fall asleep," Daisuke grumbled. "The doctor lady told me that I might have drowned if that girl hadn't pulled me out and given me CPR. Where's she? I'd like to thank her too."

"I can give you her contact information. How's your memory?"

"I'm fine, really." Daisuke touched his matted raven hair and winced. "I remember talking to you about my mom's research and everything. You're really into that stuff. Guess it makes sense since you're Dr. Crane's lab aid or something."

"Since I've been working with Abby—Dr. Crane, I've gotten really good at keeping stuff confidential. I'm dying to know what your mom learned about that journal. I won't even tell Ab—Dr. Crane."

"Ha. You bugged me about that before. I don't get why it's such a big deal. All I know is that my mom figured out which family line probably brought part of the journal over from Ireland. She says they live in the area too," Daisuke mused. "Oh, and something about the other half being in Scotland. She's planning a research trip soon."

"Yeah, you're right, that's not really all that interesting," Taban said as nonchalantly as he could while internally panicking. *Dr. Savali already knows it's with the Tolymies. Does she know where their house is? And she knows where the other half is …*

"Hey buddy, you look like you're the one who needs medical attention."

"Oh, I'm just prone to migraines." Taban lied.

To his relief, Daisuke laughed. "Should I call that nurse in for you?"

"Nah," Taban said. "We can't all be made of iron like you and a certain giant lacrosse defender I know."

"Is the defender cute?"

"Gorgeous, actually. You two could totally bond over benching Shetland ponies." Taban combed his fingers through his own hair. "By the way, the straps on the kayak were gone when I got it to shore."

"I couldn't undo them, so I just ripped them out. Then I hit my head on a rock and blacked out."

It irked Taban that Daisuke and Cassidy had managed to thwart him without even trying. "Anything I can do for you before I head out?" Taban said bitterly.

"No. I'm well taken care of," Daisuke replied, clapping Taban on the back hard enough to make him lurch. "Would you give me that girl's information though? She gave me CPR on a wave ski. That's badass."

"Her name's Cassidy. Here's her basic contact. I don't think she'll mind if I give that to you. She's headed out tomorrow morning."

"Too bad I won't be able to thank her in person." Daisuke accepted Cassidy's contact information with his Ogham. "Maybe see you around?" he asked.

"Yeah. Sure. I'll be in touch." Taban waved as he left Daisuke's room. He nodded to the receptionist and headed to the parking lot.

Once safely in his car, Taban peeled back a lid on a can of sardines. He crushed the little salty fish in between his molars, as he read about the Each Uisge Abigail had mentioned. *If the Tuatha de Danann have descendants, the Each Uisges might as well,* Taban thought. "The Each Uisge would seduce its prey then the victim would get attached to its skin. The beast would drag the prey into its home in the ocean and eat him or her alive, except for the liver," Taban read aloud to himself. "That's disgusting." He found several artist interpretations of the Each Uisge that depicted the beast as a man with a horse head. *And the wrong part of the body part is like a horse,* he concluded. *I really hope that thing isn't my ancestor. Why couldn't my genetics give me laser eye beams or make me a vampire?* In no mood to return home, Taban pulled the lever to recline his seat. Reasoning that he must be tired if he couldn't fool Daisuke about his reaction to the news about the journal, Taban prepared his alarm clock; a timer on his tablet connected to a squirt bottle. Since he could only wake up naturally or on contact with water, he had created a miniature Rube Goldberg design for occasions when Eadowen couldn't be bothered to wake him.

The scarlet clouds of a spectacular sunset greeted him when he awoke. As he drove to the Tolymie's house, he briefly fantasized about driving into a lake he passed, but there was too much at stake, with Dr. Savali hot on the trail to finding both pieces of the journal. *The Tolymies will never get rid of that stupid journal. If Cassidy won't abandon her friend Danny, maybe she can at least help me keep track of the Tolymies and Danny.*

CHAPTER 13
WHEN SOMEONE WANTS YOUR ARTIFACT

WHEN THEY ARRIVED HOME from the beach, Cassidy collapsed on the guest bed. Her body ached from the feel of the turbulent water pounding against her skin.

Downstairs, Ms. Reyes poured some tea into a cup for herself and left the pot for Danny. "Cassidy is probably sleeping, so try to be quiet," Ms. Reyes said, "And don't use the whole jar of honey this time."

Danny jumped on the counter by the sink to get a mug from the high cupboard and poured herself a cup of tea. She jammed a spoon into the honey, enjoying the sweet aroma of a honey made from lilacs. The label said that the honey came from a variety of flowers, but she could tell which variety of nectar the bees had chosen—she approved of their decision. The honey sparkled just like Cassidy's beautiful eyes whenever she saw Taban. Danny knocked her tea cup to the floor. Her ears ached after it shattered. The dark liquid pooled around the victim of her frustration. *Why doesn't Cassidy ever look at me that way? I wish I could've been the one to help her with the rescue.* Danny kicked her reflection in the tea, slicing her foot on the broken cup. The addition of blood to the tea turned the liquid a disquieting rusty shade. Again she viewed her image in the spilled tea, but when the blood swirled into her reflection it cast a red aura around her face and turned her dark eyes to a deep red. Terrified by the warped visage at her feet she threw a dish towel over the spill.

She heard a bird's chirp at the window. A song bird flapped its cinnamon-sprinkled wings against the glass, its curved black and yellow beak opened as though it were laughing."You're right, you stupid bird," she snarled, stooping to carefully pick up the shards. "She's not into me. And here I am telling her not to care what other people think." She confessed to her own hypocrisy.

"Is everything alright down there?" her mother shouted from the top of the stairs.

"Just dropped a mug. Don't worry. I cleaned it up."

"Again? You need to be more careful."

"I will! Promise." Danny called in a voice that sounded so convincingly jovial she wasn't sure it was her own.

"You need to wake Cassidy up soon."

"I know."

Danny ran out of the house into the driveway, she ran through a few forms, trying to burn out the wild energy that coursed through her veins. *I think Mom put me in martial arts when I was a kid so I'd have more control—I guess it's helped a bit,* she thought.

* * *

"Are you sure you remember the way to the Tolymie's house?" Danny asked from the passenger seat next to Cassidy.

"Yeah, turn at the gigantic trees," Cassidy laughed. Soon after her comment, Cassidy passed the dirt driveway and did a U-turn on the vacant highway. Ms. Reyes' car admonished her for performing such a maneuver.

Danny shivered as the trees closed in on them once more.

"Good evening," Eadowen called through the open door. "So glad you could make it." He skillfully moved his wheelchair to hold the door for them to enter. "I heard about your heroism on the news."

"Taban helped," Cassidy explained. She removed her boots under the tri-crystalled chandelier in the hallway.

"Cassidy performed the CPR." Danny set her tennis shoes below the golden tapestry. "She's the one who probably saved the guy's life."

"I'd love to hear more. Come to the dining room. I have something to show you both."

The crystal prisms dangling from the ceiling captured the candlelight, reflecting multicolored radiance in a glass display case on the table.

Wearing a wrinkled sleeveless shirt, Donovan sat with his elbows on the table, pressing the surface of an electronic game player rapidly. When she and Danny took chairs next to each other, Donovan padded out of the room stepping on the tattered bottoms of his faded pajama pants as he went.

"This is the journal I mentioned." Eadowen indicated the glass display, which contained remnants of ancient stone tablets.

"We usually keep it in a safe, but I brought out the remainder of the original to show you. Here's the best paper transcription copy and here's a translated English copy. I assume you can't read Latin, so here are some dictionaries if you want to check me. I'd rather you didn't use your Oghams. Latin's really tough to check word-by-word, I'm afraid."

"I took a semester of Latin because I was interested in science," Danny said. She stacked some of the dictionaries on her chair to get a better look at the stone pieces. "I'm not very good, but I might be able to check some of it."

"I'm so relieved to hear that," Eadowen replied. Resting his chin on folded hands, he allowed Danny and Cassidy time to inspect the materials he'd given them. Cassidy carefully selected random words and phrases Eadowen had translated and checked them with the Latin counterparts. Once satisfied that he'd done an admirable translation, she inspected the tablets. Danny attempted to decipher the content of the English version. In his translation, Eadowen had retained the Latin grammar structure, which made the content a challenge to decode. Eadowen assisted Danny by explaining the genetic significance of the encounter the soldier recorded.

"Do you have any other questions?"

"What do we need to do to keep Danny safe from people who want full access to her DNA?" Cassidy asked.

"Well, as long as no one knows where this part of the journal is we should be fine, though it would be wise to subscribe to Savali's news articles and Me-Site."

"There's another part?" Danny remarked.

"Well, there was an addition to this piece that indicated the Roman officer wrote a journal on wax tablets while he was in ancient Scotland. This is the second half, which he had transcribed onto stone when he returned to Rome. He bestowed it to his daughter when he passed on. His great granddaughter managed to disguise herself as part of the military in order to travel north to Scotland and Ireland in search of her Celtic identity. She must have reproduced and remained in Ireland, because my father's family brought this journal over from Ireland during the potato famine in the 1800s."

"I've been doing a little reading about Ireland, since the lecture," Cassidy said. "Didn't the Irish send children over to North America during the famine?"

"Yes, though it is distinctly possible that older members of our family came over on those boats, due to our youthful appearance."

Donovan returned, balancing a polished tray of tortilla wraps, a platter of egg rolls, a serving bowl of miso soup, a plate of spinach salad, and a silver pitcher of vinaigrette. Impressed by his ability to balance the soup bowl on his head, Cassidy rushed to assist him.

"You didn't have to bring everything in one trip," Eadowen commented.

When Danny stood to help, she felt a stabbing pain in her abdomen. "Ugh," she said, placing her hand between her hip bones as she bent forward. "I'm sorry, I need to go lie down for a minute."

Her sock chafed the cut on her foot, as she hobbled to the living room with the fireplace and the game consol. *What horrible timing,* she thought. Groaning, Danny sprawled on the sofa encircling the hearth. She felt the pleasant cold of the leathery texture through her loose shirt.

"What's wrong? Are you okay?" Cassidy asked, hurrying to her friend's side.

"Cramps," Danny explained.

"I take a pill once a month that deals with mine." Cassidy sat on the couch next to her. "I don't have anything with me for the pain, sorry. Maybe the Tolymies have something."

"No, thanks. The cramps only started a few months ago. I don't actually bleed yet. Nothing has worked so far."

"But you turn eighteen in September. Aren't you a bit late?" Cassidy said. "I guess your muscle to fat ratio and longevity genes probably delayed it."

"From what I understand from my mother, the GF genes should only have made you a little later than average, maybe fifteen at the latest. But I agree with Cassidy's assessment that it was probably a combination." Eadowen added as he joined them. "Here, put this where it hurts." He handed her the pillow that smelled of lavender like Cassidy's perfume.

"Thank you." Danny rested the pillow on her abdomen letting the warmth and pressure ease the sharp pain.

"Ginger root tea can help with pain too," Eadowen suggested. "Would you like some?"

"Make sure you put more honey in it, more than you think is possible," Cassidy instructed, too concerned for her friend to consider a polite request. "That's how Danny likes it."

Through the paneled window, the sky brightened from blue to scarlet. Cassidy admired the rosy pink ambiance the shift caused on the foliage outside.

"You want to go look at the sunset, don't you?" Danny mumbled.

"Yeah," Cassidy conceded. "But you aren't feeling well and I don't want to leave you."

"I'm fine. I actually wouldn't mind. I'd kind of like to talk to Eadowen about something."

"Oh?" Cassidy raised an eyebrow. "You want some alone time with Eadowen?"

"It's not like that," Danny sighed. "I just need to ask some advice." She waved Cassidy to silence because she heard Eadowen's wheelchair coming down the hallway. *I wish Cassidy wouldn't coddle me so much,* Danny thought.

"I'm just kidding." Cassidy shoved Danny's shoulder lightly. "I'll get out of your way for a bit, have fun." Danny's brow furrowed. "I'll be back soon," Cassidy added quickly.

"There's a lovely place to watch the sunset just behind the house." With his back to the fire, Eadowen arranged his wheelchair to face Danny. He offered her a large mug filled with a tea so saturated with honey, it looked like soup.

I bet Danny wants to talk something that has to do with being a GF that she doesn't want me to hear, Cassidy thought as she put on her boots. *I feel kind of left out, but she needs this and I should respect that.*

Shifting to accommodate her discomfort, Danny listened to Cassidy's footsteps leading away from the house. During her moving around, her hair got caught under the couch headrest and she felt a jolt of pain all the way from her scalp down her spine. To her surprise, the discomfort she experienced was far worse than when she had broken her arm in middle school. The rhythmic tapping of Donovan's game controller on the other side of the room occupied her attention, until she heard the familiar crunch Taban's car made in the driveway.

"How're you feeling?" Eadowen asked.

"During someone's period do they become really sensitive to pain?" Holding the pillow to her stomach, Danny sat up, her scalp still throbbing.

"I don't think I'm the right person to ask, but I'd be willing to look it up for you," he said. Then he blanched. "Did you say you're suddenly hypersensitive to pain? If that's the case you need to make sure you don't get sick. Please, start taking care of your health as though you have an immunodeficiency disorder."

"I'm sure it's just hormones," Danny lied. Uncomfortable by Eadowen's sudden interest in her selfcare habits, she decided to change to another subject. "Could I ask a favor?"

"Anything," Eadowen replied in a low voice. His face shifted to the bright intensity Danny had seen once before.

"Since you have a boyfriend, I thought you might ..." Danny started to say, but stopped when Eadowen shook his head. "Taban's not your significant other?" she asked.

"I would not consider my relationship with Taban a healthy one, though, it is symbiotic in some ways."

"Okay ... Well, I think you're wonderful." To Danny's confusion Eadowen frowned when she added, "Which means other people must too."

"Thank you, I—"

"You're hot too. Especially when you make the sexy face you just did a minute ago," she remarked excitedly. "You and Taban deepen your voices when you talk to Cassidy and me too. It's interesting how much of a change those little tweaks make."

Eadowen began to distance himself from her. Without thinking Danny grabbed the closest part of his body, which happened to be his thigh, to hold him in place. He flinched. She looked down, realized she'd done something socially unacceptable for their level of acquaintance, and retracted her hand. "Sorry."

"That's alright." Eadowen dismissed it with a wave of his hand. "What was that favor you wanted?"

"I guess I just sorta wanted to talk to you. I have a crush on Cassidy and I don't think she likes me back—" Danny tilted her head. "I just heard another car turn off the main road and it sounds different from Taban's. Did you hear it?"

Eadowen froze. "Donovan," he hissed. "Pull up the security camera on your screen and come over here."

Donovan's race car game changed to an image of two people walking up the steps. Danny recognized one of them. "Savali?" she whispered. Eadowen held up a hand to signal that she shouldn't speak. There was a rapping on the door. Donovan crouched behind the couch watching Eadowen over Danny's shoulder.

"Hello?" Savali said through the door. "That's funny, I just saw someone through the window," she commented to her partner when no one came to the door.

Oh no. She already knows we're here, Danny thought. *Good thing she probably didn't get a good look because of the fireplace blocking us from the window.*

Beside her, Eadowen scribbled something on a pad of paper he produced from his pocket. He showed her the writing on the paper which read: *Do you have lipstick?* Danny took the pomegranate lip balm out of her pocket and passed it to him. Eadowen ducked in thanks and started to sign rapidly to his brother. The only gesture Danny could decipher was when Eadowen tugged on his own collar to indicate "clothes." Widening his eyes, Donovan shot his sibling a dubious look and mouthed "heck no," or something less polite. Sighing, Eadowen's hands blurred as he continued to communicate in sign language. Danny understood the signs for tall, big, and walk. Grudgingly, Donovan removed his shirt and allowed Eadowen to dab a speck of the lip balm on his mouth. As Donovan lumbered to the door Danny gave Eadowen a puzzled look even though she had already guessed the plan.

He confirmed her suspicions by scribbling: *Invoking a cliché to distract Savali and make her uncomfortable.* On the television screen, Danny observed the security feed. Savali and her companion took a step back when an unshaven, muscular, and door-frame-tall, Donovan responded to their knocking. The steel-death glare intended for Eadowen, was instead redirected at Savali and her companion, who were noticeably taken aback.

"Oh goodness, are we interrupting?" Savali asked, glancing at his mouth.

"Yes."

"Hello, my name is May Savali this is my colleague Gregory Andrews, an archeologist. We tried to contact your father by Me-Site, but he seems to be unavailable. We have reason to believe your family is in possession of a historical artifact. Namely, a journal."

"Eh?"

"You don't know what we're talking about?"

Donovan delivered a perfect blank look.

"Is a Dr. Daray Eldin here?"

"No."

"When will he be home?" Savali asked.

"Don't know."

"Is there someone else home we can talk to?"

"No." If forced to hire a person to play a brick wall, Danny didn't think she could find a better candidate than Donovan.

"Should we come back at a better time?" Savali tried. "Uh, could we have your contact information?" Donovan showed her his empty wrist. "Oh, we'll just find that later."

"Thank you," he said. Instead of slamming the door in their face, Donovan watched them walk up the driveway, before he slunk back into the hallway.

"You know," Danny heard Savali say. "My son and that young man would get along well."

"He looked pretty grouchy to me," Andrews replied.

Two car doors slammed and a few minutes later Savali pulled onto the main road.

"Here's your shirt." Wrinkling her nose, Danny offered Donovan the sweaty garment. He snatched it from her and picked up a device that resembled a silver remote control.

"What's that?" Danny asked Eadowen.

"Spyware scanner," he whispered. "Donovan will check for any spyware they may have used."

Shaken by the turn of events, Danny tried to enjoy her long-forgotten tea.

"Nothing there," Donovan confirmed when he returned from outside.

"Good, that buys me about a day to come up with something better, but that was way too close. I had no idea they'd tracked us this far," Eadowen replied. "Thanks for watching them closely, Donovan."

"Whatever." Donovan flopped down in front of his video games.

"Where's Cassidy," Danny asked "... and Taban?"

CHAPTER 14
A SEA SEDUCER'S PREY

CASSIDY TIED HER TRENCH COAT around her waist. The Tolymie's didn't have any semblance of a cultivated yard. Instead, the ground was covered in a sea of moss and the trees' gigantic roots snaked through the driveway. Passing a gazebo sheltering a covered hot tub, she followed a worn path in the moss behind the house. An owl hooted high above her, sending a chill down her spine. Cassidy jumped as a crack and flash of movement in the fading light caught her attention. Surrounded by a circle of tiny mushrooms, Aydan twirled a black whip. He threw a silvery card and hit it out of the air with the bullwhip. His movements were graceful and powerful in a short lace dress. Not wanting to interrupt his work, Cassidy quietly stepped over the shreds of cards, and continued up the path. *Ronu-Mom would like him,* Cassidy thought.

The thick canopy of trees blocked her view of the sky overhead, but the grove turned out not to go very deep. She broke out of the woods, shadowing her eyes against the bright crepuscular rays that shone like a gateway to a glorious world above the clouds. Wishing she could look in all directions at once to admire the rosy skyscape, she lay on a log for a better view. Each cloud in the darkening indigo sky magnified the crimson light of the sun.

"Hey Cassi, what're you up to?" Taban approached her from the same trail she had followed. The scarlet light emphasized his cinematic allure. He scratched a place under his mouth, drawing her attention to his full lips. She briefly fantasized about having her first kiss with the current sunset as the backdrop, but promptly shoved the image out of her mind.

"Just finding a place to watch the sunset." Cassidy stood dusting herself off. "And my name's Cassidy, not Cassi."

"I was just using a nickname." With an injured expression, he dropped his chin, and shoved his hands in his pockets. In doing so, he flexed his arms. "I do that to people I like, but I won't if you don't want it."

"No. No. I'm sorry. Cassi is fine. I didn't mean to make you feel bad."

"Make it up to me by watching the sunset with me." He plopped down on the log and patted a spot next to him. Obliging, she joined him and felt a rush when his hand coincidentally brushed the bare skin of her arm.

"I really should go check on Danny pretty soon. She wasn't feeling well."

"Don't worry about her. She's with Ea, right?"

"Yeah," Cassidy agreed. "But I'm worried about her safety."

"Listen to me." Slipping his fingers into her belt loop, he tugged gently. "Ea wouldn't do anything even if she threw herself at hir," he said bitterly, as he rubbed his neck.

"That's not what I meant." She slid closer to Taban, allowing him to put his arm around her.

"Nice work today on the water."

"Thanks, I—"

"I told the news that you did everything. You should take all the credit. I mean everyone gets a lucky break sometimes. You'll be happy to know he was completely fine when I visited in the hospital. The doctors said he would've been fine anyway, but you still did a very Good Samaritan thing."

"Yeah—well, that's good to know." Nervously, Cassidy ran her fingers over the thin gold chain around her neck. She could feel the vibration in his chest as he spoke.

"You did your best though and that's good." He coiled his arms around her. "By the way, do you own a bikini? All I saw you in was that wetsuit and the one-piece."

"No."

"I find you attractive, anyway. Besides, those are, like, only meant for certain body types."

Cassidy attempted to furtively wipe her sweaty palms on her jeans. "I eat well and live an active lifestyle, but I feel fat all the time."

"It's better for someone to fall for your personality, like I did." Taban's eyes flashed in the fading light.

Cassidy felt a tingling warmth on her cheek—too delicate for her to tell whether or not he'd kissed her or breathed close to her. Afraid to discover which of the two had occurred, she didn't dare look at him. Instead she picked at the log, wondering why his flattery made her confidence dive off the deep end.

"I like the intelligent conversations we have," he continued.

"Me too," she agreed.

"You want to go into law right? That's super competitive. I'd be stressed by the brilliant people I'd be competing against."

"That's true, but I'm going to work hard."

"Good for you." Turning her face toward him, he pressed his lips more definitively to a place on her cheek close to the edge of her mouth. "I'm so glad I met you, Cassidy."

Did he just insult me? Cassidy mentally screamed. *Why's he kissing me?* She gazed into his azure eyes. His fingers caressed the nape of her neck, and then intertwined with her cropped hair.

"Wait!" She managed to say. "Aren't you and Eadowen together?"

"You don't like me?"

"I do. I really do," Cassidy explained. "But I'm not going to come between you and Eadowen."

"We're not a couple. Ea and I can't be, because I've fallen for you."

"When?" She lay a hand on his chest to ground herself in reality, which he interpreted as a request for a tighter embrace. "We've only known each other for three days?"

"Don't you feel it too?" He tilted her chin up and, mind in a fog, she touched her mouth to his warm lips. To her surprise and relief, she quickly adapted to that method of showing affection, though she wouldn't have guessed kisses tasted so salty. Any doubts in the back of her mind drowned under a wave of bliss. Again she envisioned the perfect warm sea, from his song and her dream. "What're you thinking about right now?" he asked, as the peach-colored moon highlighted his flaxen hair.

"Uh … moon hair?" A flustered Cassidy replied. "I mean, tonight rise moon pretty. No, um … the moonrise is pretty tonight." She covered her face with her hands, while Taban laughed at her. "My brain feels like it went through a whirlpool."

"Moon, eh? I read a story in a Greek mythology book about the moon goddess and a man she loved," he commented. "Would you like to hear it?"

She hung on his every word, but it took her a moment to put together his question. When she understood she opened her mouth, but no words came out so she just bobbed her head.

"The goddess of the evening star, Selene drove the moon chariot for Artemis, just like Helios drove the sun chariot for Artemis' twin brother, Apollo. One day in her trek across the sky, she saw a handsome man asleep in the field. There is some debate over whether he was a prince or shepherd, but she was a goddess, so the only thing that mattered was that he was mortal. Her sister, the dawn star, had made the foolish wish of asking Zeus to give her lover immortality. The dawn star's lover shriveled away into a cricket. The moon goddess was much wiser," he explained. "She asked Zeus to give her man eternal sleep. Apparently, if you sleep forever you stay eternally young—an interesting concept." He took her hand. "This is really romantic isn't it?"

"Yes—I think." Cassidy shook the haze from her mind. "I need to get back to Danny," she said, feeling both redundant and inarticulate.

"I told you. She's fine," Taban rolled his eyes. "Here I am confessing my feelings and all you can talk about is your friend. Do you have a heart?"

"I'm sorry. I'm sure we can stay out a bit longer."

* * *

"Good job getting rid of Savali," Aydan remarked. He walked into the living room juggling five playing cards in one hand.

"Did you see Cassidy while you were out?" Eadowen asked.

"Yeah, she walked off with Taban."

"Would you please go get them?" Eadowen replied.

"Don't block her," Aydan said. "If she wants to get it on with your cash-cow-boy-toy, let her."

"I agree," Danny said. "If you're not in a relationship with him, Cassidy can have whomever she wants." She couldn't believe how much more noble her words sounded than her bitter thoughts. The mug tipped in her hands, Eadowen stabilized it. She noticed the handle in her left hand and the cup in her right, no longer attached to each other.

"Don't worry about the mug. Under normal circumstances I'd agree with you," Eadowen explained. "But Taban has a way with people and he isn't always working for their benefit."

"Hypocrite," Aydan muttered under his breath. "Well, I can't go because Cassidy will think I followed her. She saw me working on a new trick." He leaned over the sofa. "Donovan, do you like jogging?"

"No."

"Well, you do now." Aydan snapped his fingers. "Eadowen seems to think Taban's up to something. Better bring him back."

The silence that followed Aydan's remark intimidated Danny more than any glare Donovan could've delivered. "I ... could go if it's that important ... my cramps feel better now," she offered.

"I think it would be better for your friendship with Cassidy if you didn't interrupt a potential romantic liaison," Eadowen replied.

"You're probably right," Danny said. *You couldn't pay me to be the youngest sibling in this family,* she thought as Donovan stalked out of the room. Clattering and sloshing followed his departure. Danny glimpsed him hauling a sizeable metal bucket full of ice water.

"I don't think you'll need that," Eadowen called. "He's not sleeping." A loud crash followed as Donovan dropped the bucket in the hallway.

The sharp pain in Danny's abdomen flared up again. She set the remainder of her mug on the floor and lay down to ease the pain in her stomach, knowing the pain in her chest would not go away. *I haven't cried since I broke my arm when I was thirteen—I'm not going to cry over this,* she told herself. Eadowen ran his hand along the edge of the couch next to Danny's torso. The ripple he created with his motion spread along Danny's back, easing each vertebrae of her spine. Then he joined Aydan somewhere down the hall.

* * *

"You're going home tomorrow and I'm going to miss you so much. I got this for you and I want you to have it." Setting a dainty rectangular box on her leg, Taban gave her a glowing smile. "Open it—"

A loud thumping noise cut him off, as Donovan marched out of the trees.

"Hey Donovan, what're you doing out here?" Taban asked.

"Jogging," Donovan grumbled.

"Oh my gosh!" Cassidy checked the time on her Ogham. "It's been twenty minutes. I have to get back." As she leapt to her feet, her elbow collided with Taban's mouth. "I'm so sorry, I had a Danny moment."

"Don't worry about it." Rubbing his mouth, Taban started to walk in the direction of the house, but tripped over his platforms again. Cassidy caught him. "Guess I was too busy staring at you to notice where I was walking," he said to her. "Donovan, there are some foxgloves for Ea in my car. Be a doll and put them in some water for me. The car's unlocked."

"Oh. I can do that." Cassidy made her way toward the car, giving no time for either to decline. Donovan wasn't difficult to read and she could tell he'd had a bad day. As she walked back to the house she saw Taban leaning against a large oak tree facing Donovan.

"You can continue your *jogging,*" Taban said, emphasizing the last word with air quotes. "I'll just wait here for Cassidy to get back." Stooping, Donovan grabbed Taban by the wrist and behind the knees, hauled him across his shoulders, and started to carry him back to the house. "Hey! Put me down." Taban struggled. "Where do you behemoth jocks come from?"

When they reached the house, Donovan dropped Taban in front of Eadowen and made a beeline for the stairs, presumably to his bedroom. Taban and Eadowen had a tense non-verbal conversation with a couple of gestures, but mostly glances. Then Taban muttered, "Donovan had another growth spurt." Leaving them in the hallway, Cassidy found a wilted Danny in the living room.

"Hi Danny," Cassidy said, clutching the foxgloves. "What happened?"

"What were you doing?" Danny asked with a strange rattle in her voice.

"I ... uh ... Taban wanted to watch the sunset with me. And we kissed." Danny's dark face paled as Cassidy spoke. "I'm so sorry. I thought you said you wanted time alone. That's no excuse. I'm so sorry. What's going on?"

"I don't feel like talking to you right now."

"I'm so sorry." Cassidy reached for Danny's shoulder, but she shrugged her away. "Alright, I'll leave you alone. Eadowen, may I use your restroom?"

"Yes, look left just before the dining room," Eadowen replied, taking the foxgloves from her.

Cassidy crept into the restroom and took the box from her pocket. The unlabeled gift box was bound shut with a narrow piece of turquoise ribbon. She spent several minutes undoing the ribbon so that she would not have to slice it. Winding it around her hand, she opened the box. A pair of golden teardrop earrings with turquoise inlay sparkled on a display sheet. She clipped the earrings into her ears and admired her reflection in the mirror. The gold and blue-green shimmered on her skin highlighting the bronze undertones of her neck. In the hallway, Taban caught her in a hug. "Goodbye," he whispered.

Not wanting anyone to see her watery eyes, Danny tried to find something on the bookshelf to hide her face. Inspecting a printed photograph, she recognized Eadowen sitting under a red and white beach umbrella. A boy next to him displayed a blue-colored tongue, clutching a snow cone of the same color. Danny noticed a tattoo on the boy's arm, and she realized he was a younger incarnation of Taban without the bleached hair and a darker tan.

"May I see that?" Cassidy asked timidly. "Weird, he's not nearly as attractive in this image as he is in real life."

"I'll put that away for you." Eadowen accepted the photograph from Cassidy. "I suppose we should say goodnight."

"Is everything going to be okay with Danny?" Cassidy said.

"We don't know," he said. "You're both flying back to Victoria tomorrow, correct? We'll contact you."

"How will you contact us?"

"Through non-electronic means. I know this is already obvious, but please don't even speak to each other or others electronically about this."

"I understand," Danny replied, shaking Eadowen's outstretched hand. "Thank you."

* * *

"You're about to drive into a tree!" Danny shouted, seizing the steering wheel.

Cassidy swerved the car, narrowly missing a large oak. "Oops, sorry." She turned onto the main road feeling the transition to smooth pavement. She headed home trying not to think about Taban or her first kiss. *Not relevant, Cassidy, not relevant,* Cassidy told herself. *Why can't I get him out of my head? He's insidious.*

"It isn't like you to be so quiet. I'm sorry for what I did." Cassidy's guilt heightened as she observed Danny's bleakness from the corner of her eye. "Whatever it was that I did."

"Doesn't matter now, so never mind," Danny mumbled into the window, her breath made a heart shape on the glass as her own ached.

"Is it about Savali showing up? Are you scared?"

"Yes, that too."

"I like you," Danny said slowly. She quickly diverted her gaze, so she wouldn't have to see Cassidy's reaction.

"Oh, Danny I'm so sorry."

"I know," Danny muttered. "I'm just insanely jealous of Taban."

"I'm really sorry. I just don't feel that way about you," Cassidy said, her voice trembling as she empathized with Danny's pain. "I really like you as a friend. I always have."

"I know."

"You're a great person, Danny. I know you'll find someone who is worthy of you. And I'm sorry if I hurt your feelings." Cassidy rambled, hoping something she said would help her friend. "We can still be friends right? I know I'm not a Genetic Fey, but I'm going to stay with you whatever happens. I may not be much help, but I'll give you all I've got. This isn't a token for not returning your feelings. I already committed to support you because I care about your well-being and I swear I will never get distracted by anyone again. I made a mistake."

"Sounds like I'm going to need all the support I can get."

"Well, all I can give you is mine and you have it," Cassidy said. "Please don't cry. I mean unless it'll make you feel better."

"I'm not crying!" Danny shouted.

"Would you like some music? I'll play something you like at a low volume."

"Something with flute, harp, or bagpipes, but no singing," Danny offered.

"Vehicle: Search music archives: purchase any song with harp, flute, bagpipes and no vocal."

"Are you sure you meant to search flute, harp, bagpipes and no vocal," the Reyes' car replied.

"You darn machine, find a melody with all three or I will deconstruct you until you make my fairy happy," Cassidy yelled. "Ahem. I mean, Vehicle: yes, I intended that search."

"Your results are—"

"Vehicle: Just select highest-rated song," Cassidy commanded. A sweet melody with long beats started to play from the speaker. "Good car." Cassidy petted the dashboard, as though it was a puppy. On any other occasion, Danny would've laughed. She wished she could enjoy the image.

They were silent for the rest of the trip to Ms. Reyes' house. Cassidy's concern for Danny helped her drive without getting distracted by images of Taban.

When they reached home, Danny quickly brushed her teeth, shoved her clothes in her suitcase, and got into bed.

"Good night, Cassidy," she muttered into her pillow.

"Good night, Danny," Cassidy replied and turned off the light. "Sleep well. Everything will be okay. I promise." Though she'd set her Ogham to sleep mode, Cassidy hadn't removed it to sleep, so she felt the buzz of a message. Trying not to disturb Danny, she read the messages and typed her responses.

Message from Rona-Mom: Hi sweetie, have you decided where you want to study abroad this summer? Weren't you interested in Japan?

Message to Rona-Mom: I changed my mind I'm going to apply to programs in Scotland and Ireland.

Message from Daisuke Savali: Dear Ms. Cassidy, Thank you so much for saving me this morning. The doctors told me I might not be alive if it hadn't been for you getting the water out of my system.

That's weird, I could've sworn Taban said I barely did anything for Daisuke, Cassidy thought and looked at her Ogham. *Speak of the devil.*

Message from Taban: I had an amazing night tonight. I can't get you out of my head.

Message to Taban: Thanks, you too, Cassidy tapped, unable to come up with anything better. Daisuke had the same last name as May Savali, so she decided to keep her contact with him minimal until she'd researched him.

* * *

"Goodbye, Cassidy." Ms. Reyes squeezed Cassidy's shoulders, then wrapped her arms around Danny. "Goodbye, Honey."

"I'm going to miss you," Danny said. "When are you coming to visit?"

"Soon, sweetie."

Danny stared out the window the entire flight, without uttering a word. Since Cassidy couldn't recount the events of the last three days, she recorded the trip in her journal as fiction in case anyone discovered it. *I feel kind of pathetic right now. Ever since that evening with Taban, my goals just seem so far out of reach. I've developed such an attachment to him, for almost no reason. What is wrong with me?* When she reread her entry she cringed and decided to occupy her mind with something else. Fortunately, she didn't have to threaten her tablet to obtain a suitable documentary on the subject of politics.

CHAPTER 15
HAPPINESS EVER ELUSIVE

THE SPICY AROMA of the tortilla wraps wafted through the kitchen. Taban entered to see Eadowen scrubbing dishes. Eadowen glanced in his direction and tapped a stirring spoon harshly on the side of the sink. "What did you think you were doing with her?"

"I just kissed her." Taban shrugged. "Besides, you refused me just fine, so she could've too."

"First of all, I had already lived with you for almost four years when you came onto me. I saw what you did to people and I knew all your ugly habits. And as I've said before, we're not so different."

"Were you jealous?" Taban folded his arms.

"No, I see *plenty* of you." Eadowen said, flipping a red dish towel in Taban's direction. "Dry for me."

"You know there's this thing called a dishwasher. They were around in the twentieth century too." Taban scrubbed a dish, as though he were trying to remove superglue. "*You* criticize me for flirting and yet *you* had me sing for them and you served them food. *Twice*."

"How is that related to toying with Cassidy's emotions?"

"Music triggers a boost in dopamine in the brain. Dopamine is related to pleasure. People get a higher release of that chemical from eating fatty foods than they do from an orgasm. The food you served last night was laden in peanut oil, even though Donovan's deathly allergic," Taban snapped, slamming his plate on the counter with a crash. "Do you know what that means?"

"That you should learn how to cook?" Eadowen replied, calmly passing him the broken mug. "Oh, careful with that. Danny tore it in half."

Aydan rapped his satin-gloved fist against the door frame before he clacked across the kitchen floor in black boots. "Sorry to interrupt your lover's quarrel, but don't we have more important things to figure out?"

"We're not lovers," Taban scoffed, hanging the dish towel on Eadowen's head. "Not today at least."

"Flirtacious-long-term-domestic-partners-in-an-asexual-romantic-relationship-with-matching-rings quarrel seemed like a bit of a mouthful, but hey, I'm an open-minded guy," Aydan replied. "Anyway, I heard Savali. That was way too close for comfort. What're we going to do?"

"I can't believe she found this house," Eadowen sighed.

"Do I have to buy you a new house to move to?" Taban asked.

"Somewhere secluded in Ontario please," Eadowen said. "Aydan, tell your brother to pack his things. We're leaving tomorrow morning. We'll stay at a hotel until Taban gets us a place."

"You mean all two shirts and his video games?" Aydan said. "Hey, did Cassidy punch you?" Aydan asked Taban a little too gleefully, when he noticed the mark Cassidy's elbow had left on his lip.

"Just because she's a woman doesn't mean she can abuse me. It was an accident."

"Rats. She seemed like she had chutzpah."

"She likes me," Taban said. "Which is too bad because I'm not into her, but apparently you are."

"So, you have no taste?" Aydan wound a strand of black hair around his finger.

"This is coming from the guy trotting around in a lacy dress."

"I know. I look fantastic in it." Aydan replied, twirling to show off his petticoat.

Since Aydan had a point, Taban unable to come up with a decent retort said, "Put a sock in it mini-kinky-braw."

"Is the valley-boy-siren with a tentacle monster tattoo on his arm trying to insult me, because those terms are quite flattering."

"Gentlemen," Eadowen said in warning tone.

"Alright, but will you both just kiss and make up, so we can get a move on?" Aydan said. "Whoa, okay, points for taking *that* literally. I don't need to see my sibling tonguing." Shielding his eyes, Aydan left the room.

"How was that for making up?" Taban asked.

"Rather salty and monochromatic. Good texture, but overdone."

"So, you and I are Peach Whiskies—er—Gay Frisbees or whatever those Kelpie-ish things are, aren't we? I can't believe I never made the connection before."

Blanching, Eadowen held a hand to his lips, and finger-spelled 'E-A-C-H U-I-S-G-E', in sign language.

"And you're the bastard child of both the T-U-A-T-H-A D-E D-A-N-A-N-N and the E-A-C-H U-I-S-G-E?" Taban communicated through sign.

Eadowen nodded affirmatively.

"And your brothers don't know you're their half brother," Taban signed. He hadn't realized that Donovan and Aydan didn't know about their older sibling's identity.

"Guess it had to happen to somebody," Taban said before signing another question to Eadowen. "Do your brothers know you're their half-sibling?"

"Aydan might know depending on how much he overheard when I first got my injury ten years ago." It took Taban a couple minutes to decode Eadowen's response from the sign language grammatical structure. He signed it back to confirm what he'd interpreted. Eadowen nodded again.

"Taban, you're behaving more peevishly than usual," Eadowen observed verbally. "What's bothering you?"

What's bothering me? Taban thought as he glared at Eadowen silently. *Well let's see, I bashed a seventeen-year-old's pride, because I know she's going to stick around Edana. I almost drowned a guy to learn about the journal. And for the last four years, I've been whoring myself to manipulate Abigail, who is actually a decent person, in order to keep you and my sister safe. You're welcome.* "Nothing," Taban summarized, when he realized he hadn't actually said anything.

"You know something about Savali don't you?" Eadowen accused. "You smell like Cassidy's lavender spritzer and a high end perfume you would give a woman. I know you've had *rendezvous* with several people today, including the supposed surf accident."

"Yeah, I was showing off in the water and I got laid. Not exactly news. Look, I'm just shaken up by the whole Savali appearing on our doorstep," Taban fibbed. "I seem off because I haven't been getting a lot of sleep because of homework stress and stuff."

Eadowen regarded him with sympathetic eyes. "I'll give you some chamomile tea and we can watch *Pride and Prejudice*."

"Why do you want to watch that movie? It's so boring. Don't you remember when we had to watch it in class and I passed out? Oh wait ..."

"So, you don't want to sleep?" Eadowen smirked.

"I hate it when you do that," Taban remarked through his teeth.

"Tell me what you're planning."

"What's that?" Taban avoided the command by reaching for the picture frame in Eadowen's lap. He recognized the old snapshot someone had printed of Eadowen and him eating snow cones on the beach in Malibu.

"Danny picked it up. I haven't put it back yet."

"This must be the one non-airbrushed picture of me." Taban held the photograph under the red shaded lamp. "It's weird to see my face before my dad decided my jawline wasn't good enough. I wonder what I would've grown up looking like without alterations." As he contemplated his modified face, Taban realized that if the Each Uisge charisma was tied into facial features both he and Eadowen were marred. He had been adjusted to appear better-looking but in the process some of the natural appeal his genetics had given him could have been removed. Because Eadowen's scars disrupted the symmetry of his face and body, Taban wondered if his friend's abilities had also been tarnished. *If Ea and I are flawed Peach Whiskies I don't want to meet an unspoiled one,* he thought.

"I think you're handsome then, and now," Eadowen said the exact words Taban wanted to hear.

"You're the only person who understands me."

The picture reminded Taban, he hadn't looked up his sister,Telyn, in a long time. It pained him to see her, but he searched his Ogham. The most recent picture he found horrified him. The photograph was unadjusted, but her waist looked strangely small. Her face even seemed to have gone through some unnatural alterations.

"How's your sister?"

"See for yourself."

"Oh my g—" Eadowen guided Taban into a tight embrace. "You need to go see her."

"I can't just yet," Taban explained. His father would do worse to her if he showed up, since research had been going slow.

"I'm going to go talk with Aydan about a plan of action regarding Savali. Do you want to join?" Eadowen asked.

"Just destroy the tablets and all the copies."

"No. I made a commitment to my parents and I have an obligation to future generations. Just think what would've happened if our generation didn't have that evidence. I never would've been able to help Edana," Eadowen explained.

"You're being stupid. Wake me up if you come to your senses!" Taban shouted clutching the photograph to his chest.

"Are you going to bed?" Eadowen asked.

"Yeah."

Eadowen caught his wrist. "Taban, promise me you won't go near Cassidy."

"I promise I won't visit her in Washington State. Please … Ea … I just want to be alone for a bit."

Pulling Taban toward him, Eadowen said in a low voice, "I know about you and Abigail."

"How?" Taban touched his cheek to Eadowen's so they could speak in whispers instead of signing to each other.

"Did you really think none of my friends on campus would tell me if they saw, who they perceive to be my boyfriend, making out with another person?" His fingers traced the nape of Taban's neck. "I know you're scheming something as we speak. Why won't you share it?"

"If you could spend the rest of your life with me or Danny and your brothers who would you choose?"

"Danny and my family."

"You can't go to jail if you don't know about what I'm going to do. If you become my accomplice you'll have to run away with me and you might not see them again."

"I see ..."

"And this is for picking them over me." Leering, Taban slapped his palm across Eadowen's face, but softened the blow at the last second leaving only a momentary discoloration on Eadowen's flesh.

"So." Eadowen put his hand to his injured cheek. "You would like me to act surprised when you disappear?"

"Preferably."

Contemplating all that had to be done, Taban headed upstairs. *I'll have to talk to Daisuke more. I need to know when Savali is leaving to research in Scotland and what she knows about the other piece of the journal. And then there's the matter of my father.*

PART FOUR

THREE WEEKS LATER: IN WHICH EVERYONE GOES ON ADVENTURES

Like Circe from Homer's Odyssey, Math, a Celtic magician enjoyed turning people into animals. He transformed one man into a stag. If only the stag had been silver then it would have been lucky for anyone who caught it.

–AYDAN TOLYMIE

CHAPTER 16
EXPECTING SOMEONE TALLER

CASSIDY DROVE DOWN FIR STREET from her volunteer job at the mediation clinic to her house. Wind blasted against the small electric-solar car and grey clouds loomed overhead. When she reached the one-story beach house that she shared with her mother on the outskirts of Port Townsend, she noticed white crests on the ocean. It was almost summer: May 25th to be exact. The weather didn't bother her. She'd finished her last final for school only a few days earlier, and a blustery day wasn't going to overcome that stress relief. As she got out of the car, she breathed in the smell of salt and seaweed. Untangling one of the golden earrings Taban had given her from her hair, Cassidy trudged into her house, shutting the door against the wind. After she slid her double-breasted trench coat onto a hook on the violet-painted wall, Cassidy followed the smell of sautéed vegetables into the kitchen where she saw the crockpot bubbling on the table. She turned down the temperature and headed toward the living room, passing framed electronic photo albums from family trips. A standing lamp with different colored lights fanning out like a peacock tail guarded the center of the living room. Attached to the walls, shelves of varying heights encircled the living room. They contained exotic plants and souvenirs from around the world. Rona Adisa, Cassidy's mother, reclined in a large black massage armchair, dressed in a bright red kanga. She read an e-zine on her tablet, the likely content: magic shows; her hobby, or architecture; her career.

"How was your day, sweetie?" Rona asked.

"Hi, Rona-Mom. It was my last day at work until August," Cassidy said, sitting down in an identical armchair across from her mother. "Where's Anna-Mom? I thought it was her night to cook."

"She got called in to repair blood nanobots for the hospital. She probably won't be home for another few minutes, so I just decided to make sure you both had something good to eat when you got home," Rona-Mom smiled. "I used a cooking site by Ursula Eldin that I just found."

"I got responses from my applications to the exchange programs," Cassidy commented. "A few accepted me and two offered small scholarships."

"Well, you know we'd love it if you picked the ones with scholarships, but if you can present a reason why one of the other programs is better then you should attend that one. You need to hurry and pick one. The deadlines are closing."

"I know," Cassidy responded. Then she made her way to the far end of the house to her bedroom. Last year, she'd painted her walls sea foam green, which didn't quite suit her dark-red carpet. Repainting would involve moving chaotic piles of electronic devices, doodles, and clothes, so she hadn't gotten around to it. She braced herself against her dresser to maneuver around an egg chair and over her collection of beach glass. After successfully traversing her room, she stripped down to her camisole and flopped onto her bed. To her delight, Taban had left a message during her volunteer hours. For the last few weeks Taban had messaged her often, though erratically. As usual, her heart pounded as she commanded her Ogham to read it to her.

"Message from Taban: Hi Cassidy, we haven't talked in a couple days. Would you send me a picture of yourself wearing those earrings I gave you? I never got to see you in them. How'd your last day at mediation go?"

"It went really well," she recorded into her Ogham.

Her Ogham read a new message from Taban a few moments later.

"Message from Taban: I wish I wasn't so busy. I'd love to see you. Maybe someday I can rent a place on the beach and you can come visit me. Wouldn't you love to live on the beach for a while?"

Laughing, Cassidy glanced out her bedroom window at the silver sand beach just past her backyard.

"You mean a beach that's warm all year instead of off-and-on from July to September? You know I live in *Port* Townsend, right?"

"Message from Taban: Oh right. But just imagine we could cuddle under the sun on the warm sand and I could take you shopping. If you want me to send you some clothes, give me your sizes. I'm sorry the last thing I got you was too big."

"That's really sweet, but I don't want any more gifts. I don't feel like I can reciprocate and I already have too many clothes." A row of jewelry boxes Taban had sent her covered half of her dresser. Every piece had unique and beautiful qualities. Cassidy never felt more fulfilled owning more items, but she wasn't immune to desire of possession and remained an active consumer.

"Message from Taban: I just want to make my girl happy. If you don't like shopping or jewelry, then tell me, what makes you tick? And don't list your extracurriculars again because you sound like a resume."

"I waste a ton of time playing video games, but I'm not sure I actually have a passion," Cassidy said sadly.

"Message from Taban: Well, if you make me your passion, I'll make sure you have whatever your heart desires. Hey Hon, I have to go, but I'll contact you soon."

"Talk to you later."

Under her thick comforter, Cassidy felt her journal dig into her back. Absentmindedly, she flipped through the pages. She hadn't written anything since the plane flight home from Halifax. A wave crashed on the shore, evoking the memory of her evening not watching the sunset with Taban. She rummaged for her pen. It was time to get him out of her mind and onto a page.

That conversation was a lot shorter and shallower than our usual talks. Taban and I have spent so many nights messaging each other, but he always focuses on me and my goals. Not that I don't appreciate that, but I want to know more about him. I'd do anything to see him again.

Cassidy touched her lips and stared at the page not wanting to believe she'd actually written the last sentence. Hastily, she scratched it out in black until it became completely unintelligible.

I wonder if the Tolymies contacted Danny? She'd probably tell me. At least I hope she'd still tell me. Danny and I have only been in touch a couple of times and I know she's probably upset that I turned her down. I feel so bad, but I couldn't lead her on, when I knew I didn't feel that way about her. I should contact her today. Maybe I'll give her the birthday present I got for her early. I know she'll love it.

"Hi, honey," Rona called, loudly greeting her wife, Annabelle.

"Hi, Anna-Mom!" Cassidy shouted from her room.

"How are you sweetie?" Annabelle Adisa asked in her crisp British accent as she knocked on Cassidy's door.

"I'll be out in a few minutes, I just need some time alone." Cassidy addressed a *Knots of Avernus* poster on her closed door.

The doorbell clanked.

"Hello? May I help you?" Cassidy heard Rona greet the newcomer but Cassidy couldn't discern the speaker's responses. "Yes … uh … huh? Would you like to come in? No? Okay, I'll bring her out."

"Cassidy, there's a dashing young man waiting for you," Rona whispered with more enthusiasm than she usually bestowed on Cassidy's friends. "He looks like Harlan Eldin."

"Who?" Cassidy asked, throwing on her slacks. "Oh yeah, the magician you're a fan of. I'm coming."

It's not Taban, she muttered to herself, trying to dash her own hopes. When she opened the door, she recognized Aydan Tolymie, standing arms akimbo with one thigh-high boot planted on the front step. He sported a black tunic belted at his waist by a large red sash. The wind blew strands of black hair that had escaped his low ponytail across his face. He regarded her with a feline smirk adorning his wide mouth.

"Good afternoon, Master Tolymie," Cassidy said with her best imitation of her mother's London accent. "Shall I direct you to the nearest damsel in distress or are you more inclined to rob the rich and give to the poor?" She shut the door behind her. "All joking aside, is Danny okay?"

"Taban stole the journal. We wanted to know if he'd been in contact with you."

"Are you sure *he* took it?" Cassidy raised her voice, upset by his accusation against Taban.

"He told Eadowen he'd be away visiting his sister," Aydan replied through gritted teeth. "We checked the vault where we keep the pieces of the journal a few days later and it was gone. I'm just here to find out if you've been in touch with him. Then I'll leave you alone."

"Yes, but he didn't say anything about the journal or anything relating to GFs. As far as I knew he was still with you."

"Well, if that's all you're going to tell me, then …" With a casual wave, Aydan produced a large sprig of spurred red flowers seemingly out of thin air. "I apologize for intruding. Have a nice day."

"Wait, what about Danny? Where're you going?"

"I have to take a cab back to catch the ferry to Victoria. I'll meet up with Danny in B.C. Donovan will probably *rendezvous* with her shortly."

"I'm going with you."

"No. You're involved with Taban." He offered her the sprig. "Take care."

"I don't want a flower." She brushed it away. "I want to be with my friend. If something happens to her I'll never forgive myself." She tugged on his billowy sleeve, preventing him from walking away. "Taxis are expensive. I'll drive you."

"No, you won't." Aydan leaned the flower against the door. "Thank you for your time." A silver hair pin glinted in the light as his ponytail lashed behind him when he turned to leave.

She grabbed his arm with such fervor that he halted.

"You can't be part of this because you'd tell Taban everything if he asked you." He slithered out of her grasp and started power walking toward the street. "This way you have nothing to tell him, so you can continue your relationship with him."

"That's not as important." She said more decisively than she felt. "If I give you my word, I won't tell him anything. And I give it." Cassidy swiveled in front of him, blocking his path. Aydan barely managed to stop before barreling face first into her generous chest. Emphatically making eye contact, he took a step back. "At least let me take you to Victoria," she begged. To her surprise her voice cracked. "I told Danny I'd be there for her."

When he heard her passionate plea, Aydan touched her arm with concern. "We'll take care of Danny. I promise."

Cassidy checked her Ogham to see if she'd managed to stall him long enough. "If you contact a taxi now, you'll have to wait at least fifteen minutes," she exaggerated slightly. "I know when the evening ferry leaves. You'll miss it if I don't take you."

"Fine," he acquiesced.

Cassidy opened the door to her house and called for her mothers. "Do you mind if I go to Victoria tonight? I'll stay at Danny's house."

It took both of Cassidy's mothers a few minutes to come to the door. Cassidy could hear the mumbles of conversation, the topic of which she guessed without comprehending the words.

"They're discussing whether to give you permission to go to Victoria tonight," Aydan stated the obvious.

"Well, first of all who is this gentleman?" Annabelle asked.

"He's a friend I met in Halifax—we have to hurry or we'll miss the ferry."

"I was in the area. I should've messaged in advance; I apologize for dropping in on you." Aydan explained offering his hand to shake. "Cassidy has offered to drive me back to the ferry."

"I've never seen a delphinium that wine color before," Rona remarked. "Cassidy, why don't you come inside and put it in water?"

"I'll wait," Aydan assured her. "You have my word."

Once she and her mothers were safely in the living room, Rona-Mom turned to her. "Cassidy, you're very trustworthy and responsible, you've proven that many times."

"However, we would like you to video chat with us tonight to confirm that you're at Danny's house," Annabelle said. She cleared her throat as though she was about to say something that she didn't want to say. Cassidy cringed at the sound. "You're old enough now that Rona and I can't dictate what you do but …"

"Anna-Mom don't …" Cassidy tried to assure her mothers. "I'm not going to do anything with him. He's just a friend."

"You know how to protect yourself. Remember: only do what is right for you. Don't ever let anyone tell you to do something you don't want to do."

"I'm not interested in him."

"You can always call us, if you need one of us to come pick you up," Rona said. "You can always talk to us." Cassidy's mother looked at her like she was a colt who had just learned to walk.

"I will. I promise," Cassidy said relieved that the conversation was over. "I have to get going or we'll miss the ferry." After hugging her mother goodbye, she tossed traveling essentials and the box containing Danny's present into a backpack. She inspected the hangers by the door, selecting a pirate jacket with ruffled sleeves—her best approximation of swashbuckler attire.

As Cassidy and Aydan rushed to her car, she sent a message to Danny. "I'm bringing Aydan back to Victoria. Will you please let me stay over?"

In the passenger seat, Aydan silently flipped cards in his hands. *I have to get to know him better so he'll trust me,* Cassidy thought. *I wish Danny was here. I'm not as good at this stuff.* She managed to come up with something to say.

"Rona-Mom thinks you look like a magician she likes." Not brave enough to flatter her striking companion directly, Cassidy added: "Mom called you dashing."

"I heard."

"Oh." She felt beads of sweat form on the back of her neck. "Then you also heard—"

"That your mothers think you'll sleep with me instead of hanging out with Danny?" Aydan replied with what Cassidy was beginning to realize was characteristic candor.

"No, they don't," Cassidy replied.

He spun a card around thumb and index finger. "You could've told them you like a man, with blond hair and a tan," he commented in a sing-song voice as though quoting a certain cult classic picture show.

"It's so funny that you look like Harlan Eldin and you're also a magician with eccentric costumes too ... oh ..."

In her peripheral vision, Cassidy saw the corner of Aydan's mouth curl into a slasher grin.

"So, your younger brother's sixteen and your older sibling attends college. How old are you?"

"Eighty-seven."

"No way. Really?"

"I just turned nineteen in March."

"You got me," Cassidy said, feeling very gullible. "It's getting hard to know what to believe."

Between uncomfortable silences, Cassidy spent the rest of the drive introducing Aydan to the Pacific Northwest and listening to his stories about his year with an international young magicians program.

"That sounds incredible. How did you get to be part of that program?" Cassidy asked.

"I won first place in Illusions at FISM, International Federation of Magic Societies, when I was sixteen."

An hour and a half later, Cassidy parked in Port Angeles and they walked across the street to the ferry. Aydan scanned his Ogham on the meter to pay for the parking and passage before she could reach it.

"Thank you," she mumbled. "You didn't have to."

"You're welcome. Thanks for the ride."

She tapped several codes into her Ogham to reach her digital passport. The border patrol worker checked her Ogham and approved it with a digital stamp. He did a double take at Aydan and started to scrutinize Aydan's person. "I'm a magician," Aydan said calmly, as if to explain away any discomfort the patrol worker had with him. It worked.

"Is Eadowen alright?"

"I don't know. Eadowen ... has a way of being blank." They followed the serpentine ramp to board the ferry. "Fortunately, we never completely trusted Taban. Eadowen had the presence of mind to keep a vital piece of information from him."

"What?" Cassidy asked eagerly.

"I can't tell you." Aydan gave her a cold smile. "You're still involved with Taban."

Sitting next to him in an old padded seat looking out over the stern of the boat, she watched him closely as he made a card disappear and reappear in the palm of his outstretched hand. The safety announcement boomed over the intercom.

"I've been meaning to ask. How did you guys know about Danny? You're pretty distant relations."

"Mom used to tell Eadowen and me stories about her because she knew Danny's mother would try to keep things from her. Mom took her characteristics and any information she could gather about her interests and passions and spun them into elaborate epics that made even her annoying qualities seem wonderful. I think the idea was that if we adored her; we'd protect her even if our parents weren't around."

"Huh, I wonder why Eadowen didn't tell Danny that."

"Eadowen was the biggest fan of the stories mom told. I wasn't old enough to remember the content very well and I wasn't that interested. I think Mom severely underestimated Eadowen's obsessive personality." With a distant look in his eyes, Aydan stared at the churning foam trailing the ferry boat. "Then again, I'd probably develop pretty intense feelings if I'd been told Danny was my only chance at a healthy romantic relationship." A jack of hearts disappeared in Aydan's hand.

"Hold on!" Cassidy touched his shoulder so he'd look at her. "From what I've seen Eadowen is caring, intelligent, responsible, and not bad looking. Why in the world would Danny be the only candidate for romance?"

"Well, most GFs would be an exception. I think even that statement is a hyperbole, but Eadowen being Eadowen took it to heart … Never mind, it was just something silly I overheard when I was nine." Aydan spoke as though his words had been pent up inside him for a long time. "Some guy came to our house and spent a lot of time with Eadowen. I was kind of off in my own world, so I didn't pay much attention. I'd rather you didn't mention this to Danny because it's just conjecture."

Then Eadowen wasn't being sweet on her just because of a childhood memory, Cassidy thought. "Obsession isn't healthy," she said aloud. "Shouldn't Eadowen be in therapy or something?"

"You're probably right, but to get to the root of the problem Eadowen would have to reveal our GF status. The good news is I'm pretty sure Eadowen wouldn't do anything unless Danny gave clear indication that she's open to hir overtures. Besides, she'll never live up to hir image of her."

"So, if Danny never falls for hir, Eadowen won't pursue anything ever?" Cassidy asked.

"That's why I suggest not mentioning this to Danny. A: I could be wrong."

"And B: we'd be subconsciously putting the idea in Danny's head," Cassidy finished his sentence. "I'm pretty sure she doesn't look at hir that way and as much as I like Danny she's a bit weird. I doubt she's the kind of person people fantasize about. Before I agree to keep this a secret, tell me what *is* Eadowen's personality because xie kind of doesn't seem to have one?"

"To tell you the truth, my own sibling is an enigma to me," Aydan said. "You know Taban doesn't even know the truth about how he and Eadowen met."

"And how was that?" She sighed, her curiosity allowing Aydan to shift the subject.

"Eadowen saw Taban at a school fair. For some reason xie really wanted to interact with him, but Taban was acting like he was above everyone there. Eadowen asked me to orchestrate a meeting. I tripped him and he fell right into Eadowen's arms, but he never saw me. To this day, Taban probably still thinks it was an act of fate. I wish I could undo what I did and make it so they never met," Aydan concluded bitterly.

"Were they a couple?"

Aydan shrugged.

"Oh no. I kissed him." Cassidy felt cold. "This is horrible."

"Listen, whatever their relationship, my older sibling would never judge you for Taban's transgressions."

The ferry started to roll as the ocean swelled. Perceiving the motion, she sat quietly for a few minutes to enjoy the sensation. Aydan started to look green.

"The restrooms are that way," she offered.

"I'll be okay."

"Can you show me a card trick?"

The color returning to his face, Aydan turned to her, a look of astonishment on his face. "You *want* to see a card trick?"

"Yes. I still have that card you gave me." She felt in her slacks pocket, where she usually kept the card, but it had vanished.

"Indeed you do." Aydan held up the missing card.

"Hey! How'd you get your paws on that?"

"Do you carry it with you a lot?" He asked, noticing the condition of the card. The silver shine had worn significantly as a result of Cassidy's fondling.

"It's pretty and shiny and meditative," Cassidy defended, snatching it back. "If you give these cards out a lot, shouldn't you have your site on it as a promotional thing?"

"Breathe on it—you know the way you'd fog up a window. I guess I usually mention this at my shows or to people who might become clients."

"Really?" She blew on the ten of diamonds. Violet shapes and lettering slowly appeared: a crescent moon with a v through it, Aydan's stage name, and his site.

"What's that?" She pointed to the crescent moon.

"A Crescent V-Rod. It's an ancient Pictish symbol for eternity."

They amused each other by playing a simple game, in which Aydan predicted cards Cassidy secretly selected.

"I thought you were the observant type who liked to solve puzzles, but you haven't asked how anything's done," he commented.

"I usually do but I ..." Cassidy tucked a crimped curl behind her ear. "I guess I want ... to let magic have a chance to be ... magical."

"I like that." Aydan gave her a sidelong glance.

"Message from Danny: Sorry it took me so long. I hope you're coming because ... something's wrong."

The horn sounded signaling the ferry docking.

"We'll be there as fast as we can," Cassidy said into her Ogham as they dashed off the boat.

CHAPTER 17
PAIN

SLAMMING HER FOOT into the dangling punching bag, Danny felt the satisfying crunch of the padding and heard the crack of the plastic cover. A solid punch sent the bag backward with enough force to hit the back wall. Then she went in for a knife hand strike with excellent form. The moment her hand connected with the bag she felt a jolt of sharp pain. She screamed. Danny inspected the seemingly undamaged hand she had used to break cement blocks for her black belt. *I don't even see a mark. Why does it feel like I broke my hand?* The stinging pain spread up her arm and into her shoulder tightening her muscles. She knelt to the floor. What should have been a light impact on her knee, felt like a brick had been dropped on it. Clutching her knee, she lay down on her highschool gym floor in intense pain and complete bewilderment. She crawled across the vacant gym. Using the door frame for support, she managed to pull herself onto her feet. She cradled her hand and slowly made her way to the school's main entrance. Not many students remained at the school after class, so Danny faced the vacant hallway alone. Once outside, she passed several students, all too busy looking at their tablets to notice her. Danny knew they'd probably help her if she asked, but she didn't know for what assistance to ask. The acute soreness all over her body worsened. Her legs no longer worked, so she collapsed on a bench outside her school. As she stared at the clouds, she realized her current experience was like an amplified version of the pain hypersensitivity she'd felt at the Tolymies' house.

"Oh, my gosh. Who is that?" A young woman a couple meters away from Danny said to her friend. Delighted squeaks and gasps ensued, as students looked up from their tablets. Moving as little as possible, Danny looked around to see who the latest intrigue was. Clean shaven and dressed in fitted jeans, only the retro headphones around his neck, indicated to Danny that it was none other than Donovan Tolymie. Tugging anxiously at the popped collar of his grey polo shirt, Donovan scanned the groups of students. He hunched in a futile attempt to avoid the many pairs of eyes admiring his impressive stature and defined features. Danny called to him. With a sigh of relief, he joined her. She struggled to sit up. Concern in his deep-grey eyes, Donovan cocked his head at her.

"I can only walk slowly." Danny hobbled past him. "Uh, convenient and nice to see you," she added.

The shuttle headed in the direction of Danny's apartment, pulled up to the stop down the street from the school. "Sorry, Donovan, I don't think I'll be quick enough to catch that one. We can just wait for the next one." Just then someone cat-called Donovan. Flushing to the color of a tomato, Donovan scooped her up and ran toward the shuttle. She nearly protested, but his humiliated expression forestalled complaints.

In the moment, she couldn't recall how distantly she and Donovan were related. "Leave my cousin alone!" Danny shouted at the harassers, even though it hurt to speak loudly.

"Don't bother," Donovan growled, showing a glint of teeth under a suppressed snarl.

Poor Donovan, Danny thought. *Though, I wish I was a huge guy who could just pick up people and move them whenever I want.*

She slid her arm across the shuttle scanner and let Donovan place her in the seat next to him.

"What's going on?" Danny took advantage of a moment when her pain lessened. "How's your family?"

"They're okay." He slipped her an ivory envelope, on which her name was scrawled. It opened easily with a snap of the seal. Fascinated by this form of communication, she stroked the thick textured paper and tried to decipher the cursive.

My Dearest Edana Reyes,

I hope all is well with you and Cassidy. I am afraid to inform you that Taban has made-off with the journal we had. We have reason to believe this is because Savali has discovered evidence of the other piece. Stag was talking to Abigail and he found out that she and Taban were involved. It is not clear whether Taban intended to give the journal to her or not.

Donovan and Aydan will be traveling to Scotland soon to search for the other part of the journal. We kept the daughter's addition to the journal a secret. She wrote about where her great-grandfather left the piece in Scotland. I think it would be best if you joined them, but it is your decision, of course. I have a contact, named Marja, who has signed you up for an exchange program with a full-ride scholarship. I have full confidence you will make the best decision for your needs. Stay safe.

Yours Always,

Eadowen Tolymie

P.S. Please dispose of this letter in such a way that it may not be salvaged.

A trace of Eadowen's cologne, probably deposited by his wrist brushing against the page as he wrote, caught Danny's attention. Holding the letter up to her nose, she inhaled and her pain subsided even more.

* * *

Rubbing his forehead after an unfortunate encounter with the front door of the Reyes' apartment, Donovan lumbered into the living room after Danny who held the door for him. She collapsed on the couch. The acute discomfort stemming from her arm increased. She writhed on the couch. Donovan hovered over her.

"Hospital?" Donovan asked.

"I'm starting to feel better," she lied. "Why don't you make yourself comfortable."

* * *

Fifteen minutes later, Cassidy and Aydan rushed into the apartment. Cassidy saw her friend curled in a ball and ran to her side. "Do we need to take you to the hospital?" she asked. At her present discomfort level, post consumption of pain medication, Danny no longer considered the suggestion completely unreasonable.

"That probably won't do any good," Aydan said quietly, his face somber.

"Why?" Cassidy demanded.

He looked away and muttered, "Not her too."

"What is wrong with Danny?!"

"I'm not positive, so I don't want to say."

"Danny, you should take a bath, you'll feel better," Cassidy said in an overly sweet voice. She guided her friend to the restroom and locked the door from the inside before shutting it. "Some honey would probably make her feel better. There's some in the kitchen cupboard, but it's up too high for me to reach," Cassidy lied. "Would you be so kind, Donovan?" The second Donovan disappeared into the kitchen, she grabbed Aydan's wrist. Wrenching his arm behind his back, she nudged him on the back of his knees with her foot.

"Hey—" he started to say, but she clapped a hand over his mouth. Intertwining her fingers in Aydan's silky hair, she dragged him into Mr. Reyes' vacant bedroom and locked the door as Donovan rushed back from the kitchen empty handed. He started to pull and beat on the door. Afraid he would break it down; Cassidy released Aydan's hair, but held his wrist. "I've had enough! My friend is in pain for no obvious reason and you won't tell me anything about this or the journal. If you don't want to say anything in front of her then explain everything to me." She jumped when she noticed a razor blade in Aydan's hand.

"Donovan stop banging on the door. It's okay," Aydan tucked the blade back into his hairclip. "Sorry, I'm just under five feet tall, do late night shows, and walk home in the dark a lot. That was just reflex."

"I overreacted too. I shouldn't have handled you so roughly." Guilt bore down on Cassidy. "I can't believe myself—flipping out. I swear I'm not usually like that. I just felt so helpless."

"You're forgiven. I would've done the same thing if Donovan became mysteriously ill." Aydan massaged his wrist. "So here's what I think is going on: she'll live, but her martial arts career may be over. Some of us seem to be more susceptible to a chronic malady that makes us hypersensitive to pain. The onset occurs when our bodies are weakened for some reason, usually a virus. Now put me down." He sat on the plush duvet covering the bed.

"Are you affected?"

"Yeah, Eadowen and me. Donovan washes his hands excessively because he's afraid of a virus weakening his body. Sometimes I wonder if the real key to our longevity is having a minor chronic illness," Aydan added sarcastically.

"So, what I did really hurt you?" When she stooped to touch his shoulder, she saw red marks on his wrist where her fingers had been. He winced at the contact. "I am *so* sorry. Can I get you anything?"

"No, I'll recover." He patted her hand reassuringly.

"Wait, you're hypersensitive to pain and you play with whips and knives." She helped him to his feet. "Are you insane?"

"We're all mad here." He grimaced with an icy Cheshire-cat smile. Holding the door for him, she followed Aydan into the living room. Forcefully, Donovan shoved the jar of honey he'd since located into Cassidy's arms.

"I feel bad that you're all so worried," Danny dragged herself from the restroom to the sofa. "It comes in pulses. I'm okay at the moment."

"Of course I was worried. You're like a sister to me."

"You're like a sister to me too." Danny lightly squeezed Cassidy's shoulders the way she'd seen the rejected romantic interest do in movies. She secretly congratulated herself at executing such a difficult social maneuver. "So, the opioid receptors in my brain have been affected somehow?" Danny asked.

"I don't know much about brain chemistry, sorry. Eadowen takes cold baths when xie hurts," Aydan suggested. "Did anything happen to weaken your body?"

"My period started a couple days ago. My whole body felt like the nutrients had been drained out of me," Danny explained.

"I'm so sorry to hear that. I wish there was something I could do," he said. "Have you gotten rid of Eadowen's letter?" She pulled the folded letter out of her pocket. Aydan took the paper, it burst into flame, and he calmly let it disintegrate in the air.

"Why'd you do that?" Danny cried.

"He didn't want me to read it," Cassidy replied.

"It smelled like Eadowen and made me feel good."

"I'll get you some of hir perfume," Aydan offered.

"I want hir flesh too," Danny mumbled.

"She thinks it smells better mixed with his natural scent," Cassidy clarified after an uncomfortable glance from Aydan. "I brought you an early birthday present. I hope you feel well enough to try it on." She gave Danny the box.

Danny slipped the shirt Cassidy had given her over her head. Snapping the choker collar, she pulled her other shirt out from underneath it.

"I know you really wanted one of those Strap-Shirts. This was the closest I could find in an extra small. I hope you like it."

In front of the mirror in the restroom, Danny twisted and stretched, the heavy black fabric moved with her. The front of the shirt was comprised of a solid material starting from the collar and culminating in a V-shape at her waist. Straps formed two x's across the open back to hold the front in place. She admired her back in the mirror. "Thanks Cassidy. I love it. Speaking of clothing, Donovan looks really uncomfortable." Danny pointed to Donovan, who squirmed in his jeans, while he tried to watch a soccer game on his Ogham.

"Stag didn't want Donovan walking around in the rags he usually wears," Aydan explained.

"Who's Stag?" Cassidy asked.

"He was the guy with the purple hair and the chinchilla at Dalhousie," Danny reminded her.

"Right. I remember him." Cassidy had a new idea to convince Aydan she was trustworthy. "Stag is a non-GF, who seemed to know about you all," she said slyly. "Who is he?"

Aydan narrowed his eyes to indicate he knew exactly what she was scheming. "You're not like Stag. The reason he knows about us is because he helped Donovan out in a big way."

Groaning, Danny lay back down on the couch next to Donovan.

"How did he help?"

"Some guy on Donovan's lacrosse team got jealous of him and spread such a nasty rumor nobody would room with him during away games. Stag saw what had happened and decided to be Donovan's roommate. He joined the cheer squad just to dispel some rumors and give Donovan a roommate."

"Oh," Cassidy said. *Geez, these people have high standards of loyalty.* "So, you need to know how I operate. Fine." She unlocked her journal and shoved it into his hands.

Aydan tried to give the book back to her. "This is personal, I understand."

"It is. It's horribly embarrassing. I sound like a pathetic, swooning teen, but it's all real. You don't trust me. Well, here are my feelings for Danny and Taban." She pressed it to his chest. "Everything."

"I want Cassidy to come," Danny said. "I trust her."

Aydan flipped through the journal: without commentary, to Cassidy's relief. "Would you throw Taban against a wall like you did to me, if he threatened Danny?" He asked.

Cassidy nodded apprehensively.

Desperately, Aydan turned to Donovan who gave him a blank look. At that moment, Donovan's Ogham beeped to indicate it was low on power. Fumbling around in her bag, Cassidy found her Ogham charger and tossed it to him. He tipped his head in approval of Cassidy. Aydan shot his brother a disapproving "you-traitor" look. With a defeated sigh, Aydan revealed the contents of Eadowen's letter and the location of the international studies program run by Marja. "We hid the daughter's addition to the journal, which documented where the journal was left in Scotland."

Cassidy selected from her accepted programs the closest one to where Danny would be.

"Shouldn't you tell your mothers what you're doing?" Aydan said sarcastically.

"Sure." Cassidy smirked. "Sunset accept: Message to Moms: I'm going to be gallivanting around with Danny and her fairy relatives during my exchange in Scotland."

"Message from Rona-Mom: That sounds like a very fun program. I'm delighted to hear that Danny's going too."

"Do you need a place to stay?" Danny asked the brothers.

"No. Thank you." Aydan tapped Donovan on the shoulder and they headed toward the front door. "I suppose we'll be seeing you soon."

After the Tolymies departed, Cassidy joined Danny on the sofa. "I'll protect you," she said.

"I'd rather you didn't, so much."

"What? But you're …"

"I don't like feeling helpless either," Danny explained. "And if I can't do my martial art, I've lost the one thing that made me feel powerful."

"You remember when I said I was jealous of you."

"Yeah."

"Well, I'm sorry I ever thought that. You're not helpless, but you have a burden to bear. How about I say, 'I'll support you'?" Cassidy put her arm around Danny.

"How about 'we'll support each other'?" Danny suggested.

"Done."

They clasped hands in a triumphant grip to seal the promise.

Chapter 18
Breaking and Entering in Scotland

THE FLIGHT FROM SEATTLE TO SCOTLAND left Cassidy's legs so stiff she wondered if she'd ever be able to touch her toes again. From Cassidy's second-story hotel room, Loch Ard Forest looked like a curtain of grey: no horizon, no land, and no sky. Opening the window, Cassidy could taste the thick fog as she attempted to convince her body that it was indeed early morning in Scotland, not night as it seemed. In order to arrive at the same time as Danny and the Tolymie brothers, she'd flown to the UK a week before her exchange program began. With money she'd saved from working as a barista on school breaks, she had reserved a room for a couple nights at a hotel no more than three kilometers from the exchange program's youth hostel, which Marja ran. Danny would stay at the hostel south of Ward Wood, while she stayed north of Shadon Wood and east of Muir Park Reservoir. Cassidy hoped she could negotiate with Marja for a place at the hostel instead of paying for the hotel until she had to go to the University of Edinburgh for her exchange program. *I like being on the edge of a National Park,* Cassidy thought. *It feels like I'm surrounded by wilderness, a bit like home.*

"Message from Danny: We'll meet you at your hotel in a few minutes."

In the hotel lobby, Cassidy entertained herself in the same fashion she had while awake on her red-eye flight: Videos of Harlan Eldin performances. For the eleventh time she replayed a clip of him prancing about in a peacock-feathered suit. He linked gigantic silver rings as he cast flirtatious glances at the audience.

"Hi, Cassidy." Danny poked her head into Cassidy's field of vision. "I'm wearing the top you gave me."

"Looks great. Where're we off to?" Cassidy hastily slipped her tablet into her pocket.

"Two stops today: University of Glasgow and part of the Antonine Wall," a plain looking teenager in a pink newsboy hat and loose T-shirt informed her. Cassidy looked twice before she recognized Aydan without makeup by the long black braid sticking out of the cap. "Don't really want to draw attention to myself," he explained. "That's why I left Donovan at the hotel. Have you seen any alerts from May Savali?"

"No, she's really private. Probably because she doesn't want anyone stealing her research," Cassidy replied. "I've subscribed to all the researchers with whom she seems to be affiliated. One of them named, Gregory Andrews, insinuated that she'd be meeting with him at the University of Glasgow soon. Apparently, you already knew that."

"No, I didn't." Aydan blanched. "Come on, let's go."

"Is Eadowen joining us?" Danny asked.

"No, Eadowen is busy sorting out our estate and keeping us off the map back home."

A half-hour walk took them to a bus station. They transferred buses a few minutes later and settled into their seats for the forty-five-minute commute. During the ride Aydan quietly explained that the daughter had indicated her ancestor left the tablets along the Antonine Wall. "The geographic landmarks she describe suggest he buried them somewhere just outside of Glasgow as some sort of tribute to the GF he loved. I doubt we'll find anything there, but it's one piece of evidence we have that no one else does."

Cassidy read a couple passages on her Ogham to familiarize herself with the historic site. **The Antonine Wall was a Roman military structure maintained for only about two decades.** She tugged on one of the gold earrings Taban had bought her. He always asked about the jewelry, so she felt guilty not wearing them; but due to recent developments, she felt just as uncomfortable when she did. Realizing she'd lost track of the conversation between Aydan and Danny, Cassidy tuned in.

"There're a lot of videos of you on there." Danny said as she peeked over Aydan's shoulder at Cassidy's tablet which he held.

"Give it back you little klepto!" Cassidy felt in her pocket. *I can't call him on it,* she thought, *browsing another person's virtual video and literature library is equivalent to perusing a physical shelf.*

"Well, at least you haven't read all the fan fictions about Harlan Eldin. One day Taban picked me up from a magic show and my fans had a field day."

"Oh, that's who the blond guy was," Cassidy grinned sheepishly. "Anyway, the Antonine Wall is a historic site." She changed the subject abruptly before Aydan could comment. "It's not like we can dig anything up. Besides, it's also been two-thousand years. The landscape has changed. Have you looked up a comprehensive list of all the items that have been excavated from the Wall?"

"Yes, which is the reason I decided we should go to the University of Glasgow first. A piece of a stone tablet was found about three weeks ago near the Wall. It's being studied at the university."

So, we're going to take it? Cassidy scribbled on a page of her journal. *There're probably security cameras everywhere.*

Squinting at her scrawled letters, Aydan shook his head. *If it looks like it's part of the journal we'll probably have to accidently destroy it.* He looked pained as he wrote. Cassidy decided she didn't like the idea of destroying a piece of history either.

They switched to a train which stopped close to the university. The elegant old buildings made Cassidy curse the fact that she came from the New World.

A delectable blend of regional Scottish accents sprinkled with other nationalities delighted Danny's ears. She passed a member of the janitorial staff whose voice had a particularly deep intonation.

When Aydan brushed against the same staff person, the glint of the janitorial keys, caught Cassidy's eye as she watched him drop them into his pocket.

"Do you know where they're keeping the piece?" Danny asked.

"No, but Gregory Andrews' office seems like a good place to start," Aydan replied. "Geez, this campus is huge."

The trio followed a digital tour of the school to Andrews' office. Unlike many of the North American universities, this university hadn't moved to the electronic locking systems on interior doors.

"His office is locked." Cassidy touched the keyhole with great interest. "If we break in we'll get caught on camera."

"Excuse me sir," Danny asked a faculty member who walked by. She affected a mixed accent like Eadowen's, so she could better pass as a student. "Do you know where Gregory Andrews is?"

"Ee'z uh meetin' with May Savali," he replied.

"I have a professor appreciation card to dropoff," Danny replied. "Could you tell me where to find him?"

The man appeared to give her detailed directions to find Andrews, but his fast Scottish made her wonder how they both spoke the same language.

"What?"

"Where're you from?" he said more slowly.

"Uh, never mind. I understood," Danny said, not wanting to blow her cover. "Thanks." She rejoined Cassidy and Aydan, who had made themselves scarce during the exchange. "See, I don't always need your help, Cassidy. Though I'm not sure what he said."

"Unfortunately, I can't help you with that," Cassidy replied.

Aydan translated the detailed directions with ease. "So, it sounds like they're meeting in a research lab," he said. Cassidy gave him a skeptical, but impressed look. He winked at her and led the way across the elegant campus.

Kicking a pebble in the courtyard, Danny decided she supported Cassidy and Aydan's flirtation. Regardless, it still hurt like a monster clawing at her insides. She comforted herself with the slightly sinister thought of, *well, if I help Aydan and Cassidy, no more Cassidy likes Taban.* As she contemplated her friends, they looked back at her, she grinned innocently.

"You look as cheeky as Puck from Midsummer Night's Dream," Aydan chuckled nervously. He held the door for his friends. They entered into a quiet corridor.

"Hm, it looks like most people are at lunch," Cassidy observed. "What's wrong?"

"I feel like we're being watched." Aydan glanced around and Cassidy dodged a lash from his braid. "I keep hearing footsteps that stop when we stop."

Holding up his hand to silence them, Danny jabbed her finger toward a door. "There they are." Listening closely, Danny identified both Savali's and Andrews' voices.

"The radio carbon dating shows that this piece is from the time period you mentioned," Andrews' said from behind the heavy door.

"Would it be possible to expand the excavation near the site where this was located?" Savali asked.

"Let's discuss that over lunch with some of the members of the dig."

"That would be great I'm starved." The sounds of shuffling and chair squeaking followed.

Pre-emptively, Danny backed around a corner to hide. In case Cassidy hadn't interpreted the entire conversation, Aydan wrapped his arm around her waist and pulled her into a lab across the hall. Savali and Andrews walked into the hallway just as Cassidy and Aydan crouched behind the door. The latch to lock the door clicked. Ducking her head so her long hair fell in her face, Danny pretended again to be a student minding her own business. She bumped her elbow on the wall and felt a pulse of pain as though she'd broken it. Savali rushed to her when she heard the scream Danny was unable to suppress.

"Hon, are you okay?" Savali said.

Danny nodded.

"You look familiar ... were you at one of my lectures?"

"What lectures?" Danny affected a Scottish accent covering her Canadian as much as possible. "I'm okay."

Reluctantly, Savali left Danny alone and walked down the hallway with Andrews.

"They seem like nice people," Danny remarked when she and her friends reconvened.

"Yeah," Aydan agreed. "They probably weren't involved directly in my mother's murder, but Eadowen suspects whoever is funding their research."

"Savali and Andrews seem interested in making the world a better place with their discoveries," Danny said. "It seems like we should be going after whoever is funding this project, not destroying the middleman."

"I'm open to better ideas," Aydan replied.

"I don't like doing this either, but they can move on to other research projects. It's not like we're destroying their livelihood. We're just inconveniencing them." Cassidy wiggled the door handle. "Give keys," she said, tugging on Aydan's braid like a bell rope. "We can pass this off as one of the janitors gave us keys to use the lab."

"How'd you know Aydan had the keys?" Danny asked.

"I've had plenty of experience with his abilities," Cassidy grumbled.

With a frown of disappointment, Aydan dropped the keys into her hand and they slipped into the room. Glass cabinets displayed artifacts from around the Celtic world. While Aydan and Danny searched methodically for the labeled piece, Cassidy used a light on her Ogham to search the cabinet frames. She located a handprint on the light layer of dust.

"Is this it?" Cassidy indicated a flat, fist-sized stone with Latin inscribed in it.

"That's definitely what they were looking at." Aydan checked the label then carefully inspected it through the glass. "Bad news. It's not what we're looking for."

"What?" Danny asked.

"The date's wrong and it's not a journal; it's a battle plan," Aydan replied. "I can't bring myself to destroy it on the off-chance that it is something related to us."

"That's not a risk we need to take. I rewatched Savali's lecture on my Ogham," Cassidy said. "Savali found documentation of the journal at the University of Aberdeen. Maybe we'll find something there."

"Be quiet," Danny hissed. Everyone froze. A few seconds later a young woman entered the room the hem of her long dress swaying around her ankles. Fluffing her cropped orange hair, she inspected Danny with interested eyes.

"Do you need one of those cabinets opened?" she asked sweetly in a subtle Irish accent. "I'm an aid for the archeology department, so I have the electronic code."

"Uh, no. We just ..." Danny trailed off.

"What're you looking for?"

"Nothing."

"Don't worry." The young woman put a finger to her coy smile. "I won't tell. What's your name?"

"Ed." Danny gave her rarely used alternative nickname. "We have to get going, sorry."

"You can call me Chay," she giggled for no apparent reason. "I have a book I think you'd like, but it's back at the library. If you don't come with me, I'll tell them that you stole the janitor's keys."

Captured by their new acquaintance, they followed her toward the library. Chay stopped them at security and allowed them to say they'd found the janitor's keys on the floor. The library towered over many of the other buildings on campus. Its modern architecture contrasted with some of the more classic buildings. Chay's golden slippers padded across the polished wood floor.

"Here you go." She handed Danny a paperback from a shelf labeled young adult. "Don't worry about getting it back. I'll make sure the library gets a new one. It was nice to meet you Edana and friends." She disappeared behind another bookshelf.

"You too," Danny called.

"That was weird," Cassidy said.

"Oh, I don't think her checking out Danny was at all odd," Aydan replied. "If we're lucky she was just being nice to us because she thought you were hot," he said to Danny.

"Have you mistaken Danny for Taban?" Cassidy asked. "Though, I guess she did give Danny a once over … a few times." She intentionally flattered her friend, who seemed like she needed a pick-me-up. "You're a fine lady, maybe we did get lucky."

"You've both got to be kidding. Besides, I think I'd rather be a guy than a lady."

"Do you want us to start using different gender pronouns for you?" Cassidy suggested.

"Not yet. I really haven't figured myself out." Danny inspected the small paperback as they headed back to the train station. The book's cover looked like a night sky, with constellations Danny didn't recognize, traced into the stars. When she turned it over, the cover design continued onto the back with no words. She found the name of the book on the title page, *The Moon Princess Was Wiser,* by Eamon Baird.

"So the Chay-girl was Irish?" Cassidy asked.

"Yeah," Aydan confirmed.

"I feel so guilty not being able to tell the difference between Scottish and Irish," Cassidy sighed. "I'm such an ignorant American, but I'm trying."

"Well, if anyone refers to us as 'Americans', I promise to throw a fit about being associated with United States-ians," Aydan offered. "Donovan'll meet us at the Antonine Wall soon."

Laying the book in her lap, Danny flipped through pictures of Tossachs National Park on her glasses. "The lakes are beautiful here."

"Did you know that the myths about lake monsters, like Loch Ness, originated because people would get caught in the kelp and drown?" Aydan inquired. "Sorry, guess I'm a bit frustrated. We're not going to find anything at the Wall, but I don't know what else to do. We'll have to wait until tomorrow to head to the University of Aberdeen."

Fifteen minutes later, they stepped off the train and onto a field covered with white and violet wildflowers.

"Where's the wall?" Danny asked.

"That's it." Cassidy indicated a mound covered by verdant grass.

"Like I said, I don't think there's much we can do here, but here's some sandwiches." Aydan handed Cassidy a ham and cheese sandwich.

"I like getting close to the ancient world." Danny spun to get a full view of her surroundings.

"I agree, I don't think trying to get into the soldier's head is a bad idea." Cassidy took a bite of the sandwich Aydan had prepared, and nodded her approval. "What was the guy's name? The guy who wrote the journal?"

"Endymion," Aydan replied as Donovan approached.

"Endymion, as in the lover of Selene?" Cassidy asked. "I know it was a Greek myth, did the Romans use it too?" She referenced her Ogham. "Yes, they did."

"Find anything of interest bro?" Aydan asked.

Shaking his head, Donovan showed his brother hundreds of photographs he'd taken on his tablet. Most were photographs of the dig, to which Savali and Andrews had referred, but some were artistic shots.

"It doesn't look like anyone was there. Did anyone see you?"

"No."

"Those are really nice photographs," Danny commented, making Donovan's cheeks flush. "Why don't you get some framed for your house?"

Cassidy's Ogham, which she had turned to silent during their university escapades, lit to inform her of a new message. "Five new messages from Taban," it said.

"My, he sure contacted you a lot," Aydan commented dryly.

"I swear I haven't told him anything, but I didn't think it would be a good idea to sever all contact."

"What is it about that guy?" Aydan ripped into his sandwich with his teeth. "Even *I* can't stop thinking about him. As soon as he started living with us, it was Taban this and Taban that."

"I don't know. There's just something about him that ... just sucks you in. No, that's stupid. Let me see what did I say about him ..." Cassidy turned to a particularly lusty page in her journal. In her head all the things she thought about Taban were dreamy, until she saw them on paper and realized how weird she sounded.

"You look like you took field notes?" Aydan chuckled.

"Yes. You read it."

"Isn't this the same as the tattoo Taban has?" Danny pointed to the cover of her book at one of the constellations. "It kind of looks like a giant squid. Hey, just pretend Taban's a huge tentacle monster. That should make him less appealing."

Covering his mouth, Aydan doubled over.

"What's so funny?" Danny demanded.

"Aydan, would you like to explain to Danny why that's so funny?" Cassidy asked glaring daggers at Aydan to show him she knew exactly what he was imagining.

Gagging on his sandwich, Aydan waved his hand to show he intended to collect himself.

"Hey Donovan, how did you deal with being around Taban?" Danny asked.

"No blonds."

"Well, there you have it," Aydan replied. "Donovan just assumes all blond guys are evil, even though he's a dirty blond and Taban's a brunette."

"Danny, pretend you're Taban. I need to make sure I can keep my head, since I'm going to have to respond to these messages."

She and Danny attempted to role-play a flirtatious conversation. Cassidy practiced analyzing her whirlwind romance with Taban as she fed lines to Danny. Just as Danny leaned in to try another Taban-esque phrase, Cassidy noticed Aydan watching them intently, as he chewed on the knuckle of his index finger.

"Oh, you want to see some girl *and* girl action?" Cassidy said, tapping Danny on the shoulder. Rolling up her sleeves, Cassidy approached him. Aydan, who hadn't missed the conjunction Cassidy used, dashed off. They playfully chased him around the field.

"Help!" Aydan called to his brother.

Donovan took the opportunity to take a seat and turn up the volume on his tablet. Laughing, Cassidy turned Aydan's hat backward and Danny spun him around.

"You read slash fiction about me," Aydan accused.

"That's right, you still have to show me that," Danny said.

"You'll love it," Cassidy replied. "In all seriousness Danny, how are you feeling about us?"

Danny sighed. "I still like you, but I'm just glad you're honest. I'm trying to see you as a best friend, and a sort of adopted sister."

"Anyone who's your friend is lucky to have you, Danny. I'm honored." She embraced her.

"Ow. Watch the elbow." Danny rubbed the place she'd bumped.

"Sorry."

"It's fine. The endorphins from the jogging actually decreased the pain." Danny gave her friend a good squeeze. Then they both turned and glared at Aydan, who threw up his hands innocently.

"Right now, I'm admiring the respect and trust in your beautiful friendship," he said. "You wanna chase me for that?"

On the bus back to Cassidy's hotel, Danny perused the book Chay had given her, while Cassidy and Aydan looked up recent research at the University of Aberdeen—their planned stop for the next day.

* * *

"Are you all set for the night?" Aydan asked in the hotel lobby.

"Yes, I'm sure I'll be fine," Cassidy replied. "I need to sleep off the jet-lag. Take care."

"Message Rona-Mom: Today I visited the University of Glasgow. Then I frolicked in front of the Antonine Wall with some fairies."

Taking the ten of diamonds out of her bag, she watched the silver light play across the card. She meditated about life as a Roman officer. What was it like to meet the fantastic GF and where had the journal gone? The earrings Taban had given her clanked against her neck as she threw her Ogham on the bedside table. She drifted off to sleep.

A sharp tap at her window abruptly awoke Cassidy with a start. Instinctively, she touched her Ogham to turn it to 'awake mode.' Rubbing her eyes, she saw a shadowy silhouette through the misty glass. She promptly squeezed her eyes shut, but when she looked again the outline was still there. The figure rattled her window, causing the old latch to slip out of place. Frightened, she grabbed the lamp off of the bedside table and held it in front of her. She looked down at the lamp, set it on the floor, and assumed a fighting stance.

CHAPTER 19
SWEET TENTACLES

I HAVE TWO OPTIONS, she thought. *I can try to push whoever it is out the window, or I can use one of the defensive maneuvers I know and pull them in. I wish I was as good at martial arts as Danny. I'm just an amateur and I haven't done Aikido in ages. Okay, calm down.*

The figure opened the window with a creak. Cassidy darted forward. Using knees and fists, she struggled in the darkness in an attempt to push the stranger out of her room.

"Cassidy, it's me," Taban said in her ear.

Surprised at hearing his voice, Cassidy fumbled. He pressed against her to get into the room, and instinctively she used his momentum to propel him to the floor by twisting his wrist. He tumbled to the floor, crashing into the lamp Cassidy had originally intended to use for a weapon.

"I'm not here to hurt you," he cried, guarding his face with a pitiful expression.

A cloud gave way to bright moonlight, and she was forced to look into his wide blue eyes. Shivering in her camisole, Cassidy allowed him to stand. He shut the window, leaving a trail of muddy shoe prints.

"Are you cold?" He pulled her into his warm embrace. The insecurities he'd highlighted during their night under the moon, flooded into her mind. Somehow a thought that she was lucky to have his attention, because she wasn't worthy or special slithered into her mind. She visualized a page of her journal and imagined that she wrote the toxic feeling down to figuratively read it.

"What are you doing here?" She pushed away from him. To her surprise, he let her go without hesitation. This was unfortunate because it gave her no immediate reason to fight.

"I had to see you."

"Why? You …," she started to say. *What did he do … ugh … there is no blood fueling my brain,* Cassidy thought. "You betrayed their trust." She avoided his eyes, though she knew that was the worst way to assert power.

"Yes, I stole it, but I did it to protect them." He reached out and caressed her shoulder.

"How?" She attempted to pull away, but his gentle grasp was like the soft kelp that could catch a person and slowly drown her.

"I destroyed it," he whispered, drawing closer. "Cassidy, darling, I love you. Can't you see it? I'd never do anything to hurt you."

She made the mistake of looking at his face. If ever someone had regarded her with tenderness and passionate love, he did.

"How can he love me after such a short time?" she quoted a line from her journal verbatim because her soul believed his words.

"Your spirit. Your beauty. You've changed me for the better, just by being the wonderful person that you are." He held her chin, so she would continue to look into his eyes. "Why else would I climb through a second-story window?"

The situation was not so different from a wave rolling her over in her surf kayak. Her body always surrendered itself to the plunge, while her guts tried to stay above the surface. She loved the acceleration of being pulled beneath the surf, but she always had ways to escape: a paddle or the release on her kayak.

"I want to give you everything." His soft lips pressed against hers. She tasted bitter salt. "We can live together. You can go to the best law school. I'll pay for it. I'll buy you a nice car. And I'll always be there to hold you. Anything … Everything you want."

"Friends. My friends," she said meekly, as she attempted to bring Danny, Aydan, and Donovan's faces into focus.

"Yes," he replied fervently. "They'll be fine too. Let's work together and everything will be perfect."

"I don't understand."

"Tell me where the other journal is. Then we'll get rid of it and everyone will be safe."

"I don't know where it is," she said glad to have an easy answer.

"Of course you do. Or at least you know something I don't know. You went to the University of Glasgow."

Did I tell him I went to the university. I don't remember, she wondered frantically. *I always reveal things I don't mean to with him.* When strapped upside-down to the kayak there was no time to think about moral decisions. An instinct of self-preservation dominated her mind. As she suffocated in his deep kiss, Cassidy had the same thought: air. With the core energy she'd used to right herself she pushed away from him. "I need to use the restroom." Before he could respond she ran past her room's bathroom. Realizing the mistake she'd made in her lie she added. "I mean the one in the lobby. That one's broken."

If she stayed with him a moment longer, he'd wrap her in his sweet tentacles and drown her in his psychological warfare, of that she was certain.

She dashed down the hallway of the hotel in her pajamas, with no plan of action. Contemplating how he'd know where to find her, she felt Aydan's card in her breast pocket. It was strange to be attached to an object just because it shined like jewels. *Jewelry!* She thought. *I'm such a fool. The jewelry he gave me probably had tracking chips in them. No wonder he gave me so much, so I'd always be wearing it.* She looked over her shoulder and saw him in hot pursuit.

"Come back. I don't mean you any harm," he called in his mellifluous voice.

Desperately, she tried to formulate a plan. As she rushed down the stairs, questions buzzed through her head: What would happen to her if he caught her? What would she do if she caught him? In the back of her mind another thought refused to be silent, Was he telling the truth? With her current knowledge, she realized she couldn't justly categorize Taban as evil or even of malicious intention, but she had confirmed him to be untrustworthy. Then again, how reliable were the Tolymies? *I blindly did as they asked because I wanted to protect Danny. But if I don't make a choice soon, I could compromise everything.* In her hurry to escape, she hadn't thought to grab anything she could improvise as rope to tie him up. She attempted ripping part of her sleeve to roll into a rope, but the fabric was too thick and she had nothing sharp to cut it. There was also the matter of getting him in a position where she could bind him. In order to incapacitate him, she feared she'd have to break his leg or give him brain damage with blunt trauma. She stashed the option away as a last resort, unsure that she knew the right techniques to break bones. Next she considered reporting him to a hotel staff member. Even though he had broken into her room she quickly assessed that she had a much higher chance of beating him in a physical confrontation than in a situation where he could easily out charm her. She put her hand to Aydan's card in her front pocket. *If I have to face the Tolymies and Danny, then so does he,* Cassidy decided, dashing out the hotel's backdoor into the pale moonlit night. To slow Taban, who had gained to only an arm length behind her, she slammed the heavy door into him. The handle collided with his abdomen, stalling him long enough for her to get a slight head start. The cold bit her skin. Even in summer the nights could be cold, and this was a particularly frigid night for June. She'd decided to lead him to the hostel where Danny and the Tolymie brothers stayed a few kilometers north. Cassidy touched her arm, where her Ogham should have been and realized in horror that she'd left it in her room. The rough ground chafed her feet as she ran into Loch Ard Forest. Neither elf, dryad, nor woodland spirit, she raced barefoot through a dense forest in the dark of night. Grabbing the branch of a spruce tree, she let it fly backward into Taban's face. She ducked under low-hanging branches, stumbling as she went. Based on the unsteady thudding behind her, the large roots and uneven ground were just as treacherous for her pursuer. Taking advantage of a tiny clearing among the coniferous trees, she located the cup of the big dipper and traced the stars to Polaris. Huffing, she started to feel tightness in her lungs. She'd never been a runner, as the sharp pain in her side reminded her. Her breasts ached without the aid of a sports bra. The cold night air constricted her throat and her feet throbbed. In the moonlight, she saw the blood on her slashed-up toes. How she envied Taban's shoes, which being tennis shoes instead of platforms, improved his coordination impressively. His fingertips brushed her hand. She dodged, but he managed to grab her forearm.

"Please, I just want to talk," he begged.

Twisting out of his grasp, she flung a particularly spiky pine branch in his face, and threw herself ahead of him. He fell, still calling to her. She fled. *It would be too easy for him to talk me into anything,* she thought as tears streamed down her face. *I hate that I have such powerful feelings for him.* The numbness in her body couldn't conceal the place where his nails had cut into her wrist. For another half kilometer she managed to elude him, by viciously throwing rocks and branches. The hot tears burned her cheeks. She tried to stifle them, so as not to blur her vision, but with all the other components she was fighting, they continued to fall. A sharp branch cut into her arm. The woods opened up to a large clear-cut field. Without shelter, she quickened her pace across the clearing. Slamming her foot against a hidden rock, she screamed and stumbled, but managed to continue running. Unfortunately, her momentary lapse coupled with her lack of tree branch ammo, allowed Taban to gain on her. Cassidy readied herself for the gruesome confrontation. He caught hold of her arm and twisted it behind her back. As she threw a hard kick aimed backward to his shin, she felt a pin prick in her neck. She whirled around with a hard round-house kick, but he'd retreated with a jump. Planting her bloody feet, she faced him. He held his battered shin with one hand and clutched a syringe in the other.

* * *

"Cassidy is not answering her Ogham right now. Would you like to leave a message?" Danny listened to Cassidy's awake mode for the first time. Danny's circadian rhythm hadn't shifted with the time zones, so she was wide awake at one-thirty in the morning. She'd decided to call Cassidy to see if her friend was in the same predicament, but had received only sleep mode replies until her most recent Ogham message to which she received an auto-awake mode response. *Come on Cassidy, if you're awake you'd answer,* Danny thought. *She never leaves her Ogham on by accident.*

Danny ran downstairs to Aydan and Donovan's room and banged loudly on the door. After a couple minutes of waiting, the door opened and a boxer-clad Donovan glared at her.

"Where's Aydan?"

"Showers," Donovan growled and moved like he was going to shut the door. Apparently, she wasn't the only one to enjoy the perks of international travel. Behind Donovan, Danny noticed Aydan's whip with several ripped up cards around it. She slipped around Donovan and grabbed the whip. "Why?"

"I'm worried about Cassidy."

Donovan looked her up and down coldly, then gestured to himself. "Need me?"

She shook her head.

"I'm coming," he grumbled. After he'd thrown on a crumpled shirt and sweats, they went to the communal restroom.

"Aydan!" Danny shouted to the shower stalls. "Are you in there?"

Pulling a towel around his waist, Aydan yanked open one of the curtains. His expression rivaled the annoyance his brother had shown. "What's your problem?"

"Is Cassidy with you?" Danny asked before thinking through her question.

"Why would Cassidy be in the shower with me?" Aydan replied. Danny opened her mouth to say something unrelated to his question, but promptly forgot it when he added, "Don't answer that. What's going on?"

"Cassidy isn't answering her Ogham and it's not on sleep mode."

"So she forgot to turn it on sleep mode," Aydan rolled his eyes. "Eadowen warned me not to bathe around people who have no concept of personal space," he muttered.

"Cassidy never forgets."

Giving her an incredulous look, he tightened the towel around his waist. "Are you sure?"

"Yes. She's very exact about these types of things."

"What did you want to do?" Aydan pawed at the suds in his hair, like a kitten who hated being wet.

"I want to go to the hotel and check on her. Please," Danny begged. She handed Aydan his whip.

"Pants would've been preferable," He squeezed the water out of his hair on the shower curtain and strode out of the restroom.

"Where are you going?" she asked.

"I'm procuring you a vehicle," Aydan replied. "Coming Donovan?"

His brother stepped forward affirmatively. He and Danny followed Aydan to Marja's office where the young woman worked the night shift.

"Thank you so much, Marja."

"Okay, I'm really bending some rules by letting you do this, so be back soon," Marja said. "And contact me if there's any trouble."

Dictating Cassidy's hotel address to Marja's car, Danny settled into the driver's seat of Marja's electric-solar sedan. Donovan spread out in the back. "How come she's so nice to us?" she wondered aloud.

"Eadowen has a way with people." As Aydan buckled his seat belt in the passenger seat, his arm and core flexed accentuating a figure that a gymnast would envy.

"You have a great body. May I touch?" Danny asked steering the car onto the narrow street.

"Eyes on the road," Aydan replied. "I stayed naked so Marja would see how urgently we wanted to see our friend. Besides, I didn't think you'd let me take the time go back to my room to get my clothes anyway."

"That's probably true."

"I've worn less than a towel on stage." He shrugged.

* * *

"I'm sorry, Cassidy." Taban gripped the empty syringe.

"What'd you do to me?" She threw a baseball-sized rock at him because she didn't dare try to disarm him until she knew what he had injected her with. Her hands started to tremble involuntarily and her limbs felt numb. "I could've beaten you in a fair fight."

"I know." He advanced on her as a chemically induced weakness spread through her body. She punched at him, but he blocked it easily and grabbed both of her arms. Fighting a haze more sickly than the lust she usually felt in his presence, she bit his arm in defense. He yelped and bent her arms behind her back. Struggling against him with her increasingly uncooperative body, she kicked. He took advantage of the split second when she only had one leg to balance herself and forced her to the ground. Pinning her with his entire weight, he pushed the last quarter of the contents of the syringe into her arm. Several rocks in the damp grass embedded themselves in her back, but she continued to writhe underneath him.

"I've injected you with a neuro-inhibitor. It won't hurt you, only slow you down. I made it with consideration to your size and age. I promise," Taban said in a reassuring tone, as he held her wrists. "I need information. You don't know how far Savali and Crane have gotten. I need to eliminate any evidence of the journal as soon as possible. Just tell me what I want to know."

To show her refusal, Cassidy silently turned her head away from him. The wet grass padded her cheek. He suddenly shifted, releasing her left hand. The effort it took for her to bring her left arm up to block her face felt like she was pulling it out of molasses. She tensed, ready to receive a punch for not surrendering her knowledge about the journal. Instead, he slid his hand under her block and tenderly wiped away the tear trail on her exposed cheek. "You're like Telyn," he whispered to himself. The name she didn't recognize caught her attention. "Telyn?" she repeated. His eyes widened to express that he hadn't meant to say the name aloud. A gust of wind made her, now inactive, body shiver. Taban adjusted his weight to his arms. She tried to fight, but the drug had gone into its full effect. Appearing to determine she no longer posed a physical threat to him, Taban started to feel her body. "Are you injured?" he asked testing her legs and arms. "Yes," she said quietly. He located the deep gash on her arm and produced a medical bag from his coat pocket. Padding it with antiseptic from his medical bag, he tended to her injury. She shook in her cotton pajamas. Initially, he appeared confused by this response. Then he removed his heavy jacket, lifted her up, and wrapped her in it, before laying her back down on the grass. A part of Cassidy wished he would treat her worse, so she would have more reasons to hate him—she needed all she could get.

He took another syringe out of the small medical bag. "This is sodium thiopental." He held up the syringe. "I'm going to give you a very low dose. You'll pass out for a few minutes. All it's going to do is make it harder for you to lie to me." Her screams and feeble squirming didn't stop him from shoving the needle into her arm. Her world went black. When the stars in the moonlit sky came back into focus, she found herself still restrained by Taban.

"My goal has the same result as yours. What can I give or show to convince you?" he asked, his eyes bright and beautiful in the moonlight—not so different from the time they'd spent outside in May. Exhaustion swept through her body in the warmth of his coat. She let it consume her, so she wouldn't have to answer. He lightly slapped her cheek to keep her conscious. "In your condition, there are things I could easily do to you to force it out of you." He put his weight on her again as if to remind her of his strength. "But I'd rather not." Releasing her again, he rubbed her hands to keep them warm. She attempted to force herself into sleep. All she could think to do was stall until the drug he'd injected her with wore off. This time he hit her with his open hand. "The drug won't wear off for hours," he said. "I have all night with you." For the first time, there was a dark note in his sweet voice. "You don't have your Ogham. No one knows you're missing. And you're weakened ... there's nothing you can do." He removed the coat that was shielding her from the cold. Even as the rocks and cold cut her skin, she felt her eyelids grow heavy. What time had he broken into her room? Sometime between midnight and three in the morning, she guessed. Holding her nose he put his lips over hers to slip a bitter liquid into her mouth. In her somnorific state, she recognized the tangy flavor of a highly concentrated energy drink. If she wanted to breathe, she had to swallow. Choking, she pushed on his shoulders, but he used gravity to his full advantage. In a few minutes, she felt the pulse of caffeine in her heart. Keeping quiet was getting more difficult. Taban held up another syringe. "Apparently, the sodium thiopental dose I gave you was too small." A shout distracted them both. Taban clapped his hand over her mouth and pushed her harder into the ground. With Taban's dark coat, the grass, and the uneven terrain, Cassidy realized it would be difficult for someone to spot her. As Taban pressed into her, Aydan's card dug into her chest. She wiggled her head and showed Taban submissive eyes. He loosened his grip on her mouth.

"I'll tell you," she whispered through his fingers. "I want a kiss, first." She slipped the card out of her pocket, hiding it under her hand. Though he seemed skeptical, Taban did as she requested. She let her arms fall heavily on his back, because she didn't have the control to hold them up and he wouldn't notice she held the shimmering card in one hand. Pulling back from the lip lock, he saw the card before she could hide it. With silent rage, he struck her hard enough to make her see fireflies. *Kissing is supposed to distract people,* Cassidy thought, as blood rushed to the point of impact on her cheek. Heavy footsteps hurried toward them. Someone had seen her signal.

CHAPTER 20
BLOODY MOONLIGHT

DANNY, DONOVAN, AND AYDAN rushed toward the old hotel on the edge of the Loch Ard Forest. "Message Cassidy again," Aydan commanded.

"I did. She's still not responding."

"Okay, how do you want to get into the hotel to check on her?"

"Cassidy authorized me to visit her." Danny tapped her Ogham to show Cassidy's electronic signature.

"At this hour?" Aydan asked.

"Well, it's not like I look very threatening."

"True."

"Can you guys get in?" Danny asked.

"I think I can slip in while you're showing them the authorization," Aydan replied. In response to his brother's comment, Donovan lumbered back to the car.

Introducing herself at the front desk, Danny showed her electronic signature, while Aydan ducked in through the front doors. "I'm sorry we can't let you in at this hour," the tired clerk said. Danny nodded solemnly. Once outside she listened for any sign of Aydan. Her Ogham announced a message. She silenced it and read: *I'm inside, come around to the backdoor, I'll let you in.*

"This door was left ajar for some reason. We could've gotten in this way," Aydan pointed out as he held the door for her.

"Thanks. Do you think it'll be okay if we do this?"

"This hotel is ancient. None of the security cameras I checked are even up-to-date. If Cassidy's in her room, we'll just leave. If not. We may have bigger problems. Do you remember her room number?"

Danny led the way to Cassidy's second-story room. In brass numbers, 217, adorned the painted door. Pressing her ear to the narrow gap between the carpet and door, Danny remarked, "I don't hear anything." She tried messaging Cassidy. Her friend's Ogham responded, but she didn't hear Cassidy's breathing. "Unlock the door," she directed Aydan.

"This is an electronic lock. What do you think I am, some kind of Hollywood-Houdini magician? You and Cassidy just think I'm some kind of universal lock pick at your disposal."

Danny looked around for something she could use to break the lock. She spotted a vase of flowers on a table in the hallway, and approached it.

"What are you doing?" Aydan asked.

"I'm going to break the lock."

Sighing, he produced a metal hair accessory he'd clipped inside his towel. *He wears that hair thing with every outfit,* Danny realized. *He must keep it with him at all times—even the shower.* With a pin he removed from the fastener and a razor blade he separated from the decorative component, Aydan took off the face of the lock. He fiddled with the wiring until the light on the handle turned green and the door swung open.

"If anyone asks, I can't do that. Taban would always buy such expensive stuff that he didn't need. He could always buy more, but instead he kept buying fancier locks for his bedroom," Aydan explained.

The room was void of Cassidy, but populated by pieces of a broken lamp. Scouring the room, Aydan discovered Cassidy's Ogham on the night stand. Danny indicated the muddy foot prints on the floor, while he plucked a bleach-blond hair from the window ledge.

"He couldn't," Danny whispered in horror and disbelief. "This is the second story."

"According to Eadowen, second-story windows were Taban's specialty when they lived together in a dorm."

"Did you notice any mud by the backdoor? Cassidy would probably have trouble fighting Taban since she likes him so much. If her fight-flight response kicked in, she'd probably flee in this situation. What am I saying? I don't understand people." Danny's voice cracked in distress.

"You give yourself too little credit," Aydan replied, resting a comforting hand on her shoulder. "Where would she have gone?"

"I don't know."

"Think, Danny."

"If she didn't have her Ogham and she didn't contact the front desk for help ...," Danny said. "Toward us—she'd head toward the hostel."

"Makes sense to me."

"Really?"

"Well, you were right about this." Aydan gestured around the room. "I don't know how your mind works, but I'm inclined to trust it—in this situation at least."

"Aydan ... thank you."

In nonverbal acknowledgment, he gave her a quick hug. They snuck out of the hotel and returned to Marja's car to debrief Donovan.

"I messaged her about forty minutes ago and her Ogham was on sleep mode," Danny explained. "She may have made it close to the hostel by now."

"I'll take the car back to the hostel and head into the woods from that direction," Aydan instructed. "Try to find where she would've gone into the trees. We'll message each other if we find her. Oh, and take this." He tossed Danny his meter-and-half long whip, which he'd retrieved from the back seat. "Do you know how to use it?" She swung the lash around, enjoying a whooshing sound, but no crack. "You'll figure it out," Aydan assured her as he started the car.

"Which way?" Donovan asked her.

"Aren't you going with Aydan?"

"No."

From the back door of the hotel, Donovan and Danny followed freshly beaten-down grass into the forest. Navigating with her Ogham, they hurried through the dense woods. Knowing every scratch would burn horribly due to her new intolerance to pain, Danny stayed directly behind Donovan. Aware of this fact, he cleared their path broadly and used his Ogham to light the way, while Danny told him which direction to go. "If she didn't have her Ogham Cassidy would've used the stars,"

Danny shouted to Donovan. "According to my Ogham, our hostel is only slightly east of north. On this map it shows a large clear-cut area about two kilometers in. When we get there, we should look for any trails that might be hers."

Their teamwork allowed them to reach the nearly quarter-kilometer field in good time. They edged around the perimeter looking for any sign Cassidy may have left. Behind a small rise in the ground at the far end of the field, Danny heard what sounded like a muffled comment followed by rustling grass. She tugged on Donovan's shirt and gestured in the direction of the noise. He squinted into the distance. Then his eyes widened and he dashed toward it. Danny followed, but couldn't keep pace with his impressive sprint. She prepared her Ogham to message Aydan.

* * *

Her cheek still throbbing from his strike, Cassidy watched Taban glance around frantically to locate the intruder. A look of recognition crossed his face as he slipped a vial out of the bag that held the syringes. Uncapping the vial with his teeth, Taban let the clear liquid spill into his mouth and over his face. He smeared the oily substance over his arms, hands, and chest. With a much more assured expression, Taban held another syringe, and faced Donovan's charge.

Too discombobulated to stand, Cassidy grabbed Taban's ankle. "Look out! His hand!" she shouted, before Taban delivered a back kick to her gut.

Donovan took a moment to assess the situation, but once he saw Cassidy's state, he didn't hold back. Knocking the syringe out of Taban's hand, Donovan took a swing at him. His fist made contact with Taban's chest. He crumpled on impact. With Donovan's second punch, Taban fell backward to the ground, holding his core, as though paralyzed in pain. Weakened, Taban regarded Donovan with the same pathetic eyes he had used on Cassidy. Staring at Taban skeptically, Donovan touched his fist as though the impact didn't match the outcome.

While they fought, Cassidy attempted to stand with disappointing results. When she finally managed to get solid footing, the blow she'd received to her stomach relieved her of her dinner. Wiping off her mouth, she stumbled toward Taban. Donovan held up a warning hand to her. Just arriving, Danny also advanced on Taban, ignoring Donovan's direction. He scooped up Danny, put himself in between Cassidy and Taban, and set Danny down, such that he was guarding both of them. Cautiously, he approached Taban, who lay on the ground holding his ribs.

"I don't think I can stand," Taban coughed. His whole face warped by pain, Taban crawled away from Donovan.

"What's making his skin all shiny?" Danny asked, as she supported an unsteady Cassidy. "It looks like oil."

Stooping, Donovan grabbed Taban to stop him from moving. The moment Donovan touched him, Taban whirled around. Coiling his arms around Donovan's neck, which he used for support as he kneed him in the solar plexus, Taban clung to Donovan.

Danny's comment triggered Cassidy's memory of Taban's off-color joke a month earlier. "He's covered in peanut oil!" she shouted, her voice hoarse.

Clawing at Donovan's eyes, Taban wrapped his legs around his waist. Donovan stood, trying to pry Taban off of his torso. Danny rushed forward to help Donovan. She kicked Taban in the back hard enough to make him scream. Pain shot up her entire leg.

"Stay back," Donovan growled at her through his teeth. He pursed his lips as Taban attempted to shove his oiled fingers down his throat. Though, Donovan managed to pin Taban's arms, Taban still managed to lick him on the mouth. Wrenching Taban off, Donovan threw him onto the ground with a heavy thud.

Danny inspected the whip she'd left on the ground next to Cassidy, whose drugged body wasn't faring well.

Donovan's face started to swell and he gasped for air. Each swing became easier for Taban to dodge, but Donovan continued to stand in front of Danny and Cassidy.

"I have an Epipen. If you all stop fighting me, I'll help Donovan," Taban said. Donovan made it clear with his fist that he didn't believe Taban. "You'll die, you moron!" Taban shouted at him.

Adjusting her grip on the whip, Danny hurled herself at Taban. She knew two things: 1. She was still stronger than she looked. 2. She only had one shot to beat him.

Unable to breathe, Donovan collapsed. Cassidy staggered to him. Throwing herself on his chest, she beat against him, attempting to keep him alive through clumsy CPR.

Faking a kick at Taban's groin, Danny jumped into an instep half-kick at his knee. When he faltered, she clubbed him on the head with the whip handle. He struck her chest. Her breast throbbed like a knife had been shoved in it. Choking, she caught him under the knee with a low hook kick and drove her elbow into his solar plexus. His legs swept out from underneath him, Taban fell with a heavy thud, and she landed on top of him. Though her head spun from the rebound of her attacks, she beat the whip handle against his chest. A sickening crack resounded in her ears, through her own pain, she realized she'd broken some of his ribs. His nails ripped into the flesh of her arms. Her vision blurring with the intense sensation, she swung even more aggressively with the handle. Accompanying screams bombarded her ears.

"Danny, throw me the bag in his pocket," Cassidy yelled, vomit burning on her tongue.

To prevent him from hurting her while she fished in his jacket pocket, Danny shoved the whip handle in his mouth when he screamed. She located the bag and flung it to Cassidy. It landed about a meter off mark, but Cassidy stumbled to it, located the Epipen and administered it to Donovan's thigh.

"Come on Donovan breathe," Cassidy murmured. He gasped for air, but his chest started to move on its own again. She marveled at his perseverance. Assured of his recovery, Cassidy turned her attention back to Danny. "Donovan's okay," she called, but Danny didn't seem to hear her words. Back arched with a mass of hair obscuring her face, Danny continued to clobber Taban, even though his screams had stopped. "Stop! You'll kill him!" Cassidy could tell Danny didn't comprehend a word she coughed out. Desperately attempting to move, Cassidy realized she'd used the last of her strength to pump Donovan's chest.

The creature on top of Taban had focused too much of its mind to blocking its own pain. Its body acted on the motions Edana had set it to before shutting off her humanity. Only a blur remained of her senses—hearing, sight, touch, had all faded. It had no empathy for the young man who no longer struggled.

In a hastily donned jacket and pants, Aydan burst out of the trees. "What the heck happened?!" He shouted when he saw Donovan's swollen face and Cassidy's vomit covered clothes.

"Stop Danny!" Cassidy commanded.

Aydan attempted to pull Danny off of Taban, catching a collateral elbow to the shoulder, which knocked him backward. Collecting himself, Aydan slid past her blows and spoke to her gently. "Danny, can you hear me. He's not fighting you anymore." Swiftly, Aydan avoided another backhand. "It's safe now." Maintaining his silvery tone, he carefully stroked her back. "All your friends are safe."

Inside the monster, Danny felt Aydan's caress and heard Cassidy's guarantees that she was okay. "Edana Reyes." Her own name freed her from the place in which she'd temporarily locked her soul. Scorching and slicing pain coursed through her body. Blood dripped from her knuckles onto Taban's battered body. Terror filled her when she saw what she had done. Then shame consumed her, as hot tears began to run down her cheeks.

"He's still alive," Aydan assured her as he lifted her off of Taban. He carefully laid her on the grass, where she remained motionless.

Taban's eyelids opened hesitantly.

"Why did you steal the journal?" Aydan demanded. He stood over Taban, cradling the shoulder Danny had hit.

"I destroyed it." Taban wheezed. "I need to destroy the other part."

"Why should we believe you?" Aydan replied.

"Torture me if you have to. Break more bones, except my legs, because I still have one more person to go to."

"Who're you talking about?"

"Telyn … my sister," he explained, his voice cracking. "I have to tell her that I destroyed the journal. My dad will eventually blame me for not succeeding in helping Abigail." Tears streamed down Taban's bruised face. "You wouldn't understand. You all have people who care about you. I'm just an empty shell for everyone to project their own desires onto. So is Telyn. I'm all she has …"

"There is nothing in your track record that allows me to believe your touching story," Aydan's voice was like ice.

"Torture me then. You're the one with the whip and the razor blades." There was a heavy rasp in Taban's words, as though each syllable caused him physical pain.

With a frown of disgust, Aydan replied, "I can't do that."

Regaining some of her strength, Cassidy dug through Taban's bag. "Here's something that might work as a truth serum." She held out the labeled syringe.

"Use that," Taban advised.

Aydan administered it into Taban, who blacked out. "He might have been trying to protect us," Aydan said. "As much as I despised him, there is a possibility he favored us over the researchers. I think he truly cared about Eadowen—a little at least."

"Why can't it be villains and heroes?" Danny mumbled. Only her mouth moved, the rest of her body remained still as stone.

"Life would be so much easier if it was black and white, not shades of grey." Cassidy bowed her head.

"Yeah, life sucks that way," Aydan agreed. "What should we do if we decide he is telling the truth?"

"Does he really have a sister?" Cassidy asked.

"Yes, he and Eadowen used to talk about her."

"We should let him go to his sister," Cassidy decided. "If he *is* telling the truth. Speaking of sisters, how're you doing over there, Danny?"

"What have I done," Danny said to the sky.

"You saved Donovan's life," Cassidy replied. "Taban used peanut oil to subdue Donovan," she explained for Aydan's benefit. With harsh eyes, Donovan silently informed her that he didn't want that information shared.

"You big guys all think you're invincible. Try being my size for a day and see how that works for you!" Aydan screeched. "How many times do I have to tell you to carry an Epipen with you?!"

"Usually do."

The grass rustled as Taban stirred. "How did you destroy the journal?" Aydan asked.

"I ground it into sand and burned all the paper copies."

"I'm still not sure I believe him," Aydan mumbled. "But I don't know what to do."

Taban started to choke; he gagged up phlegm and blood. "I'll do anything, just don't let me die before I can help my sister," Taban begged. His face contorted with agony and grief, Taban looked nothing like the vibrant man Cassidy had met on the plane.

Donovan walked over to Taban, grabbed a fistful of his hair, and held him up by it. Taban vocalized his pain. Leveling him to the ground, Donovan wrenched his head back and stared into Taban's blue eyes. "He's telling the truth," Donovan stated.

"Why did I fall for you?" Cassidy asked, more to herself than Taban, but he answered her anyway.

"I'm a Peach Whisky."

"A what?" Aydan said.

"You're not the only descendants of an ancient race. I'm a—oh I don't know how to say it. I can't lift my arm to look it up on my Ogham."

He swims like a fish and he's inexplicably alluring, Danny thought. "He's an Egg Frisbee!" She said aloud.

"Those sea gods that could lure people," Cassidy explained. She hadn't put together all the pieces, but she remembered her own butchered pronunciation of the deities. With a baffled eyebrow, Aydan stared at his companions.

"Each Uisge?" Donovan said.

"Yes," Taban confirmed.

"Are there more of you?" Aydan demanded.

A light breeze whistled through the grass, but Taban gave no reply.

"Are there?" Aydan yelled. The shadows from the moonlight across his face emphasized his anger.

"If there are more of you GFs then there are more of my kind too."

"Don't ever come near our family or friends again," Aydan said.

"You don't have to worry about that," Taban replied. "I hope none of you will ever see me again. Leave me here. I'll call the hospital and I'll tell them some thugs beat me up for money."

Helping Cassidy to her feet, Aydan stabilized her. The bloody scratches on his hands from battling through the forest suggested to her that he was in a great deal of pain as well. They supported each other on their trek back into the forest. Donovan picked up Danny, who was still unable to move. Once several meters into the woods, the foursome ducked behind trees to watch and make sure Taban would do as he had promised. The medical helicopter arrived several minutes later blowing brush and dirt in their faces. Huddling together, Cassidy and Danny guarded each other's eyes, as did the Tolymie brothers. The helicopter took Taban away. Cassidy didn't know how she should feel. The only emotion she distinguished was relief that Danny was safe.

At last, Danny found the power to move her throbbing body. As they made their way back to the hostel, she felt as though a piece had been excised from her soul. "Cassidy?" she said as she supported herself on her friend's shoulder.

"Yes?" Cassidy said.

"I almost killed him … if you and Aydan hadn't …"

"He isn't dead," Cassidy assured her. "You helped us all."

"But, I might kill someone else someday."

"I know you'll learn control."

"But what if …"

"What if, has yet to be seen," Cassidy replied, her own frustration deepening her voice.

"What's wrong?" Danny asked.

"I'm feeling pathetic for not being able to defend myself, and having troubled you all to rescue me."

"The only thing that's pathetic is that the expectation of women these days is that they have to be intelligent, wise, strong, ethical, empathetic, and beautiful," Aydan retorted. "Cassidy, you rescued a drowning man, held your own even after getting drugged, and stood by your friend. If you were any more powerful, I'd be dragging you in to get your genes checked for superpowers. Danny, you are an oddball, but there's nothing wrong with that. No one is perfect. Even women—but for some reason you're expected to be."

"That's why people have to work together," Donovan muttered. The rest of the group stared at him. "Yes, I can speak in complete sentences," he sighed.

"I'll take care of explaining this mess." Aydan held onto his brother's arm. "I recommend you both get cleaned up."

CHAPTER 21
GO WEST, SHEARED ADONIS

TABAN AWOKE and held his Ogham over his head to read the time: three-seventeen in the afternoon. As usual, he had slept through hundreds of alarm sounds from his Ogham. He hadn't bothered to set up a way to spray water on his face. Wrapped in the bleached sheets, he oozed from the bed to the scratchy hotel carpet and stared at the dimpled white ceiling. Agonizing pain shot through his chest. After getting treatment at the hospital, he'd flown to Seattle to see his sister. He knew, from browsing her Me-Site, that she was at a modeling gig downtown. Several messages from Abigail showed on his Ogham.

"Request for video chat," his Ogham said. He accepted it.

"Hi, Taban how are you?" Abigail said.

"I'm alright. Sorry to leave so suddenly," Taban replied, trying to give her a winning smile, but he seemed to have forgotten how. "Look, I know it's not my place, but I really think you should do research in something else. I know Savali is desperately searching for the journal, but I don't think it exists."

"Savali just contacted me to tell me she thinks she's searching for a ghost." Abigail's voice wavered.

"You have better things to do than chasing fantasies of eternal youth."

She's so smart and kind. Her one weakness is that she's too trusting, which shouldn't have to be a flaw. She'll be fine, Taban told himself. "I know it's frustrating," he said. "Why don't you work on cancer research. They've made incredible headway, but there's so much to be done." He suggested. "And there's money in it," he offered, knowing that she'd only really considered research topics from an ethical perspective, and not from a financial one.

"But this is really important to me. I don't want to get old and ugly."

"Enjoy what you have while you have it!" Taban felt as though this was the first honest conversation he'd ever had with the scientist. "You'll age beautifully and you're so incredibly smart. Take some time off please."

"Your father would hate that," she cried. "He really supports the program."

"Don't tell him. He won't know if you take six months or a year off. Just tell him you have another lead. Go look for the journal on a tropical island or something."

"I've always wanted to go to Australia," she conceded.

"No … not Australia … too many things that can kill you," Taban said, realizing that his father's sister might be a bigger threat than his father, Abigail, and Savali combined. The international privacy laws and his father's ignorance were really the only things protecting the Tolymies. *I wish I'd remembered to warn the Tolymies about my aunt,* he thought. *I forget if she has kids or not.*

"I'll think about it. You're breaking up with me aren't you?" Her eyes filled with tears, but she gulped back any sobs.

I wish she'd just punched me, Taban thought. "Yeah. I don't think I can continue this. I hope you can forgive me."

"At least I'm not as crazy in love as I was during the first two years of our relationship. My head was in the clouds so much." She covered her face with her hands. "I met a really handsome guy the other day, we went to lunch, and he told me he'd be my wingman. I guess I should accept his offer." She lashed out at him with bitterness on her tongue.

Taban let her vent her anger on him. When she hung up, he paid the escort company he'd hired to help her find a suitable companion. Taking long silver shears out of his shoulder bag, he stood in front of the full length mirror. He grabbed a fistful of his blond bangs and sliced it off. The cold metal of the blades hit his scalp as he hacked off waves of hair. Clumps fell around him and scattered across the carpet like straw thrown from a hay-baler. He barely noticed when his reflection transformed into an advertisement for *Knots of Avernus.* Leaving a large tip for the cleaning service he left the room.

Rain pattered on the sidewalk. His newly-sheared scalp felt every drop. His ribs still throbbed from the imprint Danny had left on him. His whole body ached. Even his soul ached. There was still one more thing to be done before he could disappear from his father's world. He dragged his feet along the pavement almost passing Lincoln Street where he was supposed to turn. Stopping midway through crossing the street to correct his course, he heard car horns blaring at him. It was time to tell his sister what he had done.

As he rode the elevator to the bottom floor, he looked at himself in the ceiling mirror. Without his blond hair, bright clothes, or gigantic fake grin, Taban barely recognized himself. He touched his emaciated shoulder, then his white T-shirt, to prove the reflection was him. He realized he'd barely eaten in days and still wasn't hungry. A few blocks down the street, he found the place where his sister was working. He loitered outside for a half hour. When he saw her, he felt sick to his stomach. Her waist had been altered unnaturally; her short hair was stringy from malnutrition; and her dark eyes were blank. To his horror she walked right past him.

"Telyn! It's me!" He called to her. "Don't you recognize your big brother?"

She spun around. To his relief a look of recognition showed in the sixteen-year-old's eyes. Then she feebly punched him in the face.

Okay, does anyone else want to hit me? Taban thought rubbing his cheek. *Never mind, I don't want to know the answer to that.*

"Where have you been?! You were the only person, who was there for me. Then you ran off to LA and then Canada! You're no big brother to me."

"I wanted to be there for you! I really did, but Dr. Mir … our father … wouldn't let me." Taban cried. "I love you."

A couple of passerbys stared at him. He waited for a crowd of people. "Come with me," he took his sister by the hand and led her into the Westlake Center. "Walk with me, while we talk." He draped his arm around her shoulders, so they could speak more closely, with people thinking they were a couple. "What happened to your body? Who did this to you?"

"Corset, rib removal, and laxatives," she replied after a long silence. "Dad did it, because he didn't think I was pretty enough to get the jobs he wanted me to get. He's scheduled me for plastic surgery soon. I'm going to run away. Will you help me?"

"Yes. I will. Is there anything else you want to tell me?"

"I can't go anywhere without getting attention. Even in middle school everyone acted weird around me. They called me a slut, then they wanted me to come to their birthday parties."

"You're a Peach Whisky like me," Taban explained. "You attract people and your appeal frightens them, even as it lures them. They are jealous of you and they want you."

"A Peach what?"

Taban searched on his Ogham. "This." She looked at an image on his Ogham.

"That's ridiculous. I'm not some dude with a horse head and a name that sounds like a bad-tasting alcoholic beverage."

"You don't have to believe me." He lowered his voice. "I'm going to make your life a lot better by nine-o-clock tonight. Just trust me."

"Well, I don't have much choice."

"Good. Now father is staying with you right?"

"Yes, he's been visiting a lot lately, saying you're a disappointment," she replied, regarding a chocolate shop like a wild animal. Taban took her inside the shop. The young man working at the counter took one look at her and handed her a raspberry truffle the size of Taban's fist.

"It's free," the employee confirmed. "And get her some real food."

"Where's mom?" Taban asked as they left the chocolatier.

"She's been working a lot lately." The chocolate melted over her fingers. "She probably won't come home tonight."

"Listen carefully, I want you to go home and tell Dad I'm coming over, so he'll wait on having dinner. Oh, and mention I got in a car accident last week, because I kind of look like a mess."

"Ok."

"Does mom have security cameras in her apartment?"

"She doesn't. What are you going to do?"

"If you don't know, no one can blame you," he replied. "I'll come by in a couple of hours," Taban added with a tight embrace. He released his sister and located a natural food store on his Ogham.

Electing to walk instead of ride in a taxi, he made his way up to the small shop. He bribed a homeless man with the promise of beer if he'd purchase a poisonous mushroom, false morels, for him. The rain turned to mist as he exited a drug store with old-fashioned cold medicine in a little red box. He jogged down to Pike Place Market, where he picked up three purple sea urchins and was distracted by fish throwing.

Ingredients in hand, he took a taxi to a location several blocks from his mother and sister's apartment. From that point, he approached the apartment complex. Inside the glass doors, he saw a large male security guard pacing back and forth. Taban backed behind a building. To his dismay the rain had stopped. He looked around until he found a gutter still draining water, he stepped underneath it, and let the water pour over his body. *This is a time when it's good that I'm not handsome, because men don't consider me a threat,* Taban reminded himself as he carefully stuck his now translucent shirt to the black bruises on his chest. He checked his reflection in a vacant store window. His soaked, emaciated body and uneven haircut reminded him of a stray dog. As the wind picked up, the evening sun started to shine a bright-orange onto the street. With a glance toward the sun, Taban decided the weather in Seattle was crazier than him. He returned to the upscale apartment building, put on a baseball cap, and walked right in through the front doors.

"Where do you think you're going young man?" The guard asked him. Taban slouched to make himself look as small as possible, but didn't need to fake his shivering.

"I'm going to visit my mom. I live with my dad," he gave the guard his best wide-eyed stare. "Didn't someone sign me in?"

"What happened to you?"

"Got beat up. No idea why." Taban let his voice crack to give the illusion of a younger age. "Must've mistaken me for someone else."

"What's your name, kid?"

"Connor," Taban replied. He had considered using his middle name, Ahern, but thought better of it and used the name of the movie star who had a crush on Eadowen.

"Can I see your I.D?"

With cold fingers, Taban fumbled with his Ogham as though trying to pull up his I.D. Instead, he unclasped his Ogham and let it fall to the ground in such a way that it appeared accidental—a trick he'd perfected to flirt with women. Groaning in real pain, he knelt to retrieve the device and batted it with his hand, so it slid across the floor. He scrambled pathetically to pick it up.

"Just go." The security guard gestured to the elevator.

Haha. Sucker, Taban thought, wincing as he got to his feet.

He rode the elevator to the fourteenth floor and knocked on room 1405. Telyn let Taban inside and Taban saw his father watching something on his Ogham in the expensively furnished living room.

"What brings you here?" His father said without looking up. "There better be some news about the research that Abigail hasn't given me."

"Science is a slow process, father, but we may have a lead," Taban lied. "Could we order dinner? I'm starved."

"Go ahead. Order something for all of us."

"Seafood is your favorite right, Telyn?" Taban said sweetly.

"Yeah!" Telyn jumped happily at the mention of dinner.

"She can't eat dinner," his father barked. "No food after five, to keep her weight down."

"How about sea urchin? One sea urchin only has a couple tablespoons of insides, so very few calories. How about a mushroom risotto for the main course; since she's allergic to mushrooms, she won't eat leftovers."

"Fine," his father replied.

His sister looked crushed that her brother had taken her father's side and stormed off to her bedroom. *Dr. Mir must have treated her like a spoiled princess until he decided to use her for more money,* Taban realized as he gave his father a list of ingredients to send to several delivery vendors.

"I thought you were ordering dinner not ingredients."

"My roommate at the academy was a really good cook. I picked up some stuff."

"As long as it gets on the table quickly."

"Anything good in the wine cabinet?" Taban asked, browsing the bottles.

"Pour me a glass."

"A good pinot noir should breathe." Taban selected a bottle, uncorked it, and took it into the kitchen. Once out of sight, he took the cold medicine, ground the tablet between his fingers, and slipped it into the wine. He transferred the groceries he'd concealed in his shoulder bag to the fridge. After he finished the *mise en place,* Taban crossed the living room and went into the restroom. Placing the cold medicine in the cabinet, he discarded any other pills that would treat similar symptoms. "That should be long enough for the wine," Taban remarked. He poured two glasses and presented his father with one. After inspecting the wine, Dr. Mir took a long sip. Taban waited until his father had drunk half the glass before he took a sip. To show disgust, Taban wrinkled his nose, "I think it's corked." He spat the tangy liquid back into the glass. "Let me get another bottle." Snatching up another bottle, he uncorked it in the kitchen and poured himself a glass. After pouring the rest down the drain, he transferred the poisoned wine to the other bottle and brought the tainted one back to the living room.

While they waited for the ingredients, Taban fleshed out an involved story of Abigail's lead with the journal. As he refilled his father's wine glass, Taban provided tantalizing descriptions of his relations with her to minimize the number of relevant questions his father asked.

The scent of melted butter wafted through the kitchen as Taban followed a mushroom risotto recipe Eadowen had taught him. He started the rice on the oven and set to work chopping the mushrooms. In one pan he sautéed regular morels, in the other he cooked the false morels he'd purchased earlier in the day. While he waited for the rice to cook, Taban cracked open the sea urchins. He ground some of the poisonous sea urchin spines and contaminated two of the open vessels: one for his sister, the other for his father. Scooping the risotto onto two plates, he double-checked to make sure the one containing the false morels would wind up in front of his father. He meticulously washed all of the dishes, destroying the evidence of the separately cooked false morels.

"Come have your sea urchin," Taban called to Telyn as he set the glass table with the first course. Grudgingly, she joined Taban and her father at the table adjacent to the kitchen. Her smile melted Taban's heart as she slurped the gut of the urchin off her spoon. His father seemed to enjoy it as well. Though Taban had no taste for urchin, he swallowed the cold goop anyway.

Next, Taban served his father the risotto. Telyn was thereby banned from the table. The rich creamy taste combined with subtle spice reminded Taban of Eadowen's cooking, and the relationship they had.

"What's wrong with you?" Mr. Mir asked in a pointed way that sounded like an accusation.

"Nothing. Ea … I mean, *I* could've done a better job on this meal," Taban said.

After dinner, Taban endured his father's slurred questions. Fortunately, his father was no longer in a sufficient mental state to comprehend his responses. No less than an hour after dinner, Telyn ran out of her bedroom and retched in the restroom. Mr. Mir soon followed. Taban didn't expect the minor food poisoning from the sea urchin to affect his victims very much. After all, that was part of the plan: if Telyn got sick, she would be even less likely to receive any blame.

"Must be a stomach virus that stupid girl gave me," Mr. Mir gestured to his daughter.

"You should take something for that," Taban suggested. "I don't want to get sick."

As Taban had predicted, his father downed the classic cold medicine without noticing it had been changed out for a newer version. *Classic cold medicine has a warning label against consuming alcohol with it,* Taban thought. *Unlike a lot of medications, it's not because the company is warning against combining depressants; in this case, a chemical reaction occurs that can destroy a person's liver.*

Green from the urchin spines, his father lay on the sofa, sweating and holding his stomach. Telyn retreated to her room with a stove pot in hand. Taban waited until his father had to return to the restroom, before he crept into Telyn's room after her. Receiving the brunt end of her glare as she lay on her bed, he bent over her.

"You're just going to have a little food poisoning," Taban whispered in her ear. "You'll be okay by morning, dad won't be. I love you, Telyn. Goodbye."

"Where are you going?" She caught his sleeves in her fists.

"Away." He put her hand on his cheek and slipped a scrap of paper into her palm. "Here keep this secret and safe. It's the name of someone, who will be there for you whenever you need hir."

In the dim light, she squinted at the paper. "Who's Ea—?"

"An old flame," Taban interrupted her. He heard his father shuffling out of the restroom, so he kissed his beloved sister on the forehead, and left her.

"I have a gig out of town, so I need to go catch my flight. I hope you feel better," Taban informed his father. "Don't worry. The last time I got a stomach bug, it only lasted a day."

Grumbling something unintelligible, his father doubled over holding his abdomen. Taban shut the door to the apartment decisively—he'd made his choice. People would investigate his father's murder. They might not be able to charge him, but they'd certainly track him down.

Using the cold June evening as an excuse to don a cashmere scarf, Taban passed a different security guard as he left the apartment building. He bowed his head under his cap and scarf, doing his best impression of a non-descript, depressed teen. Once outside, he looked up at the fourteenth floor. "Go west to hell, father," he said, and pulled his jacket's hood over his head.

Large drops of rain dripped down his collar, soaking him before he had walked two blocks. The icy water, and a breeze that tasted of salt rejuvenated him as he hurried to distance himself from the scene. Twenty minutes later, near the ferry dock downtown, he passed a brightly lit café. The late hours of a place that smelled of freshly brewed coffee caught his attention. The rain caused tiny waterfalls on the uncovered sidewalk tables in front of the café. The few patrons enjoyed their coffees indoors on fluffy red sofas, except one who sat hunched under a hooded raincoat sipping a tiny espresso at one of the outdoor tables. Taban lingered. Something drew him toward the café.

"Good evening, Taban," a familiar melodious voice said. The outdoor patron pulled off his hood and shook out his bangs. "That's the worst hair cut you've ever had," Eadowen remarked as Taban self-consciously ran his hand over his bare scalp. "And you've never looked better."

"Ea?" Taban approached the table in disbelief. "Did you track me with a chip or something?"

"No. Aydan told me about what happened in Scotland," Eadowen explained. Taban felt his heart sink to his stomach—Eadowen already knew what he had done. "Your sister is the one person you had left. I knew you'd go to her as soon as possible. So, I booked a flight to

Seattle. I also knew you'd return to the sea. This road leads directly from your sister's apartment. You were always one for taking the fastest route." While he spoke, Eadowen wove the ends of Taban's scarf around his hand. He let the cashmere slide through his fingers, drawing Taban closer. "I waited for you, yesterday and today."

"Here." Taban set his Ogham to transfer money. "This is enough to send Donovan and Aydan to university and for you to live on for at least four years."

Eadowen waved his hand in refusal. The bloodstone ring on his ring finger flickered in the dim street light.

"Take it!" Taban almost shouted, then realized he didn't want to draw attention to himself, and switched to a harsh whisper. "Please, Ea, just accept it."

"No."

"Where're you headed?"

"Australia."

Addressing the sidewalk, Taban muttered a phrase he thought he'd only say honestly to his sister, "I love you."

With intent hazel eyes, Eadowen regarded him silently.

"Take it, because I love you—like family—you bastard." Taban snapped up and addressed his friend through gritted teeth.

"If I do, will it relieve you of a burden?"

"Yes."

Swiping his arm over Taban's, Eadowen allowed the monetary exchange to occur.

"Why aren't you answering me?" Taban tasted the salt of his own tears washed by the rain into his mouth. "Tell me you love me too," he commanded. "Even my own sister doesn't care for me."

"It seems I was the one who kept our deal," Eadowen replied with tenderness, in both his voice and expression.

"What deal?" Taban asked as they embraced. He consciously tried to capture the memory with all five of his senses. He nuzzled Eadowen's warm neck, heard Eadowen's breath against his cheek, and inhaled the scent of thistle mixed with hawthorn. "You'd better hurry. You're too valuable to get thrown in jail," Eadowen said. His lips brushed Taban's jaw as he spoke.

The ferry horn sounded in a long, low drone as Taban hailed a taxi to the airport. Locked in the cab, Taban stole one last look at the table where Eadowen had been sitting. His friend was gone. His ring felt like ice, as he touched it to his lips. *This time of year, it will be winter where I'm going,* he thought, as the taxi took him far away from everyone he held dear.

CHAPTER 22
THE MOON PRINCESS WAS WISER

THE ICY WATER RUSHED from the showerhead over Danny's body, soothing her pain. Completely drained of energy, Danny sat on the tiled floor of the last shower stall in the hostel. Wrapped in a towel, Cassidy scrubbed her much-abused feet in the stall across from Danny's. Neither pulled the curtain completely closed—neither wanted to be far from the other.

"I can't believe what I did." The water turned red from Danny's battered knuckles. "We aren't any closer to getting that darn journal."

"You're powerful, Danny. And there's nothing wrong with that." Cassidy winced as she cleaned dirt out of a cut. "I know you'll find your control. Maybe we should go back to that martial arts summer camp."

"We're a bit old."

"We could be summer camp counselors."

"I'd like that." Danny dragged herself out of the shower to help Cassidy with her injuries. As she washed her friend's feet, she saw her reflection in a dusty mirror at the far end of the restroom. Under harsh neon lights and framed by a thick mop of long, dark hair, her cold gaze reflected back at her. She touched her chest and contemplated whether she'd rather be male. Just then a knock echoed down the corridor of empty shower stalls.

"It's me," Aydan called. "May I come in?"

"Yes," Danny confirmed.

"Marja is a medical student," Aydan said. "She knows about our situation. She says that she has to make sure that the drugs in your system will wear off with no adverse effects. Do you mind if she comes in too?"

"No, not at all."

A lanky woman entered, carrying an emergency kit, and a wrinkle of concern between her brows. With a colorful clip, she fastened her sunny blond hair in a loose bun. "Hello, Cassidy." Marja shook her hand. "It's nice to meet you. After I check your vital signs, I'd like to call a medic."

"Is that really necessary?" Cassidy asked.

"Yes, I understand this is meant to be secret, but I can't compromise your health. I'll help you figure out a way to get an examination without having to answer too many questions. There's a room upstairs that I've had prepared for you to stay here the rest of the night."

Cassidy noticed Danny inspecting her body in the mirror.

"Do you know anything about being gender queer?" Danny said to Aydan.

"I know I'm a platypus of gender expression, but I don't know what it's like to feel like you're not the gender you were assigned at birth," Aydan replied.

"You're welcome to talk to me," Marja remarked as she checked Cassidy's blood pressure.

"Why?"

"I always knew I was a woman, but I wasn't born that way," Marja explained. An amused half-smile graced her mouth as the friends glanced at her in surprise.

"Oh." A flicker of warmth bloomed in Danny's heart. "Thank you so much."

"You're welcome. I'll give you my contact information, okay?" Marja finished her quick check-up and started to bandage Cassidy's injured feet. "You seem to be recovering just fine, but let's get you to your room and call a medic."

Marja then attended to Danny's knuckles and the nail scratches on her arms. Danny yelped when she carefully applied the anesthetic. Cassidy and Marja chatted cheerfully about the significance of law in public health as they headed to Cassidy's room. Lagging behind, Aydan remained in the restroom with Danny.

"You like Cassidy don't you," Danny commented as soon as she knew Cassidy was out of earshot. While waiting for him to reply, she slipped into a tank top and sweats.

"I don't know her that well, but I like what I do know," Aydan admitted, shoving his hands in his coat pockets. "I know you like her too."

"We're just friends because that's the relationship we can both share. It's just tough to see her like you so much."

"I wish I could help you feel better. I'm sure you'll run into lots of people who think you're pretty special … I mean all of us appreciate you." He touched her shoulder. "Is there anything I can do?"

Tapping her lip, Danny considered his offer. "You know what." She gave him her best mischievous leer. "There *is* something you can do for me."

"Anything."

Enjoying his conditioner's hazel and lilac scent, she whispered directions into Aydan's slightly damp hair.

When she finished, he drew back. "You sneaky little …!" With a twinkle in his eyes, he clasped her hand, and kissed the back of her fingers. "You're the only person for whom I would honor *that* request. Consider it done."

Danny chuckled gleefully and then changed the subject. "What does Donovan like to drink?"

"Hot chocolate with lots of whipped cream."

"Is there some around?"

"Check the kitchenette."

As Aydan had suggested, Danny found a supply of coffee, hot chocolate, tea, and all the associated amenities in the kitchenette. After scanning her Ogham to pay for access, she poured cream into a silver thermos and added the cocoa mix. Deciding the mix lacked the rich smell she associated with chocolate, Danny melted in a seventy-percent cocoa bar that she'd retrieved from her suitcase. She stirred the ingredients together and sprayed whip cream across the table as well as in its target location. A few minutes later, she found Donovan sitting on a moonlit windowsill—his expression distant as he looked out into the forest. She presented the hot chocolate and hopped up on the sill beside him. He took a long drink.

Wiping off a whipped cream mustache, he held up the thermos. "This is good." His solemn expression returned. "I hurt him."

"We all did," Danny replied. "He hurt us too." Curling up on the windowsill, she attempted to imitate the empathetic face Eadowen had made when she'd told him about her interest in Cassidy. The moon sank closer to the treeline while they remained in a meditative silence, with much fidgeting on Danny's part.

"Squirrel," he said with a gentle tug on her bushy ponytail to get her attention. Pouring the hot chocolate into the cup-lid of the thermos, Donovan offered it to her. They tapped lid and thermos together and finished their hot chocolate.

* * *

The medic departed, leaving Cassidy alone on the queen-sized bed. Marja had provided her with one of the rooms reserved for people running the hostel, but due to short staffing, the room was available. *I hope I did the right thing,* she thought as she adjusted her loose tank top. Since Danny's clothes were too small for her, Marja had let Cassidy choose from her wardrobe, which conversely was too big everywhere except her chest. Cassidy opened her journal.

I wonder if I did the right thing … I wonder if we're all doing the right thing? The researchers don't seem like bad people. They're just doing their job. Did I jump to conclusions by siding with the Tolymies to protect Danny? Eadowen is very good at selling an idea. I was certainly quick to believe him …

"Mind if I join you?" Aydan tapped on her closed door.

"Sure."

Cinching the waistband of a large peasant skirt around his hips, Aydan strode across the room to the window. The closed curtains blocked most of the light, so Cassidy could only discern a faint outline of his figure in a baggy tunic. "Do you mind if I open the blinds?"

"Of course not …" Cassidy replied hesitantly.

Theatrically, he pulled back one of the curtains and secured it on the window frame. As he casually patted the frizz on his slowly drying hair, he turned his torso perpendicular to the window. Leaning back slightly, he positioned himself so the moon highlighted every muscle on his chest and abdomen as he pulled the embroidered tunic over his head. "I'm just giving you the clothes I printed for you. It turns out the hostel has a three dimensional printer for emergencies," he said. "If you don't like them I promise not to be insulted if you recycle them tomorrow." Aydan threw her the shirt with a grin. Combing his fingers through his locks, he tilted his head back letting the light illuminate his profile. The bed creaked as Cassidy shifted nervously, trying to decide whether she was supposed to look or not. The ethical dilemma she had been recording in her journal was a distant memory.

"Hey, Cassidy, this show's for you. It'd be kind of a shame if you didn't watch." Aydan regarded her out of the corner of his eye. "If this makes you uncomfortable, I'll stop. Fairy-princess-juggernaut decided this was my punishment for receiving your attention on this trip."

Her face heating up, Cassidy clapped her hand to her forehead. *Danny convinced Aydan to do this. I guess Danny's more mischievous than I thought.* "Exactly, what did my lovely friend tell you to do?"

"Show off the result of years of work. And before you think it … yes, I was compensating for my height and having to live with Taban." Aydan ran his hand down his torso. Letting his thumb slide into the skirt, he pulled it down just below his hip bone.

"I hope you didn't feel like you were pushed to do this."

"This? As in have my body admired by someone, who also seems to care about fitness, at the polite request of a friend? Nah."

"My body isn't as good as you—" Cassidy stopped herself. "I guess that's not qualifiable since everyone has different phenotypes."

"Keep in mind I know how to use lighting and body makeup." He grabbed a chair from the desk in the corner of the room and moved it next to Cassidy's bed.

"You used makeup?"

"Yeah, a little dark foundation along my muscles and under my cheekbones. Couldn't tell could you?" Aydan replied. "By the way, I heard you used the card to signal Donovan. Nice magic trick."

"Thanks," she said sadly and took out the beat-up card. "I really liked it."

"Do you want my deck?"

"Um … well … err." She noticed a stack of cards in Aydan's hand. "Oh, *deck*. Are you sure? I don't know what I'd do with a whole … pile of cards."

It took Aydan a half-second to understand what gave her pause. "No, I really want you to have my *deck.*" With a slasher grin, he did a waterfall shuffle. "You're welcome to play with *it* as much as you want." He stroked her arm as he placed the stack in her hand. "I can teach you some mind-blowing techniques."

Cassidy pretended to glare, but she knew the quiver of suppressed laughter on her lips betrayed her. *Did he have that in his skirt the whole time?* Cassidy thought. "Speaking of gifts," she said. "I think some jewelry Taban gave me had a tracking chip in it. I need to destroy it."

"He gave you jewelry and you dragged around a ratty card?"

"Well, now I have your *deck* under my control." She cut the deck and let the cards flow together cupped in her hands. "It's a very nice one."

"Touché. How'd you manage to turn him down?"

"I reread things about him that I documented in my journal. 'Field notes,' as you so aptly called them."

"So, you beat a monster of oral tradition using the written language? Impressive."

"Can we pretend I planned that?" Cassidy tugged on the foreign tank top in contemplation. Aydan's eyes briefly flickered down. "Taban offered me a lot of things I desire, but not what I really want."

"Mm?" Subtly adjusting the skirt, Aydan rested his forearms on his legs. "And what do you want? And 'world peace' isn't allowed."

Cassidy considered the question carefully. "Community. I don't need approval from everyone, but I do need my friends." She paused. "What about you?"

"Me? I just want to bring a little magic into the world."

"You bring magic into my world," she replied. "I'm sure you have a great reason for not magic-ing up some clothes for yourself instead of wearing mine, but you don't have to tell me."

"The powers that be won't let me do anything that decreases my audience's pleasure."

Danny tapped on the door. "May we come in, or do you two need some more time?"

"Come on in," Cassidy called.

Draped in duffle bags, Donovan carried in two fluffy pillows. Danny set her suitcase on the ground and did a summersault onto

Cassidy's bed. "What a pretty deck," she commented. Cassidy blew on the top card and showed Aydan's stage name to Danny. "Hey, that crescent moon-ish symbol looks like one of the symbols on the book Chay gave me."

"What's the book about?" Cassidy asked.

"It's one of those jaded conqueror-meets-sexy-native stories. Here let me get it." Danny rifled through her suitcase. "Hey, Aydan. Where did you come up with your stage name?" Danny asked.

"It's just my middle name and my dad's bachelor name."

"What's your dad's name?"

"Daray. Why?"

"The book is dedicated to someone named 'Lug Eldin.'"

"Spell 'Lug.'" Standing, Aydan stretched his arms over his head and flexed his back.

"L-U-G-H."

"That's my dad's first name. He goes by his middle name, Daray, because a lot of people in North America pronounced it 'Lug' instead of 'Loo.'" Aydan started to fold the skirt he'd been wearing. Before she could stop herself, Cassidy looked down and discovered that he'd somehow managed to change into pajama pants. She glanced at his face apologetically.

"Don't get greedy," Aydan chided and playfully tossed the skirt at her.

"The soldier's name was Endymion right?" Danny commented as she flipped through the book. "I didn't notice it before, because I thought it was based on the Endymion and Selene myth, but the narrator of the story is Endymion. The setting is in an unnamed place, but the weather described is colder than I'd expect near the Mediterranean."

"Who's the author?" Cassidy asked.

"E. J. Baird."

"Eamon Jason Baird," Aydan read off his Ogham. "That name sounds really familiar. He lives about two hours from here by public transportation, plus a cab. It might be better if we ask Marja for her car. Since it's five in the morning, we could message him now, but we should probably wait at least another hour before heading out. Besides, we should all try to get some sleep first."

"Danny, do you want to sleep on the bed with me?" Cassidy asked. When no one answered her query she saw Danny and Donovan on the floor. Donovan had monopolized the pillows, originally intended for both Tolymie brothers, and allowed Danny to use his torso as a mattress. "Well, they look cozy. Do you want to join me up here?" She asked Aydan, a note of shyness in her voice.

"I'd like that." He folded back the covers on the other side of the bed. As soon as his head hit the pillow, Aydan started to breathe in a sleepy rhythm. She tried to do the same, but anxieties kept shooting through her mind. *I really hope Danny will be safe. What if Eamon Baird is a false lead? What if we don't find anything at the next university?* she wondered. *I don't think I'll ever be able to forget about Taban. I feel like I'm missing half the story.* A warm hand on her back returned her to the present.

"Can't sleep?" Aydan whispered.

"No, can you?"

"Not with you tossing and turning like that. And you're lying on my hair. It hurts."

"Sorry." She carefully rolled off of his hair, which had spread across the bed. "My mind just won't settle down."

"Me too. Want to chat for a bit?" Aydan propped himself up on his left elbow to face her.

"Right now I just need a distraction." Sitting up, Cassidy used the headboard as a backrest. "I need to be functional tomorrow. Anymore Celtic-y stuff I should know—or might find interesting?"

"A lot of the Celtic lore features men sleeping with wise women and powerful goddesses for luck, magic, or assistance." Lounging back onto his pillow, Aydan folded his arms behind his head.

Relieved to have a topic divergent from her internal monologue, Cassidy replied, "That happens in other mythologies too, but it's nice to hear about something other than Zeus and his lovers—though Ganymede always made it more interesting." She wound a strand of Aydan's hair around her hand, letting the smooth texture slide through her fingers.

"Speaking of which, wise and powerful Cassidy, we have an hour ..." Aydan inspected his nails. "What would you like to do?" The way Aydan regarded her was reminiscent of a cat hearing a can opener, not exactly hunger or excitement, more like—gimme.

Chapter 23
Of Crescent V-Rods

CREAKING SPRINGS AWAKENED DANNY. She dismounted Donovan and stood up to find Aydan dancing to Knots of Avernus on the bed. Cassidy sang from a seated position because her injured feet would not permit such vigorous activity. A couple of peacock feathers protruding out of Aydan's braided bun, bobbed in sync with his bouncing. Cassidy, with extravagantly colored eyelids, silver tinsel eyelashes, and bronzed cheeks, looked prepared to grace a cocktail party in Wonderland.

"You did each other's hair, makeup …" Danny gagged on a sharp scent. "And nails?"

"Yes, I've never done so much before." Cassidy scratched the air with ruby talons. "And I'm not sure I will again anytime soon, but I have no regrets."

"When I was half-asleep I heard Aydan say something that sounded kinda suggestive. Did you do each other too?"

"He didn't offer me his Ogham, so I knew he didn't want to sleep with me."

"I wouldn't go as far as to say, didn't want to," Aydan remarked as he straightened a peacock feather with his chrome fingernails. "It just seemed wrong to proposition someone who'd just been sleep deprived, beaten up, and drugged. Anyway, I'm glad I actually got a chance to get to know you better." He leapt off the bed landing in front of Danny. "Do you want me to show you a way to wear a Strap-Shirt at your height?" He unzipped his duffle bag and motioned for Danny to turn her back to him. "Cassidy told me that's why she bought you that other shirt."

"I've been wondering, do you have a title like 'Harlan the Amazing' or something like that?" Danny asked.

He took two of the thin straps and pulled them over her shoulders like suspenders. Wrapping the other thin straps together he secured them horizontally across her chest. He finished by twisting the longer straps together into a belt.

"My fans just call me Harlan Eldin, but the magician community has a dark sense of humor. They call me Harlan the Fanservice."

After coiling one strap around his neck, Aydan hung two thin straps over his shoulders and crisscrossed them on his chest in an x. Then he knotted the thick straps that were too big for him behind his back. "And if I don't feel like having a tail ..." He wound the thick straps down one of his pant legs.

"You should wear that today. It looks good," Danny commented.

"At least I have pants this time." He narrowed his eyes in Danny's direction.

"Speaking of which, here's your bullwhip back." A knot tightened in Danny's stomach when she touched the weapon. She drew away from the whip as she recalled the carnage she had caused by surrendering to her anger and pain. *I'm never going to let that happen again. I can learn control,* she thought.

"I don't think either of us want it anymore. It can stay here with our secrets." Aydan checked his Ogham. "Marja says she's waiting for us outside."

A couple of early bird hostel goers observed Aydan's costume with great interest. Cassidy waited for him to use his versatile, I'm a magician, explanation. Instead, he grinned and cordially informed the young ladies that he was Canadian.

"Don't look now, but I think they're booking flights to North America," Cassidy snickered.

"I'm driving you this time." Marja leaned against her car, with folded arms. "If anything like last night happens, I'll be with you. Oh, and don't let me forget to stop by the hotel, so Cassidy can get her things."

* * *

Marja dropped the foursome off at the bottom of a small hill dotted with crimson wildflowers. "His house should be just around that hill. You know how to contact me. If I don't hear from you, I'll pick you up this afternoon."

"I can't believe we're cold-calling this guy," Cassidy remarked.

"He's our best lead," Danny said. Hopping over toadstools, she led the way up a worn cobblestone path.

"I know. I just appreciate hearing someone else say it." Cassidy followed close behind Danny, until the path widened enough for her to walk next to her. They approached a quaint stone cottage with a well-tended flower garden.

"If a witch offers us sweets, we hightail it out of here got it?" Aydan buttoned up a short, grey peacoat to conceal his other attire.

While Danny used the knocker on the emerald-green door, Cassidy noticed a quarter-sized Crescent V-Rod carved directly above the door knob. A bee buzzed around Danny's head, irritating her, when she would normally appreciate it for the elixir it concocted. Slipper-covered feet padded to the door. A salt-and-pepper haired gentleman weathered by approximately half-a-century filled a significant portion of the open doorway. He greeted them with an unassuming smile spread across his round face. A shiver went down Cassidy's spine when she met his warm hazel gaze. She recognized a subtler version of the glowing allure she had until that moment believed unique to Taban. *Does he count as witch with candy?* she wondered.

"Hello." Danny thrust out her hand. "We're here to meet Eamon Baird."

"Guid morning. I'm Eamon."

"We want to ask you about this." Danny said waving the paperback at him.

He plucked the novel out of Danny's hand and swept his arm out behind him. "Then come in."

Cautiously, Cassidy followed her friends through the door and into a cozy living room. A fire blazed in a stone hearth heating the room so effectively that Cassidy hastily removed her jacket. Sitting in a wooden rocking chair, Eamon Baird folded his hands in his lap. "Please, make yourselves comfortable," he said.

Danny and Cassidy claimed a sofa across from him and Aydan grabbed a red armchair next to the sofa. Donovan remained standing, but rested his hand on the back of the couch behind Cassidy.

"Who do I have the honor of entertaining today?"

"I'm Aydan and this is my brother Donovan."

"Tolymie?" Eamon asked. Cassidy felt the cushion behind her head tighten as Donovan clenched it in his hand. "You must be Edana Reyes. How is your relationship with Eadowen?" Eamon continued.

"What relationship with Eadowen?" Danny asked.

Giving Eamon a possessive look, Cassidy put her arm around Danny. "She isn't in one with him."

"Oh … I see." Eamon's voice remained monotone, but his brow furrowed. "What's your name, lassie?"

"Cassidy Adisa."

"She's a friend," Aydan explained. "And a very good friend to Edana."

Eamon's almond-shaped eyes searched Cassidy's face the same way her mothers regarded her when they suspected she'd told a lie. Though she had no intention to mislead, she flinched under his gaze. "Tell me, Ms. Adisa, what is carved on my door?" he inquired.

"It's a Crescent V-Rod," Cassidy answered. "An ancient Pictish symbol likely meaning eternity."

"Follow me," he instructed, rolling up the green rug between the sofa and the rocking chair. This revealed a wooden trapdoor with the same crescent moon symbol carved into it. Eamon opened the door and descended down a stairwell. When no one followed him, he said, "How can I trust you, if you don't trust me?" Reluctantly, they obeyed. Aydan, unable to bear the heat any longer and doffed his coat.

When they reached the bottom of the stairs, Eamon pushed open a heavy door and Danny gasped. Underneath the tiny cottage was a gigantic room protruding below the hill. Amplifying the light from a couple of floor lamps, a large chandelier, like the one she had seen in the Tolymie's home, hung from the ceiling. Chay sat cross-legged in a large armchair sipping tea, next to a floor-to-ceiling book shelf. Against the far wall, Danny followed her nose to find a table with a decorative platter of fruits, breads, and cheeses.

A man rested his head on the back of another armchair. Only a couple strands of white in his long black hair suggested he might be over thirty, though his posture and the frailness of his limbs were that of a much older man. His grey eyes flitted to the entrance as though to assess the commotion, but the way he stared in their direction without registering them suggested to Cassidy that his sight was limited.

"Who *is* that?" Cassidy breathed to no one in particular as she admired the man's elegance.

Aydan whirled around defensively to see who had caught Cassidy's interest then he sighed. "Sorry, you can't have him, he was married … to my mother. And he doesn't look good at all—I didn't even recognize him on first glance." Leaving Cassidy on the steps, Aydan rushed to his father's side.

"Dad!" Donovan shouted and ran to him. The man pushed against the padded arm of his chair, but failed in his attempt to stand. With great care, Donovan helped him to his feet. Once standing Daray wrapped a shaking arm around Aydan's shoulders and rested his pale hand on Donovan's waist.

"I'm so happy to see you." He kissed both of his sons, tears rolling down his cheeks. "I regretted leaving you so much."

"It's okay, we found you."

"The letters …"

The brothers waited patiently for their father to complete his thought but he sunk back into the chair as though he had already communicated the full sentence.

"Did you receive the letters I wrote for Daray?" Eamon filled in for Daray.

"Yes, thank you," Aydan addressed both his father and Eamon. "We had trouble decoding them, but they gave us hope that you were safe."

"Tell me." Daray tugged at one of the straps on his middle child's attire. "Is this in vogue now or is it just you?"

"That's the dad I remember," Aydan squeezed his father.

Not wanting to disrupt the family reunion, Cassidy shrunk against the wall. A cold, sharp edge dug into her neck. Startled, she turned to find a few still photographs and a couple of framed video loops adorning the stairwell wall. Most of the pictures featured a man who on closer inspection she recognized as a younger version of Eamon. The young Eamon looked arrogant, but also intriguing in a vibrant way that resembled Taban even more than Eamon's present self. In one still photograph, a sturdy woman had one arm around the younger Eamon and the other around Daray who looked about the same, but healthier. Based on the suppressed glare with which Eamon regarded Daray and the way Daray's arm coiled around the woman's hips, Cassidy inferred a romantic rivalry. *I'm glad I wasn't caught in that love triangle,* she thought. *I don't know which one I would have picked.* Next to the still she found a video of Eamon and a man with azure eyes waxing their surfboards on a coast that looked far too warm to be in Scotland. She put her hand to her chest, as she looked at the face of the azure-eyed man, but dismissed her beating heart and his similarity to Taban as a figment of her imagination caused by her residual attraction to the Each Uisge.

"Daray and I were quite something weren't we?" Eamon said behind her. He indicated the formidable woman between Daray and himself. "That's Artio, Aydan and Donovan's mother." The mirth in his expression suggested to her that he had been watching her gawk at the photographs from his youth for a while.

"Um, who is this?" She pointed to the man with the surfboard.

"Tynan Mir. He was a fun guy, but either he got worse or I started to notice his lack of connection to people. It was too bad. I felt a sort of connection to him. I probably told him more than I should have ... Well anyway, we lost touch many years ago," Eamon said.

"I knew someone like him. He even had the same last name."

"You did?" Eamon rested one hand on the wall next to Cassidy's shoulder while he tilted her chin up to look at him with the other. Better prepared for his penetrating scrutiny she stared back at him defiantly. "He was your lover ... or at least you wanted him to be." He withdrew from her to a more normal conversation distance.

Her lack of discomfort during her close proximity to him all but confirmed her suspicions. "You're a descendant of a Peach Whisky aren't you?" she demanded.

"A what?" He considered her mangled pronunciation. "Each Uisge?"

"That thing. It sounds so much better with a Scottish accent."

"I wouldn't be surprised if I'm spawn of an Each Uisge." He slipped his hands in his sport coat pockets and looked at the picture frames.

She edged away from him, down the stairs.

"Don't be afraid." He shook his head with a forlorn chuckle. "I'm not what I once was. Now I'm just a harmless middle-aged man."

Says you, Cassidy thought. She checked around the basement. Preoccupied with their father, it was likely that neither of the Tolymie brothers had noticed her exchange with Eamon. Danny's attention was divided only between her plate of food and Chay. "The guy I mentioned was a Peach Whisky," Cassidy said. "So I'd appreciate it if you'd tell me what it's like to be one."

"For Tynan and me it was as if we gained our energy from bending others to our will. I can't even describe the elation when someone fell for whatever trap I'd set. It just felt so natural." He tenderly rested his fingers on the photographed face of the woman he had called Artio. The skin around his eyes wrinkled when he tensed his cheeks as though to swallow a painful memory. "But when someone got hurt in my games—which was often—it hurt me too. That is where Tynan and I were different—I was torn between my love of people, and my drive to manipulate and control. He had no such misgivings, and at the time I envied him."

"You were jealous that he didn't feel burdened by the consequences of his actions."

"Yes." He offered her his arm. "Walk with me." The basement seemed like a ballroom the way he lead her across the polished floor toward the fruit platter. By supporting herself on his arm she eased the pressure on her still throbbing feet. "Must be hard to be supernatural," he commented.

"What … I'm not …"

"The Tuatha de Danann died out." He handed her a small cluster of champagne grapes from the platter. "If it weren't for humans the Tuatha de Danann genes wouldn't exist anymore. Humans are the paranormal race to the Danann because they came later and survived."

"Well, that's a different way of looking at it." Cassidy popped one of the tiny spheres between her teeth releasing the bittersweet juice on her taste buds. Picking the grape skin out of her teeth with her tongue, behind a paper napkin, Cassidy pondered her mix of relief and frustration at meeting an Each Uisge who seemed to be kind. *I suppose taking pleasure in charming people doesn't inherently make someone evil.* She thought as she admired Eamon. *If all Each Uisges were bad, it would be so much easier for me to rally against them, but I guess I can't shove them into that small a box.*

"Don't romanticize me, Ms. Cassidy," Eamon whispered when he noticed her expression. "Your intelligence, sexuality, and empathy are all aspects of your being an Each Uisge can and will use to manipulate you."

Just then Aydan interrupted them by calling her. "Cassidy, Danny, come meet my dad," Aydan yelled across the room.

Followed by Eamon, Cassidy strode over and extended a hand. "Hi, nice to meet you."

"What a splendid young woman." Daray said as he brought her hand to his lips, Cassidy noticed how thin his skin had become when compared with the photographs. She feared the touch of a feather would rip him open. "You remind me of Artio." With a shaking hand, he held her palm to his cold cheek as though to recall the sensation of his late wife's caress.

"I thought she did too," Eamon agreed.

Leaving Chay with her plate, Danny joined her friends and waved to Daray.

"Oh, Edana," He took her hand his face lighting up with joy. "You've grown up so strong and radiant." Daray's eyes fluttered closed as he spoke. "I'm sorry everyone. I'm very tired."

"That's alright." Aydan patted his arm. "We'll just sit with you."

"Eamon, I'm grateful to you for taking care of me all this time so I could see my children again." Opening his eyes as though there were lead weights attached to his eyelids, Daray admired his sons. "Donovan, Aydan, I love you. I wish my other child were here. I love Eadowen just as much."

"Eadowen knows that and someday you'll be able to reconnect in person." Eamon tucked a pillow behind Daray's head.

While Daray drifted off to sleep in his armchair, Cassidy finished her grapes and occasionally fed one to Aydan. The fatigue she had suppressed made her feel unsteady on her feet, so she sunk into a leathery armchair near Daray and his sons.

"There's a guest room upstairs," Eamon said producing a set of keys from his pocket which he dropped into Aydan's hand. "Why don't you make sure she makes it there. In fact, you look pretty worn-out yourself. If you don't come back down, I'll knock on the door when Daray wakes up." Stroking his father's sleeping forehead, Aydan hesitated.

"I'll look after him," Donovan assured him from the other side of Daray's chair.

Convinced that his father was in good care, Aydan guided his sleepy companion back up the stairs, through the living room, and into a small boudoir with white mosquito netting over the bed.

"Thank you," Cassidy mumbled.

Rubbing the dark circles under his eyes, Aydan yawned. Cassidy pulled back the blanket invitingly. "If you join me, I promise to let you sleep this time and I won't lie on your hair." She helped him undo the Strap-Shirt, while he sponged off her makeup with a damp washcloth.

She lay on her back attempting to either sleep or resolve everything that had ever made her anxious in her life. The thoughts jumbled together incoherently in her sleep-deprived, post- adrenaline rush brain. Repositioning herself to her stomach she tried to find a comfortable position for her neck. Next, she attempted sleeping in a few different configurations on her sides, all the while taking great care not to tangle herself in Aydan's tresses. Her bedmate cleared his throat, and she realized she'd monopolized the blankets.

"I can't sleep when you're doing a horizontal ballet." Aydan rolled on his side and gave her a sultry look over his shoulder at her. "Would holding me help?"

Laying one arm over his torso, she let him rest his head on her arm. Hooking his foot around her calf to anchor her in place, he wriggled closer to her until their bodies sandwiched together. Face buried in his hazel and lilac-scented hair, her breathing began to synchronize with the rise and fall of Aydan's chest.

* * *

While Cassidy spoke to Eamon, Danny returned from the buffet table with a plate full of food. Using the floor as a table for her feast, she listened to Eamon mention the pictures on the wall to Cassidy.

A hand touched Danny's arm, distracting her from their conversation. "I knew you would figure it out." Chay's layered dress tickled Danny's hand.

"Hi." Danny stood, excited to see the young woman from the university. "How did you know to give me the book?"

"When we heard about the researchers, I got a position as an aid in the archeology department to keep an eye on them. I doubt I would've been able to do anything, though, since I was just an assistant to the department," Chay explained. "Artio and Daray told me stories about you and their children. I recognized you three from your pictures, so I followed you. I was afraid to make a mistake or that you wouldn't trust me. I figured if you were the right people, you would make the connection to the book."

"How'd the journal wind up as a novel?" Danny offered her fruit plate to Chay, who nibbled a slice of apple.

"The first half of the journal—what you were looking for was destroyed a long time ago." She joined Danny on the floor. "Fortunately, it was kept alive through stories in my family. Eamon realized we might be able to communicate the story in an untraceable way if he published it as fiction."

"Why'd you give it to me and not Aydan or Donovan? They would've recognized their dad's name sooner."

"Er ... in retrospect I should have." Chay's green eyes sparkled, as she rubbed the back of her neck bashfully. "I guess I kind of wanted a chance to talk to you."

"Me? Why?"

"Well, Artio and Daray told me all about you. You're a black belt in different martial arts, you're fluent in Latin, you once rescued a squirrel at summer camp, and you're really pretty. Oh, geez ... that must have sounded really creepy."

"I'm flattered, but I'm only a black belt in Tae Kwon Do. I can piece together a couple of Latin phrases, but I'm not fluent. And Cassidy was the one who saved the squirrel at summer camp. Do you think I'm pretty, or did Aydan's parents tell you that too?"

"Well you're … different than I expected," Chay said, as she rolled a wild strawberry between her fingers. "Is the second half of the journal safe?"

"It's destroyed too."

"That's probably for the best."

Danny fidgeted. "Can we go outside?" she asked. Chay nodded, but Aydan summoned Danny to meet Daray.

"We can go for a walk after you say hi to the Tolymie's dad," Chay assured her.

* * *

After Cassidy and Aydan went upstairs, Danny met Chay in Eamon's garden. She detected the smell of sage, rosemary, and lavender, but realized she could only identify the distinct purple shoots of the living lavender plant. The other two smells she recognized as only spices from the grocery store.

"So, how do you know Eamon?"

"I met him through Artio, Aydan's mom. My family and her family have known each other for a long time." Chay plucked one of the yellow flowers. "This is St. John's Wort."

"Oh, I've seen pills of that."

Pinching the bridge of her nose, Chay shook her head and sighed.

For the next several hours, Danny enjoyed learning the histories and uses of different flowers and herbs from Chay. When Danny was tired of absorbing information, they strung lavender cuts together in bundles that could be dried from the ceiling. They entertained themselves in that way until the afternoon, and were ushered inside by a somber Eamon.

CHAPTER 24
HE'LL BE WITH THE ONE HE LOVES

CASSIDY AWOKE TO BEES BUZZING outside the window. Judging by the square of sunlight on the satin comforter, she correctly predicted late afternoon before checking her Ogham. Aydan yawned and she gently rolled him off her arm. For the first time in several days, she felt rested and refreshed. Her bliss promptly changed to concern when Danny entered without the usual spring in her step. Chay trailed in behind Danny.

"What've you been up to?" Cassidy asked, as she shook her arm to relieve the pins and needles from the pressure of Aydan's head. She rubbed the sleep out of her eyes bringing into focus the tear stains on Chay's cheeks.

"I hung out with Chay ... until ... Aydan ... I'm so sorry," Danny mumbled.

"What happened?" Aydan threw back the covers and jumped out of bed.

"Daray died this afternoon," Danny managed to say. "He looked so young. I don't understand."

"He wasn't young, but a neurodegenerative disease took its toll on him before he lost his youthful face," Aydan explained his voice cracking. "It's alright Cassidy, he was in his late nineties. I'm glad he didn't have to suffer more."

The company made their way back to the garden where Daray's body lay surrounded by wildflowers that Chay and Danny had helped organize for the last few hours. Aydan cried out and slumped onto the cobblestone path. Kneeling on the ground next to him, Cassidy pulled him to her chest. She felt his sobs against her shoulder, while a handful of elderly people gathered in the yard to mourn.

"They're my neighbors and Daray's friends," Eamon explained gesturing at the new arrivals. "I've been keeping an eye on his body the whole time, but it's highly unlikely any of them know about his origins." He sat down next to Cassidy and Aydan. "The way your father acted around you today is the most functional I've seen him in two years. I think he was just hanging on to see you again. I'm sorry."

"Cremation was his choice and is necessary for the protection of his DNA," Aydan explained to Eamon.

"You don't need to worry about the formalities. I organized all of the burial proceedings for your mother as well."

"You were the friend who told us about Mom, weren't you?"

"Yes. I did everything I could to save Artio, but she passed away in my arms." Eamon quietly shed tears behind his hand. "I would like you to accompany me when we take his body to the crematory in an hour."

Breathing shallowly, Aydan squeezed Cassidy's waist when Eamon discussed Daray's body. In that moment, Cassidy felt more helpless when confronted with Aydan's anguish than she had felt drugged and pinned to the ground by Taban. "I understand why it's a good idea to get rid of Daray's DNA as soon as possible, but I didn't know it was possible to get someone's body cremated so quickly," Cassidy commented.

"I'm very good at getting what I want. In this case, what I want also coincides with what all of you want: Peace for your father."

When Eamon wiped his eyes the bright sunlight hit his face at the right angle to wash out his wrinkles. For a split second Cassidy thought she was looking at Eadowen. She pondered for a moment if Eamon could have fathered a child with Artio. The way he'd looked at Artio's photograph and his reference to her dying in his arms seemed very intimate. From memory she concluded that Eadowen didn't give off the same striking charisma she'd noted with both Taban and Eamon. She accepted that her observation of Eadowen did not entirely rule out that he was Eamon's child. *Why would Eamon protect and care for the man who married the woman he loved?* Cassidy wondered. *I know I'm probably jumping to conclusions, but what if Eamon killed Daray now that he has Daray's sons. What if he's going to reveal their whereabouts?* Her throat tightened. She wanted to trust Eamon but she didn't want to be duped by an Each Uisge again.

To avoid facing thoughts of death or grief, Danny made herself busy moving the fruit platter and table outside for the guests. On one of her trips, carrying an arm load of various citrus staples, Danny noticed the neighbors surrounding Donovan to hug him and express their condolences. To provide him with the opportunity to mourn alone, she dropped an orange on the path. The juicy thunk was not loud enough to disrupt the entire gathering, but it distracted enough people to allow Donovan to escape. Then she received a message on her Ogham from Cassidy which read: **I think E.B. might have something to do with what happened to D.T. Help me talk to him.** Danny decoded from the message and the dark look Cassidy gave her that she was supposed to help Cassidy interrogate Eamon.

"Eamon there's something I need help with in the basement," Cassidy said to Eamon loud enough for Danny to hear.

"Certainly," he replied and followed Cassidy through the front door.

Danny darted up to Aydan who remained seated on the steps staring at his father from a distance. She hugged him and unfastened his silver hairclip. "I need to borrow this," she whispered. "Don't take your eyes off your father."

Pulling the razor blade out of the hair accessory, Danny trailed after Eamon. He turned when she opened the door. Seeing the razor blade he looked at Cassidy uncomfortably. "What can I help you with?" he asked.

"You did something you're not letting on," Cassidy accused. She and Danny advanced on him until he backed into the sofa. Amenably sitting on the couch in front of the two women, Eamon looked from one to the other with a baffled expression. An exasperated frown formed on his lips when, he caught Cassidy looking in the direction of the open trap door with the staircase decorated by photographs.

"You think I'm responsible for Daray's death don't you?" He sighed.

"You were his romantic rival, weren't you?" Cassidy said.

"Yes, but Artio has been dead for four years, what purpose would killing him possibly serve?" He rested his arms on his bent knees. "I loved her *and* I wanted to protect Daray. He was a kind and wonderful man who was also my dear friend." Cassidy's heart ached at the sincerity of his tone, but she maintained a skeptical expression.

"Then what about the money that could be made by selling longevity?" Danny asked.

"There was no price worth betraying those I cared about." He started to stand, saw that neither Cassidy nor Danny was willing to believe him and sat down again. "Chay!" he yelled.

"Coming," Chay called from outside. A few seconds later she opened the door and her eyes widened before squinting with concern. "What are you doing to him?"

"I'm fine," Eamon assured her. "They think I killed Daray."

"Listen." Chay walked over to Danny and rested her hand on Danny's arm. "There's no reason why Eamon would shelter Daray for this long just to hurt him. Eamon could've sold him out years ago."

"Do you find Eamon attractive?" Cassidy asked. "That could skew your judgment like it did mine."

"Ew. No." Chay wrinkled her nose. "I'm gay. Besides, he's practically my uncle."

"And she's a Genetic Fey," Eamon added. "I swore to Artio I would do everything in my power to keep her family safe. I am many things, Cassidy, but I do not go back on my word." As he spoke the last phrase his face became resolute, an expression which emphasized the similarities between his and Eadowen's features.

"I apologize," Cassidy said. "I'm adjusting to not always trusting an alluring and sincere face."

"Thank you." Eamon smiled and stood up from the sofa.

"You don't seem very angry at us," Danny commented on his sudden cheerfulness.

"I haven't been called alluring in ten years."

"Flattery will get you everywhere with Eamon," Chay said, giving him a light punch on the shoulder.

"Why did you think she'd find Eamon appealing?" Danny asked.

"He's a Peach Whisky."

"Really? Like Taban?" Danny said. "Ugh."

"What's a Peach Whisky?" Chay asked.

"He doesn't seem to be all that terrible though," Cassidy replied.

"Thank you for the vote of confidence," Eamon replied dryly. "I can understand how past experiences would lead you not to trust me."

"You seem like a pretty nice Peach Whisky," Danny observed.

"Why do I get the awful feeling that the butchered pronunciation of Each Uisge is going to stick?" Eamon said. He headed down to the basement for another fruit platter for the guests while the young women returned outside.

* * *

When the neighbors finished their speeches and goodbyes, Eamon and Aydan boarded a hearse to transport Daray's body. An hour before sundown, Aydan and Eamon returned with Daray's ashes. Upon their arrival, Cassidy sent a message to Marja asking her to take them back to the hostel. She and Aydan cuddled in one of the large armchairs, while they waited for Marja to arrive.

"Where's Donovan?" Aydan said into Cassidy's shoulder.

Enlisting the help of Danny and Chay, they frantically searched every cranny of the house. "You know it's kind of embarrassing that we lost an almost seven-foot-tall guy," Cassidy remarked to Danny as they went out to investigate the garden. Eventually, Eamon located Donovan, who had taken refuge away from human interaction in a coat closet. Though Cassidy had already checked the same storage space, Donovan had evaded her by concealing himself under several trench coats and a kilt.

"Hm, the closet is the last place I'd expect to find you," Eamon remarked, then looked disappointed, as the younger generation stared at him blankly. "That would've been funny thirty years ago," he muttered.

The friends bid Eamon goodbye at the door and Chay followed them out to Marja's car. She smiled at Danny. "I had a really good time spending time with you. I wish it hadn't ended the way it did."

Danny kissed the tear stains on Chay's cheek. "I'm going to be around for a few days. Maybe we can spend more time together. Feel better, okay."

"I'd *really* like that," Chay gave Danny a quick peck on lips.

* * *

Journal Entry by Edana Arthur Reyes:

We're on the plane back to North America, and Cassidy suggested I write about our trip in her journal. We—that is Cassidy, Donovan, and I—spent two weeks traveling and exploring with our respective programs. After we left Eamon's house, Aydan caught the first flight back to Nova Scotia to communicate to Eadowen what had transpired. Aydan is so cute. I don't think Cassidy has stopped thinking about him this whole trip. Not that she'd ever admit it. Chay stopped by when Cassidy and I weren't being whisked off to the next site or activity, which unfortunately wasn't very often. I really like Chay. We flirted a lot, but we didn't get serious because we probably won't see each other for quite a while. It was still great to socialize … and make out. I have to admit, I'm not sure whether Chay liked me for me or for the stories the Tolymie's parents told her about me. Chay and I promised to keep in touch. It's nice to know another Genetic Fey outside of the Tolymie family. I think I'm going to start really studying biology. Maybe I can figure out my whole pain thing and help out Chay, Aydan, and Eadowen with theirs. Whatever happens, I'm so glad Cassidy will be there for me. I hope I can be there for her too.

Epilogue
A GF By Any Other Name

THE FULL MOON CAST a cool glow over the page of Cassidy's journal, as she wrote in the front seat of Ms. Reyes car.

We flew back from Scotland this morning. Danny and I are spending our layover in Nova Scotia before we fly back to Victoria. It's about five in the morning. Ms. Reyes picked us up at the airport and took us back to her house. I'm just waiting for Danny to finish cutting roses from her mother's garden, so we can go to the Tolymie's house.

"All set." Danny climbed into the passenger seat clutching a handful of different-colored roses.

"Message to Anna-Mom: My study abroad was very rewarding," Cassidy reported in response to the message her mother had left her. "I learned more than I'll ever be able to tell you." She gave Danny a wink as she fastened her seatbelt. "I feel a little bad about waking the Tolymie's up at this ridiculous hour." Cassidy commented to Danny as she turned Mrs. Reyes' car onto the highway.

"We warned them. Besides, that's what flowers are for, right?"

"I suppose," Cassidy chuckled. "Hey, Danny?"

"Yes?"

"Thank you for rescuing me."

"You're welcome," Danny replied. "I don't know what I would've done without your support."

"Then I guess we'll just keep rescuing each other. That sounds so sickeningly sweet."

"But it's true." An owl's cry punctuated Danny's remark. "So, are you going to lay one on Aydan like you told me last night?"

"Uh …"

"Aw," Danny teased. "Are you too shy?"

"Actually, I was worried about your feelings," Cassidy sighed. "I know I don't need your permission, but I wanted to check in. I don't want to hurt you and I still feel bad about the whole Taban affair."

"Thanks for thinking of me, but I told you I'm alright. You're my GF, after all."

"But I'm not a Genetic Fey or your girlfriend."

"Guardian Fey," Danny explained. "You're the Guardian Fey to my crazy pixie."

"Hm, Guardian Fey, I like it. I've always wanted to be a fairy godmother."

"So, university applications is our next adventure I guess. Think you can be my fairy godmother for that?" Danny asked.

"We're definitely going to need each other for that terrifying quest."

Cassidy found the Tolymie's driveway on the first pass. As they drove up, she saw Stag, in a sequin cheerleading uniform, having a disagreement with Donovan. The giant jock was doing his best imitation of a brick wall at his friend. As Stag moved, the moonlight made the v of sequins on his chest and his chrome shorts shimmer.

"Well, what'd you know? A silver stag—we must be lucky," Cassidy remarked. "How do you like them antlers?"

"I definitely do," Danny agreed.

There was a red coupe parked in the Tolymie's driveway. Cassidy pulled in next to it and turned the key in the ignition. The sky had turned from black to indigo, and a pink glow highlighted the horizon through the trees.

Dressed in his lacrosse uniform, Donovan held his lacrosse stick across his chest while Stag desperately attempted to push a garment bag into his hands. When Stag heard them approach, he turned, and his entire face lit up. Donovan took this opportunity to give the garment bag back to Stag. Unfortunately, he did it with enough force to knock Stag over before he could catch the cheerleader. Stag bounced back up, gave Donovan a warning look, and trotted up to Cassidy.

"Good … morning-ish," Cassidy said.

"Hey there! I'm going to be on the Olympic Peninsula soon and I do believe I owe you a latte," he said to Cassidy, then turned to Danny. "And my chinchilla misses you."

"Well, hand over your contact information," Danny commanded. "You're a Guardian Fey, we have to stick together."

"A Guardian—?" Stag started to say, but he correctly interpreted Cassidy's nod as a signal to accept Danny's creativity. "Okay." He tossed his Ogham-Flex to Cassidy. Trying not to giggle as she put in her information, Cassidy passed it to Danny, who threw it back to Stag. She managed to miss her target by about two meters, so Stag let Donovan catch it in his net.

"I'm gonna miss you," Danny said, jumping to put her arms around Donovan's neck.

Dropping his lacrosse stick and athletic bag, Donovan caught her under her legs and lifted her up to perch on his arm. "Squirrel," he squeezed her affectionately.

Danny hopped down and he gingerly wrapped his arms around Cassidy's shoulders. She hugged him around the waist.

"Bye Donovan." Cassidy took a white rose from Danny's hand and hesitantly offered it to him. *Donovan's the only one who I'm not sure will appreciate this, but I want to give him one in case he does,* she thought. Donovan accepted it and looked confused. "Uh … thanks?"

"How nice of you, Cassidy," Stag filled in helpfully. "That will look great in the suit he's *supposed* to be wearing for team pictures today."

Reminded that she had a handful of flowers, Danny presented Stag with a pink rose.

"Oh, pretty. Thank you so much. You know I …" Stag seemed like he wanted to continue chatting with them, but Donovan had other ideas. He scooped Stag up and unceremoniously carried him over one shoulder toward the red coupe parked next to the Reyes' car. Stag clung to the hanger of the lacrosse players suit.

"We're late," Donovan muttered.

Propping himself up on Donovan's shoulder, Stage checked his Ogham-Flex. "You're right," he sighed. "See y'all later!" He waved. "Donovan, don't think that means you're getting out of wearing the suit. The coach will have your head if you show up without it, since you never wore it to away meets."

"Games?" Donovan corrected.

"Yes, those."

Donovan set Stag in the passenger seat. A few moments later, the coupe made a quick turn and sped down the driveway.

"Edana, Cassidy—come on in," Eadowen beckoned them from the doorway. "You were absolutely brilliant to have figured out the journal." He accepted a yellow rose from Cassidy. "Thank you." She hugged him, sneaking a whiff of his infamous cologne to discover Danny hadn't exaggerated its seductive draw.

"Your bloodstone ring is gone?" Cassidy observed under her breath.

"It never fit me anyway," Eadowen replied with his usual unassuming smile. Yet, this time, Cassidy found it slightly unnerving. As she observed him slouched over the yellow rose, she decided that on the off chance he was Eamon's child he had not inherited the Each Uisge genes, or at least not enough of them to be a threat.

"Aydan is outside in the back," Eadowen said. "I'm sure he'll want to say goodbye." Cassidy headed toward the door with a meaningful glance at Danny. As she walked back down the hall, she noticed a missing panel in the wall underneath the table holding the foxglove vase. She recalled Aydan mentioning the daughter's addition to the journal had been hidden where Taban wouldn't find it.

As soon as Cassidy was out of sight Eadowen straightened his broad shoulders. Danny sniffed the air detecting a buttery aroma. "You have breakfast for us," she said to Eadowen, who laughed and nodded.

"Where're you all going now?" Danny led the way to the kitchen.

"We don't know yet, but we need to disappear for a while." He started to put fresh croissants in a cloth bag. "We're certainly going to demolish this old house ... probably burn it too."

"That's too bad."

"Yeah it is," he agreed pensively. "I'll send you a physical letter at our new address. We should continue minimal correspondences that way."

* * *

Cassidy slipped her ten of diamonds into her décolletage. The indigo sky showed shades of violet through the canopy of trees. Cassidy found Aydan in his fairy circle, his hair bound messily by a twig, and wearing the same tunic she'd seen him wearing when they met. She watched his bare feet on the mossy ground as he spun in circles, maneuvering a whip to make cards appear out of the air. *Give me courage Danny,* she thought.

"Greetings," Aydan said, coiling the whip, as she approached.

"Hey magic man," she said, stepping into the fairy circle. Before she could stop herself, she grabbed the strings of his tunic and pulled him toward her. "If you give me a kiss I'll give you good luck." He stood on his toes, wrapped his arms around her shoulders, and gave her a long peck. When they released each other, he tucked a loose piece of his hair behind his ear and cleared his throat. Surrounded by a circle of mushrooms, they both shifted awkwardly.

"Uh. Consider it a compliment," Cassidy said, at last.

"My first kiss—best compliment I've ever received." He looked at her with his bold, dark eyes and they both started to laugh.

"Well, I *am* the biggest fan ..." Cassidy slid the twig out of his hair and watched the cascade of ebony fall over his shoulders. "... of Aydan Tolymie, though Harlan Eldin is pretty cool too."

He ducked in a graceful bow and accepted the red rose from her. Holding the rose between his teeth he posed extravagantly with one hand on his hip. Then he stuck out his tongue sabotaging the image. She laughed. The sun began to warm Cassidy's skin, through the trees. Towering clouds on the eastern horizon glowed bright orange.

"Wait. That was your first kiss?"

"Yeah, can't go spreading my genetic material around, not to mention I can't exactly tell people what I am. And the whole pain-at-the-drop-of-a-hat, doesn't help either."

"May I have another?"

The spirited lip lock that followed made her knees weak, but didn't have the same tidal force as the canoodling she'd experienced with an Each Uisge. She realized she appreciated both sensations, and hoped she could forget the former.

"Don't forget this." He flicked a ten of diamonds into her hand.

"Hm, I thought I'd put it somewhere you couldn't get to," Cassidy laughed. She turned the card over in her hand. The diamonds no longer shone silver; instead a message illuminated by the rising sun read: *Go see Knots of Avernus concert.* She rolled her eyes. "I don't want to see them." She flipped the card over. On the back the message read: *I know you want to.*

* * *

Danny rested her hands on the counter. The morning light warmed her face and illuminated the red tones in her dark-brown hair. "I'm happy for her," she said, watching Cassidy laugh with Aydan in the distance. "It's nice to know there are people like them in the world." She felt Eadowen's gaze and turned. His dull demeanor had melted away, revealing a passionate intensity he made no effort to mask. "What?" she asked.

"I'm just admiring you."

"Thanks, Cassidy bought the top for me," Danny explained.

"I was referring to what you said, but the top is nice too." He rested his chin on his hand, his hazel eyes copper in the sunlight. "I hope you'll be open to the idea of a romantic relationship someday."

"Of course I will. It'll happen when it happens." Edana couldn't help but smile as she recalled Chay's blushing face. "But I'm not ready yet."

"You seem wistful," he commented.

"Oh. I was just thinking about someone cute that I met." The corners of his mouth turned down. "Did I say something wrong?" Danny added hastily.

Eadowen glanced at the floor. "You said nothing wrong." When he looked up again he wore the most benevolent expression Danny had ever encountered. "I just want you to be content."

"I have plenty of other dreams and goals to chase," Danny said. "Don't worry about me." She embraced him heartily, but he only grazed her shoulder with one hand.

"This is for you." He slipped a tiny vial into her hand, the scent of which, she immediately recognized as hawthorn and thistle. "So you'll remember me next time."

"I won't forget." Danny picked up the bag of croissants. "I wish I had something to give you."

"Unfortuately for me, you don't owe me anything," Eadowen said. Danny tilted her head to the side to encourage him to elaborate, but he only added, "Goodbye, Edana."

"See you around." Danny ran out into the morning light to join Aydan and Cassidy. She saluted Aydan, who reciprocated the motion.

"Those croissants smell delicious." Cassidy reached for the bag, but Danny dashed past her waving the bag tauntingly. "Come back here you little fey!" Cassidy chased after her best friend.

Danny threw a genetically modified blue rose to Cassidy and slipped the remaining violet rose in her own ponytail. "Catch me!" She called.

Cassidy chased after her.

THE END

GLOSSARY OF SEXUALITY & GENDER TERMS

Gender: Is a social construct that manifests as roles or expectations of how a person should act based on the gender they are labeled.[3]

Sex (Assigned Gender): Is the label a person is assigned at birth based the person's physical body.[3]

Cisgender: A person who identifies with the gender they were assigned at birth based on their genitalia.[1] For example, Aydan has male genitalia and identifies as a man.

Gender Queer: A person who does not identify with the gender they were assigned at birth.[1] For example, Eadowen has male genitalia and identifies as gender neutral not as a man.

Gender Neutral Pronouns: Pronouns used by someone who identifies as neither a man nor a woman. The pronouns used in this book are xie (the equivalent of he or she) and hir (the equivalent of him, her, his, and hers).

Pansexual: A person who has the potential to be attracted to anyone regardless of gender identity or assignment.[2]

Polysexual/Bisexual: A person who is attracted to some genders, but not all.

Queer: An umbrella term for a sexuality other than heterosexual, however, in this book it is primarily used to refer to people who are only attracted to people with the same gender assignment.[1]

Questioning: A person who is deciding on their sexuality or gender identity.[2]

SOURCES:

1. "LGBTcenter," last modified 2013, http://lgbtcenter.ucdavis.edu/lgbt-education/lgbtqia-glossary. Date accessed: June 20, 2013.

2. "University Montana Glossary," last updated 2013, http://www.umt.edu/umallies/glossary.php. Date accessed: June 24, 2013.

3. "World Health Organization," last modified 2013, http://www.who.int/gender/whatisgender/en/. Date accessed: June 24, 2013.

FURTHER READING

BOOKS:

Cotterell, Arthur, and Rachel Storm. *The Ultimate Encyclopedia of Mythology*. Ed. Emma Gray. N.p.: Anness Publishing Limited, 1999. Print.

Frazer, Sir James, and Theodor H. Gaster. *The New Golden Bough Abridged*. New York: S. G. Phillips Inc., 1959. Print.

MacKaillop, James. *Oxford Dictionary of Celtic Mythology*. New York: Oxford University Press Inc, 1998. Print.

Nozedar, Adele. *The Illustrated Guide to Signs & Symbols Sourcebook*. New York: Harper Collins, 2010. Print.

VIDEO:

Great Courses: Exploring The Roots Of Religion .Narr. John H. Hale. The Teaching Company , 2009. 3 Discs. DVD-ROM.

Little People of Flores. Nova, 2005. Web. 24 June 2013. <http://www.pbs.org/wgbh/nova/evolution/little-people-flores.html>.

ARTICLES:

Borrell, Brendan. "Faroe Islands Aim to Sequence Genes of Entire Country." Discover. Discover Magazine, 12 June 2013. Web. 24 June 2013. <http://discovermagazine.com/2013/julyaug/01-faroe-islands-aim-to-sequence-genomes-healthcare#.Ucj5eDvIEmA>.

Grammer K, Fink B, Neave N. Human pheromones and sexual attraction. European Journal Of Obstetrics, Gynecology, And Reproductive Biology [serial online]. February 1, 2005;118(2):135-142. Available from: MEDLINE, Ipswich, MA. Accessed: 20 April 2013. From: EPSCOhost

Pallett, Pamela M., Stephen Link, and Kang Lee. "New 'golden' ratios for facial beauty." Vision Research 50 (2009): 149-54. Web. 20 Apr. 2013.

BONUS STORIES

Cassidy & Danny's Summer Camp Adventure

SET THREE YEARS BEFORE CASSIDY MEETS THE TOLYMIES

"BYE, SWEETIE," Rona Adisa, Cassidy's mother said. She and Annabelle Adisa wrapped Cassidy up in a big family hug. Squished between her two mothers, Fourteen-year-old Cassidy wanted nothing more than to break free. She squirmed out of her mothers' grasp hoping the arriving students had not seen her with her parents. In the heat of the August sun, the University of Victoria swarmed with high school students lined up for martial art camp room keys. Experts on martial arts from Krav Maga to Aikido had flown in from all over the world to teach courses and lecture on their given specialty.

"I can't believe our little baby is going away to summer camp." Rona affectionately stroked Cassidy's long cornrows, which she promptly tucked behind her shoulder out of reach of her mother.

"Remember all those fun camps we went to as a family when you were younger?" Annabelle, Cassidy's normally more stoic mother, sounded wistful.

"No," Cassidy lied in an attempt to hurry the goodbye process along. She'd attended University of Victoria's Summer Explorations in Martial Arts the summer before and considered herself a veteran.

"Now you're all on your own again," Annabelle continued the thought as though Cassidy had not given the sharp reply.

"Yup," Cassidy agreed. "See you in a week." Cassidy grabbed her suitcase, started toward one of the check-in lines, and gave her mothers a backhanded wave. When she heard her mothers' car drive away Cassidy felt a surge of adrenaline—for one week of the year she had no parents and no adults to tell her what to do. At the check-in desk, she obtained her name badge and transferred the room key to her Ogham.

"Hi, are you Cassidy Adisa?" A twenty-something with platinum blond braids and a radiant grin tapped Cassidy on the shoulder. "I'm Jake, I've been assigned to your camp family. Want to go find your dorm room," she said.

College student counselors don't count as adults as they are more like smart, attractive, and mature teenagers, Cassidy thought, as she followed Jake toward a grey, brick building. *I can't wait to go to university.*

"Want some help getting your suitcase up the stairs?" A muscular college student with orange freckles asked them.

"Nah, we got it. Thanks, Ashley." Jake smiled and hefted Cassidy's suitcase over her delicate shoulder. "In college, if you ever want to move furniture into your dorm room just offer one of the athletic teams pizza to move your stuff—cheapest labor ever."

Cassidy laughed. "Has my roommate arrived yet?"

"I don't think so." Jake set Cassidy's suitcase by one of the two beds. This year Cassidy was prepared for the bareness of the tiny dorm room, but she recalled the previous year when she had been shocked that camp expected her to live in a closet-sized room with another person. The two twin-sized beds comprised the furniture of the room. A table was folded up over each bed as a desk. True desks had fallen out of fashion, due to space constraints and almost everything being in digital format. All dorm rooms had three screens, one for each wall that didn't have a window, which rolled down with the push of a button. A three dimensional projector hung from the ceiling next to the overhead light. The three dimensional projectors functioned similarly to three dimensional printers, differing mostly in their purpose: the projector helped an individual experience an image tactally through the use of specialized gloves. After all, three dimensional gaming, movies, and course work were necessary, unlike antiquated tables and chairs.

Your first activity, Aikido, starts in an hour," Jake said. "Afterward you can come to the dining hall for dinner. Lights out at 11 p.m. but I won't bug you if you're just talking quietly with your roommate. We just don't want anyone else in your room after 11 p.m. Your mothers signed that it was okay for you to be in gender neutral housing, so there are male-bodied people on this floor if that makes a difference to you when you go to the bathrooms, which are just down the hall."

"I'll be there." Cassidy called as Jake left the room. She changed into the starched martial arts uniform her parents had tailored for her then flopped onto her bed to play a three dimensional game she'd brought.

* * *

Backpack slung over her shoulder, Danny bolted from the car before it came to a complete stop.

"Danny be careful!" her father admonished.

"Bye, Dad," Danny shouted over her shoulder. "Thanks for dropping me off."

Her dad pulled the car to a stop, hurried out, and rushed after her. She hugged him.

"Contact your mom or me anytime," he said.

"I will," she promised. Danny had never been away from her parents before. She put on a brave front, but felt panic stir inside her gut when her father's car disappeared down the road. Her school had given her a scholarship application to the summer camp, which she had filled out never thinking she would actually receive it. If she hadn't received a scholarship, her family would not have been able to afford to send her to the camp. *Ugh, I don't want to meet a bunch of rich snobs,* Danny thought, as she watched a teenager with long cornrows adjusting her perfectly fitted new uniform while walking toward a sign labeled: "Aikido meet up." *The actual martial arts stuff should be cool, though,* Danny decided. She glanced at her Ogham and realized she didn't have enough time to go to her dorm room or check in, so she followed the girl with cornrows at a distance.

Inside the University of Victoria's gym, Danny followed the signs and the other girl to a basketball court covered in red, blue, and gold mats. The instructor wore a *karategi,* the white martial art training uniform, and *hakama*, pleated fabric tied in a knot at the waist by four straps. She stood in the center of a circle of seated students.

"Glad you decided to show up," the instructor said to Danny and the other girl as they trailed into the gym. "We are partnering up, so you two can be together. Please find a place on the mat and introduce yourself to your partner."

Reluctantly wandering over to a mat, Danny met the other girl's gaze for the first time. The other teen's striking brown-eyed gaze and vibrant complexion made Danny feel the little green monster of jealousy bite her.

"I'm Cassidy Adisa," the girl offered.

"Edana Reyes, but I prefer Danny."

"Please bow to your partners as a sign of respect."

Danny and Cassidy both bent at the waist—neither relinquished eye contact.

"I'm taking real martial arts like Tae Kwon Do and Judo—I'm just checking this one out for fun," Danny explained.

"I'm taking this, Tai Chi, and Karate because I think there's much to be learned from both offensive and defensive martial arts."

"In Aikido, it is important for you to learn how to fall ..." the instructor started to say.

"I want to learn how to punch and kick," Danny said under her breath.

The instructor turned to face Danny, with a complacent expression. "Punch me," the instructor invited. Danny obliged shoving her fist toward the instructor's abdomen. The instructor gracefully sidestepped, caught her wrist, and guided Danny to the floor.

"In Aikido you will also learn how to use someone else's momentum against them," the instructor explained.

Impressed by the power of Aikido, Danny became the best partner Cassidy could have hoped to have in just the first session together. She watched Cassidy's movements and body rolls meticulously, making thoughtful observations and suggestions when needed. By the end of the first session, both Cassidy and Danny felt comfortable with the front roll and Cassidy had successfully executed the back roll several times with Danny's careful spotting.

* * *

After grabbing food at the dining hall and a taking shower, Cassidy swiped her Ogham across the door to her dorm room. She noticed Danny dabbing her thick hair with a towel while seated on the other bed. Cassidy felt a twinge of envy, when she observed Danny's sharp-featured profile and freckles.

"So, you're my roommate, eh?" Danny said sprawling across the bed.

"Yeah." Cassidy pulled on her baggy pajama shirt over her uniform then slipped it off from underneath the night shirt. "Can you believe how cramped these rooms are?"

"This is the size of my room," Danny muttered.

Cassidy glanced uncomfortably at her roommate. "At least you don't have to share your room with anyone," she said in an attempt to cover up her faux pas.

"True. Sorry you have to share."

"But I am happy to be rooming with you," Cassidy added quickly. "You're going to be awesome in offensive martial arts."

I have to share a room with her for a week and I do like chatting. I should probably try to be civil, Danny thought. "What are you taking besides Tai Chi and Aikido?" Danny asked. "You know that one extracurricular thingy we get to do."

"Kayaking," Cassidy replied. "This is just going to be regular river kayaking, but I really love surf kayaking."

"What the heck is surf kayaking?"

Cassidy hit the button to make the screens go down. She and Danny selected three dimensional imaging on their respective Oghams and put on their visors. "Sunset: Show image of wave ski and gear," Cassidy demanded of her Ogham. An image of a flat kayak appeared in front of Danny and Cassidy appeared in front of them. Danny put on the gloves usually used for gaming and attached them to the three dimensional projector. She ran her hands along the image of the kayak while the printer made imitations of the material she touched on her fingertips. The sensors in the screens changed the appearance of the straps to hold the person's feet and waist, as Danny clipped and unclipped them.

"So, surf kayaking is surfing on your butt with ski gear on? Weird sport."

Danny's conclusion made Cassidy chuckle.

"I'm doing fencing," Danny offered.

"That sounds fun. You'll have to tell me how it goes. I love swashbuckling movies."

"Me too!" Danny lay with her head and shoulders upside down over the edge of the bed her hair cascading toward the floor. "Which ones?"

"Gosh anything with sword play. Even if it's colorful light swords used in an ineffective but cool looking style. I like anime too. What else do you like to watch?"

"I'm more into Western cartoons," Danny replied. "Oh, and documentaries about flora and fauna are fun too. What else do you like?"

"Okay, if you promise not to tell anyone …" Cassidy began and Danny nodded eagerly. "I like all those hit pop songs everyone makes fun of."

A frown spread across Danny's upside down lips, as though she expected Cassidy to tell her something much more tantalizing. "I listen to pop music when I work out all the time," she replied with a shrug. Pulling herself to a seated position using only her abdominal muscles, Danny stretched. "You know, I've never been kayaking, so I look forward to hearing about it too."

"We should probably get to bed. I have Tai Chi at 5 a.m.," Cassidy commented.

"Who is the person who set up that insane schedule? I don't have to get up until 10 a.m. to do fencing."

"They want us to practice with the sunrise." Cassidy stuck out her tongue and wrinkled her nose to show her disgust. "I'm a sunset girl myself."

"Well, goodnight then."

"Nice talking to you." Pulling the covers up to her neck Cassidy snuggled into her pillow. "Since I have to go to bed early, do you want to have dinner together?"

"Yeah, let's meet up in the dining hall after activities," Danny replied. *Okay, maybe this Cassidy person isn't so bad after all,* Danny thought as she drifted off to sleep.

* * *

Yawning, Cassidy rolled her shoulders back and exited the dining hall in where she'd had a hearty breakfast thanks to the appetite she'd worked up from Tai Chi. Her whole body felt at ease under the warm late-morning sun. *I don't know why I don't do Yoga or Tai Chi every morning,* Cassidy thought. *Who am I kidding? I like to lie in bed as long as possible.* She took a shuttle to the outdoor activities area of the camp off of the University of Victoria campus. She would be kayaking, but other students would be doing, fencing, canoeing, and archery. Aware that she would be about an hour early, Cassidy wore her tankini under her clothes. Thanks to modern technology her suit would dry in less than two minutes when no longer submerged in water, so it would be comfortable to wear back to the dorms.

When she arrived at the riverbed she made herself comfortable on her towel to consult her Ogham about the best swimming spot in the river within five minutes walking distance. As she scanned the river with her Ogham, Cassidy heard a shrieking sound. Fearing the sound came from a child, Cassidy changed her Ogham's settings to find the origin of the sound. A map appeared on her Ogham with a dot indicating the direction of the sound. With that information, she made her way to the river, where she saw a large log from which the strange shrieking sound emitted. She bushwhacked her way to the other side of the log where she found a Douglas Squirrel with its bloody leg twisted at an angle that almost confirmed it was broken. The squirrel's mangled leg had gotten caught on the bark, in an attempt to get free it had gotten stuck upside down. Each time the current rose it dunked the squirrel's head under water. The creature's dark eyes filled with even more terror when it noticed Cassidy. Waving its arms and tail it struggled more violently than before, tearing up its injured leg even more.

Cassidy inspected the turbulent current across the deep river. The rotting log started big enough to support human weight by the shore, but soon tapered out. The unfortunate squirrel had gotten itself caught a third of the way into the river where the log looked possibly thick enough to hold a cat. Cassidy had walked on logs enough to know that they were less dense than water, but once rotten and soaked they became significantly less buoyant. She also knew that even if the log could support her, balance would be the challenge in the river. Taking off her outer garments, Cassidy decided to walk as far out on the log as she could comfortably, then get into the water and use the log to keep the swift current from dragging her away. The rotten wood squished under her toes and moldy bark slid off the sides of the log as she walked out. The lapping sound of the river, while soothing on the shore, started to intimidate Cassidy as it splashed against the log with enough force to make the log sway. Bending her knees, Cassidy gripped the log firmly with both hands, and slipped into the river. With one arm over the log she made her way toward the squirrel. Water splashed in her mouth as the small waves from the current slapped against her face. At last she reached the squirrel, which froze when she got close.

It's probably not a good idea to actually touch a wild animal, Cassidy realized as she dug at the bark that held the squirrel's leg. "Really got yourself in there didn't you?" Cassidy addressed the squirrel through gritted teeth. Her fingers stung in the cold and the tips started to bleed from the abrasion of the wood. Summoning all of her strength, Cassidy grabbed the entire chunk of bark and ripped it from the log successfully, but lost her hold on the log. As her face submerged under water she saw the squirrel dart to safety. Before the current could drag her under the log and down the river, Cassidy managed to anchor herself to the fallen tree again. She attempted to pull her head above water, but realized some of her hair had gotten stuck underneath the log. Frantically she tried to dislodge it, but underwater and only by touch proved difficult as she struggled for air. With desperate brute force, she managed to rip enough of the cornrows out of the log for her to catch her breath, but not enough to break free.

* * *

Danny pulled one of the flat chest guards over her head. After several attempts, she managed to get her arm through the correct holes on the plastron, an arm guard used in fencing. Another student passed her a small fencing jacket, which she put on with more ease than the plastron. Holding her hair back she wiggled her head into the oval shaped fencing helmet to complete her uniform. For the last two hours, she and the other students had practiced some of the basic footwork for fencing without uniforms. *Finally, we get to use the swords,* Danny thought.

The instructor set four swords out on the grass. "This is a foil, an epee, and a sabre," he explained indicating the three thin weapons. "They are used for different types of fencing with different rules depending on which is used."

"What's the real sword?" a middle school aged boy asked.

"This is a broadsword." The instructor held up the flat sword with a long sharp blade the boy had indicated. "It is not used in fencing, but I brought it as a comparison to the fencing weapons."

The instructor put the broadsword away in his bag and continued to explain the differences between the weapons. Danny lost focus on the interesting lecture when her Ogham lit up to show an urgent message: **Message from Cassidy: Danny, I'm at these coordinates. I need your help now. I'll get in trouble if they know I went into the river without supervision. Bring a knife.**

Danny turned to the brunette girl next to her. "I need to go check on a friend," Danny whispered. "If the instructor finds out I'm gone, say I went to the restroom." The brunette nodded. Danny snuck around behind the instructor and the rest of her class. No one was allowed to bring weapons to the summer camp, so she had to leave her pocket knife at home. She did, however, know of a certain sharp blade she could use. While the students crowded around the instructor to touch the other swords, Danny dug the broadsword out of the instructor's bag and charged off with it.

The Ogham map indicated that Cassidy was twenty minutes away, but Danny made it there in half the time by dashing at full tilt toward the location. I'm running with an unsheathed broadsword, I wonder if this counts as running with scissors.

"Cassidy!" Danny panted when she found her friend.

"Bring the knife," Cassidy gargled from the river.

As she stared into the turbulent river, Danny felt her knees get weak with fear. She took a deep breath. Her friend needed her to do this. *At least it isn't an ocean,* she told herself. *It's just a big pool, Danny.* She crawled across the log until it started to bend pushing Cassidy farther under water. Holding the blade she carefully guided the hilt toward Cassidy.

"That'll work," Cassidy muttered, as she took the sword. To Danny's horror, Cassidy put the blade up to her neck.

"What are you doing?" Danny yelled as Cassidy hacked off part of her cornrows. She passed the sword back to Danny, who took it and edged back to shore. Freed from her restricting hair, Cassidy joined Danny on land a few minutes later.

"Thanks for finding me." Leaving a gap between their bodies so as not to soak her friend, Cassidy embraced Danny.

"Sorry about your hair." Danny caressed the frayed ends of Cassidy's shorn hair.

"Will you help me fix it?" Cassidy held up the rest of her long cornrows. "I want the kayaking people to think my hair was always short."

Hesitantly, Danny painstakingly sawed off Cassidy's hair as evenly as she could. "You look really good with short hair," Danny decided when Cassidy turned to face her.

"Thanks." Cassidy inspected herself in a mirror screen on her Ogham. "Maybe I'll cut it really short or shave it sometime."

"I told them I was going to the bathroom. How am I going to explain taking this?" Danny held up the sword and laughed.

"Tell them you were afraid of bears when you went to the bathroom," Cassidy suggested.

"Sounds good," Danny sighed. "See you at dinner."

"You too."

Cassidy casually arrived at her kayaking class right on time. Ashley, the red-head she'd met earlier, who turned out to be the instructor, gave her hair a second glance, but didn't question the change. She heard from Danny later that no one bought the bathroom story, but found it too funny to try to uncover the truth about her borrowing the broadsword. There was one fact Cassidy did know: she and Danny would be friends for a very long time.

THE TOLYMIE'S WINTER HOLIDAY

SET FIVE MONTHS BEFORE
CASSIDY MEETS THE TOLYMIES

TABAN FINISHED TACKING the last cedar bough to the wall of the Tolymie's hallway while Aydan desperately tried to untangle holiday lights. Provided Aydan's success, the pearl bulbs would certainly add a soft ivory ambiance to the hall, once intertwined with the cedar boughs.

"Hey Houdini, can't you magic out those knots?" Taban called.

"Magic takes great patience and skill. Though I wouldn't expect you to have either of those qualities, so you wouldn't know," Aydan retorted. He inspected the mess of lights and wires until he found a worthy opponent to unravel. "As I recall, you were the one who put these away last year," he muttered under his breath.

Ignoring Aydan's accusation, Taban jumped off the stool he'd used to tack up the boughs. As he did, one of the nails caught on his swim team sweatshirt causing him to kick the stool and fall on top of it. The most recently placed bough followed shortly, hitting him in the lower back. Taban could already feel the heat of a bruise when Aydan burst into a fit of laughter.

"Donovan, Eadowen—come look at this," Aydan called with tears in his eyes. "This is one of his funniest falls yet."

Carrying a couch-cushion-sized menorah, Donovan poked his head out of the living room. Though he almost managed to hide his smirk, the twinkle in Donovan's grey eyes was completely conspicuous, especially in the flickering light emitted from the burning lighter he held in his hand.

"Are you okay, Taban?" Eadowen asked once he'd navigated his wheelchair out of the kitchen.

"I finished decking the hall," Taban groaned. He pushed the bough off of himself and untangled his legs from the stool. "Now I'm going to deck Aydan."

"Play nice, gentlemen." Eadowen offered Taban his hand. "Donovan, do you want to invite Stag for dinner or a sleepover?"

"Probably busy," Donovan grumbled, as he placed the foxglove vase from the hall table on the carpet. In its place, he set the golden menorah and lit the Shamash, the central candle, with the lighter. He produced a candle from his pocket which he tilted into the Shamash to light it and placed it in the farthest holder to indicate the first night of Hanukkah.

I wish I could fit a candle that size in my pocket, Taban thought. *Oh, that sounded so wrong, even in my head.*

While, Aydan recited the blessing for his brother, Taban picked cedar bough debris off his clothes.

"Stag said his calendar was open when I picked you up yesterday," Eadowen commented to Donovan when Aydan finished.

With interested eyes, Donovan regarded Aydan, who sighed. "Prestidigitator," Aydan addressed his Ogham by name. "Message to Stag: You wanna stay over tonight and help us decorate the tree?"

"Message from Stag: When?"

"Now is great."

"Message from Stag: See you in a few, beautiful."

"I look forward to it, handsome," Aydan teased giving one end of his tangled light project a gentle tug. The string of lights unraveled evenly, as Aydan wound the strand around his arm with a satisfied kitty smile.

"Will you help me carry something?" Eadowen beckoned Donovan who nodded and followed Eadowen into the living room. They returned with two large cardboard boxes, which they hauled outside.

Starting from the kitchen entrance and working their way down to the front door, Aydan and Taban wrapped the lights through the cedar boughs. Aydan dimmed the tri-crystal chandelier in the entryway so they could better admire their work. The ivory glow of the pearl lights and the firelight from the other room coupled with the sharp scent from the boughs and the crisp winter air gave the usually dark hallway quite a festive ambiance. Aydan donned a long velvet coat of a deep indigo shade. The salt-and-pepper faux fur trimmed hood framed his raven hair while the double breasted lines of brass buttons emphasized his triangular silhouette. He completed his snow-princess-steampunk-vampire-look with silk gloves covered in lace and thigh high boots with matching faux fur trim and pointed brass toes.

Too lazy to go upstairs to get the winter coat he'd left on his bed, Taban grabbed Eadowen's trench coat from a hanger in the living room. A brisk wind greeted the two young men when they joined Eadowen and Donovan by a pine tree adjacent to the Tolymie's house. Despite its height being only about two feet taller than Donovan, the pine's branches spread as wide as trees decades older than it. *Ea doesn't like the idea of cutting down a tree so we have to decorate it out here in the cold.* Taban gave Eadowen a bitter look. *I suggested a fake tree inside, but no, Ea has to have the living tree.* "Why do you burn trees for the bonfire in your living room if you don't want to cut down one measly tree?"

"We collect tree branches and bark that won't kill the trees," Aydan replied. The moonlight shone in his silver-eyeliner as he rolled his eyes at Taban's question. "If you collect bark from a tree by taking off vertical pieces the tree will be fine, but if you take bark from all around the tree in a ring around the trunk you'll kill it."

Shaking his head at the Tolymies, Taban shivered and turned a couple of dials on the side of the house to heat the hot tub next to the house.

Eadowen slipped off his heavy winter coat and cashmere sweater. "My trench coat isn't going to keep you warm. Taban, put on my sweater underneath the coat," he commanded.

Taban admired the moon and surrounding constellations as he slipped the paleblue sweater over his head. Stealing Eadowen's clothes was preferable to wearing his own Taban decided; he got to enjoy Eadowen's hawthorn-thistle perfume and the benefit of the extra room Eadowen's broad-shouldered clothing provided.

The sound of Stag's coupe approached, getting louder as it neared the Tolymie's driveway then faded away for a few minutes, before returning. The four housemates chuckled when they simultaneously realized Stag had missed the turn to their driveway. Eadowen set index-finger thick candles in silver candleholders, which he passed to Taban. Humming a holiday tune, Taban clipped the candlestick holders to the branches, while Aydan and Donovan hung biodegradable tinsel. Rhythmic metallic clangs resounded through the night as Stag carried his pet carrier into the house.

"Oh, yay!" Aydan's ears pricked up. "Stag brought his chinchillas."

Soon, Stag came around the side of the house. Upon seeing the moonlight tree decorating party, he broke into a sprint. Almost mirroring him, Aydan raced toward Stag. They yelled excitedly and clasped hands to jump up and down in a fashion Taban thought was reserved only for girls at bars and preteens.

"My ears," Taban grumbled as Stag and Aydan rejoined them.

Ignoring his comment, Stag flung his arms around Donovan's neck to exchange a quick squeeze greeting with his best friend. After giving Eadowen a quick kiss on the cheek, Stag started rummaging through one of the decorating boxes. "May I put the top on the tree?" Stag asked in a sweet Georgia accent. Locating the object he sought, Stag held a hollowed out crystal that Donovan had carved into a unicorn horn to his forehead.

"I don't know it looks quite pretty where it is," Aydan commented motioning for Stag to bend toward him. When Stag obliged, Aydan brushed Stag's purple bangs into place around the horn. "There we go." He snapped a picture with his Ogham.

Donovan placed his hands on Stag's hips, "Ready?" he asked. Stag smiled over his shoulder at Donovan and timed a jump as his friend hoisted him up. After some manipulation of the branches, Stag managed to fit the horn over the top of the pine.

"Show us one of your cheerleading moves," Taban demanded.

"I'm usually a catcher. I'm not a good flyer," Stag replied.

"Show Taban and Eadowen that thing you and Donovan figured out," Aydan suggested.

Still carrying Stag, Donovan backed away from the tree, nodded to Stag, and launched him up in the air. Stag twisted around in midair and landed facing the other direction in Donovan's arms. Laughing, their audience clapped and resumed decorating.

To distract himself from his frozen fingertips, Taban started quietly singing, "Baby, It's Cold Outside." Soon Eadowen recognized the tune and started to sing in his sweet baritone. As he accepted another candle from him, Taban gestured up to help Eadowen adjust himself to the correct pitch. Stag, who had joined Aydan and Donovan on tinsel duty, searched his Ogham to find an instrumental version of the song. Once the melody played, Stag was able to join in at the chorus. Though Stag's voice could not compare to Taban's trained and talented vocal cords, he matched Taban's tenor adequately for the occasion.

"Why didn't you two join in?" Stag asked.

"I didn't know the words," Aydan explained.

"We could project the words on the side of the house," Stag offered holding up his Ogham.

"Since we're doing stuff, we could sing something we all know," Aydan suggested.

"Winter Wonderland?" Donovan suggested.

"Sure," Aydan agreed.

The quintet sang under the starlit sky. Donovan's bass blended with Eadowen's baritone, but the deeper voices sounded a bit off when juxtaposed to the two tenors singing the exact same words. Secretly, Taban was grateful to Aydan who used his counter-tenor to echo the lyrics. Taban wished the others had as much training as he had, so they could create a beautiful masterpiece with their different ranges. *I guess that's not supposed to be the point of singing holiday music together,* Taban decided. When they finished caroling, the tree's branches, so laden with tinsel and candles, drooped painfully. Despite the strained branches, the pine glittered so brightly in the candlelight that it appeared to be moments away from lighting on fire.

"I think we over did it," Taban remarked.

"Nonsense," Aydan replied. "Looks great."

"I think we should take a few candles off, but the tinsel is fabulous," Stag decided titling his head to look at the tree from another angle.

"Well, enjoy your glitter tree, boys." Taban sighed and turned in the direction Eadowen had been. "This is the last time we let a cheerleader and a costume-happy magician be in charge of anything sparkly, eh Ea?" Taban glanced around the tree, but Eadowen was nowhere to be found. "Ea?"

"Bringing hot chocolate," Donovan explained.

"Thanks." When he spoke Taban saw his own breath more clearly than before. A shiver pricked at his scalp and slithered down his spine. He glanced longingly at the hot tub with seating for eight he'd bought for the Tolymie's during his first winter in Nova Scotia. The luxurious tub complete with miniature water falls in two corners, steamed only a few meters away under a turret-shaped gazebo Donovan had constructed to protect it from the elements. Aydan, who apparently had the same idea, started to work on the straps to the padded cover. Taban and Stag heaved the top off the cedar finished tub.

"Are you getting in, Donovan?" Stag asked stripping off his coat and long-sleeved shirt.

"Uh ..." Donovan inspected the ground. "Getting a swimsuit," he muttered.

"Suit yourself." Stag casually slung his pants and underwear over one shoulder the way someone might usually carry a jacket. The bruises he'd received from catching cheerleader's falls adorned his chest in purple splotches. In anticipation of getting wet, Stag slicked back his hair then programmed his nano hair dye to hold his bangs in place.

Retrieving some hangers he'd stashed in the gazebo roof, Aydan carefully hung his clothes over Stag's folded ones. The winter weather made Taban reluctant to remove his clothes, but his desire to be engulfed in warm water soon superseded his former misgivings. He wasn't excited about being nude in front of Stag and Aydan, but he succumbed to the peer pressure and tossed his clothes in a heap next to the Jacuzzi. As he settled in against one of the water falls, he noticed that Aydan used his legs to hide his genitals unlike Stag who made no effort to cover anything. "Hey Aydan, you could totally pull off a The Birth of Venus look if you just used your hair to cover yourself," Taban jeered.

Moving a handful of his hair in front of his body, Aydan seemed to take the idea quite seriously, but fell short of covering himself by a few centimeters.

"Wow, you guys massacred your body hair. What did it ever do to you?" Taban wondered aloud. "I mean I know I don't have a lot and I groom it, but you guys ... *everything* is like waxed."

"I've had sequins and glitter in places I didn't know I had."

"Ditto for some of my outfits," Aydan explained. "Not worth getting anything caught."

"Fair enough." Combing his wavy hair back with his fingers, Taban leaned back to let the waterfall of warm water flow over his face and shoulders. As he licked salt off his lips, he celebrated his splurge to buy seaweed enzymes and sea salt instead of bromine for sanitation. The scent of the treated water evoked images of tropical oceans in his mind's eye, though the pine smell convoluted it a little.

Donovan joined them a few moments later carrying a stack of towels for everyone. The water rose noticeably when his large frame displaced it. *He's gotten so big recently,* Taban thought as his eyes traced the stretch marks on Donovan's back. *I can't believe he doesn't turn seventeen until mid-May.*

"Hey Stag, when did you turn eighteen?" Taban asked.

"My birthday was a couple weeks ago." Cupping his hands Stag scooped up some of the frothing water and let it pour over his dark arms and torso. The foam trickled down his wet body highlighting every muscle on his wiry abdomen.

Donovan had already commandeered the highest seat in the hot tub allowing him the most leg room, but only shallow water to cover his torso. When Stag decided to sit, he had to contort his body because his seat did not accommodate his legs—long even in proportion to his six foot four inch frame.

"Aren't you and Donovan in the same year?" Taban leaned back into a bubble jet to target a particularly tight knot between his shoulder blades.

"Yeah, I had trouble coming into school mid-year when my dads and I first moved to the United States from Amman."

"Couldn't you have done an online thing?" Taban asked.

"I was eleven and wasn't self-motivated enough … and school is kind of hard for me. I'm not a very fast reader. Math is tough too."

"You're just going to major in girls in university aren't you?" Taban laughed.

"Do you mean gender and sexuality studies, women's history, or were you insinuating he'll be having a lot of sex?" Aydan sneered from his end of the Jacuzzi.

"From what I hear Stag needs no formal education in the last of those three categories," Eadowen cut in as he rolled down the path toward them in his swimsuit. Despite the bumps of the uneven path, he managed not to spill a drop of the hot chocolates sitting on a tray balanced in his lap. He set the hot chocolates afloat in the Jacuzzi on the buoyant tray, then hoisted himself from his wheelchair into the effervescing water.

"Guess cheerleaders like their own kind," Taban joked expecting Stag to chuckle.

Instead, Stag suddenly averted his eyes as though he found a spot in the foam from the jets fascinating. Running his hand through his hair bashfully Stag said in a quiet voice, "Apparently they do."

"Oh really?" Taban, interested for the first time, half-stepped and half-swam toward Stag who held his right arm with his left hand guarding his chest as he continued to avoid eye contact. Chin submerged in the water, Taban looked up at Stag expectantly, this gesture only made Stag try to make himself even smaller against the side of the hot tub.

"Uh … they just sort of … well, one of the ladies on the team asked me to. Then she told her friends and more people asked me. I like them so I mean I was fine with it, but I didn't know I would be so …well … you know …"

"Popular," Taban filled in. "Why are you embarrassed? You're male-bodied. There aren't as many double standards around sex that you have to deal with. The only people who would call you a slut are jealous guys. You don't even want to know how many people I've slept with."

"You're right I don't," Stag said coldly.

"Your face lights up when you look at women and you always look really interested in whatever the person you're talking to is saying. No wonder they like you."

"I *am* interested in what people have to say, but I used to always look away from people I found attractive because I didn't want them to think I was objectifying them. Eadowen told me differently. Apparently, it's better to acknowledge that I find her attractive with a smile or a more subtle expression."

"Since, to you, women are just as much people as men, it's already obvious you don't just view them as objects and most people like a compliment—even a silent one," Eadowen assured Stag.

"I didn't realize Ea was coaching you." Taban plunged his fingers into the whip cream on one of the hot chocolates and licked them off thoughtfully.

"Wait. I think I overhead something a few months ago," Aydan commented. "Did you contact Eadowen when you were in some sort of a crisis recently?"

"Yeah." Putting a hand up to his face as though to conceal a blush, Stag laughed sheepishly. "I was so scared before my first time that I was practically in tears, so I called Eadowen." Stag turned to Eadowen. "Thanks so much for the suggestions," he added.

"You got tips from Ea? Smart move. I wish I'd thought of that," Taban replied. He wanted to continue quizzing Stag because it made the cheerleader so uneasy, but Eadowen grabbed Taban's ankle and pulled him back to the seat next to him. Relief spread across Stag's face and his shoulders relaxed once Taban had been removed from his personal bubble. Craning his neck, Taban nuzzled Eadowen's cheek, to which Eadowen responded by draping his arm over Taban's shoulders. Donovan peeked at them and then looked away. To cheer his friend, Stag pushed the tray of hot chocolates toward Donovan who took one and regarded Stag expectantly with his piercing eyes. Acting on the nonverbal cue Donovan had given him, Stag started a conversation with Aydan about new car models, while Donovan listened intently.

The friends admired the moonlit tree from their warm refuge with only the sound of the breeze and the gurgling bubble jets.

"Stag, Donovan, wanna play Elvish Robot Quest after this?" Aydan turned his back to the rest of the company to warm his chest on one of the waterfalls. His hair made a delta in the bubbles as it flowed out around him.

"That's the three-dimensional partial sensation video game where you have to team up with the high elf vampires and colorful miniature horses to fight giant robots in a steam punk universe right?" Stag asked.

Donovan nodded affirmatively.

"Y'all have the gear for that?"

The lacrosse player bobbed his head again.

"Awesome."

* * *

A drizzle snuffed the trees candles out while they each took turns washing off in the outdoor shower. Wrapping a towel around his waist, Taban gathered his clothes and followed the others inside.

Donovan, Stag, and Aydan went into the living room and started dressing in the gloves, vests, and visors required to experience the video game.

"I call an elf," Aydan said.

"Then I'll be a unicorn!" Stag replied. "What do you want to be Donovan?"

"Sphinx."

As a centaur Taban joined them, but soon grew bored of the game and abandoned his character. Upstairs in his room, Taban started to change into his pajama pants, but when his bare feet touched the icy floor, Taban decided he needed to seek out a better place to relax. He padded across the upstairs common area to Eadowen's room.

"Uh … mm … Taban?" Eadowen said groggily from under the covers.

"It's cold in my room," Taban muttered. He closed the door behind him shutting out the light from the hallway. Using his Ogham to see in the darkness, Taban made his way to Eadowen's bed.

"Well, you do have the second draftiest room in the house. Be glad you aren't Aydan in the attic."

"That kid's tough." Taban pulled back the silky comforter and slid in next to Eadowen.

"Can I get in?"

"Okay," Eadowen replied after a brief hesitation. They lay next to each other in silence listening to the wind pounding against the window pane in a pulsing rhythm. The light drizzle morphed into large half-frozen raindrops, which crashed against the glass. Taban shivered when he felt the subtle change in temperature caused by a gust of wind blowing through the unsealed sides of the window. Sliding closer to Eadowen, Taban guided Eadowen's arm around his waist. Eadowen rolled on his side to accommodate the movement of his arm and allowed Taban to rest his head on his bicep. Inspired by the pounding wind, Taban pressed himself against the length of Eadowen's body.

"Whoa, am I really that attractive?" Taban laughed and snuggled even closer.

"I was fast asleep. It'll calm down if you stop squirming," Eadowen replied wrapping his other arm around Taban's waist.

Reaching behind his head, Taban stroked Eadowen's jaw. He rotated his upper body so he could just see Eadowen's face from the corner of his eye. "Wanna mess around?" Taban asked.

"How much do you want to do?"

"You know me. I'm a sensual soul." Making a backrest out of pillows, Taban reclined against the headboard. He ran his hands over his own chest and regarded Eadowen through his lashes. "In other words ..." Taban's thoughts were interrupted as Eadowen caressed his chest with his teeth. "As long as it feels good." Playfully pushing Eadowen's head down to his abdomen, Taban ran his fingers through Eadowen's bangs. "You know where my limits are."

"Do I?" Eadowen flicked his tongue just below Taban's navel and exhaled slowly above the wetted spot. The tingling sensation Taban felt as Eadowen cooled his skin made him quiver involuntarily. Chuckling at the reaction, he propped himself against Taban's chest. At eye-level with him, Eadowen repeated his question in a more serious tone: "Do I know your boundaries?"

"You always ask me that. I trust you." To guarantee the veracity of his words, Taban assured him with a peck on the lips. "Now stop talking and make me feel good."

Eadowen slipped one arm between the pillow and Taban's back while his other hand held the side of his waist. As they kissed deeply, Taban wrapped his legs around Eadowen's hips and stroked his smooth jaw with his finger tips.

"To what extent do you trust me?" Eadowen's deep voice had a much more sensual tone than his previous question. Sighing, Taban flopped back on a pillow and looked up at the dark ceiling. The tie Eadowen had left hanging from his bookshelf tickled his nose. Taban yanked on the end and it slipped off the shelf and into his hands. He made a French bullion knot around his wrist.

"This extent." He offered the untethered end to Eadowen.

Laughing, Eadowen accepted it and began to retie the knot. "One wrist tied to the bedpost won't hold you, but I suppose that's not the point."

"It's symbolic. Okay?"

* * *

No more than fifteen minutes later, Taban heard a clattering and yelling from the living room below Eadowen's bedroom, followed by rushed footsteps coming up the stairs. The door to Eadowen's room burst open a few moments later. Holding his white chinchilla, Stag stood in the doorway looking frantic at first, then surprised to see both Taban and Eadowen dressed only from the waist down in bed together. "Sorry," Stag muttered. "The house is on fire you should probably head outside even though I think Aydan and Donovan have managed to contain it."

"And here I thought you two had nothing in common," Eadowen commented looking from Stag to Taban. "I wonder why I ever bothered shutting doors." He transferred himself from the bed into his wheelchair before Stag could cross the room to offer assistance. "I'm fine, I'll be faster than if you tried to carry me."

"Great. The house is on fire and I'm tied to a bed," Taban grumbled. "Isn't anyone going to help me out?"

"Go like this." Eadowen made a quick sweeping gesture with his arm. Imitating the motion, Taban pulled his arm away from the bed post and the knot came undone.

"Oh," he said realizing Eadowen had tied a slip knot.

"I wouldn't ruin a good tie on you. Now hurry up."

To check on the status of the fire in the living room, Taban sprinted downstairs ahead of Eadowen and Stag who took the lift. He smelled smoke, but when he poked his head into the living room, he saw that with several buckets of dirt and the hose, Aydan and Donovan had managed to put out the fire. The grey chinchilla had taken refuge from the fire on Donovan's shoulder where he'd kept it out of harm's way.

"It looks like they have it under control," Taban called to Stag. "I can't believe you got us out of bed for that." He waved at the charred floor by the central fire.

"How many times do I have to tell you to put out the fire before you play video games that make you lose your orientation to real objects?" Eadowen chastised.

"We're really sorry," Stag and Aydan replied in unison hanging their heads.

Donovan nodded in agreement with the sentiment and hit a button to roll up the two movie theater-sized screens they'd used for the game.

"How am I going to teach you three not to..." Eadowen began, but Stag's white chinchilla, interrupted him by jumped into his lap. Tickling the rodent's fluffy fur under her chin, Eadowen's face softened. "In the holiday spirit, I'll let you guys off on this one. Just please be more careful. What is this chinchilla's name?"

"I call her Aglet." Stag and Aydan exchanged smirks, clearly aware that Aglet had rescued them from punishment.

"Give her a treat, you need to reinforce this behavior," Aydan said under his breath.

"I get Aglet as a chinchilla name, but why is the other one Grenadine?" Aydan asked as he gestured to the grey rodent who still perched on Donovan's shoulder.

"Named after my favorite drink."

"Roy Rogers?" Aydan guessed.

"Nope, Shirley Temple." Stag grinned.

Fixing his messed hair, Taban noticed Stag glance in his direction with a furrowed brow and pursed mouth. "What is that look for?" Taban demanded.

"I thought you were heterosexual."

"I pretty much am. Not that I expect you to believe me."

"So, Eadowen's like your one exception? Or does your heterosexuality include hir in it because xie is gender-neutral?"

"Hm not really. Where we were when you came in is usually the extent of our physical relationship."

"So you're an asexual romantic with male-bodied people, but otherwise heterosexual?"

"Sure. Whatever. Does it really need a label?" Taban shrugged. "And now I'm going to go back upstairs with Ea." He started to walk down the hallway, but soon realized Eadowen wasn't following him, so he returned to the living room.

"I'm going to make everyone cheesecake." Eadowen stroked Aglet's grey tinted ears.

"Even better," Taban replied.

Sitting cross legged on the floor, Stag made a clicking noise and tapped his nails on the wood. Aglet hopped off of Eadowen's lap and bounced over to Stag followed by Grenadine who launched herself off of Donovan's shoulder. Exhausted from the fire fiasco, the two nocturnal rodents napped in Stag's lap while the friends watched Connor Haswell's latest action movie on one of the big screens.

THE END

FOR CHARACTER PROFILES,
TRIVIA, AND MORE, VISIT
WWW.CULLYNROYSON.COM

ACKNOWLEDGMENTS

Thank you to Lawrence Abrams for providing research support for the Celtic Mythology, Scottish history, and Celtic languages. Abrams is a student of history at the University of California Davis.

I benefited greatly from the support of Professors Michael Mills, Kate Reavey, and Elizabeth Williamson.

I deeply appreciate my family's support of my writing.

Thank you to beta readers: Andrew Oswalt, Brandon Diltz, Brent Williams, Elisabeth Thomas, Jennifer Gabriel, Megan Cullinan, and Michael Rose.

Finally, thank you to Bill Ransom, Katelyn Campen, and Molly Gort for insights and encouragement.

MORE GREAT READS FROM BOOKTROPE

Dead of Knight **by Nicole J. Persun** (Fantasy) King Orson and King Odell are power-stricken, grieving, and mad. As they wage war against a rebel army led by Elise des Eresther, it appears as though they're merely in it for the glory. But their struggles are deeper and darker.

Changeling Eyes **by L.A. Catron** (Fantasy) An epic tale of loss, self-discovery, revenge, and magic. The first book in the Aesir Chronicles.

Charis: Journey to Pandora's Jar **by Nicole Walters** (Young Adult - Fantasy) Thirteen-year-old Charis Parks has five days to face her fears against the darker forces of Hades and reverse the curse of Pandora's Jar to save mankind.

The Chosen (Book One of the Portals of Destiny Series) **by Shay West** (Fantasy) To each of the four planets are sent four Guardians, with one mission: to protect and serve the Chosen, those who alone can save the galaxy from the terrifying Meekon. An epic story of life throughout the galaxy, and the common purpose that brings them together.

Doublesight **by Terry Persun** (Fantasy) In a world where shape shifters are feared, and murder appears to be the way to eliminate them, finding and destroying the source of the fear is all the doublesight can do.

CPSIA information can be obtained at www.ICGtesting.com
Printed in the USA
LVOW06s0035040913

350720LV00004B/139/P